I0581223

BOOKS BY EMMALINE ROSE

Dear You

Benevolence Society Series
Gabriel's Empath
Michael's Warrior
(coming Spring 2022)

GABRIEL'S EMPATH

Emmaline Rose

BENEVOLENCE SOCIETY SERIES
BOOK ONE

This is a work of fiction. Names, characters, places, and incidents are either the product of the author's imagination or are used fictitiously. Any resemblance to actual persons, living or dead, business/companies, or events is entirely coincidental.

Gabriel's Empath
Copyright © 2021 by Emmaline MacBeath
Cover Design by Elena at L1graphics

ISBN 978-1-7324073-8-1

eISBN 978-1-7324073-9-8

Printed in the United States of America

FOR RYAN

Who is always gracious enough to be my

personal psychology dictionary so I know how

my characters should feel at all times.

You are the best!

PROLOGUE

Eight Years Earlier

Desperately hoping to avoid the touch of the man next to her, the young girl hugged the side of the coach as closely as possible. Good Lord, he stank.

That was the least of his faults, and with her unnatural ability, the girl would know.

She stared down the darkness through the window as she bounced on the coach seat to the rhythm of the dirt road. Even though it was a necessity they travel at night, it was dangerous. Evil came out to play in the dark. Her brown leather gloves creaked when she squeezed her hands more tightly together—keeping the fear at bay.

The girl flicked her eyes to Sarah, her maid, who sat on the opposite seat. Huddled as she was deep in her thick woolen cloak, little of her was visible. She had nodded off an hour ago. Lucky girl. The man had also fallen asleep— hands resting on his overstuffed belly, head laying on the seat back, all while loud snores and nasty fumes erupted from his gaping mouth. A jarring bump in the road caused the man to close his jaw for a moment and then resume snoring.

Holding herself stiffly, the girl looked out of the window and whispered to herself, "I can do this. I can do this." The obsidian sky did not answer.

What ifs, worry, and dread all churned together in her stomach, making rest impossible. She wanted to make the driver turn around and take her back home, but she knew she would never get better if she did not reach her destination.

Finally, half an hour later, the coach turned onto a private drive bringing what had seemed an eternal journey to an end. In the moonless dark, there was little to see other than dim candlelight peeking out of a window or two and lamplight on either side of the front door.

"Whoah," the coachman called to settle the horses as he pulled to a stop. The young girl did not take the time to wait for the footman to help her out properly. She threw open the door and hopped down to the ground, gulping in fresh, cool air and soaking up the wide-open space.

Calmer, she looked up at the looming brick structure in front of her. One could hardly call the dark, square menace a home, or even a house. Spying bars on the first-floor windows, she amended her assessment. A prison maybe?

It was too late for these sorts of thoughts. For better or worse, she had arrived. The front door slowly creaked open, and a monstrous figure loomed from the shadows.

The girl screamed.

ONE

Signor Silvano's Sayings Number 1
When your life is no longer in your control,
take a deep breath to calm yourself.
Repeat.
Keep repeating until you feel stronger.
Then go on to act as if your life is not in a
broken heap lying at your feet.

~Ten Miles Outside of London, England 1816~

Lillian awoke with a start and immediately strove to calm her wild breathing. *One slow breath in, one slow breath out. Repeat.* Just as Signor Silvano had taught them.

Her mind was still halfway between sleep and wakefulness, making her briefly believe she was on the carriage ride to Silvano's School eight years ago that had invaded her dreams. She shook her head briskly to clear it and remembered she was indeed in a carriage, but heading in the opposite direction. At seventeen, she was no longer a little girl, but that thought did not make her stomach feel any less queasy to be returning from that journey she had made so long ago. A lifetime ago.

She had just enough time to look up and notice Sarah was napping on the seat across from her when a loud *crack* rent the air. The coach listed immediately to one side and gradually slowed until it came to a stop. None of this woke her maid.

Lillian took a moment to envy Sarah's ability to sleep through anything before unlatching the carriage window and letting it slide down. It was a typical early spring in England—overcast and cold. She shivered as the frigid late morning air hit her face. "Mr. Thompkins? Mr. Thompkins, what has happened?" she called out to the hired driver.

She heard muttered cursing, then felt the vehicle rock from side to side. Lillian grabbed the strap attached to the ceiling to steady herself. The driver appeared in front of the window.

"It's that sorry I am, my lady. We hit a stone in the road what's large enough to bust the axle."

Lillian knew nothing of the mechanics of a carriage other than it had wheels and was pulled by horses, so she asked, "Is this a very bad thing, Mr. Thompkins?"

The man chuckled, but it was not a happy sound. "Aye, my lady. The coach can't go nowhere without the axle bein' whole. The wheels won't turn."

"What is to be done then?" Lillian asked. She clutched the strap tighter and bit her bottom lip.

"There's nothin' for it but to find someone to fix it, my lady," Mr. Thompkins said as he removed his cap and scratched his balding head. "We passed a village a couple miles back."

Sarah woke like a contented cat who had just taken the best nap of her life. The slight girl stretched her arms above her head and took a deep breath, saying in a slow lazy voice, "Are we there already?"

"Do we look like we are there?" Lillian snapped.

The tone of her lady's voice brought Sarah to full attention. "What has happened?"

"The coach has sustained some damage and we cannot go forward," Lillian said. "Mr. Thompkins said there is a village nearby where perhaps we can receive assistance?" The question in her voice was aimed at the coachman.

"Aye, that be the case, my lady," he said. "It's close enough I can walk there and come back with help." He squeezed his cap tightly in his hands and shuffled uneasily from one foot to the other. "But I don't like the idea of you being here alone, my lady."

Before Lillian could answer, Sarah interjected, "We could walk into town as well."

"Yes, but what about our things?" Lillian asked. "Everything I own is strapped to this coach, and I do not wish it to be left for anyone to come along and snap up." She closed her eyes and took a deep breath. Then she looked at Mr. Thompkins. "We shall remain here. If the village is as close as you believe, you should be able to return in less than three quarters of an hour, yes?"

"Aye, my lady. I can do that. I'll be back as quick as a wink."

Lillian closed the window again to keep the chill of the morning out. Squeezing her hands together in her lap, she said to her companion, "I cannot help but think this is a bad omen."

Sarah patted her dark blonde hair, ensuring everything was in the right place. "You are being silly, Lillian. Coaches break all the time. This is nothing special." Even though Sarah was only sixteen years old, a year younger than Lillian, her friend was often the more level-headed of the pair. This was not the first time she had had to keep Lillian calm in a crisis.

"How would you know?" Lillian grumbled. "How many of the coaches that you have traveled in over the past eight years have sustained damage?"

Sarah thought over the question, then said, "None?"

Prince Albert, Lillian's pet ferret, who had also been sleeping like the dead on the coach seat next to her, popped up and nudged her arm. She picked him up and cradled him in her arms, stroking his brown and white fur.

"Precisely," Lillian said before slumping back into the seat with a large sigh. "I am sorry to be so bad-tempered. I am nervous enough as it is to return home for good after all these years away at school, Sarah. Unexpected events do not help."

"I know." Sarah looked at her with compassionate eyes. "I suppose there is nothing else I can say to help ease your mind."

"No, I suppose not, but as Signor Silvano says, we must move forward, which means I must arrive home today. If I do not get there before my mother begins her plots and strategies in earnest, I will be doomed to whatever life, or husband, she chooses for me."

"Surely the situation cannot be so dire," Sarah said.

"Remember what happened the last time I visited home and she had decided to put me in charge of the new literary society she was forming?"

"Yes," Sarah huffed out a laugh, "and all the best ladies of the *haute ton,* the highest of high society, attended, much to your horror."

"None of those ladies appreciated my thoughts on the merits of the French novel, *Candide,* which I had chosen to speak about on that day." Lillian grimaced.

"How were you to know it was considered scandalous?" Sarah said with laughter in her hazel eyes.

"Or the time before when she thought I should learn to practice good works and forced me to accompany her to the poor house."

"That was an unfortunate choice," Sarah agreed.

Lillian remembered now all the wretched souls crammed into one building with barely enough room to move. There was little chance she could remain untouched in such a setting, and she had ended up having an episode in the first ten minutes.

"I must hurry home to steer my mother away from this ridiculous notion that I will be getting married. I do not want a husband."

She could see Sarah's sigh; this was old, familiar ground. "Society dictates that a lady cannot make her way in the world the same as a man," Sarah said. "What other choices does she have than to marry?"

Lillian did not answer. She closed her eyes, leaning her head back against the leather seat. As a woman, as the daughter of an earl, and as someone with her peculiar condition, could she ever have any true freedom?

"You know I am very skeptical about this latest plan of

yours," Sarah said. "I feel it is far more reasonable for you to find a decent husband you can live with, then find independence within your marriage. Many ladies do the same."

Lillian cringed at the idea. She would never be like other ladies, so why should she follow in their footsteps? "I feel I must at least try to become self-sufficient, Sarah. It is my only hope for long-term survival." Married life would make her die inside a little more each and every day. She could only imagine what would happen each time she touched her husband.

"We shall see how it works out," Sarah said in her matter-of-fact way, which meant she did not expect Lillian's plan to work at all. Her friend of nearly ten years was always more practical than she, who liked to think up big ideas and plans.

Her latest one was quite grand. For some time now, Lillian had been collecting herbal remedies from every herbalist, midwife, and scientist, she could get to write her back, as well as family members of her fellow students who came from abroad. She had read every book on the subject she could find. She had even tested many of the medicines she had prepared herself on her fellow schoolmates at Silvano's when they were sick or injured.

Now, she was writing a comprehensive herbal. She had heard women could make a decent living with their writing —if they wrote under a male pseudonym, that was. This herbal was her chance to live a life she could tolerate, a life where she could keep herself separated from people.

First, she needed to thwart her mother's latest attempt to

make her daughter fit into society like a normal lady. If that did not work, Lillian had high hopes her little problem would do the job for her. If she allowed herself to have one of her spells at every social gathering, she would quickly become an outcast. That was what she truly wanted, was it not?

Prince Albert scuttled out of her lap and onto the floor and spun in a circle several times. He was probably ready for a walk.

Lillian stared out the window at the dreary scenery of the dirt road and the wall of trees along it, thinking. What she would like above all things was to return to Silvano's where it felt like home. Where she could be understood and insulated. Where she could be free to live how she wished. She broke the silence. "I still do not see why Signor Silvano felt it best to close the school now and move everyone to London under this silly name, Benevolence Society."

"You know he said it was no longer safe in the country where we all stuck out like a sore thumb," Sarah said. "He said it would be better to blend in."

"Yet the whole reason for the school, to begin with, was for students with unnatural abilities to get away from the public. These are completely opposite philosophies."

Sarah shrugged. "Who can ever understand a man's mind?"

Lillian snorted at this. "Too true, but the problem is I liked his initial philosophy so much better. I was content to stay in Shropshire forever. I mean, a few more feet and we would have practically been in Wales." Lillian's voice turned wistful.

"Perhaps we should have simply moved the school there."

"It never would have worked. The Welsh are a suspicious lot," Sarah said. "Could you imagine what would happen the first time Christopher accidentally changed the weather?"

Lillian huffed out a laugh at the idea. "Oh, I suppose you are correct," Lillian attempted to smooth out a wrinkle in her skirt, "and I suppose it does no good to wish for what cannot be. But I am not ready to give in yet to all these changes." She thought longingly of her now former life. There would be no more solitary rides on horseback. No more peace and quiet away from the touch of others. No more keeping her ability hidden. She looked out of the window again, seeing nothing. "I will find a way to remain separate from all society, just you wait and see."

"If you say so," Sarah said.

After several minutes, she turned back. "Do you ever dream of a different life, Sarah? A better life?"

Her maid gave her an odd look. "My life could be no better than it is now."

"If you were not stuck with me, you would not have to work so hard."

Prince Albert jumped into Sarah's lap and she rubbed his ears. "I would end up in a less pleasant situation, that is for certain."

"But I am such a troublesome creature," she complained, giving her maid a mock pout.

"Lillian," Sarah said in exasperation, "I have been allowed

to go to school at your side, receiving a first-rate education, and become friends with people from all levels of society. I have the role of friend and companion rather than a maid who must work her fingers to the bone from sunup to sundown, and I enjoy my work. I promise you, the daughter of a tenant farmer could never ask for better."

Lillian gave her a skeptical look and echoed her friend's words. "If you say so." After a prolonged silence, she said wistfully, "All I have ever wanted is to be an ordinary woman."

"Oh, Lillian." Her friend gave her a fond smile. "The last thing you will ever be is ordinary."

That was the problem. Sarah saw that as a good thing, whereas she would give anything in the world to be like everyone else.

Several minutes later, they heard the rumble of wheels outside.

"I believe we are saved," Sarah announced.

Lillian allowed the warmth inside the rustic little inn to envelop her upon entering the doorway. She did not think she could have withstood the chill of the early April weather much longer.

Mr. Thompkins had been able to find a man with a cart who was willing to bring them and their belongings back to the inn until repairs could be made to the hired coach. Lillian had no idea how long that would take, but she knew she needed to get home today, no matter what.

"You will figure this out, Lillian. You always do," she whispered under her breath as she looked around. To her right was a taproom, currently empty of patrons, and to the left was a common room with several tables spread out where men were eating or drinking tankards of ale while they conversed. It had been a long time since she had had any contact with strangers. Being even this close felt uncomfortable. If she had her way, this would be as close as she ever got to any of them. It was key for her sanity.

She was about to turn to Sarah to find out what they were to do next when a gruff male voice came from behind her.

" 'Ere miss, you're blockin' the way."

She had no time to respond before a strong hand grabbed her by the upper arm and yanked her to the right.

Her familiar world disappeared.

The lantern in Joseph's hand was the only light as the man bent over his work, digging furiously into the hard ground. Digging, digging, digging.

"Can't you go any faster?" Joseph asked.

"Do you wanna be the one down 'ere breakin' yer back with a shovel in yer hands?" he asked.

"No," Joseph said sullenly.

"I didn't think so, so shut your gob," he barked.

That shut the other man up right quick. He kept at it, the eerie light flickering over the scene as the hole grew larger, and finally large enough. He jumped out of the hole and without a word grabbed the man lying dead on the ground by the boots and dragged him to the opening.

"It's a shame about the boots," Joseph said. "They're awful nice."

What an idiot. "You keep these 'ere boots and they'll know what happened to Tom. You'll be done for his murder. That what you want?" Joseph shook his head. "Then shut up."

He positioned the dead man alongside the hole and rolled him over. The body fell with a whump. That done, he began to fill the grave in again with the pile of dirt.

He hadn't set out to kill a man tonight. He laughed softly to himself. But it had felt mighty good. Mighty good indeed. And if Joseph couldn't keep this a secret, he might just have to enjoy himself like this again.

They had only just entered the inn and already it had erupted into chaos. Chaos had been an all-too-common occurrence since the day Sarah was employed by the Hargraves family. Not that she was complaining. Her job was much easier and far more pleasant than most from her social class had to face, and she was doubly lucky that she and her lady had become friends—the lady who was now in distress once again.

Lillian was unconscious and shaking on the floor, the large-as-a-bull man who had just shoved her was calling out, "I didn't do nothin' to her, honest," and the men at the tables were scraping back their chairs to stand and get a better look at the spectacle.

If Lillian had been conscious, she would have been mortified, but Sarah did not have time to think about that. She needed to take command of the situation. Putting down the herbal case she had been in charge of, she knelt on the floor and leaned over her friend. She needed to get her to a safer place until this vision passed. Sarah quickly scanned the room, hoping an answer to the situation would present itself, and saw one of the young guests was hurrying forward.

He bent down and made ready to pick Lillian up off the floor, but Sarah stopped him with a tug of his coat sleeve. "Please, you cannot touch her," she said quietly.

"Why not?" he asked.

She swallowed hard and replied with silence. Sarah was used to keeping anyone from touching Lillian, but it did not make sense now when her friend was already in the middle of an episode.

She must have taken too long to answer, because the man snapped, "I am not going to leave her here by the doorway to be trampled on," and without waiting for a response, he scooped the still-trembling Lillian into his arms and turned toward the innkeeper who had come bustling from behind the bar by this time. "Show us to a room with a clean bed," he ordered.

"Right this way, sir," the innkeeper said and started toward the stairs.

Sarah grabbed up the herbal case and the bag in which

Prince Albert was sleeping and followed. The pet was used to being thumped about during one of Lillian's spells, but she could only hope the fall to the floor had not caused him an injury. She counted three doors upstairs before they entered the fourth.

"This room is our quietest, away from the inn yard," the innkeeper said.

Sarah scanned the room and saw that it was small but clean and free from the smell of damp.

"This will do," the man said. "Send up some hot water."

Sarah had no idea what use it would be, but it seemed in every difficult situation, people always called for hot water.

After reaching the bed, situated against the wall in the middle of the room, the man gently placed Lillian upon it so her head reclined on the pillow. He backed up a couple of steps and turned toward Sarah. She saw he was quite young, probably early twenties, with dark wavy hair. She had a fleeting thought that she might call him handsome.

"This is a common occurrence for her?" he asked.

Sarah gave a quick nod, tightening her hand on the case.

"She has regular fits?"

What could she say? The truth was too unbelievable. She nodded again.

"What needs to be done for her?" the man clipped out, seeming to be exasperated at her lack of words.

"Nothing. She will be fine after some rest," Sarah said.

The man nodded and appeared as if he would leave, but stopped himself. "What has brought you to this inn?"

Now that the urgency had passed, Sarah had a moment to think more sensibly. Should she tell this stranger anything about their situation? Signor Silvano was constantly telling them that being polite to strangers was important, but to stay safe, one must keep one's business to oneself. On the other hand, the entire inn most likely knew the whole of their business by now.

She placed the case on the floor and Prince Albert on the bed. "Our carriage axle requires repair. We plan to be on our way as soon as our coachman has taken care of it."

The man made a tsking sound. "This inn is not large and does not keep a man employed in the stables who is skilled enough to accommodate travelers in need of such services. It could be several days before your driver can have a new axle brought in for the repair."

Sarah squeezed handfuls of her dress fabric in her fists. If Lillian had been awake, she would not have been pleased by the delay. "We are expected in London by this evening."

"If your lady is abed, I do not see how you could continue your travels. You might as well take a room and stay until the repairs are complete," the man said.

"That is not possible. We need to be in London as soon as may be."

The man smiled gently. "Sometimes plans must change."

"Yes," is what she said, but in her mind she thought about what Lillian's response would have been. This man could not possibly understand her lady's urgency and she felt no desire to explain, especially since she actually agreed with him. Sarah doubted returning today would make any difference. Her doubt was even stronger that Lillian could change her parents' minds about marrying her off. They were no different than every other lord and lady who expected to connect through their children to the highest title with the most money. Highborn parents had been doing it for centuries.

The man nodded. "I will check in with you a little later to see how the lady fares. In the meantime, is there anything I can do to assist you?"

She clutched harder at her dress. It would be the very devil to iron out the creases later. She had no wish to ask for anything, but they were rather at his mercy. "Would you please speak to our coachman and see if there is anything to be done about the carriage?"

"I do not hold out hope for a swift resolution, but I will speak to him on your behalf," he said.

"Thank you. I do appreciate the assistance."

As soon as the man left the room, Sarah checked on Prince Albert who was sleeping the contented sleep of a ferret inside his cozy little nest. Then she sat down on the side of her friend's bed. "Oh, Lillian," she whispered. "I do not believe your grand plan is going very well so far."

TWO

Signor Silvano's Sayings Number 2
You can travel the world,
but if you cannot be comfortable
with yourself wherever you are,
there is nowhere far enough away
you can run.

Gabriel breathed in deeply as he leisurely scanned the length of the English coastline through his borrowed looking glass. The air here smelled different than the coastlines of Europe or the Americas. It was familiar—like an old friend.

"Looks like smooth sailing the rest of the way, Guv'nor," the large man beside him observed. Jersey, a few inches taller than Gabriel's own six foot two, was his valet, bodyguard, and man of all work. He was often a contrary fellow, but he did his job better than anyone else Gabriel could have chosen for the role.

"Yes, and a bit of sunshine as well," Gabriel agreed. "A nice homecoming, that."

The two men fell silent, drinking in the perfect morning. The ship rocked gently below their feet. Much of the voyage had not been nearly so smooth, and fierce storms had forced Gabriel to spend too much of the past fortnight below decks. He had felt like a caged bear. Now he could breathe as much fresh air as his lungs could take in and be at ease. The wind tousled his too-long coffee-colored curls as he lifted his face to the sun. He needed a haircut. It was likely the first thing his mother would notice when he arrived home.

Home.

He had not laid eyes on it in four long years. He had only been eighteen years old when he was forced to flee, but Gabriel would think on all that later. For now, he enjoyed the little time he had left before everything would begin again. Before allies were gathered and plans were made. Before enemies were run to ground and destroyed. And they would be destroyed. He would let nothing and no one stop him or stand in his way this time.

"Let us go below, Jersey, to be sure all is ready for our departure."

"If you like, Your Honor," the man said with a cheeky grin. "But it's not as if our bags haven't been packed and ready for two days."

Gabriel sighed and pinched the bridge of his nose. So much for his calm and peace of mind. "Jersey, just one time, could you call me by my proper title and do as I ask without commenting?" Jersey opened his mouth to comment once again, but Gabriel held up his hand. "Never mind. I believe you just answered my question." The two men left the top deck with Gabriel muttering under his breath, "How did I get saddled with the most impudent servant on the entire seven seas?

The casual observer would have seen a man dressed in the clothing of perhaps a clerk or a merchant—just a simple man carrying his luggage off the ship and down the gangplank. That observer would have seen exactly what Gabriel wanted him to see. Jersey would follow later with the remainder of their belongings.

He scanned the Plymouth docks, currently a hive of activity, for any sign of trouble as he headed for solid ground in a relaxed manner. Then he eyed the sole coach waiting. It was a plain vehicle—black with no markings except the thin silver stripe across the top of the door, telling Gabriel it was the correct one. His blood beat more quickly in anticipation, and he picked up his pace. At the back of the carriage, he hefted his trunk up and strapped it on. He gave the back panel a series of quiet knocks. He waited. When the correct sequence of answering knocks were given, he walked around to the side, opened the door and jumped in—not bothering to pull down the collapsible steps. He said nothing until the carriage left the docks and the driver signaled with two knocks that they had not been followed.

"Hello, Barnaby," he said to the short, golden-haired man on the opposite seat. "Tell me the latest updates."

Barnaby shook his head slowly and made a sound of disgust as he pushed up his round spectacles. "Just like you, Gabriel, to get right down to business. No 'how are you' or 'how is the family.' "

Gabriel folded his arms across his chest and sat back

with a grin. "Fine. How are you, Barnaby? And how is your family? Oh, wait. I know you have not married since I left, your eldest brother has been making a ruckus in parliament, and your youngest brother has been sent down from school. Again. Your sister is what, fifteen years old now?"

Barnaby snorted. "Point taken. You seem to know more about my life than I do. You are incredibly up to date for someone who has been aboard ship for the past fortnight." He gave a nervous laugh, then fell silent. Nervously silent.

"What is it, Barnaby? You have news." Gabriel knew stalling when he saw it.

The other man squirmed in his seat. "How did I end up in this position as the messenger?" Barnaby muttered to himself.

"Out with it!"

Gabriel's barking command caused Barnaby to jump and blurt out, "We have lost contact with Gemini."

"What do you mean you have lost contact with Gemini?" Gabriel asked with a glower.

Barnaby worried the top button of his plain brown waistcoat. He spoke to the floor in almost a whisper: "We last heard from Gemini three weeks ago when he gave his usual report through our courier. Then nothing. He checks in once a week. This is the longest the Network has gone without hearing from him."

There was an audible grinding as Gabriel clenched his teeth in anger and frustration. "What about the agent who was supposed to be watching Gemini's back? Where is he?"

"She."

"What?" Gabriel snapped out, causing Barnaby to look up and answer.

"Gemini's backup is a she."

Gabriel was struck speechless for a full minute. "What happened to the man who was previously on watch?" he finally ground out.

After several throat clearings, Barnaby said, "Falcon fell off his horse when it unexpectedly reared on him. He broke his leg." He rubbed his button a little harder. "We knew we had to replace him quickly with the best person on our team. Lady X—"

"Lady X?" Gabriel's voice grew louder and more menacing if that was possible. "You had Gemini covered by a woman named Lady X? What kind of code name is that?"

"S-She chose it herself," Barnaby stammered. "She is very good—well versed in all manner of hand-to-hand combat, weaponry of every imaginable kind, disguises, codes." He paused, looking to the side. "Actually, there is very little she cannot do."

"Except keep track of Gemini, it seems." Gabriel uncrossed his arms, and draped them across the back of the carriage seat. He drummed the fingers of his right hand on the leather to calm himself. The rocking of the vehicle made him feel as if he were still aboard the ship. "Your primary mission was to keep Gemini safe."

Barnaby cringed at the rebuke. "We have no reason to believe that Gemini is in any danger. You know him better than anyone. The likeliest scenario is that something tipped him off and he is lying low as an extra precaution."

Gabriel stopped drumming his fingers and thumped his fist on the seat so explosively it caused Barnaby to jump. Again. He raised both eyebrows at the man's skittish behavior. "What has been done to recover Gemini or discover his location?"

"N-nothing, sir. We decided that if Gemini were in deep hiding, it would be best not to actively search for him, thus compromising his position."

Gabriel took several deep breaths to control the emotions swamping him. This was not how he had expected his first moments on his home soil to go. Once he had allowed himself to cool down somewhat, his rational brain began to work again. Gemini would not have done anything to put himself in danger or jeopardize their mission by allowing himself to be seen in public—especially when he knew Gabriel was on his way home to wrap things up. He had to hope that if Gemini was out of contact it was for a darn good reason.

Putting this current migraine to the side for the present, he asked in a softer tone, "Barnaby, what has you in such an excitable state? You are usually a cool-headed and quick-thinking man, but in the past ten minutes, you have been fidgeting and squirming like a six-year-old who has been cooped up inside the nursery during a week of bad weather days. This must be about more than Gemini. What is going on?"

Barnaby stopped pulling on his waistcoat button and smoothed a hand down the front of the fabric. He cleared his throat, then tapped his hands lightly on the top of his thighs —like a man buying time. "It's like this, Gabriel. I love being a part of the Network—saving England from enemy spies and all that—but when I started, I was doing fieldwork. When I am out there, I am in my element. I feel like I can do anything. But I believe putting me in charge at home base was a mistake and I—"

"You were—you are—the only person I felt I could trust to adequately relay information to me regarding day-to-day operations and keep tabs on our key agents," Gabriel interrupted.

"I am honored by your trust, truly, but this job has me constantly tied up in knots. I worry." He ran a trembling hand through his hair. "I am forever wondering if I have made the right decisions. I spend far too much time considering which information to pass on, which to hold back, and exactly how it should be said. I am honestly not cut out for this work."

Gabriel leaned forward, smiled, and slapped Barnaby on the knee. "Well, old chap, it is a good thing I have returned then. I shall take my proper place in the Network and you will go back to the field and spread your wings once again as Eagle. Raven can take charge of the ferrying of information between the field and me."

Barnaby let out a long slow sigh of relief that filled the carriage.

"Your first assignment will be to discover the whereabouts of Gemini and keep an eye on him," Gabriel continued. "He is still working on ferreting out the French spy ring along the west coast, is he not?"

"Yes, as far as I know," Barnaby said. "I would say it is not a wise idea to search him out, sir, since we do not want to compromise his position, but you always know best." He pulled the window curtain to the side to look out. "It appears we are nearing our first rendezvous point."

"Good," Gabriel said. "They can update me on any Network business in the southwestern corner of England while I get my land legs back. Then we are off to London?"

"Yes, sir." Barnaby reached for his top button again but stopped himself. "How long until I can go back to the field?"

"I shall need you by my side for the first few days and then we will see what can be done to send you on your way."

Letting out a puff of air, Barnaby said, "My growing ulcer thanks you."

Gabriel opened the door and stepped out of the unmarked carriage. He had taken an extra day in Exeter for a proper haircut and a visit to a tailor. He was not ready to take London society by storm, but he was once again dressed in the familiar garb of an English gentleman.

Not yet wishing to alert all of London of his return, he had chosen to enter his home through the back gardens. Jersey and his belongings had caught up with them in Exeter, but Gabriel chose to leave the bulk of his luggage with Barnaby to send on later. He wanted an inconspicuous homecoming

—to get the lay of the land, so to speak.

His valet hefted Gabriel's trunk onto his shoulder and followed him through the back gate. All was quiet in the half light of the evening. As planned, they arrived at five o'clock, well before the dinner hour, when the servants would be at their busiest. Gabriel went around to the side of the house and unlocked a rarely used door. Once inside, he headed to the left where another door led to the back staircase. The men made it up two flights of stairs without gaining anyone's attention. It was as Gabriel had hoped. He did not want the staff to know of his arrival until he had spoken to his mother. She should be the first to know that he was home.

Although his suite of rooms was at the end of the long hallway of the family wing, Gabriel stopped at the third doorway and knocked. Jersey continued walking past. "Come," a familiar voice called out, causing a lump to form in his throat.

Four years. He had not heard that voice for four long years.

Gabriel shook himself and opened the door, his eyes quickly landing on his mother reading by the fire in her favorite chair—her legs pulled up beneath her. She did not look up when he entered. Gabriel spent a quiet moment drinking in the sight of her during what he knew was one of her rare chances for relaxation. She was achingly beautiful, her hair still dark with no signs of gray even though she was into her fourth decade. Her eyes, a golden brown he had not inherited, were kind. She had a soft smile on her face, obviously enjoying her book. Probably some comedy. Mother always did prefer literature that made her laugh.

He was silent too long. Soon his mother looked up and gasped in surprise. Then she gave him a dazzling smile. "Gabriel!" She jumped up awkwardly from her chair. He stepped forward to steady her, returning the smile.

"Mother. I have returned." He bussed her on the cheek. "You are looking extremely well." Pulling her hands wide, he looked at all of her at once.

"Shall I turn around and then show you my teeth as well?" she asked in a wry tone.

"Forgive me, Mother. I missed you very much."

"And I you. More than I can say, especially with Michael and your father gone." Her smile faded. "But that is a topic better left for later." She picked up the book that had fallen in her haste and sat again. "Come, sit by me and tell me of your journey home."

Gabriel took the wing-backed chair across from her and sank into it. Home. He briefly closed his eyes and savored the feel of a chair he had not sat in since the last time he was in this house. Yes, four years was far too long.

"Well, Gabriel, I am waiting!" The side of his mother that was a duchess through and through had appeared.

No matter that he was now an adult at twenty-two years old, Gabriel Lionel Trentham Ramsay, the fifth Duke of Wyvern—'Lion' in the Network—shrank in size to a boy still in short pants when his mother used that tone. Without delay, he told her everything she had not yet heard since his last letter home.

After reluctantly leaving his mother to dress for dinner, Gabriel went to the ducal suite. He had inhabited these rooms for scarcely a month before leaving for distant shores, which was just as well. He did not feel comfortable here in his father's domain. He took time to scan the bedroom that was now his while Jersey busied himself organizing his things. The room was fit for a king with a bed so large that it could easily fit four people, dark red velvet curtains covering the windows, and heavy mahogany furniture. Gabriel felt like an intruder.

"Would you like to change for dinner, Your Most High Excellency?" Jersey asked.

He sighed at his valet and once again mused over what an odd man he was. It was not only his eccentric manner, but with his great height and muscular build, he looked far more like a prizefighter or a bear handler than a gentleman's gentleman. Gabriel shook his head at the ridiculous thoughts and moved further into the room. "Yes," he said.

Jersey sauntered into the dressing room and returned with a set of more formal wear—shirt, waistcoat, evening coat, neck-cloth, and knee breeches. Gabriel eyed the knee breeches with distaste. He would have to wear silk stockings with those.

"Her grace does like the old tradition of dressing fancy for dinner, you have said," Jersey pointed out, noticing where his eyes were fixed.

"Why is it you call my mother by her correct title, but you cannot do the same for me?"

Jersey shrugged with a cocky smile. "Perhaps I have a higher respect for the ladies."

Gabriel started to say something he might regret later when Jersey snapped his fingers.

"I just remembered. A message came for you from the club today. "

"Read it to me while I dress," he said.

Jersey pulled a small pair of spectacles from the inside pocket of his jacket, put them on, unfolded the letter he had picked up from a side table, ran his hand over the letter repeatedly to straighten out any creases, then cleared his throat several times.

"Just read it!" Gabriel barked out. His valet took every opportunity to annoy him.

"Yes, Captain." He rolled his shoulders then began.

It has come to our attention that your cousin, Howard Ramsay, has been living beyond his means and has accumulated considerable debts to the point he has visited more than one well-known unscrupulous moneylender—

"Help me with this and tell me what you currently know of my cousin," Gabriel interrupted. He held out his first sleeve. The man would already have all the details of his cousin's life without needing to read it on paper.

"Ramsay struts around as if he owns the world in your absence. Wines, dines, and spends time with the ladies if you know what I mean," Jersey said as he secured the first cufflink. "He's not especially liked, but tolerated because of who he is related to and the fact he's your heir, and it seems he takes right fine advantage of that fact."

"How considerable are his debts as of now?" Gabriel asked and held out the other wrist.

"Over ten thousand pounds," Jersey said.

Gabriel cursed under his breath. "How has this been allowed? His income is not large and he has no charm or wit to convince others to extend him credit."

"Ah, but he has expectations. No one but you stands between him and the dukedom, so everyone believes. The knowledge he will inherit a great deal of money can buy him a lot of beefsteak and fancy clothing on credit."

A growl came from Gabriel's throat. "I want you to put it about that the estate will not be paying his debts any time soon and no one should be extending him additional credit. Howard can learn to live within his means like everyone else under my care."

"Right you are, Sire," Jersey said as he helped Gabriel into his coat.

Gabriel tugged on the lapels in annoyance. He did not have time for this nuisance. Babysitting a family member he had never even liked was not on his schedule.

The soup spoon was nearly to his lips when his mother spoke. "Perhaps now that you have returned, we can discuss the upcoming social events you will need to attend."

Gabriel frowned, looking at the duchess over the long table's centerpiece of flowers. He never understood the need for such ornamentation when they were merely here to eat. "I have only just arrived, Mother. I have so much to catch up on—list upon list."

He swallowed the mouthful of the delicious artichoke bisque, which was light and creamy with just a hint of lemon. He had missed good English food, although this course was probably more French.

The duchess wrinkled her forehead. "Why would you have so much to do, Gabriel? Have you not been keeping up with your business through correspondence while you were away?"

"It is not the same. Many things have been put aside to await my personal attention. I also need to call upon several people, check up on work that I have been told is complete, and see that all is running as it should."

"Do you mean to visit all your estates then?"

"I shall, eventually—but not all at once and not all now. I have several pressing matters to attend to that will take much of my time, and you know I have an important ongoing investigation to complete."

The footman removed the soup bowls and replaced them with plates of salmon and asparagus with a cream sauce.

"Yes, I know your urgency is quite strong on that matter, but I prefer not to speak of it this evening so I can enjoy your homecoming." She took a bite of the delicate salmon and after swallowing said, "I hope you mean to update your wardrobe. Clothing from four years ago is considered extremely out of fashion, you know." Her eyes twinkled, but Gabriel knew she was quite serious.

"Although I am not wearing clothing that ancient—they do have new clothing in other countries, you know—I had already begun work on a new wardrobe before I arrived yesterday. Unfortunately, I shall have to spend at least a little more time attending to that chore, much to my chagrin." He grimaced and drank from his wine glass.

"Men." The duchess sighed and shook her head. "Always preferring to hurry in and out of the shops while we ladies choose to peruse, compare, and buy to our hearts' content."

"Your hearts are never quite content or the shops would not stay in business, now would they?"

Both chuckled at this.

Gabriel had a sudden realization. "Where are the great aunts? Do they no longer dine with you in the evening?"

"They most certainly do; however, they are currently in Bath visiting a friend. Gertrude and Gemma will be very pleased to see you when they return."

"And I them," Gabriel said fondly.

His mother delicately wiped her mouth before speaking

again. "On a more serious matter, Gabriel, now that you have returned, you must consider taking a wife."

Gabriel choked on a mouthful of asparagus. He finished chewing and coughed several times to clear his throat. "Must I, Mother?" he squeaked out. "I have only just arrived."

"There is no time like the present," she said. "You need an heir other than your cousin Howard to whom you may pass the dukedom, and all this getting married business"—she waved her hand in the air to indicate the list—"the courtship, wedding, et cetera, et cetera, take time. With the social season about to begin, it is best to create a strategy straightaway."

He knew his mother was right, but this was one part of his life Gabriel did not want to deal with at present, and if he had learned how to do one thing well over the last four years, it was to delegate. "Fine," he said. "Since you will know all the best ladies of society, perhaps you could arrange something for me."

His mother's fork clattered on the plate. "Arrange a marriage for you?" she asked, astonished.

"Why not?" He shrugged. "It is done all the time, and one lady is as good as another, in my opinion, as long as she meets the basic requirements."

The duchess let out a strangled gasp. "Are you quite serious? What about affection or even love? Your father and I loved each other dearly."

His gaze softened. "I know, Mother, but I can never hope

to have what the two of you had. My life is far too wrapped up in my work."

"As was your father's," the duchess said quietly, "but we made it work and we were all the happier for it."

The beef course was brought in and the wine changed to a red. He tasted it and savored the richness. "I am currently far too busy, so if you wish to see the deed done promptly, you will have to handle the matter yourself." He gave his mother a cheeky grin. The look had always worked for his brother.

She sighed loudly. "I shall think on it and let you know what I have decided, hmm?"

"Thank you, Mother. Now, I wish to give my full attention to this delicious cuisine. Monsieur Brisson has outdone himself tonight."

"He is pleased to have you home to cook for once again," she said with a smile. "He says I do not eat enough to keep a bird alive."

He finished chewing the perfectly flavored meat and swallowed. "Then I shall endeavor to keep him busy." Of course, what he was truly looking forward to was the dessert course. His sweet tooth had gone too long without satisfaction.

Later, he sat back while the plates were changed out once again and went through his mental list of what needed to be done on the morrow. It was true he had many things he must check to be certain they were running smoothly, but his prime objective was to create a systematic way of eliminating suspects in his investigation. Nearly everyone under suspicion had time, opportunity, and motive. He inwardly snarled in frustration. This was going to be like finding a needle in a haystack, and he did not have the patience to look through every piece of grass. However, he was willing to do it, especially if it meant his family would finally have justice.

THREE

Signor Silvano's Sayings Number 3
When faced with adversity, look at it as an
opportunity rather than a calamity.
It is a fact that bad things will happen.
Why not be the one to take charge?

As she always did, after one of her events, Lillian awoke groggy and disoriented. She breathed deeply, trying to get a sense of where she was. Curtains of the window near the bed were parted, letting in gentle light.

Some of what had happened came back to her: A man's voice; His hand gripping her arm; A vision of his life. A vision she had no wish to see. She shuddered. A murderer had put his hand on her, and he could very well still be nearby.

She sat bolt upright. "Where am I?" she gasped.

Sarah was by her side in an instant. "We are still at the inn where you collapsed. I took a room so you could recover yourself."

"I could have recovered just as easily in the carriage on the way to London," she said, feeling hard-pressed. She was desperate for her plan to stay on track.

"You do remember the broken axle of our hired coach, do you not?" Sarah asked. "Unfortunately, Thompkins said a new axle will not arrive so the repair can be made for at least two days."

"Two days! There is no telling what devious schemes my mother will concoct in that amount of time. The letter I received from her yesterday said it was time to consider marriage, which means she does not have the man picked out yet but she will very soon. No, I need to find another way home."

Lillian swung her legs around and let them fall off the side of the bed. Her head was swimming, causing her to wobble. She grabbed fistfuls of the bedcover to steady herself. At the sound of Prince Albert scampering across the floor, she looked up to see him chasing his small ball of yarn from one side of the room to another.

"What time is it?" she asked, hoping the light from the window meant there was still enough daylight left for travel.

"It is nearing five in the evening."

That was good. Now if they could just find a way to get home.

"Lillian, I do not understand why you had an episode today," Sarah said quietly into the silence of the room.

There were several heartbeats before Lillian answered in a subdued tone. "It has changed."

Sarah did not need an explanation of what 'it' was. Her faithful companion already knew; she had witnessed the effects of Lillian's ability for years. "How?"

"How has it changed, or do you mean how could it change?" Lillian asked.

"Either. Both." Sarah shrugged lightly.

Lillian took a deep breath and let it out before explaining. "I have noticed a difference over the past several months, but I do not yet know what to make of it. The touch of bare skin was almost always the cause of my violent visions of a person's past, but now clothing is not always a barrier. When I am near someone, I often get a physical sensation from the person's memories. In this case, that man touched me through two layers of clothing and a heavy cloak."

"Oh, Lillian, this is awful!" Sarah said with a distressed look on her face.

"Stop." Lillian's voice was hard, her face stern. "Remember, no pity, Sarah. I have never wanted it and that will never change."

The anger at the truth of her life gave Lillian the energy to push herself off the bed to a standing position. She went to the small mirror hanging on the wall and smoothed her straight brown hair back into place. Once she assured herself that she was presentable enough, she went to the door. "Take me to the innkeeper, please. We must find out what is to be done so we can arrive home on time."

"You are still determined to reach London today?" Sarah asked.

"Of course," she said as she marched out into the hallway. "That was the plan, and you know I always stick with my plans."

The innkeeper was in the taproom. He was a short, stout man with a rounded belly and thinning hair that had been combed over the top of his head. He turned to serve full tankards of ale to two men sitting at the bar.

Lillian did not see the murderous man, but she took a glance about the inn to be certain. She breathed a sigh of relief at his absence.

The innkeeper beamed at the sight of her. "You look as if you are feeling better, my lady."

"Yes, I am, thank you," she said. "Can you tell me if there is a conveyance available to bring us to London since our hired coach is out of commission for the present moment?"

The man's smile fell. "The only things you'll find hereabouts are rough farmers' carts or gigs too small to carry the likes of you."

"I would not mind riding on the back of a cart if it gets us to London tonight," she said nearly in a whisper to Sarah, standing beside her.

"My lady, no. It would not be proper for a lady to arrive in London in such a vehicle."

She sighed at Sarah's practicality. "I suppose not, but we need to find something." She spoke to the innkeeper again. "Is there nothing to accommodate us? Perhaps a village or inn a little further away has something we could hire?"

He shook his head. "Not that I know of, my lady."

A deep, smooth voice from behind them made Lillian jump. "Perhaps I can be of assistance?"

Pivoting on one foot, Lillian slowly turned toward the speaker. He stood at least a head taller than she, and she had to look up to maintain eye contact. He was a very handsome man with dark wavy hair and twinkling blue eyes. There were patches on the sleeves of his jacket and his boots were scuffed, although he looked quite clean. She thought he might be a local farmer or merchant.

Next to him stood a slight, dark-haired young man who kept his head shyly lowered.

Pulling up from inside herself everything Signor Silvano had taught them about engaging with people, Lillian stood a little taller and faced the stranger. "I thank you for your offer, sir, but it is not required. We can manage on our own."

For some reason, this caused the man to chuckle. "Far be it for me to contradict a lady; however, I believe I did overhear you asking for a conveyance which could transport you to London, and I believe I may have a solution for you."

Well. What could Lillian say to that? They had no transportation and she did need to get home as soon as possible —needed it like the very air she breathed.

"What is your solution, sir?" she asked.

The man pointed toward the door. "A carriage pulled into the yard not too long ago to rest the horses. The driver currently has no passengers, as he is returning the vehicle to London for his master. I am sure I could easily convince him to take a lady such as yourself the few miles remaining."

She looked dubiously at the stranger. Could she trust him? She had no other way to get to London.

Squeezing her hands into frustrated fists, Lillian took a deep breath. She wanted to weep at all these obstacles blocking her path. She hated weeping, but if ever there was a good time to do it, it was now.

Lillian took a second look at the man, who was waiting patiently for an answer. She changed her earlier assessment, thinking now that he was a gentleman of sorts. It was in the way he stood and the fine accent of his speech. She could not discern the full truth about him as she could with many others just by standing nearby, but when Lillian probed her intuition, it said he was an honorable man. She mentally slapped herself. Trusting what she called her curse to tell her if someone had good or evil intentions was just insane!

She turned to Sarah for an opinion, and as always, her maid had one. "I say we stay at the inn until the hired carriage can take us to London, but I know that once you have your mind set on something, there is no changing it," she said in a quiet voice. "You must decide if your urgency to return home is more important than your own safety."

Translated that meant: 'You are stupid for trying to get what you want regardless of the consequences.'

Lillian inwardly smiled at her friend's small chastisement. She had too much of her mother in her makeup. When she wanted to accomplish something, she let nothing stand in her way.

After several heartbeats, she made up her mind. "Yes," she said to the man. "I would be pleased if you would inquire on our behalf."

The man bowed, the youth bobbed his head, and they disappeared.

Sarah leaned in and hissed, "Lillian, do you think this is

such a wise idea? Although he previously assisted us, it does not mean we should trust him. We have no idea what he could be up to."

"Previously assisted us?" Lillian asked, confused.

"I did not have a chance to tell you. He is the gentleman who carried you to the room upstairs and offered us further help if we should be in need."

"That was very kind of him," Lillian said with a grin, "and it appears we shall be taking him up on his offer."

Sarah rolled her eyes.

Several minutes later, Lillian felt a rush of cold air as the stranger came back through the front door. "The driver has graciously agreed to convey you to London," he said, "but he is about to leave. How soon will you be ready to depart?"

"As soon as we can move our luggage to the carriage," she said.

"I will speak to your coachman about the arrangements and see that your luggage is transferred. It should take no more than ten minutes," he said.

The innkeeper beamed from behind the bar. "A happy solution, sir," he called out. "I thank you for it."

Once they were left alone again, Sarah turned to Lillian and opened her mouth as if to argue. Lillian stopped her with a raised hand. "I am as skeptical as you about going anywhere in a strange carriage, but I feel we shall be safe."

Her friend looked unsure. "I shall not say another word, except to say you have already been through enough today. I would hate to see you in further difficulty."

Lillian wanted to say how her entire life felt like one enormous difficulty the size of the highest, most treacherous mountain that could never be climbed, but she kept it to herself. Sarah had been with her through it all and she did not deserve her scorn or sarcasm.

Lillian settled her bill with the innkeeper, leaving a little extra for an ale or two for the stranger, and less than a quarter of an hour later, with her bonnet firmly tied below her chin, she was handing her case of herbals and her large bag with Prince Albert into the coach to Sarah, who was already seated. She scrambled inside before the stranger could offer his hand to assist her. She poked her head out and said, "I do greatly appreciate your assistance today, sir, and I shall never forget your kindness."

He bowed formally. "May the remainder of your journey be free of trouble." He secured the door and the coach wheels turned.

Lillian opened her bag, letting Prince Albert have his freedom. Many thought a ferret was an odd choice for a pet, but he was very loyal and affectionate and he never ate the furniture. Almost never. There was an occasional chair leg or two. She stroked down his furry back and sighed. The best part about her pet was she did not worry about what visions would appear whenever she touched him. She could not say the same about humans.

She closed her eyes and let the surrounding countryside

outside the window envelope her. She wanted to not have to think about that part of her life, at least for a little while.

Lillian breathed an enormous sigh of relief when the carriage finally reached her family's street in the prosperous Mayfair area of London. By the time the horses stopped in front of the gate, night had fallen and the air was chilled enough she could see her breath. The days were still short in England and the nights cold.

She did not wait for assistance, but opened the door and hopped down herself. Prince Albert was once again in the bag over her shoulder.

The coachman reached her side. "I will jest see to the luggage, my lady." He went to the back and began unstrapping the trunks and bags.

Once the last bag was at her feet, Lillian reached into her reticule and said, "We are very grateful for your generosity in seeing us home. I do not know what we would have done without your assistance." She handed him a half crown coin.

The driver tugged at his cap and beamed. "Thank you, my lady. It was my pleasure." He climbed up onto his seat and disappeared down the street with a flick of the reins.

Standing just outside the iron railing in front of Wentworth House, Lillian looked up at the three-story structure she had had very little time to enjoy during her lifetime. Most of her years had been spent either at the family estate in Norfolk or at Silvano's. Theirs was a pleasant townhome made of red brick, with six steps leading up to a two-columned portico.

Rain began to fall, so she hurried through the gate to the front door where she could be shielded. She rapped the brass lion's-head knocker and smiled when James, one of the family's footmen, opened the door of the house. Upon seeing her, his face broke into a wide, friendly smile and he opened the door wider to allow them to enter.

"Hello, James," Lillian said, taking her cloak off and handing it to him. In spite of herself, she was pleased to be home in familial surroundings, and it would be good to see her cousin Anne again.

The young, dark-haired footman gave a deep bow. "It has been some time since you were home last for a visit and it is a great pleasure to have you returned to us, Lady Lillian, if I may say so."

"You may say so, James," Lillian said. "No more short visits, I am home to stay. Our trunks and valises are out front being rained on and Sarah will take my case upstairs. If you will tell me where my parents are to be found, I shall greet them straight away." There was no time to waste before she set her plan into motion.

"They are in the drawing room, my lady."

"Very good." Lillian tugged her gloves to ensure they were on tightly and advanced past the front door where the butler stood in the foyer waiting to greet her. "Higgins, you are looking well."

"Thank you, my lady." He slowly performed a stately

bow. Lillian could hear him creak as he did so. *Is that his bones or some sort of corset?* she wondered. *And when did he get so old?* She had been away too long. Higgins' white hair was quite a bit thinner on top, although neatly combed and pomaded as always. "You were not expected home for at least another sennight."

"Yes, well, I decided it was best to arrive as soon as possible."

James passed with their bags and Higgins stepped forward to shut the door. Sarah took Prince Albert from her shoulder and followed James up the stairs.

"I shall go in to greet my parents now. Who is at home?" Lillian asked.

"Ahem," Higgins covered his mouth with his fist and looked up at Lillian's bonnet.

"Oh, yes." She pulled on the strings to remove it.

"Lord and Lady Wentworth, Miss Anne, and Lord Simon are all here at present," Higgins said.

"Oh, excellent. It shall be a joyous homecoming." She handed the butler the bonnet and her reticule. "Lead on, Higgins. I am sure the family has waited long enough to see me, and I am quite anxious to see them as well."

He bowed again, then creaked slowly down the long white marbled hallway, Lillian following.

As they approached the double doorway to the drawing room, another footman she did not recognize opened both doors. Higgins entered first and announced, "Lady Lillian has arrived." He bowed to the room and retreated, leaving Lillian standing to face the family she had hardly seen over the past eight years while she was closeted away at Silvano's.

Her mother and Cousin Anne sat on the settee near the fire —blonde-haired Anne with a broad smile and her dark-haired mother with a look of shocked surprise. Her father sat in a wing-backed chair, a drink in his hand. He raised his dark eyebrows at her entrance. Her heart softened at the sight of her stout father and his familiar long, bushy sideburns. Finally, her brother Simon, who stood with an elbow propped on the fireplace mantle, looking bored. It was no surprise when he scowled at the sight of her. They had often clashed.

She took a moment to feel affection for the family who had done their best to nurture and protect her over the years. Then she followed Signor Silvano's advice and used her entrance as an opportunity. Sweeping into the room, like the Queen herself, she stood tall with her chin high and announced to the occupants, "Hello, family! No need to worry about an expensive social season at the marriage market. I have no plans to marry. Ever."

Lillian's grand plan crashed to the floor like a basketful of eggs, now a broken and disgusting mess.

At first, nothing but silence greeted her when she stood before her family for the first time in months and made her declaration.

That was until her mother came out of her shocked state. "Whatever are you about, child?" she screeched.

"It will not do," her father blustered.

Her brother simply glared, while sweet and kind Anne jumped up to give her a hug and tell her how good it was to see her, ignoring her declaration completely.

Lillian had tried to assert herself, she truly had, but her parents had a counterargument for everything.

Now seated on the settee, she looked at her mother and said, "You know I cannot marry with this curse hanging about my neck."

"Nonsense," her mother said, patting her knee. "It will all work out and you will be happy in the end. You will see."

"We only want what is best for you," her father said.

What is best for me? she thought. *If that was the case, they would buy me a hermitage in the Orkney Islands, where I would never have to see another person again.*

"Besides," her mother said kindly, "you are no different from any of the other ladies currently looking for husbands in London this season."

Her mother was delusional.

Lillian refrained from pointing out that normal ladies had the luxury of looking for a husband because they did not have to worry about bumping into people at parties. Normal ladies did not have to think about whether to offer their hand to a gentleman when they were introduced. Normal ladies were able to live ordinary lives.

She was not a normal lady.

After what felt like an hour of an exhausting argument with her parents, including an attempt to promote Sarah from lady's maid to her companion now that she was older, Lillian had been well and truly conquered. She had gained absolutely nothing but the choice of husband if she agreed to one social season in London.

She was to endure three whole lovely months of torture, which would be set into motion the very next day, as Lady Wentworth was determined to have Lillian fitted for an entirely new and fashionable wardrobe at Madame Favre's.

Anne took her hand. "It will not be so bad. You will see. We can have ever so much fun together."

Her cousin and Sarah were two of the people who had always been able to touch her without consequences. She had no problems with her mother either. Her father, on the other hand, was one of the first people with whom she had experienced an episode. It was not because he was a man as she had once thought—she had since had plenty of visions with women too. She did not understand why her ability was triggered by some and not others. It just was.

Lillian looked down at Anne's hand, her own in heavy gloves, her cousin's bare. It was a stark statement about the contrast in their lives, but now was not the time to squash Anne's dreams. She looked up. "Perhaps. I know I will at least enjoy your companionship."

Not long after, she complained of a headache and went upstairs to her bedroom. It was not far from the truth, as the day's events had left her exhausted. She had spent little time in this room during her lifetime. It was decorated with a delicate peach and green floral wallpaper with matching cushions and drapery. It was the room of a little girl. Perhaps it was time to redecorate.

She sank onto her bed and sighed at the memory of her defeat. It had simply been easier for her to give in.

She had worked so hard to come home in time to stop this madness, but it was all for naught. She had gained nothing, while her family had gained everything they wanted. Well, perhaps not everything they wanted. Their daughter was still not anything like the other ladies of society. Their daughter was still a walking nightmare.

Sarah gave her a sympathetic smile. "It has been a long day."

Lillian snorted. "That is an understatement. I now wish I had stayed at that little inn and waited for Mr. Thompkins to find a brand-new axle. At least it would have delayed this torture by a few days."

Sarah laughed, her hazel eyes sparkling. "I do hate to tell you I told you so."

"You do not. You love telling me that." Lillian wrinkled her nose. "I will admit I made a tactical error. I assumed my mother was persuadable by the use of logic."

She allowed herself to fall back onto the bed. Now that argument had failed, Lillian needed to adjust her strategy. She had to find a way. Because she possessed one conviction that would never change: Lady Lillian Ruth Hargraves, only daughter of the Earl of Wentworth, would never walk down the aisle to her own wedding.

FOUR

Signor Silvano's Sayings Number 4
When in an unfamiliar or comfortable situation,
pretend you know exactly what you are doing.
If nothing else comes of it,
you will at least look impressive.

~London, England, Four Weeks Later~

"Come on, Lil. We will be late for the Grantley ball!"

Lillian sighed at her cousin Anne's animated voice coming from the doorway. She was still working her way through the many layers a lady needed to dress for a ball—stockings, chemise, petticoat, corset, and finally the gown itself followed by gloves and shoes. Thank goodness gowns were simpler than a few decades ago when women had to wear awkward panniers and multiple layers of petticoats.

Another evening, another ballroom filled wall to wall with hordes of people. Hordes or herds? It felt like being in the middle of a herd. Or a plague of locusts.

Whatever one called it, it had turned out to be all that

she had ever dreaded before coming to London, plus much worse. However, as predicted, she *was* enjoying every minute of being with Anne again.

Lillian sucked in a sharp breath as Sarah pulled on her corset strings. "Too tight," she rasped out. "I need room to breathe."

"Sorry," Sarah said, and she felt the loosening of the evil contraption.

Next, Sarah slipped the ball gown over her head and tugged everything into place. Tonight's dress was an odd pale green that was unmistakably the color of cabbage. She had no idea what her mother had been thinking when she ordered it.

She sat at the dressing table and allowed Sarah to make last-minute adjustments to her hair.

Anne had come into the room and stood beside her now. "You do look lovely, Cousin," she said with her always friendly smile.

"Do I?" Lillian took a final look at herself in the mirror. Her dark hair was nicely fashioned in a loose knot with cascading curls thanks to Sarah's handiwork with the curling tongs. Her complexion was so pale. "My brown eyes are far from fashionable though, and I wish I had your blonde hair."

Anne met her eyes in the mirror. "Your eyes are not simply brown, they are more like a dark golden brown." She paused, then added, "Besides, what does fashionable even mean, Lillian? It means everyone is trying to look like everyone else. But those with true beauty and character do not need to be a copy of others. They merely need to be themselves."

"You may only be a year older than I, but you have always been infinitely wiser." Lillian gave her cousin a fond smile that fell when she added: "But none of this—hair, eyes, dress —truly matters. I could be all that society wished for me to be and I would still never fit in."

Anne was silent now, because what else was there to say? She understood the stark truth of what Lillian's life was like.

Blinking away these self-involved thoughts, Lillian slipped on her white evening gloves and pulled the specially made extended short sleeves of her gown over them so that no skin would show. She had attempted a rebellion over the fabric colors for her wardrobe at the dressmaker's, but nothing had come of it, and tonight she was wearing the color of a vegetable. Instead of blending into the woodwork, she would stand out like a weed in the Royal Gardens.

She gave one final tug to the arm of each glove. She no longer needed to make 'accidental' contact with anyone at the ball, since her reputation as an odd duck had already taken firm hold from previous incidents. She frowned slightly over the thought. After her more recent visions, she was no longer certain her gloves offered much protection anyway. True, she could still touch some people without consequences, but she could never predict which ones.

Prince Albert had jumped up onto the bench next to her, bobbing up and down, looking for attention. "Sorry, my little imp," she said softly, "but you know if I touch you, my hands will smell like ferret all evening, and although I do wish to keep people away from me, my mother will send me upstairs again to change before we can even leave the house." She altered her voice to mimic her mother's high pitch and drew the words out: "It simply will not do."

Anne giggled. Sarah rolled her eyes.

Lillian swiveled on the rosewood bench seat to look at her cousin and said in an exaggerated manner, "Is the season not over yet?"

Anne gave a tinkling laugh. "Come along, Lillian. If we keep your mother waiting any longer, she will send out the cavalry to fetch us."

Lillian stood. "I am as ready as I ever will be. Let us depart." She turned to her maid with a cheeky grin and practiced her curtsy. "May your evening be more pleasant than mine, fair lady."

Sarah shooed her away with a laugh.

Lillian picked up her dark green shawl, embroidered with small white daisies, and the matching reticule from the bed and joined Anne in the hallway. They walked slowly side by side to the staircase.

If Lillian needed a living example of what was currently fashionable, her cousin would be it. Tonight, Anne was dressed in a white gown typical of young ladies coming out in society for their first social season. It had beautifully embroidered pink roses along the hem and the neckline. She was blonde, blue eyed, and curvy, but not plump. Plus, she had grace and poise to match her beauty. But her cousin was not only fashionable, she was extremely likable. She made everyone she spoke to feel at ease, even the most socially awkward.

Anne interrupted her observations by asking, "You do not much care for attending balls, do you?"

"No," Lillian said with an ironic chuckle. "No, I do not. Mostly because there are too many people all in one room, creating too much heat until one can hardly breathe. By the end of the evening, I want nothing more than to hide in a secluded spot to regain my composure. But I know you do not agree."

Anne shook her head, her curls bouncing. "No, I do not. I find it all so interesting."

"Interesting?"

"Yes. I love observing people and there are always so many new ladies and gentlemen to meet. I wish I could dance with them all."

"With all the ladies and the gentlemen?" she teased.

Anne laughed. "Silly. Just the men, thank you very much. At every event, there is such a handsome collection available."

Lillian snorted. "You speak as if they are keepsakes to be put on your sitting room mantle." She tugged at her gloves to ensure a tight fit. "I find them all to be decidedly similar to the point where I often cannot remember their names," she paused, "and all of them are after the same thing."

"What is that?" Anne asked with a perplexed expression.

"A rich and beautiful bride who they can leave in the country with a small brood of children while they enjoy themselves in town," Lillian said, shrugging. "A bride who they can parade about perhaps a few weeks out of the year to show all their peers how well they have chosen for themselves. Preferably a bride with little brains, but one who can keep a well-run home and dresses in the latest fashions. The perfect jewel, in other words.”

After she thought on the matter, Anne protested. “How very cynical of you. That may be true for some men, but not all. I intend to only marry a man who is wildly in love with me and who could never be parted from me for even a moment.” Her eyes gleamed at the thought.

Lillian did not have the heart to destroy her cousin’s dream by telling her how unlikely it was to find such a man. Instead, she said, “Then you shall wait for the right man, Anne. Nothing will do but to have the exact husband as you describe.”

Anne giggled. “Precisely.”

“Whoever he is, he will be the luckiest man in the world.”

Anne put her arm through Lillian’s and hugged it as they descended the staircase. Lord and Lady Wentworth and her brother Simon were waiting in the foyer, their cloaks donned for departure.

“Ah, there you two are,” her mother said with obvious relief. “I was one minute away from sending someone up to summon you. We must be going. Hurry, hurry, hurry.” She clapped her hands and herded everyone toward the door. Two footmen quickly stepped forward with the new arrivals’ cloaks.

It was a very short distance by carriage to the crowded street in front of Lord and Lady Grantley’s home. Lillian was the last to leave their conveyance, accompanied by Simon. The lamplight glowed on his wavy golden hair. Like an angel. Lillian wanted to snort at this thought. Although he was not evil like many men she had encountered, he was no saint either. She had seen more than she had wished to know about her brother.

She stiffened her spine, ready to survive the evening. She ignored Simon's offered arm. He bent his head and said in a low, sneering voice, "You know, I shall not always be present to look after you. It is high time you married, Lil."

"How utterly ridiculous and how well you know it!" she exclaimed, then lowered her voice to gain control of herself. "You know how impossible that would be." She tightened her hands into fists and resisted the urge to tug on her gloves again. They had had this conversation before—several times over the past few weeks in fact. Simon's continual desire to bring it up frustrated her. Enough was enough.

"You know my opinion on the matter," Simon added. "That is all I shall say for now, as it is almost our turn to go inside."

Lillian took a deep breath, lifted her head high, firmed her chin, and sailed up the stairs into the house. Her brother had no choice but to keep pace or tug her back and cause a scene.

The foyer was a stark study in black and white—plain white painted walls, a white marble floor, black marble stairs, and a crystal chandelier above their heads. The Grantleys had no imagination.

She and Simon handed their cloaks to a waiting footman

and caught up with their party in the receiving line, which was moving quite slowly.

"This is the largest crush we have seen yet this season is it not?" Anne whispered when Lillian reached her side.

"Quite," Lillian said tightly. Already, she felt concern over how many people would be within touching range. She wished she could be closeted away in her room with a good book instead of facing down this ball.

When it was their turn, Lillian curtsied coolly to their host and hostess—hoping she would not be required to stop and converse—and sighed in relief when they all moved on and up the stairs to the ballroom.

This room was quite a contrast from the front of the house, with light pink painted walls, alternating every few feet with a mint-green silk damask wall covering, and gilding on every possible surface. Lillian's eyes widened at the garishness.

She had taken one step toward the matron's corner to sit with the older ladies and chaperones when her mother stopped her. "Can you not simply stand at my side and meet eligible gentleman this evening, Lillian? How are you ever to find a husband hidden away in a corner at every event?"

"With this many people, Mother," Lillian said, "I would be jostled about like sheep in a pen. That would serve none of us well."

Her mother harrumphed but said nothing further. Arguing with the truth would have been pointless.

Lillian did not understand why her mother persisted in

forcing her to attend these events. Perhaps she hoped that one evening her daughter would magically be replaced with an ordinary woman. Many of the ladies had given her the side-eye over their fans as she had walked through the crowd; they all knew she was not normal.

Simon led her to a seat apart from the rest of the attendees where she could avoid the jostling of the throng and discourage offers to dance. Not that she received many such offers any longer now that her reputation had begun to tarnish. Her backup plan was working nicely. She merely needed to skate through the season with no suitors so her parents would agree to her terms for independence. She had every confidence they would.

Each party, ball, and musicale in the past several weeks had knocked Lillian lower on the social scale. Her first grand entrance into society included an incident soon after being presented to the Queen, which had ignited the rumors about her. It would have been fine if she could simply faint gracefully like other ladies when she saw images of the past, but her problem always brought on uncontrolled tremors that made her look demon possessed, or so she had been told on more than one occasion. When she had had another event at her come-out ball, where she was formally introduced to society, the gossip about her strange fits spread, just as Lillian had hoped.

She pulled a painted fan out of her reticule now, sat back in the chair, opened it, and slowly fanned herself as she surveyed the crowd.

This particular ball was indeed a spectacular crush as Anne had said. Lord and Lady Grantley were popular hosts, but even for them, this turnout exceeded all expectations. Lillian wondered at this until she overheard some gossip from two older ladies sitting nearby.

"Yes!" the first voice stated quite loudly. "He has newly returned to town and is expected to make his debut social appearance tonight."

"Are you certain?" the second voice asked.

"Yes, yes. I heard it from Cook, whose sister is on very friendly terms with his housekeeper. It is a sure thing, it is! The news is on everyone's lips tonight. Such anticipation!" she crowed.

The second lady began to speak again, but the first cut her off. "It is said he has an income of thirty thousand pounds a year. Can you imagine it, Frances? Thirty thousand pounds! He is as rich as the king! Oh, if I only had a daughter to marry off." She sighed dreamily.

Before Lillian could hear more about the mysterious lord, a pair of ladies stepped between her and the gossipers, cutting off the sound. If what the woman had said was true, it explained why so many had come this evening. Everyone wanted to be one of the first to see this nobleman with such an extraordinary income. As if the man himself were of no matter.

Lillian renewed her fanning in an attempt to waft some of the growing heat away. A newcomer was of no interest to her regardless of his income. Surviving the evening without melting into a puddle—or worse—was much higher on her list of priorities.

"Why do we come to these miserable affairs again?" a familiar voice said—her friend had slipped so easily into the seat next to her without notice.

"To keep up appearances, Francesca dearest," she mimicked her mother. "What would people say if you stayed home like a recluse?"

Francesca joined in, "They would think we had hidden you away from the public eye because there is something wrong with you." They looked at each other and laughed.

"I wish we truly could hide away," her friend complained, more serious now. Her eyebrows were knit together and her eyes partially closed as if she had a headache. She probably did.

Francesca, Fran to her friends, and Lillian had attended Silvano's School together, and being the same age of seventeen, had both recently come out into society—though neither had wished for it. Fran had just as much reason as Lillian to want to stay away from people—maybe even more. Fran could hear people's thoughts.

In the peace and quiet of the country, her friend was a lively and adventurous girl with a very laid-back manner. She often encouraged others at the school to get involved in some lark or another, which frequently got them into trouble. It was common to find her leading a brigade of cherry-pit-spitters from the mezzanine at church or sprinkling itching powder on the boys' sheets. Although Silvano always punished her, Fran's charm saved her from the worst of consequences.

It was especially difficult for Fran that Silvano had closed the school in Shropshire and moved it to London now that she was surrounded by so many voices.

"I agree wholeheartedly, Fran. I would give anything to go back to the country, preferably for the rest of my life."

Fran snorted. "Except there is nothing to go back to."

Pain squeezed Lillian's chest at the thought of her beloved school now burned to the ground. She had learned after the other students arrived in London right behind her that the reason Silvano had packed them all up was due to one of Catriona's visions. They had left just in time to avoid burning with the building, set aflame by zealots who thought they were practicing witchcraft. It felt like the persecution of her kind would never end.

She looked more closely at Fran, who was unusually pale tonight. With her peach skin and dark red curls, Fran was incredibly beautiful. As tall as many men, she had been the tallest of the girls at school, and she reminded Lillian of a queen towering over her subjects. No one would think her regal tonight, slumped as she was in her chair.

Lillian resumed waving her fan while both girls sat back to watch the mass of people. What strange creatures they all were—some more outrageous than others. Mrs. Mattingly was wearing peacock feathers in her headdress that were so tall one could easily spot her from the other side of the room.

Lillian leaned over to whisper, "Lord Dashford is wearing that foul pomade in his hair again. I can smell him every time he passes by. The odor is ten times worse than that of Prince Albert on his worst day."

Fran chuckled.

Many of the ladies and gentlemen crammed into the ballroom were overdressed in over-ornamented and over-bright clothing, as if they were to appear on a stage. This was the society her parents wished her to become a part of.

"I suppose you know about the person everyone is anticipating tonight?" Lillian leaned toward Fran again and whispered behind her fan.

"Yes of course." Fran leaned in and lowered her voice as well. "The Duke of Wyvern. No one has seen him in ages. He has been on the continent or in the colonies—the rumors cannot seem to agree—for the past four years and is now returning to take up his responsibilities." She looked about to be sure no one could hear before adding, "Apparently, there was some scandal that caused him to flee, but the funny thing is, no one seems to know what it was."

"Not much of a scandal if no one remembers it," Lillian said.

"Exactly!" Fran looked as if she would say something else, but sat back instead. After a minute she added, "It would serve everyone right if he were fat, ugly, and balding. All here are slobbering over a man I doubt most have ever met."

The fates of bad timing were against her friend. The musicians stopped playing and the room fell silent just as she grew louder at the end of her speech, but no one turned to look at her. Instead, all eyes were on the doorway in which a beaming Lady Grantley stood. She posed at the threshold—for all to see—on the arm of a tall stranger with dark, wavy hair. His height made the lady, who was nearly as wide as she was tall, look like an overweight child.

A footman broke the silence with an announcement that echoed above the heads of the guests. "His Grace, the Duke of Wyvern."

The crowd clapped at his entrance—clapped! As if he had performed some spectacular trick. The duke nodded regally to the said crowd like he was the Prince of Wales, then bent his head low to speak to Lady Grantley.

"He is not as happy to be here as everyone else is to have him," Fran said. Her ability gave her insights into a person's mind beyond what could be observed.

"Indeed?" Lillian asked casually while she continued to watch. A gentleman who did not enjoy a ridiculous show being put on for his benefit was certainly intriguing.

He continued to stand in the doorway, scanning the room. *Perhaps he is sizing up the enemy*, Lillian thought. Finally, he leaned in to say something else to Lady Grantley, who then signaled to the musicians to resume. They lifted their instruments and struck the first chords of a cotillion. Then, very slowly, she led the duke on a circuit of the perimeter of the ballroom.

The crowd followed this walk with their eyes as if they were the predators and he the prey. The thought made Lillian very uncomfortable on his behalf. She squirmed in her chair and worked her fan.

"Well, he makes ordinary black and white eveningwear look extraordinary. So much for my theory of a grotesque duke," Fran said dryly.

For some reason this characterization caused Lillian to burst out laughing. "What a moniker," she said. "The grotesque duke. It sounds like the name of a character from a fairy tale and is far from the truth."

She looked up again to size up the handsome man, a large smile still on her face, but found him staring straight at her. *Oh dear*. Of course the one time she had allowed herself a bit of freedom to be her true self in public and it had caused her to be noticed.

As the couple came closer, her mind was distracted by the realization that the duke looked very familiar. Lillian studied his features in more detail, and it came to her like a flash. A country gentleman with twinkling blue eyes. Could it be? How was this possible if the duke had only just returned to England as rumor suggested? Perhaps he had never left the country at all, she mused to herself. Perhaps everything about this man was a mirage. She had heard of his name before. Who with a copy of Debrett's Peerage had not? All ladies and gentlemen were required to memorize it, but since she had mostly been away from society, they had never had a chance to meet.

The duke leaned down once again to speak to Lady Grantley. What he said caused the lady's eyes to grow wide in surprise. She nodded, then led him in Lillian and Fran's direction.

The closer they drew, the more certain Lillian became that this was the man who had assisted her a few weeks ago. He was a little more tanned, and his hair and clothing were more fashionable, but it had to be him. Perhaps he too had recognized her and this was the reason he was heading this way. Lady Grantley and the duke stopped right in front of her chair.

"Lady Lillian, his grace would like an introduction," the formidable lady said with pursed lips.

"Of course," Lillian answered. She would like to find out more about this man who had helped her in such difficult circumstances.

She stood and made a deep curtsy as Lady Grantley spoke. "Your grace, may I introduce you to Lady Lillian Hargraves, daughter of the Earl of Wentworth. Lady Lillian, His Grace, the Duke of Wyvern."

"Your grace," Lillian said, "I believe we have met before?" She looked up at him in expectation.

A perplexed look came over the man's face, then his jaw firmed in what looked like anger. Was he offended that she had brought up their previous acquaintance since they had not been properly introduced at that time?

His face relaxed, unreadable once again, and he said, "I do not believe so, my lady."

Lillian did not offer her hand, so the duke could only bow as she stood back to full height. "I have no wish to dance this evening," he said, "but I see you are also not dancing?" Lillian nodded. "Perhaps then, you would honor me with a stroll about the room?" He held out his arm and waited for her to take it as if her assent was a given.

She had to think quickly. He gave no explanation for or acknowledgement of their prior meeting. Perhaps he did not wish to hurt her reputation, but it still irritated her. If this was how he wished to play it, she would give back as good as she received. This man was a duke and usually such high-born men seemed to prefer empty-headed women who cared for nothing more than fashion and flattery and giving flattery in return. He had singled her out for some reason. The best way to repel him was to be exactly the opposite of what he would expect. She inwardly smiled and turned to introduce Fran, who would appreciate the strategy, but the seat was empty. The wretch had slipped away!

Lillian took a deep breath, stepped forward, and lied. "I would be honored, your grace." She hesitated, then carefully placed her hand on the duke's elbow, barely touching it. Lifting her chin, she kept pace with him while inside her head she thought, *This poor fellow has no idea what he is in for.*

FIVE

Signor Silvano's Sayings Number 5
Do whatever it takes to get what you want.
Make no apologies. Take no prisoners.

Have balls always been this tedious? Gabriel eyed the too-thick crowd as he walked beside the mystery that was Lady Lillian—a woman who claimed they had met previously. This was either a new ploy ladies of society used to get a foothold into a duke's good graces, or somewhere, somehow, she had met his brother. If the latter was the case, he had a bone to pick with Michael, who was supposed to be in hiding.

The first question out of Lady Lillian's mouth to him had been: 'What do you feel are the political implications of Prince Leopold marrying Princess Charlotte?'

He was stunned. Most ladies waited for him to flatter them, at which he had little skill. Instead, he was able to give an informed opinion on the topic in question, which he hoped had impressed her. She was a refreshing change from other ladies who simpered or flirted or did that fluttering thing with their eyelashes young ladies had been practicing on him all his life to gain his attention. He now wondered if the lady of his mother's choosing might work out after all.

Gabriel had not planned to come to this event, since the next man on his list of suspects was not expected to attend, but his mother had insisted he become acquainted with his prospective bride. She had informed him that Lady Lillian was a sensible and levelheaded woman. Still, he wanted to investigate her on his own terms before raising her family's expectations, especially since the two mothers were old friends. He was worried the lady might turn out to look like a gargoyle or laugh like a hyena. So far so good on those two points.

The ball was to serve an additional purpose. His mother had also urged him to establish himself in society immediately to keep the gossip about his absence to a minimum. He would really rather not waste his time on any social functions that did not serve his personal agenda, but in the end, what the duchess wanted, the duchess got.

Earlier in the week, he had tried once more to work against her on this issue while they dined, but her logic won out in the end. "Mother I only just returned. Why can I not wait a few weeks more before making a grand appearance?" he had asked.

"Because, Gabriel," she had said with that tone that made him feel like he was still a small child, "the Grantley ball is one of the largest events of the season. This would be the perfect chance to show you have returned and you are well."

"That I am well?" he asked, one eyebrow raised.

"Oh, yes. There are many rumors that have been swirling

about since you left, such as that you have gone mad, requiring you to be locked away. My least favorite is the one where you killed your brother and had to leave the country, or else be hanged. I do not know where people get such ideas!"

Gabriel snickered like a schoolboy. He did not understand ladies and gentlemen who had nothing better to do than to make up such nonsense.

His mother glared at him from across the table. "It is no laughing matter, Gabriel."

"Of course not, Mother." He attempted to remove all signs of amusement from his face. Sometimes it was difficult to take gossip seriously.

"You must attend the Grantley ball, show them all you are in excellent health and spirits, and put silence to all the rumors." She paused until Gabriel looked at her directly. "Besides, Lady Lillian will be attending, and since you refuse to meet her informally at a family gathering, this would be the perfect opportunity to be introduced."

Gabriel sighed. "I was merely hoping for more time before pursuing the matter of a wife. You know I wish to concentrate all my time and energy on my investigation."

This caused his mother to sober under the weight of sadness, but then she rallied like the duchess she was. "If this were a typical situation, I would agree with your desire to wait. You are only two and twenty years old, after all, but with only Howard as heir to the title, I say the dukedom is in dire straits until you are successful in your mission to make it safe for Michael to return. Would you not agree?"

Gabriel sat back and rubbed his temples with a thumb and forefinger of one hand. "I agree he is not a suitable heir, Mother. I shall go to the Grantley ball and be introduced to Lady Lillian. There. Will that satisfy you?"

The duchess had given him a beaming smile, and he had seen the gleam of triumph in her eyes. "That will do for now, my son. Let us discuss what you will need in preparation for the ball."

Once his mother got started on a project, there was little he could do to stop her. Which he supposed was why she made a perfect duchess and why he was now at the Grantley ball like a good son. The only thing that had been missing was a pat on the head from his mother on his way out the front door earlier this evening.

He realized he and his companion had been silent too long. He took a moment now to assess her once again. She had dark brown hair and dark eyes and had been especially pretty when he saw her laughing smile earlier, but she was not smiling now. Perhaps she would appreciate more conversation from him.

"Are you—"

"How are—"

They simultaneously spoke.

"Ladies first." Gabriel gestured for her to begin.

"I simply wished to ask whether you are pleased to have returned to England, your grace," she said.

Gabriel smiled. "I am indeed pleased to be back. I very much missed my family and the comforts of living in my own home."

"Do you have a large family?"

He grimaced at this question. "Sadly no. I lost my father and brother a few years ago leaving only my mother in my immediate family as well as two great aunts who live with us."

"I am sorry for your loss," she said.

"I do have a scattering of aunts, uncles, and cousins, however," he added.

"It is not the same, is it?"

"No, not the same," he agreed. "What about your family?"

"I have my parents of course, my brother, Lord Simon, older than I by four years, and my cousin Anne, a year older, who lives with us. She is as close as any sister could be."

Gabriel noticed the pleasant rose scent Lady Lillian wore as he steered them around a knot of people who were blocking their way. There was scarcely enough room to do so. "You are blessed indeed to have siblings. That is something I miss." He sobered. How he wished a thousand times over he could have Michael back so that he might be tormented once again by his antics.

They walked on, but in silence once more. Gabriel decided to attempt to push for some information. "When we were introduced, you said that perhaps we had met before somewhere? Where would that have been? Perhaps I have forgotten."

"I believe I must be mistaken," Lady Lillian said. "I was assisted on my way to London a few weeks ago when I experienced a carriage mishap. The gentleman resembled you, that is all."

"Yes, for if it had been me, I would not have forgotten you so soon," Gabriel said with a grin.

The lady gave him a slight scowl before looking ahead again. He had always assumed most ladies enjoyed a bit of flattery, but obviously not this one. He should not have attempted it. Michael was the one who knew how to charm women. When Gabriel tried using the same words his brother regularly practiced, they always fell flat.

What was he doing wrong?

He went back to a more usual topic of idle conversation. "Do you like riding?"

She jumped as if she had gone somewhere else in her thoughts and had been interrupted. "Yes, I very much enjoy riding, especially in the country."

"What makes riding in the country superior to riding anywhere else?" Gabriel used his height to push his way through another large group of guests. It seemed that more and more people were filling the ballroom and yet none were leaving. If this continued much longer, there would be no room to move at all.

He knew he was still the subject of speculation. As they drew past new groups of people, he could see them staring at him, whispering—heads together or behind fans. He looked forward to the time when society found someone new to gossip about and the interest in him faded.

Lady Lillian's voice trembled slightly as she answered his question: "The country affords quite a bit more freedom.

One can gallop to their heart's content and not concern themselves with running into others."

"Unlike this ballroom," he said flatly. "Shall we attempt to find a spot on the terrace to converse? The din of voices is making it hard to hear you, and it is becoming increasingly difficult to move through this mass of bodies."

"And increasingly ho—" Lady Lillian's words were cut off when a gentleman stumbled backward and bumped her off balance.

No, no, no, Lillian screamed in her head as she began to fall. Everything had been going so well—no major incidents in sight. Until now.

Even though the room was nearly wall to wall full of people, instead of someone reaching out to steady her, everyone stepped back as if afraid, allowing her to fall to the floor— as they should, given the rumors that swirled about her, some of them true. Because she was thrown backward away from the duke's side, his attempt to pivot quickly enough to catch her was unsuccessful.

Her bottom met the floor with a hard *thump*. Thank goodness for the layers of fabric to cushion her fall.

"Lady Lillian," the duke said while glaring at the offending gentleman, "are you unharmed?"

"Quite all right." She let out a small groan and took several deep breaths. "Give me a moment to regain my senses."

The duke stepped forward as if to help her stand, but before he could reach out, the other gentleman pushed him aside. His slurred speech was an obvious sign that he was worse for drink. "I am so shorry. Sorry. Let me help you."

The last thing Lillian wanted was for the man to come near her, but before she could push herself to a standing position, he grabbed her by the upper arm and hauled her upwards like a sack of potatoes. It was too much. It was only a matter of seconds before Lillian began to convulse violently. Visions of intense rage and brutality appeared in her head.

Gabriel saw the exact moment Lady Lillian's body began to shake. He assumed it was the doing of this stupid, drunken man who had no business in a civilized ballroom. He stepped forward just in time to catch her as the man dropped her like a hot poker. "It wasn't me," he slurred. "She, she …" He gulped, looking for words. "She's cray, crazy! Everyone knows it."

Gabriel glowered at the man, who had turned white as a sheet. Lady Lillian's body continued to convulse in his arms. Gabriel had no idea what was going on, but he knew the middle of an overcrowded ballroom was no place to find out. He put his other arm under her legs and lifted her against his chest. This time he did not need to use his height to force people to move out of the way. The crowd parted like the Red Sea, allowing him to carry the lady out of the room to the hallway. He immediately saw Lady Grantley, who was returning to the ballroom. When her eyes landed on them, they widened and her mouth opened in surprise, but no sound came out.

Gabriel took charge. Why be a duke if he did not use the authority it afforded after all? "I need a quiet room in which to lay her down, and a doctor, and send someone to fetch Lady Lillian's family." After the lady gave no response, he added tersely, "If you please!"

Lady Grantley, who had just begun fluttering her hands, stood to attention. "Yes, this way." To her right she called, "Bertram, fetch the doctor. John, find Lord and Lady Wentworth or Lord Simon. Quickly!"

She bustled as fast as her short legs and wide girth would allow. "Oh, this will be talked about for weeks. My ball is ruined. Absolutely ruined!" she moaned.

Gabriel had no desire to discuss the woman's inconsequential ball as he followed. Lady Lillian's wellbeing was his primary concern. They reached a room which Lady Grantley sailed through, throwing open the double doors as she went. It looked to be a sitting room. Another footman came inside and began to light candles scattered about. Gabriel spied a settee on the far side of the room and strode toward it.

With Lady Lillian continuing to shake violently in his arms, as if in a fit, he was not sure what he should do. If he put her down on the settee, she might fall off and injure herself. He made an exasperated sound which Lady Grantley misinterpreted.

She began sobbing into her handkerchief. "I am so sorry you have had to deal with this miserable event, your grace. You can put her down there and when her parents come they will take charge of the situation."

He stared her down. "I shall do no such thing, my lady. Lady Lillian was in my care when that bumbling fool knocked her down. I shall stay until I see she has been properly cared for. A warm blanket would be a nice start, do you not agree?" He raised a ducal eyebrow.

The lady opened her mouth to say something, but only a small squeak emerged. Then she closed her mouth, took a breath, and stood a little taller. "Quite right. You there," she pointed at the only footman in the room, "find a warm blanket and a pillow for the lady. Hurry. His grace cannot hold her forever." She clapped her hands to speed the liveried man on his way. "Here." She hastily grabbed a square pillow from a chair by the fire and placed it on the settee. "Put her down now."

Gabriel again raised an eyebrow. The lady's face slowly turned red from the neck up as she realized she had just given an order to a duke.

"Lady Lillian continues to shake. I think it best that I hold on to her." Gabriel took his charge to a large chair by the fire instead and sat down, settling her across his lap. "This should do."

"Your grace," Lady Grantley protested. Her squeak had now turned into an annoying squawk that sounded like a crow. "This is highly improper!"

Gabriel glared at the woman and said in his haughtiest

tone: "Are you quite serious? This woman is ill and in need of our care. Or would you rather she incur additional injury falling off the settee?" He held her gaze.

Lady Grantley looked away, wringing her handkerchief in her hands, and whimpered.

Several people spilled into the room.

Lord Grantley eased up casually next to his wife, taking her hand. "What is it, my dear? I heard we have a small to-do."

Seemingly unable to answer, the lady merely pointed to where Gabriel sat, holding the still-tremoring Lady Lillian on his lap.

Lord Grantley opened his mouth like a dying fish: open, close, open, close.

Behind Grantley, two ladies—one young and one older—hurried across the room. "Lillian!" the younger lady exclaimed. She knelt beside the chair taking Lillian's hands in hers. She looked up to Gabriel, concern and dismay in her eyes. "How long has she been like this?"

"Less than a quarter of an hour. I have sent for a doctor, but I have no notion what else to do for her."

"No. No doctor is necessary," the older lady, presumably Lady Lillian's mother, said, looming over them. "We shall take her home and she will be fine in no time." She looked up, scanned the room, and found whom she sought at the door. "Ah, here is my son Simon. He will take her from you."

"You are certain she does not need a physician, my lady?" Gabriel asked. "This shaking and trembling cannot be good for her body or her mind."

Lady Wentworth looked offended at his insinuation that anything might be wrong with her daughter. "No harm will come to her. This happens from time to time and within approximately half an hour she comes out of it as if she were merely sleeping." To her approaching son, she said, "Simon, please take your sister from this gentleman and we may leave."

Simon did not immediately do as his mother asked. He looked straight into Gabriel's eyes. "How did this happen?" The question was not quite an accusation, but the tone was very close. If he had not understood the man's protectiveness, he might have taken offense.

"Lady Lillian and I were crossing the ballroom when a drunken fool knocked her over. She was fine until he grabbed her by the arms to haul her up. The idiot," he said under his breath. "Then she had this fit."

Lord Simon nodded, seeming to be satisfied with the information. Then he reached down, and pulled Lady Lillian into his arms. "Mother, run ahead and get our cloaks please."

"Yes. Yes, of course." She bustled out of the room.

"Thank you, sir, for attending to my sister so graciously. Many men would have left her to the care of the servants." Simon bowed his head.

An older gentleman had entered the doorway and saw Lady Lillian and her brother. *This must be the father,* Gabriel thought. They had gathered quite a party in the sitting room. Seeing that his daughter was fine, Lord Wentworth turned to follow Lord Simon out the door.

Gabriel hurried forward and stopped the departing men. "Please, I would like to check on Lady Lillian's progress tomorrow, if I may?" Lord Wentworth looked taken aback by the question. What was the matter with all these people? They acted as if the lady had the plague.

Lord Wentworth pulled a silver card case from his jacket pocket, fumbled with shaking hands, then managed to pull a card out and hand it to Gabriel. "I am sure she would welcome the visit." He spun on his heel and hurried after the departing group, so intent on his daughter, he had barely acknowledged Gabriel's presence.

Gabriel stood in place for a long minute. *What the devil is going on here?*

"You know, they say she is quite mad." Lady Grantley had slithered up next to him like a snake, ready to whisper venom in his ear.

Curiosity got the better of him. "Why do they say that, pray tell?" he asked.

"This is only what I know, and not from gossip, mind you—" Gabriel wanted to snort at the blatant lie—"but she cannot stand to be touched, and if someone accidentally touches her, she has fits like this. It is all quite bizarre if you ask me. What kind of girl goes mad from physical contact? And have you noticed how she is covered in fabric from neck to toe?"

"Perhaps she is modest," Gabriel said.

"Ha! Not only is it not fashionable, it is unusual I can tell you. Also," the lady leaned in to whisper, "during the day she is never seen without specially made leather gloves. It is mad, I say."

Gabriel stepped back and gave the woman a narrow-eyed gaze. "Because the lady prefers modesty and to wear quality gloves? You cannot judge her based on that alone."

Lady Grantley only gave a shrug as if to say she could. Lord Grantley was looking like he would prefer to be anywhere else but there.

Gabriel resisted the urge to pull on his hair in frustration at this ridiculous conversation. "This is utter rot." He had had enough. He bowed to his host and hostess. "I wish you a good evening, madame, my lord, and I beg you to invite a smaller crowd in the future to prevent such events as drunken men knocking over respectable young ladies." Without a backward glance, he left the room. He was far too angry to continue conversing with the woman.

While waiting for his outer garments in the foyer, a hand touched his arm, startling him out of his agitated state.

"Wyvern!" Gabriel turned toward the voice and smiled. "I thought that was you I saw speeding toward the doorway. Was the ball too much for you?"

"Quite, Hartley," he said to the tall, slender man with dark blond hair and sideburns. "Well met!" He took the offered hand and gave it a firm shake. "I came by your townhouse for a visit upon my return but was told you were out of town."

Valentine Montgomery, Viscount Hartley, and he had known each other their entire lives. He had been there when Gabriel needed him on more occasions than he could count, both as a part of the Network and as a good friend.

"Was, but now I am not." Hartley took his hat, cloak, and gloves from the arriving footman. "If you have no use for any more balls tonight, why not come to the club and we can talk? It has been four years since we have seen each other."

Gabriel put on his gloves and cloak and held the top hat in his hands. "Indeed. Far too long. I would be pleased to join you. Do you have a carriage or would you prefer to share mine?"

"Yours is far more comfortable than mine," Hartley said.

"Excellent. Let us be on our way." The two men strode out of the overheated, overcrowded ballroom and allowed the carriage to take them to the one place where he had hoped to end up all along by night's end. A place where many plans and strategies had been devised in the past.

Right now he would have given anything to find the perfect solution for how to find his father's murderer. Up to this point, all the work in his investigation over the past four years had been fruitless. His frustration was now at a boiling temperature.

Gabriel had returned to England with only one goal in mind. He would not stop until he captured his father's killer, so his brother could finally come home.

SIX

Signor Silvano's Sayings Number 6
You must have all the necessary facts
to make the best decisions.
Never be afraid to be nosy.

The carriage was well on its way down the street when Hartley spoke from the opposite seat. "What was happening back there?"

"What are you referring to?" Gabriel casually feigned ignorance while he watched one home after another go by through the window. He was not quite sure what to make of the whole evening.

"I saw you carrying Leprous Lillian out of the ballroom. It was all anyone could talk about."

Gabriel whipped his head around to look at his friend. "What did you call her?"

Hartley held his hands up in surrender. "I did not create the moniker, and you know me—I am not one to spread tales. But it is what they call her."

"Who is they?" Gabriel ground his teeth.

"Those who enjoy the destruction of others in hope of

gaining a higher position in society. In other words, most everyone," Hartley said with a shrug.

"Why the devil would they call such a pretty young lady a name like that?"

"It has nothing to do with looks," Hartley said as he tossed his top hat beside him onto the leather seat. "It is because she is untouchable—literally, or so the gossip says. At least twice she has had to be carried away from social events because someone touched her, causing her to have a fit. Tonight makes three times, if my understanding is correct."

Gabriel shook his head slowly. "That does not make a lick of sense. She held my arm during our entire stroll."

Hartley shrugged. "I do not pretend to understand the whole of it." He leaned forward. "There are some who say she is demon possessed."

"That is absolutely ridiculous and you know it. There has to be a perfectly reasonable scientific explanation for her condition, and the days of witch hunting are over."

Hartley sat back. "Too true, but there is definitely something odd about her. Everyone avoids her out of fear."

Gabriel thought for a moment, then said, "She was closely conversing with another lady at the ball, so it cannot be everyone as you say."

"Taller than average, red-haired girl?"

"Now that you mention it, yes, she did fit that description," Gabriel said.

"They call her—" Hartley started to say, but Gabriel held up a hand to stop the man.

"Do not tell me. I have no wish to know. Let us talk of more pleasant things than ladies. How is Network business?"

"You will see once we are at the club."

Gabriel raised an eyebrow. "That serious, eh?"

"It depends on your definition of serious." Hartley grew quiet, which he often did when thinking deeply on a problem.

Gabriel allowed the silence until the carriage stopped in front of a red bricked townhouse that looked like every other building in a long row along the street.

Once inside, the butler took their outerwear and bowed low. "We are that pleased tae have ye back, yer grace."

Gabriel eyed the large Scottish block of muscle with a smile. "Frazier. Did the place fall down around your ears without me to babysit?"

"Of course nae, yer grace," he sobered, "but it has nae been the same without yer presence." His eyes darted to the open door of the salon. Gabriel saw some warning there and nodded to Frazier in thanks.

"Does the kitchen still make an excellent cup of coffee?" he asked.

"Yes, yer grace. That they do," Frazier said.

"Good. Please send up a tray with coffee and food. Lots of food. I have need of sustenance."

Frazier bowed. "Yes, yer grace. Right quick that'll be."

Gabriel followed Hartley down the hall into the salon where the members of the club generally met and stopped dead in his tracks. Only two tables were occupied tonight, and Cousin Howard was sitting at one of them enjoying a cigar and chatting with two other long-standing members. This must have been what Frazier was hinting about. What in the devil was Howard doing here? Gabriel did not allow the displeasure to show on his face. He needed to keep the upper hand. Instead, he called across the room: "Cousin! What brings you here on such a lovely night?"

Howard looked up. Gabriel saw an annoyed look in his eyes before he flashed a smile—all friendliness. "Cousin, I had heard of your return, but have not yet had the opportunity to see you. Welcome home."

Howard Ramsay took after his mother's side of the family in looks and build. He was of average height and thin rather than tall and muscular like the Ramsay men. He had small eyes and a long nose which always reminded Gabriel of a rat. The only thing he and his cousin did have in common was the dark wavy hair, but Howard had always slicked his back.

Gabriel casually walked across the room. "I have only just returned this week from a tour of my estates. I had much business to catch up on."

"No time for even a short note to me, your heir?" Howard said with an exaggerated pout like a little boy being refused a treat.

"I apologize. I would have come to visit you soon, but I see that is now unnecessary," he said.

"What are you doing here on an evening, Cousin?" Howard asked. "Are there not many balls clamoring for the attention of the Duke of Wyvern?"

"The ball grew tedious and I am in need of refreshment."

Howard blew a cloud of smoke that wafted towards Gabriel. He waved it away. "We have a designated smoking room down the hall, Howard."

"I know," he said languidly, "but I asked the other gents and no one said they minded if I lit up in here."

"Be that as it may," Gabriel said through clenched teeth, "I do mind, and this is my club. If you would please put the foul thing out or take it down the hall, I would be very obliged."

"Fine." His cousin got to his feet in a huff and took his time walking to the door. "I was not quite finished, so I shall take myself off for a bit."

"Thank you," Gabriel said with a short nod and walked the rest of the way across the room. He greeted the other four men present with a shake of hands, then moved to his favorite chair at a table in the corner. He flipped up the tails of his evening coat and sank wearily into the chair. Hartley joined him in the opposite seat.

The dark red carpet and smokey green painted walls of the room were not ostentatious like many other gentlemen's clubs. This room was meant for comfort rather than style. Each of the tables was surrounded with plush leather chairs, one of which Gabriel relaxed more deeply into now.

"We have much to catch up on," Hartley said. "You were away for a long time."

"You can start by telling me why the devil Howard is sitting in the middle of my club as if he owns the place," Gabriel said in a harsh whisper. "He is not a member nor shall ever be. He is not Network material and I do not need him in the middle of our business."

Not all the men belonging to the club were a part of the Network. Many men, from all walks of life had been invited to join so they could be of use to the organization, although they did not know it. Some were subtly probed for information and others were asked discreetly to carry out activities that would hold no consequences for them but would benefit the Network in some way, such as ferrying messages. As an unpredictable layabout, Howard was not one of these useful men.

"I am afraid it was done while I was out of town on business." Hartley kept his voice low and looked around to make certain no one was listening. "One of the other members thought since he was your cousin he should be afforded membership without any objection and brought him along. No one else questioned it, and Howard has been like a barnacle ever since. He has not taken the hint to go away even when I told him I alone approved all memberships."

Gabriel gave him an incredulous look. "I know Howard can be stubborn when he wants something, but it is not acceptable for him to intentionally insert himself here. The last thing I need is for my cousin to learn the true purpose of this club and all that we do on behalf of the Home Office."

"I know. This was one of the things I wished to inform you of immediately."

Gabriel looked up as Frazier brought in the tray of coffee along with sandwiches and cakes. He laid everything out on the table between the two men before bending down to whisper, "I watched them prepare it all meself."

"Good man," Gabriel said.

The large Scot straightened. "Happy tae oblige, yer grace." He bowed again and left.

Hartley smiled. "That man would die for you, you know."

"Yes. It is one of the reasons I keep him in the position he has—a very well-paid position I might add."

Gabriel poured each of them a cup of coffee and took several sandwiches. He sipped the rich brew and a sigh of pleasure escaped his lips. "I have not had coffee anywhere close to this good in four long years."

"I suppose doing without your usual comforts makes you appreciate them all the more."

"Exactly." Gabriel sat forward. "We have quite a bit to catch up on, but now is not the time. Can you meet me at Wyvern House tomorrow morning, say ten o'clock?"

"Of course," Hartley said.

When Howard reentered the room, it was to find Hartley and Gabriel having a jovial conversation on whether the speed of a high-perched phaeton was preferable to the comforts of a curricle. Their performance was good enough for the stage.

It was shortly after one in the morning when Gabriel let himself into his locked study. He pulled the bell rope to summon his valet. He knew it was late, but there was pressing business he felt could not wait. After a quarter of an hour, a sleepy-eyed Jersey entered the room.

"You called, your grace?"

Gabriel looked up from the desk where he had started working. "Yes, I am sorry to have woken you, Jersey, after promising you could turn in early, but several things have come up and need immediate attention."

"Of course, sir. Sleep is highly overrated anyway, if I do say so myself."

Gabriel lifted a brow at this gift of information, but Jersey only grinned.

"First, I need you to find out everything there is to know about a woman named Lady Lillian Hargraves, daughter of the Earl and Countess of Wentworth."

"The usual information?" Jersey asked.

"Yes, but also dig a little deeper. There is something going on with her that society only guesses at, but I do not believe anyone truly knows. I want to know. Second, I want an around-the-clock tail placed on my cousin Howard. He has taken it into his head that he belongs to my club."

Jersey whistled. "The cheek of the man!"

"Exactly. He just inserted himself like a pole through a carriage wheel, and I do not like it. I do not wish to spend my time guessing at what he is up to while I give my concentration to the investigation."

"Consider it handled. Anything else, Your Most High?" Jersey asked.

"Any update from Eagle?"

"Not since the last one, but you know Gemini isn't going to make it easy to find him."

"Yes, yes I know. I but worry. Let Eagle know that I have reason to suspect Gemini was seen on the road outside London a few weeks ago. It is not much to go on, but it is more than nothing. Do you have what I asked for regarding the suspects?"

"On all but two of them. Do you want what I've got so far?"

"Yes, I will read over it before I turn in for the night."

Jersey went to the small desk where he often worked and retrieved a stack of papers. He bowed formally before Gabriel and held them out. "Here you are, Your Highness. Additional details on the twenty-six of the twenty-eight names of those who were present during the house party at which your father was murdered, and have yet to be eliminated as suspects."

He waved Jersey away. "That is all. You can go back to bed. Take care of my cousin first if you please and then the other matter. I know you will keep me apprised of any contact from Eagle."

"Without question, Your Lordship." With a tip of an imaginary hat, the valet was gone.

Gabriel rubbed his hands over his tired face, then sat in the silence of the room for several minutes listening to Jersey's heavy footsteps as they sounded farther and farther away. There were quite a few irons in the fire to oversee now that he was home. Certainly, he had done an adequate job while working from abroad, but it was not the same. Now, with every day that passed, more things popped up which required his attention.

Then there was Lady Lillian. He would find a way to take care of that business with as little work on his part as possible. He was sure the duchess would not mind handling the details. If he felt a twinge of guilt over the matter, he would ignore it as usual.

Hartley showed up at exactly ten o'clock the following morning. The man was on the dot punctual in all things.

"I have had coffee sent up," Gabriel said as his friend sat in the leather armchair before his desk. "How is your mother?"

"Feisty as ever."

"And your sister?"

"Elizabeth is well. She will be coming up to town next year to be presented."

Gabriel whistled in amazement. "I have most definitely been gone too long. When I left she was a mere girl."

"Sixteen now and already turning men's heads back home. I told my mother it would be less bother to keep her under lock and key, but she refuses to listen to me."

Gabriel chuckled. He had never had a sister, but he could well imagine how difficult the job of elder brother to one might be.

Jersey came in with a tray of coffee. Once the gentlemen were served, he stood off to the side to listen discreetly. Gabriel always kept him apprised of all his business.

After a gulp, Gabriel put down his coffee cup. "What updates do you need to impart this morning?"

"We have agents following leads on the group of young noblemen who are wreaking havoc all over the country."

"I have only just heard of this new matter from Eagle. What do we know of these men?" Gabriel asked.

Hartley took a sip of his coffee as if thinking over his answer, then said, "The men are younger than the usual crowd of this sort, but what they are up to is not petty. We are talking about out and out crimes. Kidnapping of women and children who are sold into slavery, sabotage of competitors in business, murder, selling government secrets to the highest bidder, and worse.

Gabriel's eyebrows rose. He could only imagine what worse could mean.

The viscount continued. "All that they do appears to be purely driven by the motive of acquiring money, which means there should be a financial trail to follow, but so far they have been able to remain anonymous in their dealings. We only have rumors to work from."

"What has been uncovered so far?" Gabriel asked.

"Precious little, from what I gather. It is most difficult for an operative to ask questions without giving away their purpose. The preliminary report was vague at best. I will let you know as soon as more comes in."

"Very good." Gabriel sat back with his elbows on the arms of his chair and steepled his fingers together. "I assume you have also heard that Gemini is missing?"

"Yes, and I am sorry to hear it," Hartley said.

"Thank you. If I know Gemini, he will land safely on his feet and we will all have a laugh over this at the club later. Is there anything else to report?"

"Not at the moment."

"Good. I'd like to talk to you about my pursuit of my father's killer. I am beyond the point of frustration and would like your assistance. Jersey has already discovered a great deal about each person who attended the house party, but I need more if I'm going to solve this."

"I know we have discussed this in the past," Hartley said, "but what makes you think it was a guest as opposed to a killer for hire? The best assassins can slip in and out of anywhere, none the wiser."

Gabriel sat back, anger taking over his face. "Not with my father. You know he was the best in the business. He would have known if an enemy had gotten into the house. He would have reacted and there would have been signs of a struggle." He ran his hands through his hair back and forth, then down his face. "That there was no struggle is evidence the killer was able to get in close. He had to have known him. Or her. We cannot discount the women."

Hartley nodded thoughtfully. "No one remembers seeing anyone enter the study where your father had been writing letters?"

"Other than the maid who brought him tea earlier, no, and she has been cleared of suspicion."

Hartley let out a whoosh of breath. "It is not much to go on, Wyvern."

"I know, but killers always make mistakes if you push them hard enough. I need to keep pushing.

Hartley gave a short nod. "Tell me what you would like me to do."

Gabriel nudged the report Jersey had given him the night before across the desk. "I need more information. I need to know what these men eat for breakfast and which tailors they buy their clothing from. I need to know more about them than they know about themselves. It will only take one vital clue to solve this, and other than Jersey, you are the best of us all at ferreting out obscure information."

"Consider it done," his friend said.

"Thank you, Hartley."

If he had had his way, he would have more actively pursued the killer four years ago, but his brother had convinced him the two of them should stay out of sight for a while—

choosing safety over pursuit, that the killer might grow complacent. At the time, Gabriel had not realized he would be gone so long in service of the Crown. It was only because the war with Napoleon was now over that he had finally been able to come home. He only hoped so much time had not passed that the trail went cold.

"You will solve this," Hartley said, breaking into his thoughts. "I have never known you not to accomplish something you set your mind to." He placed his cup back on the tray. "If there is nothing else, I would like to get started."

Gabriel shook his head. "That is all for now, thank you."

His friend gave a short nod and left the study. Jersey sat at his own desk and began scribbling—most likely another report. Gabriel slid a stack of correspondence from one side of the desk to the space in front of him. He missed the days when letters had a hard time finding him. He was going to be here a long while. Like Barnaby, he wished he were back out in the field in hot pursuit of his quarry.

SEVEN

Signor Silvano's Sayings Number 7
When the horse bucks you off, you have two choices:
Get right back on that horse and show it who is the boss,
or go home and hide your head under the covers.
Which one you choose determines your character.

By the time the Wentworth carriage was well on its way home, Lillian had awakened. She found herself lying with her head on her mother's lap. The gentlemen and Anne sat across the carriage on the opposite seat. *Poor Anne must be crushed between them*, Lillian thought absently before the realization hit her that she had had another episode.

She abruptly sat up. "What happened?" she asked, but then groaned and put her hands to her head. "Never mind. It is all rushing back to me like the worst sort of nightmare."

Was there a better sort of nightmare?

This one involved a devil who beat one of his female servants so badly while in a drunken rage she ended up bloody, with several broken bones that would probably never heal properly, and a face that was no longer recognizable by the time he was finished with her. Those evil hands had touched

Lillian tonight. She shuddered at the thought.

"Would you care to tell us how this happened?" her father asked softly. Lillian could hear the disappointment in his voice. "I thought you were supposed to learn at Silvano's how to prevent these sorts of episodes, but instead they are occurring more frequently."

Lillian was not about to tell him that not only had she never learned how to prevent the visions, but they were growing worse. She feared his reaction.

"I am sorry, Father," Lillian said in a rush. She felt the need to explain herself as quickly as possible, like a little child trying to avoid what she felt was undeserved discipline. "I am now surrounded by more people than I have ever been before. The duke asked me to take a stroll about the ballroom, and I could not very well tell him no. Then the room became increasingly crowded as we walked. There was little I could do to avoid being bumped. We were attempting to go out on the terrace for more space and cool air when the incident occurred. I told you taking a part in the season would never work and here is proof of it."

"Wait," her mother gasped. "Did you say you took a stroll with the duke and then he offered to take you to a secluded terrace?"

"Yes," Lillian said, blinking her eyes slowly—surprised this was the only part of her recitation that seemed to matter.

"We are speaking of the Duke of Wyvern, are we not?" her mother asked.

"Yes," Lillian repeated. She could not tell by her mother's tone whether this was a good thing or a very, very bad thing.

"Oh, Lillian!" her mother waved her hands back and forth in excitement. "He asked to call on you tomorrow to see for himself that you are fully recovered." She fell back against the seat and fanned her face with the hand which was no longer clutching at her daughter. "I had hopes, but I did not know if you would be to his liking, and he was not the least bit intimidated by your incident." She gave Lord Wentworth a conspiratorial smile.

She had hopes? What does that mean?

"A simple walk among a crowd of people does not suggest he has plans to marry me, Mother," Lillian said sarcastically. No one seemed to hear her every time she sternly put her foot down against marriage—marriage to anyone, let alone a duke, who would be the worst possible choice for a lady with her curse. A duke needed someone who not only could run his household properly but appear in society at his side.

The last thing she needed was for her mother to begin scheming again. That always turned out as well as Lillian's attendance at large parties. Lillian had no such luck.

"You shall go to bed right away," her mother continued as if Lillian had said nothing just moments ago, "so you will look your very best in the morning."

"Calling hours are not in the morning, Mother," Lillian interrupted.

Lady Wentworth glared at her daughter. "A duke may call whenever he wishes and we must have plenty of time to prepare."

"Mother, I have a Benevolence Society meeting tomorrow. I cannot sit in the parlor sewing samplers while waiting for a person who may or may not come" —*and who I have no wish to see again*. She would die from the embarrassment alone.

A sniff from her mother was a sure sign her anger was flaring. "Not just anyone. A *duke*. Your Society can do without you for one day."

"I shall be very happy to entertain him in your absence," Anne said with a teasing smile. "From what I could see of him across the room, he is very handsome."

Her mother sniffed again. Apparently, Anne's suggestion did not meet with her approval.

To miss a meeting, any meeting, with the Benevolence Society—with her friends—was like missing a week's worth of meals. She could not do without.

She turned and appealed to her father. "Father, you know how important my meetings are to me." Sadly, the inside of the carriage was too dark for her father to see the pleading look. This strategy often helped tip the scale toward her cause.

"This time I must agree with your mother, Lillian," her father said with a strong tone that was rare for him. "The duke seems an excellent chap and very interested in your welfare. This is *not* an opportunity to be missed." He softened his voice. "It is high time you took a husband, my dear, as you well know."

Lillian could feel her brother's smug smile of triumph at

this proclamation. *Not fair, not fair, not fair*. It was at least three against one in the confines of the moving vehicle. How was she to win?

Lillian tried once more for reprieve. "I highly doubt the duke would show any particular interest in seeking my hand in marriage."

"Why not?" her mother asked. "You are an earl's daughter with an excellent lineage and a proper dowry. You are intelligent and poised and—"

"—and a woman with a serious flaw, Mother," Lillian broke in, her panic rising. They had been over and over this, but no one was listening. "You cannot deny this is a problem that will not be overcome. No man wants a woman who has fits and cannot bear to be touched." She tugged on her gloves.

"Enough," her father snapped, causing Lillian to look up at the uncharacteristic harshness. "As I said, I agree with your mother. You will be available for a visit tomorrow. If you must miss a meeting, so be it. There will be many more meetings in your future, but I do not expect another visit from a duke." The carriage fell silent, and then, "Not that you are not worthy of any duke," he added as an afterthought.

Lillian knew her father loved her and had championed her from the start. Her mother had done all she could in her own way to help her overcome her problem, but she could not allow this—this blatant attempt to push her into a life she had no desire for. She squeezed her hands tightly together in her lap while in her head she considered ways to avoid being forced into a betrothal with a duke.

The light was just beginning to creep through Lillian's bedroom window when Sarah came to wake her. "I can tell you, I do not like this scheme of yours to run away today," she said as she held out a woolen robe. Lillian slipped out of bed onto the cold polished-wood floor and gratefully allowed Sarah to help her into the warm garment.

"You do not have to like it, Sarah, but I want you to help me regardless." Lillian moved to the dressing table and sat before the mirror. She unbraided her waist length hair while Sarah picked up the brush from the table. "Besides, a little horseback ride that may or may not take us to the Benevolence Society for the remainder of the day will be enjoyable for both of us."

"Would it be so bad to be married to a handsome duke?" Sarah asked pragmatically. "You would at least have the power and freedom the position of duchess would give you."

"It would be a disaster for me to marry anyone, but especially a duke. Imagine all the public responsibilities that come with being a duchess." Lillian removed her sleeping gloves and applied cream to her pale hands. She held them out for further inspection and shook her head. Maybe she should go gloveless in the garden on occasion.

For the first time she wondered when she had become so afraid of touch that she continued to wear gloves to bed. It was not as if there was anyone to avoid when sleeping in her own home. It had been different at the school when she shared a room with other girls

"Stop your moving about or I shall end up pulling out your hair," Sarah fussed.

"Sorry." Lillian stilled. Then she noticed something missing on the surface before her. "Where are my day gloves?" Sarah's first job of the morning was to put a new pair of gloves on the dressing table.

"Oh, I was in such a tizzy to have everything ready so early this morning that I left them with your clothing."

Lillian quickly put her hands in her lap and clutched them between her legs as protection, trying to hold off the panic. This had to stop. Fear was controlling her life.

"Not to worry. Let me put this last pin in and I shall fetch them for you. Besides, there is no one here but you and I." Sarah hurried to the dressing room.

"I know, Sarah, but I worry out of habit," Lillian called out in a shaky voice.

"Of course you do," Sarah said as she returned with the gloves, "and you have had good cause for it. I know that."

Lillian grabbed the offered gloves, hastily donned them, and breathed a sigh of relief. She took another deep breath for good measure.

"Which would you like first? To break your fast or put on clothing?" Sarah asked.

"I am in a hurry. Clothing first I think, then I will consider food."

Sarah had poured a cup of tea before Lillian could blink. "A sip of tea will fortify you for the day," she said briskly.

She brought the cup to the table and set it down, then went back to the dressing room to fetch all that would be needed for the day.

Lillian took a sip of the warm liquid. "Ah, you were quite right, Sarah." She took one more sip, then stood and allowed her maid to work the same magic on her clothing as she had on her hair.

With Sarah following at her heels, Lillian crept down the servants' staircase. Although she dearly hoped not to run into anyone, she knew it was unlikely she would succeed. By six in the morning, most of the servants had already started their work lighting fires, cleaning rooms, and preparing the kitchen for breakfast.

"Good morning, Jack." She smiled at the boot boy, a young lad of eight years old, as they passed him. He sat near the kitchen fire while he shined her father's boots, or brother's. How could one tell?

Lillian walked through the rest of the kitchen as if she did this every morning at sunup. The cook's helper gave her a curious look, but said nothing. Once out the back door, she picked up the pace toward the back of the garden.

At the gate, she pulled the key from its hiding place beneath a hollowed-out rock and slipped it into the lock. An alley which led to the mews where the horses were stabled was on the other side of the garden wall. Lillian relocked the gate and hurried down the narrow lane.

They had just reached the door of the stables when a most unwelcome voice asked, "Going somewhere, Sister?"

Lillian pasted on her friendliest smile while her heart beat wildly. She whirled around. "Simon! What are you doing out so early? It is unlike you to be out of bed before noon if you can help it."

"Nice try, Lil, but you will not distract me. I can see you were planning to sneak off. You do realize what an incredibly stupid idea this is, do you not?"

She tried to make light of the situation and gave him a cheeky grin. "Why? It seemed like a perfect plan to me."

Her brother crossed his arms and set his jaw. "You know what I am talking about. You will only be postponing the inevitable. Mother and Father will simply find another way for you to meet with the duke." He continued in a gentler tone, "All they want for you is to be able to live life like every other young lady with a husband, a home, and a family. Why are you fighting so hard against it?"

She felt the panic rising in her chest. This was what she was trying—what she needed—to prevent. "Please, Simon. No one understands the consequences of allowing Mother and Father to marry me off. No one understands what I need."

Simon reached out to grab her arm, but thought better of it, pulling on her cloak instead to bring her inside the stable door. "What could you possibly need that you do not have? Mother and Father have given you a comfortable home, fancy clothing, a special school. They have invested an immeasurable amount of time and money into you."

Lillian balled her hands into fists. The leather of her gloves creaked. He continued to miss the point. "You are the one who has everything and can do whatever he chooses. You do not have to worry about what will happen every time you come close to another human being. You are the perfect and normal child in this family."

He was breathing hard now. Brown eyes, so like her own, held her gaze. "You have no idea what you are talking about."

What does that mean?

After a long pause, he uncrossed his arms. "You were told to be available today for a visit, and so you shall be. Now, do you plan to walk by yourself or shall I toss you over my shoulder like a sack of flour?" He raised an eyebrow and waited.

She took a deep breath and blew it out slowly. "I was hoping you at least would listen to me and understand. I see now that is not the case." She turned back to the garden, not waiting for a reply. "I will figure something out. I always do," she muttered under her breath. Over her shoulder she called, "Come, Sarah. I wish to have a nice walk in the garden before today's torture begins."

Lillian's favorite spot in the garden was the rose arbor, but rather than sit and enjoy the morning's bird song, she began to pace. Something had to be done about her family's conspiracy to get her married off. They may have all had good intentions, but her plan to avoid acquiring a husband would never change.

The skirt of her riding dress swished against her ankles as she turned to pace again. She looked up to see Sarah sitting on the bench, her eyes closed, relaxing.

"Sarah, you know me better than anyone. What do you think is keeping me here, bowing to my parents desires? Why have I not simply run away?"

Her friend smiled without opening her eyes. "Because I believe that deep down you would truly like to fit in like any other young lady of society and you care about your family and their good opinion of you. Perhaps there is a spark of hope in your mind that you can have both."

Lillian shrugged. "I suppose so, but when it comes to marriage, I see no way for us all to have what we want. Someone has to lose." Why would her family simply not let her go hide away in obscurity? It did not make any sense. She put her hands on her hips. "Either way, I will have to adjust my strategy. Engaging the duke in intelligent conversation last evening did not appear to repel him. I need some way to ensure he is not interested in me."

"Lillian," she said, "perhaps you are getting in a lather over nothing."

She sat down next to Sarah. "Over nothing? You think my mother attempting to throw me at a duke is nothing?"

"What I mean is the duke may visit, see that you are well, and then go away." She flicked her hand to illustrate her meaning.

Lillian huffed out a breath. "That is all good and well this time, but what if he does go away and my parents bring another suitor to court me and then another? What then? I thought my plan was going perfectly, but now I see it was flawed. I had not counted on the possibility of any man seeing past one of my episodes. I expected the duke to be like everyone else and run in the other direction. Instead, he is coming to call on me."

"Relax," Sarah soothed. "I still believe you are making this too complicated and getting too far ahead of yourself. Meet the duke and see what he wants. Then you can make further plans if needed."

Lillian did the same as her friend and closed her eyes, drinking in the cool air and the sounds of the morning, and let her mind wander. Birds were singing, and in the distance she could hear the rumble of carriages. It was a shame the roses were not yet in bloom. She so enjoyed the scent of roses. She took several calming breaths—as the beloved headmaster of her school, Signor Silvano, had taught her to do—then let out an "Ah."

After several minutes, she said, "As always, you are sensible, Sarah. I should not be assuming the worst will happen. I shall do my duty as a good daughter and wait upon the duke while praying he comes well before the Society meeting and goes away promptly. I would be very disappointed to miss it."

Sarah patted her arm in support. "Excellent."

"I shall, however," she added, "let his grace believe I am a lady with no conversation, who used up everything in her arsenal last night. Perhaps he will find me completely uninteresting."

"Oh, Lillian," Sarah laughed. "You are absurd. I knew you would not stop thinking until you came up with some tactic to use today. How very like you."

Lillian opened her eyes and grinned at her friend. "I refuse to surrender without any resistance." She stood, shook out her arms, and rolled her shoulders. "Let us go inside for some breakfast. I could really do with a strong cup of tea about now." If she was going to be forced into this interview with the duke, she planned to be at her very best.

EIGHT

"Mother, how much longer must we sit here in this room? I am feeling quite claustrophobic." Lillian had so far spent the entire morning and part of the afternoon with her mother and Anne in the drawing room looking at fashion periodicals, embroidering cloth, and catching up on correspondence —including a letter to Fran demanding to know why she had run off before Lillian could introduce her to the duke.

Her mother looked up with a narrow-eyed blue gaze. "You have never been claustrophobic a day in your life."

"Not true, Mother. When I am in a crowd of people, I most definitely feel claustrophobic."

"I am terribly claustrophobic all the time," Anne chimed in with a cheerful voice. "Ever since I was accidentally locked into the linen closet when I was seven."

All eyes turned to Anne. "That was a tragic event," Lillian said with a frown, remembering that day when no one could find her cousin. The servants had searched every nook and cranny in the house until one had thought to try the locked closet. Anne had fallen asleep on the floor, curled in a ball, with streaks of dried tears down her face. She had refused to leave Lillian's side for weeks afterwards.

Anne waved her hand as if it were nothing. "All is well now. I never hid in a closet again and have no reason to do so as an adult."

"Oh, never mind, the both of you," her mother said, exasperated. "I very much expect we shall not need to wait much longer." As if on cue, the front knocker echoed throughout the house. Lady Wentworth put her sewing to the side and patted her dark hair. "Sit up straight, girls, and put your things away."

Lillian, still feeling resentful that she had to attend this visitation, stood, lifted the cushion beneath her chair, shoved her sewing underneath, and flopped unceremoniously atop it. Her mother had seen what she had done but only had time for a gasp before the doors to the room opened and Higgins announced, "His Grace, the Duke of Wyvern." The butler bowed and moved to the side to reveal the same duke from the night before. Lillian was hoping he might have turned into a toad overnight. A duke, even an ugly one, might be exciting, but a handsome duke was beyond her mother's wildest dreams. It made her all the more nervous the family would be eager to push her into his path at every opportunity.

All three ladies stood promptly and curtsied.

He bowed before fully entering the room and heading straight for Lillian. "I see you are much recovered."

"Yes, your grace," Lillian said, clutching her skirts like a lifeline. What did one say in a situation like this? There were no rules in the etiquette books for how to greet someone after they witnessed the consequences of a mysterious ability she should not have in the first place. But as Silvano liked to say, 'Courtesy is always a good idea.' "I must thank you for lending your kind aid to me last evening."

The duke put his hands behind his back and raised an eyebrow. "Kind? I believe it was the least I could do under the circumstances."

"There are many who would not have done so," Lillian said softly.

Lady Wentworth interrupted them with the clearing of her throat.

"Oh, yes, your grace," Lillian said. "May I introduce my mother, Lady Wentworth and my cousin, whom I believe I mentioned before, Miss Anne Hargraves." The two ladies curtsied again for good measure.

The duke nodded. "It is a pleasure to make your acquaintance, as there was no time to do so last evening."

"Will you sit down, your grace?" Lady Wentworth motioned with a sweep of her arm to the chair located next to Lillian's. "Tea will be brought in shortly." When everyone had settled into their seats, she said, "May I also, as a mother, offer my thanks as well as those of Lord Wentworth for the assistance you gave to my dearest Lillian?" She clutched her handkerchief to her bosom in a dramatic fashion. Lillian sighed inwardly. Her mother would stop at nothing—including overacting—to see her plans bear fruit.

"It was nothing, madam. I am only pleased that no lasting harm has fallen upon your daughter." He looked at Lillian with a raised eyebrow and question in his eyes.

"No lasting harm at all," she assured him. "You see me quite fit this afternoon." Wishing to shift the subject away from herself, Lillian was relieved at the entrance of Higgins and the tea tray with a maid following behind carrying a vase of white roses.

The girl set the vase down on the small table beside Lillian and leaned in to say, "With best wishes from his grace." The room was silent until all was set out before them and the servants left.

At least Lillian could say the man had good taste, drat him. He was already thwarting her plan to have nothing to say today. "Roses." She leaned over and breathed in the scent. "In May. My very favorite flower. Thank you, your grace, but you need not have."

"It was my pleasure. I asked them to be put in water before being presented to you."

Her mother beamed at him from across the tea table. "How kind of you. How do you take your tea?"

"I take it plain, if you please, and not meaning to be greedy, but several of those biscuits would not go to waste." Lillian was reaching for said biscuits, but grabbed her hand back like a guilty child at his request, remembering the guest should be served first. She was quite hungry after being stuck within these four walls all day.

"Do you also have a sweet tooth, your grace?" Anne gave him a dimpled smile.

The duke returned the smile with a genuine one of his own. Anne had that effect on people—she always put them at ease. "I admit that I do have a bit of a sweet tooth, but I also have missed the tea cakes of England, as I went without for so long. I find, now that I have returned, I have not yet been able to get enough." Everyone chuckled, except her mother, who tittered. Lillian wished very much to roll her eyes.

"We are very spoiled in our country with such lovely teas with all the yummy things to eat, are we not, your grace?" Anne asked.

"We are indeed." He took a sip of the offered tea, then a bite of a lemon biscuit. The ladies watched with rapt attention as he enjoyed the treat—as if a duke taking tea was a novel experience.

"Where did you go on your travels abroad, your grace?" her mother asked, finally handing a cup of tea to her daughter, then to her niece.

"Oh, a little bit of here and there. The war with France hindered much of my travel to Europe, but I did have a chance to see Spain, Portugal, and Italy." He paused to take another sip of tea. "I also spent a good deal of time in the American colonies, although I suppose I should say the United States of America. They are a bit touchy about that over there." He smiled.

"Oh, but you must tell us more about your travels to the Colonies," her mother tittered again, resembling a young girl. "Excuse me, I mean the United States. It is not often one gets to hear firsthand accounts."

Lillian looked at the clock again. She wanted to scream. It was nearly three o'clock. If her mother had her way, the duke would be here through dinner.

He had just finished his story about crossing home from Spain to England when he said, "I just now remembered I have two questions I have come to ask. First, my lady," he directed this question to Lillian's mother, "my mother and I would like to invite your family to dine at my home. It would be just a small intimate gathering. As it is already Wednesday, would Friday be agreeable?"

"Yes, indeed," she assured him enthusiastically. "My family would be more than happy to join you on Friday. How delightful!"

Lillian wanted to shout 'No!' but once again no one had asked her opinion.

"Excellent." The duke then turned his attention to Lillian. "My second question is whether you would do me the honor of a walk in the park this afternoon? After I finish off every crumb of these delicious biscuits on my plate, that is." His

midnight-blue eyes twinkled. Just as she had seen on an exact duplicate of his face not so very long ago. She still did
not know what to make of it. "Lady Lillian?" he prodded.

"Sorry, I was woolgathering." Her eyes flicked to the
clock. It was now half past three. Did she have time to walk
with the duke and still make it on time to her meeting? Her
mother took the decision out of her hands.

"Of course Lillian would love to walk with you. She is a
very fine walker and enjoys the outdoors."

The duke looked to Lillian for confirmation. This was not
going according to her hopes that he would—as Sarah had
said—just go away, and she had no valid reason to refuse
him. "I would be honored, your grace."

Her mother looked as if she would like to stand and
dance a jig, but somehow she controlled the urge. Lillian
herself felt as if she was being led to the gallows.

While a footman helped Lady Lillian up into his curricle,
Gabriel thought briefly of the list of things needing his attention that did not include escorting a young lady outside. But
he required a wife, and if he could decide this week for certain
about Lady Lillian, that would be one less responsibility.
Not to mention it would keep his mother busy and off his back.

On the surface she appeared to be the right lady for the
job. She was pretty, intelligent, and listened more than she

spoke. She never giggled or simpered or gushed as if his title were the only part of him that mattered, and she talked to him as if he were a real person. The only problem was this mystery surrounding her that was shrouded in innuendo and rumors, but mysteries rarely baffled him for long. He would get to the bottom of it soon.

Gabriel walked around the curricle and climbed into the driver's seat. He nodded at the footman to release the horses he had been holding steady. "I apologize if I have taken you from something important," he said to his companion.

Lady Lillian was still attempting to arrange her skirts, but looked up at the question. "I beg your pardon?"

"While we were taking tea you kept watching the clock as if you had somewhere else to be."

He could see her mind working as though she were deciding between blatant honesty or a white lie. The truth won out, and she said, "I do have a meeting scheduled at five o'clock."

He gave her a gentle smile. "Why did you not simply tell me 'no' when I invited you to walk?" He slapped the reins and the horses started forward.

"Your grace, if I had said no, I do believe my mother would have had forty fits right over the tea table. There are times when it is best to do what is expected rather than what one wants." Lady Lillian put her hand to her mouth as she realized what she had just admitted to. "I did not mean to imply I do not wish to walk with you."

Gabriel glanced at the lady and lifted an amused eyebrow.

"I believe that is exactly what you meant to imply." She began to deny the charge, but stopped herself. "Were you so eager to keep your appointment, or is it me?" Then after a pause. "Or something else?"

When Lady Lillian did not answer, Gabriel looked at her. Her face was turned away and her straw bonnet hid any expression from his view.

Finally, she said, "I hardly know you, your grace; however, there is nothing I find objectionable about spending time with you."

"Except?"

"It is complicated."

When no more information was forthcoming, he decided to press harder. This lady was a tough nut to crack, but he would have fun trying. "I do not mind complicated. We have a little time in which you could explain it to me."

He glanced to the side again and saw Lady Lillian was squeezing her hands together. Perhaps he had pushed too hard, but he had not yet discovered an answer. "You said you wish to attend a meeting today rather than walk in the park?" The lady turned and narrowed her eyes at him. Ah, he was thoroughly enjoying himself.

"Yes. It is a weekly meeting, and very important to me," she said.

"May I ask the nature of the meeting or is that too personal a question?"

She hesitated again as if considering her words. Another mystery then. How intriguing.

"It is called the Benevolence Society," she finally said. "We meet to begin and continue projects that will be of help to those in society who are not as fortunate as we are. The projects are wide in variety and scope."

Gabriel could tell it was not the full truth. Her explanation sounded rehearsed. He slowed the horses and eased the curricle through the park entrance. Hyde Park was quite busy at this hour, with ladies and gentlemen promenading along the pathways or riding on horseback. "Forgive me for saying so, as I know nothing of these things," he said, "but you are very dedicated to the cause of helping unfortunates if you do not wish to miss even one meeting." He gave a friendly smile to put her at ease.

Lady Lillian's nostrils flared slightly in annoyance. Later, he would have Jersey check out this so-called Benevolence Society and find out what they were truly up to. If he were to marry this woman, he wanted all the facts.

"The Society is also beneficial to those who attend. I enjoy the time spent with those I consider my friends," she said tightly.

"Oh? What is it you do with them?" he asked.

"We do not simply sit around and discuss the unfortunates. We have lively and intelligent conversations and discuss our own lives as well. Quite a bit of problem solving occurs during our meetings."

"Ah, you have a problem you wish to discuss today, perhaps?" Gabriel asked lightly.

Lady Lillian closed her lips firmly and looked down at her lap. He had pushed her to the limit.

"I am sorry. I have offended you," he said, deftly maneuvering his curricle around an open-topped landau stopped on one side of the carriage drive. Lady Lillian started to answer, but he continued before she could do so. "Shall I stop this equipage so we can get out and walk a bit? It is such a lovely and warm day."

"Indeed," she said.

He pulled the curricle into an empty space out of the way of other conveyances. Once he tied off the reins, he jumped down. Reaching Lady Lillian's side, he saw she was nervously looking at the ground and rubbing one hand back and forth along her skirt.

"It is not so far down as all that," he said lightly, holding his hand out to assist her. She bit her lip and looked at his hand as if it were a snake.

At this rate, they could spend all day staring at each other, getting nowhere. Gabriel chose to take the matter into his own hands. He reached up, grabbed her by the waist and whirled her down to the ground.

"Your grace! Was that entirely necessary?" she protested.

"You did say you were on a tight schedule today," he said with a grin. "I was only helping to move things along."

"Hmm." Lady Lillian said skeptically as she opened the lavender parasol she had brought to filter out the sun.

Why did ladies do that? Their enormous bonnets seemed protection enough.

He held out his arm for her. She hesitated before finally taking it and they began their way down the walking path.

"I shall make an agreement with you," he said. "If you will take a short turn about the park with me, I promise to return you in time for your meeting. What time did you say it was to start?"

"Five o'clock, your grace, and thank you." She smiled up at him. "That is a fair deal."

"Before I take you back, let us give the old tabbies something to talk about, shall we? I have always gained a large amount of enjoyment from making society wonder about my actions. 'Why is the duke escorting a young lady in the park whom he barely knows?' they will whisper behind their hands."

A small laugh escaped Lady Lillian's lips. "That is quite absurd. Very few people actually wish to be talked about."

"Oh, on the contrary, my lady. Everyone wishes to be talked about. However, they all wish to be talked about in the most positive light."

"This is true, I suppose." They walked in silence a few moments before she added, "What is it you enjoy doing in your spare time, your grace? Other than giving the ladies something to talk about, that is."

"The usual gentlemanly pursuits—riding, time at the club, and such. I very much enjoyed my travels but am always glad to be home again. I also have a small hobby of solving mysteries." The latter was something he often told people. The idea enabled him to hide in plain sight, so to speak. A duke with a hobby was a safer explanation than a duke who led a spy organization on behalf of the British Crown.

Lady Lillian looked up at him, "Oh? What sort of mysteries?"

"Whatever comes my way. A missing piece of jewelry, sounds in the night thought to be a ghost, missing persons. The usual sort of mysteries."

"How fascinating. How does one go from being a duke to a man who solves such puzzles?"

"I was not always a duke," he answered solemnly. "At one time I had quite a bit of spare time on my hands. If you want to know the true beginning, it all started with my mother's lost pearl ring. Her mother had given it to her and so it was very dear. I put my skills of analyzing and problem solving to good use to locate it. I was hooked from that day forward."

"Where was the ring found?" Lady Lillian asked.

"In a jewelry shop where the thief had sold it."

"Did you find the thief?" she asked.

"Unfortunately, no. He had left no trail."

"But the most important thing is that you were able to give the ring back to your mother."

He smiled down at her. "Indeed. Thus began my reputation as a man who could solve mysteries."

Lillian felt an all-too-familiar sensation interrupting her concentration on the duke. She spun around and called sternly to the young man with light brown hair who had just passed them, "Turpentine, give it back!" Her mischievous friend stopped, his hands in his pockets, his shoulders drooping. Lillian was so engrossed in her conversation with the duke she might not have noticed him at all if she had not felt the odd whooshing though the air.

The boy was barely sixteen years old, but he should have known better than to take risks like this. Using his ability was fine at Silvano's among others like them, but not in Hyde Park.

Turpentine looked up through his lashes at Lillian, with that way he had of trying to charm people. She was not falling for it. She held out her hand. "Now!" She wriggled her fingers to emphasize the point.

"What is happening here, Lady Lillian?" the duke asked from behind her shoulder.

"I will explain later, please," she whispered out of the corner of her mouth.

Turpentine slouched toward them. "Ah, come on, Lil. I didn't mean no 'arm. I were just 'aving me some fun."

"Having fun at someone else's expense is just mean, and stop talking like a child from the streets, which you most certainly are not." She continued to hold her hand toward him, palm up.

Having reached Lillian, her friend put the item in her hand, which she quickly closed.

"Is that my pocket watch?" the duke asked, half in curiosity, half in disbelief.

"Apologize to his grace, Turpentine," Lillian said, her lips thinned.

Her friend bowed low with one leg forward as if he were at court. "I do beg your pardon, your grace. I meant no harm to anyone and only wished to tease Lillian. I would never have kept it." He winked at Lillian as he came out of the bow.

"I do not begin to understand what has occurred here, but I accept your apology for Lady Lillian's benefit," the duke said.

"I suggest you make yourself scarce, Turpentine, before you end up in trouble." Lillian shooed him away.

He ran a hand slowly through his straight hair and said, "If I've told ya an 'undred times, I'll tell ya again: me name's not Turpentine. It's Xerxes." With that he turned and sauntered away, whistling as if he had not a single care in the world.

Lillian returned the watch to the duke, who absently pocketed it in his waistcoat. "Now would you care to tell me what is going on?" he asked. "Did that lad just pick my pocket?"

Not exactly. "I do apologize, your grace. Turpentine is the son of a wealthy merchant, but he likes to play the part of street urchin on occasion." She held up a hand. "Before you ask, I have no idea why."

"You know this young man?" the duke asked in surprise.

"Yes. His real name is Jack Walker and he is a member

of the Benevolence Society. I know he has given you a very poor first impression, but he is a dear friend."

The duke raised an eyebrow. "It is a dangerous game he is playing," he said. "One that could very well get him hanged if his luck runs out."

"Oh, I agree," she said in a rush. "One hopes he will grow out of it very soon."

The duke merely grunted in response and held out his elbow to her, so they could resume their walk. Lillian could only imagine what he might be thinking about that whole episode with her friend. Turpentine thought it was a great joke to practice his skills in public, as he was one of the few of Silvano's students who had any control over his ability. Lillian would give anything to be counted in that number.

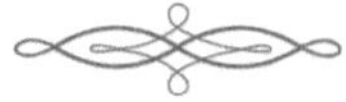

The mysteries surrounding Lady Lillian were beginning to pile up. Turpentine was not at all the type of friend ladies of the *ton* usually spent their time with, so now he was doubly curious about this Benevolence Society she had mentioned.

Gabriel stopped with her along the banks of the Serpentine, a manmade lake in the middle of Hyde park.

"I am pleased you brought us here," Lady Lillian said. "I find it soothing to be near the water and watch the ducks at play."

"It is a shame I did not think to bring breadcrumbs," he said.

"Oh, do not worry over much. I believe these ducks are likely to be the best fed birds in the world. They need no additional crumbs from me." She moved closer to the water's edge. "I envy the ducks," she said on a dreamy sigh.

Gabriel stepped up to her side. "How so?"

"Look at them." She pointed to a cluster of three in various shades of brown, beating their wings against the water. "They are free to enjoy themselves in any way they wish and their lives are so uncomplicated. They eat, they swim, they sleep."

"Would you truly wish for such a life?" he asked.

Her forehead creased. "Whatever do you mean?"

"I think you would enjoy it for about three days, and then boredom would set in. I have a feeling you are more like me, Lady Lillian: always looking for the next thing to keep your mind stimulated."

"You are correct, but I do wish I could be this free."

"Yet, these birds are not truly free are they?" he pressed. "They are chained to their nature as birds. If they wish to leave the water and live their lives as a fox in a den does, they will not long survive."

Lady Lillian smiled. "You are determined to contradict me today, are you not? From your perspective, ducks are not as free as they appear. You have spoiled my illusion."

Gabriel chuckled lightly. "I have committed two sins then —contradicting a lady and destroying your dream of living as a duck. Perhaps I should redeem myself and get you to your meeting on time." He held out his elbow again. "Shall we return?"

Once he helped Lady Lillian up to the curricle, he went to the other side, climbed up, and untied the reins. "I believe I will have you home with a little time to spare."

"I thank you for your kindness once again, your grace."

Kindness. That was not a virtue he was often accused of having.

Gabriel had not expected to enjoy today's outing as much as he had. This lady had been intriguing him from the first moment they had met, and he could not wait to learn more. As soon as he returned her home, he would set Jersey the task of discovering what he could not. There was more than one way to solve a mystery.

NINE

Signor Silvano's Sayings Number 9
When your world is turned upside down,
you can do one of two things:
Go in the new direction
or fight like mad to get your former life back.
Only you can decide which will serve you best.

As always, Lillian was excited to be back with her school friends at the Benevolence Society. She noticed some sort of commotion was brewing when she and Sarah entered the building in the Soho neighborhood.

Sarah had been at Lillian's side since her curse showed itself, and though she had no strange ability, she was considered a Society member. Without a word, she went off to chat with friends while Lillian stood and assessed the large room where their meetings were held.

Although the area was residential and there were bedrooms upstairs for those who lived at the Society, nearly the entire downstairs area of this home was set up like a theater with chairs lining the room, facing a podium at the front.

Today it felt like all twenty-two members of the school

were talking behind their hands and staring at Lillian. Considering each student of the Society had their own peculiarities, this was an odd occurrence.

Lillian chose to ignore whatever had gotten her friends so excited and headed for her usual seat, but she stopped in her tracks when a burst of flame shot across the air.

"Sorry!" Luciana called out sheepishly. The eight-year-old from Spain was still having trouble containing her ability to create fire.

Lillian glanced around the room at the clusters of people, who varied in age from six to late twenties. By her calculations, she had been the last to arrive.

" 'Ello, Lil," Sarah said from beside her, except the voice was wrong.

"Stop it!" Lillian scolded. "It scares me when you do that, Samuel."

Twelve-year-old Samuel frowned and said in his Yorkshire accent, "I was just 'aving some fun. I didn't mean to upset ye."

"I know, and I am sorry if I sounded so harsh," she said in a gentler tone. "None of us can help these problems we were born with."

"Not all of us think of 'em as problems," Samuel said with a grin. "My ability allows me to get away with all sorts of things."

Lillian laughed lightly. "It gets you into no end of trouble too." Silvano had had to give Samuel strict rules about using his ability after he had once snuck into the girls' dormitory at school in the guise of Catriona, a student from

Scotland who had the second sight. Samuel now lived at the new London location of the school.

Across the room Lillian spied Neera from India who could speak to animals. Next to her was Christopher from Egypt. He had the ability to change the weather. Then there was Lottie who saw ghosts. She was from Ireland. Lillian shuddered at the thought of constantly being surrounded by dead people. Her own problem was a little better, she supposed. She saw people from the past, but at least they did not speak to her. Turpentine was from London.

Every person in the room, from all walks of life and from all over the world, was plagued with what the world considered to be abnormal or even evil abilities that none of them had asked for. They had undergone nearly insurmountable trials in their lives because of them. For years they had huddled together like homeless waifs at Silvano's School, more formally called Silvano's School for Exceptional Children, hiding away from the rest of humanity. For Lillian, the school had been a place to fit in. For some of the others, it had been a place to heal from the abuses endured because of their abilities. The school represented safety and belonging.

When she had first arrived at Silvano's in Shropshire, at the age of nine, all students boarded there. It was a necessity for their survival that they stayed away from the world. A few of them, like herself and Fran, had now returned home, and from stories she had been hearing from her friends in the past few weeks, she was not the only one having trouble adjusting to the return to society. She still thought the move to London was crazy, but none of them had had a say in the matter. The days of hiding were now over for her, but Lillian would have given anything to have them back.

Signor Silvano interrupted Lillian's musings with a loud clap of his hands as he appeared at the front of the room. "Come gather around, my children. Let me look at you all." He spread his hands wide, indicating they should take their seats across the room.

Lillian took her usual place next to Fran and glared at her. There was no time to give her a piece of her mind for abandoning her at the ball, for their mentor—who was dressed today in a green pin striped coat, matching green pants, and a waistcoat with brightly embroidered peacock feathers—was giving one of his often-used Shakespeare quotes: "I am amazed, and know not what to say." He swept his gaze slowly across the occupants in the room.

Although Signor Giuseppe Silvano was a thin man of average height, he was larger than life. He had to be at least in his fifth decade, but his hair remained as black as a raven's, perhaps due to his Italian heritage. Although he told the parents of his students he was the grandson of an Italian nobleman to give himself a higher social standing with them, the truth was he was the son of an English actor and an Italian opera singer.

Regardless of his background, Silvano had become a man they looked up to with great respect.

Not only did he care for a motley group of energetic kids, he and the other teachers provided them with an excellent education, which included many subjects traditionally only taught to boys. Under his care, Lillian had received classes in Latin, mathematics, and even fencing. Plus, all of them attended weekly lectures on how to lessen the effects of their abilities.

Unfortunately, she had begun to realize no amount of lectures would ever be enough to tame their oddities.

Silvano nodded briskly then looked to the back of the room where Halvar, a man from Scotland, stood guard against any strangers who might wander in. The man was a giant compared to Lillian, not only tall, but strong. She imagined he could easily crumple an average-sized man with his bare hands, like a piece of paper. He was the first person Lillian had met at the school, and he had scared the life out of her, looming in the doorway at night like a mythical god. Lillian shook herself to clear the memory.

Halvar nodded that all was secure.

"Very well." Signor Silvano rubbed his hands together. "Who would like to begin this evening?"

"Lillian had another incident in public," Fran offered.

Lillian gave her friend's ribs a sharp jab with her elbow.

"Ow!" Fran rubbed at the sore spot.

"Why are you picking on me, Franny?" Lillian hissed. Her friend hated being called that.

"Just trying to help, darling," Fran said with a grin and

did not look the least bit apologetic.

Her friend was in an odd mood tonight, Lillian thought. She scowled at her and then turned back to Silvano. "Yes, I had an incident that was quickly taken care of. No harm done."

There was no deterring Signor Silvano. "Tell us what happened."

With a big sigh Lillian began: "I was strolling through a crowded ballroom—"

"—on the arm of a handsome duke," Fran inserted.

"Stop that," Lillian shot at her friend. "If I need your help, I shall ask for it."

Fran gave a huge smile, like that of a cat playing with a mouse, and waved for Lillian to continue.

"I was strolling through a crowded ballroom when a man bumped into me knocking me to the floor. I was fine at that point and would have remained fine if the dolt had not attempted to drag me off the floor by the arm."

"Was the man not wearing gloves as well?" Signor Silvano looked pensive.

Lillian scrunched her eyebrows, trying to think back. "I barely remember, but he must have been. I fell into a vision and everything happened as usual."

Signor Silvano stared intently at Lillian. "I know you always wear your gloves, but did you slow your breathing and find a focal point in the room to attempt to prevent an incident?"

"There was no time, signore. It all happened very quickly. I was trying to get up on my own, the crowd was pushing forward, the duke was attempting to assist me, and then this man unceremoniously hauled me up like an animal carcass. I hardly knew what was happening."

"You know, avoiding crowded rooms would be the best way to prevent these incidents in the first place," Silvano said in a wry tone.

"Oh, I most certainly know that," she said with a sigh. "I wish I could avoid any and all public events, but according to my parents I have no say in the matter."

"Yes, I understand." He waved his hand in the air in frustration. "We will come up with a new practice strategy to help you deal with the kind of situations you are faced with in London. Anything else to report, Lillian?"

Lillian licked her lips. "My ability is changing."

Signor Silvano looked up quickly, intrigued. "How so?"

"I no longer need the touch of bare skin for me to see into someone's past and I have recently begun to notice strong sensations of intense emotions when I am near a person—without any touch involved."

"Do you see images like when you are touched?"

"No, signore. At first, I did not understand what I was experiencing. There has been no time since to explore the problem."

He nodded. "It sounds like you and I have some work to do." He turned to Fran. "Who is next to report? Francesca? What do you have to say?"

"I say you should stop thinking such negative thoughts, sir. I can hear you." She smirked.

"You are still wearing cotton in your ears?" Silvano asked.

Fran pulled wads of cotton from each ear and held them up to demonstrate. Then she returned them. "Indeed I do, but they do me absolutely no good."

"Are the voices still too loud then?" he asked with a frown.

"Not only that, but like Lil here, my gift is getting stronger, and I am not pleased about it. I can never turn it off."

Signor Silvano looked around the room. "Is this true for others? Who else is having the same difficulty?" More than half of the room's occupants lifted a hand. He shook his head. "I wonder if being in London has created this effect," he muttered. "I did not expect this."

"Trying to stop our gifts from happening as you have always taught us is nae working," Catriona said. "They come when they wish to and it cannae be predicted."

"Except in my case," Fran piped up in a deceptively cheerful manner. "I can predict mine will always come."

Christopher spoke up. "Excuse me, Signor Silvano, but maybe we have been working backward all the time?"

"Speak louder, Christopher," Signor Silvano lifted his hands several times to demonstrate. "What do you mean?"

Despite his reserved manner, fourteen-year-old Christopher carried himself like one who had authority as he was doing now. He had light brown skin, tightly curled short black hair, and high cheekbones. Lillian believed he was either from a royal family of Egypt or a well-to-do one.

"Maybe, Signor Silvano, we should not make quiet the gifts,

but learn how to use the full power? Do you know what I am meaning? I have tried this and it has been working well for me."

Signor Silvano held up one finger. "Let me think about this for a moment. You are saying you should practice *unleashing* your gifts rather than suppressing them, and it has worked?" He held his thinking pose, hands clasped under his chin for several minutes. Then abruptly he said, "I understand if some of you wish to attempt this strategy in the coming week. You can report your results during next week's meeting. We will dismiss early today so I can consider these new problems you have brought to my attention as well as Christopher's idea." Groans echoed throughout the room. The Society meeting was the highlight of everyone's week. He threw one hand in the air. "Feel free to stay and practice your abilities, my dear ones, or simply talk to each other if you prefer." With a courtly bow he left the room.

Lillian shook her head. The man certainly had a flair for the dramatic, following his own whims wherever they took him.

She turned on Fran and hissed. "What is your problem to-day? You are supposed to be my friend and yet you mock me?"

Fran did not react but coolly placed her elbow on the back of her chair and rested her cheek on her fist. "I have no clue what has you so upset, my dear. I was merely stating the facts." It was not usual for her friend to be so insensitive.

"And another thing. Where did you disappear to the minute the duke showed up, Fran? You must not have gone far if you knew about the incident," Lillian said in an accusing tone.

"You know me. I could not bear the noise in the room any longer. Not to mention I did not want to hear the inner thoughts of a man showing interest in you. I might have spoiled every-thing, you know."

"You need not have told me anything," Lillian said.

Fran snorted. "Dear one, if he had a wife and seven children, I would tell you. If he had killed a man for wearing prettier boots, I would tell you. There are just some things which should not be kept to oneself. I could not handle the pressure, so I went to another room." She paused. "If you want to know how I knew about the incident, that is easy. I could hear every word from where I was supposedly finding peace and quiet."

Lillian opened her mouth in shock. "It has become that strong?"

Fran slowly nodded.

"Dear God. What is going to happen to us? Will we all slowly go mad?"

"Darling," Fran said, "I think we already are."

Lillian slumped, feeling very depressed. "There has to be something we can do."

"If my mother were not keeping me captive in town," Fran said, "I would run away and hide in the country—just myself and the cows for company. At least they have no thoughts. Sheep neither. Nor the trees or grass. I could live happily there."

Lillian gave a small chuckle. "I am sorry, Fran, but you

were not meant for the bucolic life. I know how you enjoy the colorful array of gowns and the pretty ballrooms."

"Yes, but unfortunately all the people and their abundance of loud thoughts rather ruin the experience for me." Fran sighed. "I do not have the answer, but I do think a little holiday might be very refreshing."

"Oh, Fran, I completely understand."

Christopher came upon them then with his usual bright smile. He bowed and said, "Do you wish to hear of my success?"

"Yes, please do tell," Lillian said, pasting on a smile for him. Christopher was like a little brother to her. They had grown up together at the school.

"I get tired of creating weather accidents, so I begin to practice every day. Little bits at first like one cloud or changing the rain into snow. The more I practice, the stronger I get, you see?"

"Are you saying by practicing you are better able to control when the ability happens?" Lillian asked.

"Yes, yes! Each day I get a little better. I believe soon I will not create the weather unless I wish to."

Fran let out a hard sigh. "My ability never stops. I do not see how that would work for me."

Christopher turned to Lillian. "Here, you try." He held out his hands palms up.

She looked at them as if they were covered in spiders. She hated spiders.

"Come, come. Do not be afraid, Lillian. Take my hands and try to see on purpose." He held them out.

Some of the other kids had come to watch.

"It cannot be any worse than what you have experienced so many times in the past," Fran said with a shrug. "And how bad can it be if you are seeing into Christopher's life? He is the most harmless person in the room."

Christopher gave her a worried look. That was interesting.

Licking her dry lips, Lillian said, "I am willing to try." With shaking hands, she placed her palms down upon his.

"Now," he said, "Look at me and try to see."

Lillian had never attempted to look into someone on purpose. She had always kept far away from the possibility. Regardless of the consequences for her, who would want to see the evil deeds hidden away in a falsely innocent shell? Knowing how corrupt humanity truly was made life look very bleak indeed.

She took a deep breath to steady herself, then met Christopher's dark eyes. She locked on them while feeling the hands beneath her—the size, the shape, the essence. A great force slammed into her, and she gasped for air. The room fell away and was replaced with open desert and the night sky. She wanted to hide away and pretend this was not happening as she usually did, but the feeling of Christopher tightly squeezing her hands and his sure, strong voice kept her present. She struggled to catch her breath.

"Concentrate on what you see," she heard him say. "Breathe slowly."

She tried to focus her mind. One breath in, another one out. One breath in, another one out. *I can do this. I can do this.* She repeated this several times until she could look once again at the scene around her.

Several dark-skinned men were sitting around a fire in discussion. Although she knew they were not speaking English, she could understand every word.

"The child is cursed. You have seen what he has done," one man said in a raised voice.

"He is but a child," another man said. "Can he be blamed?"

A third man said, "This is not about blame. It is about self-protection. We must cast the child out. Before he kills us all like he did the goats."

Several heads nodded as silence fell.

A fourth man spoke up quietly, "Are we to be responsible for the death of a child then? Who here wants that upon their soul?"

The third man spoke again, "He will not die by our hands if we give him to someone else to become their problem."

The men looked at each other, then gave nods of agreement.

The world around her changed again. They were in the same place on another day. Only two men sat in front of the fire. One man held a little boy who could not have been older than three or four years old while the second man spun the metal handle of a brand which he held into the fire. It was glowing red with heat when he pulled it out

"Hold him firmly," he said to the first man, who lifted the boy to place him face down over his knees. He put one hand on the boy's back, pulled down his loose pants, and held his other hand firmly over the lower legs.

The first man pressed the metal to the back of the boy's upper thigh. A child's scream filled the night as the word was imprinted on his skin. Lillian could not read the language, but she knew it to mean 'unclean.'

Still whimpering, the child was bundled into a rough blanket. The second man handed him up to the first, who was seated upon a horse. He rode off into the night to dispose of the child—to save them all.

The room returned in a flash, knocking the wind out of Lillian. She staggered back and would have fallen onto the floor if she had not had enough presence of mind to lean to the side and let herself slump into a chair.

Her breath was coming in quick pants and she could feel sweat rolling down her back. If this was the way to control her problem, she wanted none of it. Nor did she wish to know such intimate details of her friends' lives.

She could hear Christopher's voice as if it were coming from across the room. "This is good. You are awake."

In truth she would rather not have been. Why oh why did she always see the worst inside of a person? She would give anything to see their happiest memories, even if it happened only once.

Finally, bringing her breath to a more normal speed, she looked at Christopher and said, "I must think about this. What good is it to hurt myself on purpose?"

"I believe if you practice like this," Christopher said, "you can choose to see or not when you are touched. Trust me. The more you practice, the easier it will become. I am happy to say it has started to work for me."

Lillian turned to Fran. "Would you do this? Purposely hear people's thoughts to see if you can control it?"

Her friend shrugged. "I could not say. However, what I do know is if things get much worse for me, I may no longer be able to live with it."

Lillian gave Fran an empathetic look. What a bleak future stood before all of them.

"Thank you, Christopher, for your insight. I believe it is time for me to return home. I am in need of a nap," Lillian said, feeling deflated.

The young man bowed as he left their company and Lillian rose to retrieve Sarah, who was still across the room with some friends.

Once they were settled in the carriage, Sarah asked, "Are you well?"

She wanted to nod, but it would have been a lie. "Not now, Sarah," she said instead.

As they rode home, she thought seriously on the matter of her problem. She wanted to discuss it with Sarah, but needed time to work through it in her head first.

Her entire life, Lillian had dreamed of the day she could make her ability disappear. However, she now knew keeping it stored away and unused was the best she could ever hope for.

Silvano had worked with all of them on strategies to diminish or hide their abilities, and it had seemed in the past that the work was successful, but it had been an illusion. It was a completely different scenario living with their abilities in the country away from people. Based on her own recent experiences and the raising of so many hands in the Society's room this evening, it was clear being in London was having devastating effects.

Was how they had been approaching their problems this entire time wrong? Was Christopher right? Was the only way to control the thing you did not want was to learn how to use it?

Lillian put her palm over her eyes and leaned her head back onto the leather seat. Everything she thought she had known about her world as true was now being brought into question. Now she had a decision to make about her curse—whether to deliberately use it to try to control it or continue on as she had been. She was afraid all her carefully laid plans were about to be shattered into pieces.

TEN

An undercut to his left jaw had Gabriel seeing stars. He jumped back and shook his head to clear it.

"Been out of the country too long and forgot how to fight? Come on, Gabe, get those fists up," his opponent taunted with a congenial smile.

Gabriel took advantage of Davis' relaxed stance to lunge forward and give him a right, a left, and a final blow to the stomach. The man let out an "oof" as the air was forcefully pushed out of his lungs. Gabriel did not stop to let his friend catch his breath. He followed with an undercut to his jaw while putting out his left foot to trip Davis as he began to fall back. He landed with a hard thud.

The spectators were silent—waiting to see if Davis would rise again. The men were left disappointed. "Pax!" his friend cried from his prone position on the floor. "You win." Davis was a short, stocky man, which did not give him much of an advantage in a boxing match, but he was also tenacious. Gabriel knew he would not have given up so easily if this had been a real fight, with his life on the line.

His friend's surrender caused Gabriel to smile and say, "You should have learned by now never to egg me on Davy." He leaned down with an outstretched hand to help the man up.

"I am a slow learner it seems." Davis rubbed his sore jawline. "Glad to see you back in fine form."

Both men removed their boxing gloves and picked up towels from a bench on the side of the room to wipe sweat from their faces and necks. Davis ran the cloth several times over his short brown curls. The ladies had always loved the man's hair, which made Gabriel want to roll his eyes.

Several club members slapped Gabriel on the back in congratulations as they walked by to leave the room now that the show was over.

The cellar of his club had been cleared out and transformed into an exercise room. It was a place where his men from the Network could stay fit for when they needed to be out in the field. The room was equipped with all manner of apparatus, but the men, who were from all walks of life, spent most of their time in one-on-one combat such as boxing, fencing, and wrestling.

Gabriel grinned. "I do not believe I was ever *out* of fine form."

He and Davis had been friends since their school days at

Eaton. Most of the boys who attended were sons of the nobility or the rich middle class. Davis, on the other hand, was the bastard son of an earl and his mistress, which meant he started there as an outcast. Those born out of wedlock were usually treated as the lowest people in society unless they found a way to earn their place higher up. Being a charismatic person, Davis had quickly done just that. He became the favorite of the school with all the boys. Even the bullies respected him.

His friend held out his hand now, which Gabriel shook firmly and said, "I would spot you a drink upstairs, but I have a meeting and quite a bit of business to attend to, as you might imagine."

"Indeed, indeed," Davis said as they turned to the stairs and began the climb to the main floor. "Do you think that last hit will bruise? It might garner me sympathy with the ladies."

Gabriel chuckled. "Not that you need the help with the ladies, but if it does bruise, just do not tell them it was I that caused it."

"Oh ho, no. Fighting off footpads makes for a much better story, don't you think?" Davis said with a laugh. "Especially if I came out of it better than they."

"You should know it is bad form to lie to women to win their favor." Gabriel shook his head with a smile, then sobered. "I will catch up with you as soon as I have heard back on the progress of this out-of-control lordlings problem. I may need you to assist." He paused his steps. "Come to think of it, I could use more men on my personal investigation. Since you seem to have nothing better to do right now than woo and win ladies, perhaps you can help. The more bodies we have in the search, the faster we will get the bastard."

Davis put his hand on Gabriel's shoulder and squeezed. "You know I would do anything for you Gabe. You only need to ask."

Gabriel let out a breath he had not realized he had been holding. "Thank you. I will send word as soon as I know my next move."

At the top of the stairs, Frazier met them with their outerwear.

"Certainly, Gabe. In the meantime, stay out of trouble." He winked, put on his hat and was gone.

Frazier turned to his master and said in a low tone, "Received word from Raven. Says you're late and he needs tae speak tae ye right away. He is a stickler for being on time, that one is."

"Thank you, Frazier. The day got away from me, but now I am on my way."

As the carriage rattled down the street toward home, Gabriel thought about how good it had felt to get pummeled this morning. He had truly needed that to get his mind back into the game. Lady Lillian and the possibility she might become his wife was nothing but a distraction. Finding his father's murderer was the only thing that needed his full attention, and he had already decided that other than the upcoming dinner he would stay as far away from that distraction as possible.

Hartley was waiting for him when he entered his study.

He called for coffee, then shook his friend's hand. "What have you to report?" Gabriel asked as he sat behind the desk.

"I have completed some initial inquiries regarding the men and women on your list of suspects. I put one of our men on the financials, as they can often lead to all sorts of interesting finds."

"You have found something?" Gabriel asked.

"Nothing conclusive," Hartley said, "but about three months after your father's death, Lord Alston purchased a stud farm."

Gabriel frowned. "There is nothing unusual about that."

"Not usually, no, but in this case, Alston was deeply in debt at the time. You said yourself he owed your father a great deal of money."

"Perhaps he won some money at cards?" Gabriel turned his attention to his valet, who had just come in with a tray of coffee. "Jersey, what do you know about Lord Alston's gambling habits?"

Jersey shrugged and poured coffee into the cups, passing them over to the men. "There isn't much to tell. He has no great talent at cards, but that's probably because he doesn't spend much time at it. His vice is more in the line of buying expensive toys for himself and his lady."

Gabriel took a sip of the hot brew and turned back to Hartley. "If not from gambling, where did he get enough money to pay off his debts and buy a property stocked with horses? Those do not come cheaply."

Rarely one to be flustered, the viscount slowly and thoughtfully rubbed his hand along the arm of his chair several times before saying, "That is what we have yet to discover. The money just appeared out of nowhere without the usual trail."

Gabriel uncapped the inkwell on his desk and dipped his quill pen inside. "Let me pen a short note to the Home Office and inquire as to whether they have any information about Lord Alston's activities. Perhaps they will know more, especially if there are illegal operations at play. Is there anyone else you can tell me more about?"

Hartley shook his head. "It is early days yet."

"I plan to visit Lord Chumly this afternoon to follow up on some information Jersey uncovered for me." He threw the quill onto the desk. "I am vexed at the slow pace at which this entire investigation is going."

"When a crime has but a small handful of suspects, it can take weeks to make a proper inquiry, yet you have twenty-eight," Hartley said. "It will take time if you wish to be methodical about it, Wyvern."

"I know, I know. My father taught me well not to be impatient, but I am having a difficult time following his advice." Gabriel finished off his coffee and handed the cup out to Jersey to signal for a refill.

"If that is all, Hartley, I have an enormous pile of correspondence to deal with this morning."

The viscount rose from his seat and reached across the desk to offer his hand. "I will let you know immediately if I find any new information."

"Good. And Hartley …"

"Yes?"

"Thank you."

The viscount nodded and left the study.

"Jersey, follow up on this business with Alston. You know more about the dirty dealings of the aristocracy than anyone. Perhaps you can find the mysterious source of the money."

"Sure thing, Sergeant." Jersey gave a military salute and moved to place the empty cups on the tray.

"Well, Jersey, has it not felt wonderful to be home and in the thick of things again?"

"Home for you, Guv, not for me." Jersey said.

"Where are you from again?"

With a wink, his valet picked up the tray and said, "Don't believe I've ever said."

Speaking of mysteries, Lady Lillian was not the only one in Gabriel's life.

Lillian felt ready to confront her dilemma the next day. Sarah and Anne were two of the people in her life she could trust without question, so she called them to a meeting in her bedroom to discuss it.

"What is all this about a secret meeting?" Anne asked, breezing into the room with her usual bright smile.

"If it were all that secret, you have now given us away," Sarah grumbled as she closed the door.

"Oh, I am sorry. Is this truly meant to be a clandestine meeting, then?" Anne asked with a frown. She moved closer to Lillian, seated at her escritoire, where she had been working on her manuscript.

Lillian turned in her chair. "Not so much clandestine, Anne, but private. I have an important decision to make and wish for your opinion on the matter."

Anne clasped her hands in front of her bosom. "Is it about the duke?"

Sarah snorted.

"Not the duke," Lillian said. "Today he is the least of my problems." She rose. "Come, let us all sit on my bed like when we were little girls sharing secrets. I have missed our time together while away over the years."

Anne sighed wistfully. "It truly has been miserable only seeing you a few weeks at a time each year. I am ever so glad to have you home."

The three lifted their skirts enough to kneel onto the bed and sit tailor-fashion—something they could have never gotten away with if her mother were in the room. It felt good to have the freedom to break the rules.

"Now, what is this all about?" Anne asked after squirming around until she settled.

Lillian took several breaths to focus her thoughts. "I have not told you about this, Anne, but my problem is growing stronger. When I first attended Silvano's School, he taught us strategies for how to hide our abilities so they did not appear so often. However, the constant wearing of gloves, the avoidance of touch, the slow breathing—it has all been for naught.

I only need to be *near* certain people now for it to rear its ugly head."

"Oh no," Anne said. "Does this mean everything is so much harder for you now?"

"Yes. With all the balls and parties and outings Mother has us attending, there is no way to avoid being in close proximity to others. I now live in constant fear of being in public." Lillian looked down and plucked at a loose thread on her skirt. "At this week's Society meeting, it was discussed the possibility of embracing the problem instead of running away from it. Christopher showed me how to attempt to do so. It was overwhelming, almost more than I could bear—but I did not have a fit, nor did I faint during the vision."

"It sounds like doing so may be a practical solution. What do you need from us?" Anne asked quietly. "You know I love you dearly and would go to the ends of the Earth and back if it would help you in any way."

Lillian looked up and saw the love shining in her cousin's eyes. She was so lucky to have her as a friend. She looked at Sarah, who had been at her side since the beginning of this journey. Sarah, loyal to a fault—another dear friend.

"Thank you, Anne. That means the world to me. What I want to ask from both of you is if you think I should pursue this practice. It would mean exhausting myself daily as well as seeing so many events of the past I would rather not. Christopher said he found success this way and has been able to bring his gift under his command."

"Who would you practice on, Lillian?" Sarah asked. "If you need people who have dark thoughts and deeds, you cannot simply walk up to strangers and say, 'Can I look into your black heart if you please?' "

Anne giggled. "Sarah, you do have such a way with words."

"Thank you, Anne," her friend said with a grin.

"You do have a good point, Sarah," she said. "Who would I practice on? First, I still do not understand what triggers the episodes." She frowned in thought. "I do not know why I can touch some people like you and not others. Besides, what would I say to people? Most of the servants know rumors about me, but none know the entirety of my problem." Lillian paused in thought. "Perhaps I should just start with friends from the Society."

She blew out a hard breath. "Oh, I simply do not know. This is not something I have ever considered before and the decision is overwhelming me."

Anne reached out and took one of Lillian's gloved hands. "I think one thing you are truly wondering is if short-term suffering will bring you long-term gain. Let me ask you this. If you had control of the problem, would you be able to live life differently than you do now?" She squeezed the hand and let go.

"I have no idea." The thread she had pulled continued to unravel. She wondered where it would end. "You know I have no wish to marry. Yet, there is no other prospect for women of our class but marriage. The other choice is to hide away in obscurity, which has been my plan all along, regardless of whether my parents continue to push me upon men who have no idea what they would be getting."

Sarah batted at her hand. "Stop that, Lillian. You will have your entire gown pulled apart before you know it."

Lillian squeezed her gloved hands together to keep them from fidgeting.

"Are you not the least bit interested in the concept of marriage? Of falling in love?" Anne asked.

"No, not when it is all too impossible," Lillian said.

"Well, I think the duke might be the one man who could change your mind," Anne said. "He is awfully handsome and charming." She clasped her hands together in front of her bosom and sighed dreamily, which she did every time she mentioned the duke. *Maybe Anne should marry him.*

Lillian waved her hand in the air as if to push the idea away. "It does not matter whether he has fine attributes or not. What is the point of considering him as a suitor if I cannot even contemplate the idea of marriage? Imagine how awful it would be for him to be saddled with me. No, it is best to stop thinking about it altogether."

"You will write your book and live away from society all your life then? There will be no husband, no children, no outings," Sarah pointed out. "Is this really what you want for yourself?"

Anne perked up. "Book? No one told me about a book."

Prince Albert scampered up the side of the bed and turned

several times in the circle the girls made. Then he jumped onto Sarah's lap.

"I have yet to tell you of my plan," Lillian said. "One of my schoolmates has a cousin who is a book publisher. He told me there are plenty of women who write under pen names to protect their reputations and earn decent livings as authors. I have been writing an herbal for some months now, collecting information from letters I have exchanged with people around the world. Once finished, I will send it to this publisher and thus gain my freedom to live as I wish."

"That sounds very exciting," Anne said. "I know you have been talking about your interest in healing herbs for some time, but as Sarah said, is a life as a successful author who lives as a hermit what you want? What if you *could* have a husband and a family instead?"

Lillian bit her lower lip and worried it between her teeth. If she could control her problem, would she want a husband? She had stopped considering it a possibility years ago when she had understood the negative consequences of her so-called gift.

"Before you answer that, there is something I think you should know," Anne said quietly, interrupting her thoughts.

She turned to her cousin. "Yes?"

"I was not sure whether to tell you this, as I do not know all the facts; however I have decided you should be forewarned." Anne took a deep breath and let it out. "The other day after you left with the duke for a walk, your mother told me she has been conspiring with the Duchess of Wyvern to create an alliance between you and her son. It appears he is allowing her to choose a wife for him and he will simply approve the woman and show up at the altar on the day of the wedding."

Lillian's nostrils flared. Once again, her mother was scheming to take her choices away. "I assume I am to have no say in the matter." She rubbed her open palms up and down her thighs. "This is all so ridiculous!" She slapped her hands on her knees. "How am I supposed to fight my mother's strategies, plan for my future, and figure out how to best deal with my problem? How could anyone have the energy to keep up with so much?"

"I find It difficult to say what I would do if I were dancing in your slippers, as I truly have no idea what it has been like for you," Anne said, "but know this: whatever you decide, I know I speak for Sarah as well, we will stand your friends and help you."

Lillian reached out both her hands toward the girls until they put theirs into hers. She squeezed them both and said, "I am fortunate to have you in my life. Thank you." She let go and flopped back onto the bed with a loud sigh. Prince Albert climbed onto her belly. "I have much to think upon."

When she slipped under the covers later that night, Lillian could think of nothing but her decision. She had never dared to dream about other possibilities, always assuming she would live her entire life away from society.

If controlling her problem could give her the freedom to have anything she wanted in life, what would that look like? Did she want a husband and a family of her own? That could mean passing on her ability to her children. She inwardly groaned at the idea.

She rolled and pushed herself onto one elbow, then attempted to plump up her pillow. She lay back down again and thought of having a husband. Would he be anything like the duke—intelligent, commanding, and sociable—or perhaps someone more like her, who preferred a quiet evening at home with her nose in her research? She sighed out loud.

Unable to sleep, Lillian got up and padded to the window. She pulled the curtain to the side, tied it back, and sat down on the bench. She had no idea what to do now that all her plans had been turned upside down. Perhaps it would be better to wait until the next Society meeting to see what Signor Silvano had to say. He had always shown great wisdom about how to deal with the difficulties of life. She laid her head against the windowpane and sighed again.

Gabriel could not sleep. He got out of bed, put on his robe, and went to the window. He saw the moon was bright tonight as he pulled back a curtain. He was not the least bit worried about the Network. It would keep moving forward. It always had. He was more anxious than ever to tighten the noose around his father's killer's neck. But how? All that he had tried in the past had reaped no positive results, and everything was moving too slowly now. He needed to try something different.

What was it his father had always said? 'Son, if you continue to do the same thing and gain the same unwanted results, you must find a new approach. Only then can you gain what you want.'

His father was right.

One man was dead and another in hiding due to the murderer's evil actions. The thought made Gabriel rub at the ache in his chest. He did not want to suffer any more losses. Taking a deep breath, he cleared his mind of all the puzzles without solutions. Tomorrow. Tomorrow would bring him fresh ideas. Then he would spend every waking moment chasing down the devil so he could send him back to hell where he belonged, and bring his brother home.

ELEVEN

"Lil, what are you doing?" Anne asked from Lillian's sitting room doorway. "We are going to be late, and you know the worst thing possible for our reputations is to keep a duke waiting." She said this last part with a wry smile.

Lillian had been ready for at least half an hour but was now at her escritoire attempting to add a few new pages of the information she had received this week from one of the Spanish herbalists to her manuscript. The feeling of desperation to finish her book was increasing, especially now that she knew about the new scheme her mother had concocted regarding the duke.

"Just a minute," she said to Anne. "Let me just complete this sentence."

She wrote a few more words while Anne talked to Sarah

across the room and then placed the new page atop her growing stack. She took several deep breaths and stood.

This evening was not to be just any dinner, and Lillian was nervous. She was wavering between following her desire to get out of marriage—any marriage—and considering the possibility of a normal life. The first had a certain outcome and the second was fraught with too many possible outcomes, both good and bad.

She blew out a breath. She needed to choose the correct path and stay on it, like she always did.

"I am ready, Anne," she said. "Do you think this simple amethyst necklace is elegant enough paired with this lilac silk? I could not decide whether I should try to impress or go out of my way to look my worst, so I settled for something in between. What is your opinion?"

Anne gave a small laugh as she came closer to inspect Lillian. "I think it is too late to attempt a strategy of repelling the duke with bad looks. He has already seen how pretty you are, and tonight you look lovely."

"You are impressive enough for any duke," Sarah added. "Whether you choose to grab his attention or send him away, you are battle ready."

In the end did it really matter how she was dressed? She sighed aloud and ran her hands, covered in dark lavender gloves, down the skirt of her dress to smooth any wrinkles. "I thank you both for your kind words." She stood tall and lifted her chin. "I say let us go to this dinner and get it over with. Perhaps the duke will have no interest in me and tonight will be the end of the acquaintance. Then I can go on as before."

"Or perhaps you will fall madly in love with him and live happily ever after." Anne giggled.

"Bite your tongue, Anne," she said with mock sternness. "The last thing I need is to invent fantasies in my head about a future that might never happen."

"It could happen," Sarah said, reasonably.

"Hmm," was all Lillian said. She was tired of arguing the point and wished to move on.

She and Anne walked arm in arm down the stairs, finding they were the last to be ready as usual.

In the carriage, her mother had plenty of advice she felt the need to impart. "Now remember, you want to be very attentive to his grace tonight, but at the same time give equal attention to the duchess." She rapped her fan against Lillian's side several times as if making a point. "The key to winning a man is to first win over his mother."

"Is that what you did, Mother?" Lillian asked to be contrary.

Her mother's smile faltered as she quickly glanced at her husband, then away. "Well, my situation was vastly different, since your father was not as close to his mother as the duke is."

Her father coughed into his fist. There was obviously more to this story than she had ever been told, and this made her wonder again why she had never met her paternal grandparents.

"Besides, this evening is not about me," her mother said in a defensive tone. "It is about you. If you can win a duke for yourself, think what it would mean for your brother and for Anne—the whole family, for that matter."

"How can my snaring a duke help anyone?" Lillian asked quietly. She felt like sticking out her lower lip and pouting like a little child.

"You must know that a ducal connection can help your brother when he one day takes a seat in parliament and when he looks for a good bride," her mother said. "Furthermore, it will certainly allow Anne to look nearly as high as she wants for a husband."

"I believe Anne's beautiful disposition already allows her to look as high as she wishes." Lillian reached to the side and squeezed Anne's hand. Anne squeezed back.

"Be that as it may, having a duke in the family certainly cannot hurt," her mother said.

It cannot hurt anyone but me, Lillian thought. Not a single member of her family noticed the elephant in the room—or in the coach in this case. She could not help bringing it up.

"There is a not-so-small fact that being married would not only be impossible for me," Lillian said, holding back the angry tears that now threatened, "but might be a living hell. Do none of you realize this? Or do you simply care more about getting me off of your hands?"

"That is enough, Lillian," her father said sternly. "This is not a discussion for tonight. Tonight let your mother have her hour to shine as the duke's guest. Tomorrow, we can consider the details."

She could not believe her ears. Her mother had just said this dinner was not about her, but her father's words had said the exact opposite. Her anger was reaching the boiling point, and soon she knew it would spill over on everyone around her. "You mean *you* can worry about it tomorrow. You may be able to easily put these concerns aside, but I live with them every moment of every day." She wanted to shout, but a carriage was not the place for it.

"No more, Daughter," her father said in a quiet, even voice. "This discussion is over."

Knowing Simon, she could sense his smirk from across the carriage. She dearly wished to kick him. She might have done so if her heavy skirts had not prevented it, because if nothing else, it would have made her feel better.

She managed the remainder of the ride in silence. Lillian interlaced her fingers and kept them in a tight ball in her lap. This was an argument that was never resolved. Why would her family not listen to her? They were so focused on giving her the life of a normal lady that they missed how much emotional pain she was in.

The only time she felt supported was with the other Society members. They understood exactly what it was like to be an oddity of nature. Her family never had.

Lillian expected an old and stodgy butler to open the door of Wyvern House, but instead a rather young man wearing an old-fashioned white wig took their things, introduced himself as Pennywhistle, then announced their entrance to the drawing room. It was a lavishly decorated room—as one would expect from a ducal home—with gilding at every turn.

The duke strode over quickly to meet her family. She noticed he wore a dark blue waistcoat that matched his eyes with his black and white attire this evening.

He first bowed to her parents, nodded at Simon then took Anne's hand, bowing over it, and said, "Miss Hargraves, it is a pleasure to see you again." This caused Anne to blush and give a small giggle. At the last, he turned to Lillian. "My Lady, I hope all is well with you."

She did not offer her hand but curtsied and said, "Of course, your grace, and I hope the same for you."

"We are all well here." He turned his attention to the group once again. "May I introduce you to our small family party?" He led them across the room to a settee where three ladies sat. "Mother, I would like to introduce you to our guests. The Earl and Countess of Wentworth, whom you already know, their son Lord Simon, daughter, Lady Lillian, and their niece, Miss Anne Hargraves." Looking at the Wentworth party he said, "My mother, the Duchess of Wyvern." They all curtsied, and the duchess gave a regal nod of her head.

Lillian saw that the duchess was a very beautiful woman who must have turned many heads in her youth. She had dark hair like her son, but darker eyes.

"May I also introduce my great aunts, who were very gracious to join us this evening." The older ladies tittered like schoolgirls at his remark. "Next to my mother is Great Aunt Gertrude and next to her is Great Aunt Gemma. They do not wish for formal introductions, as they would expect you to call them by Aunt."

The women, dressed alike in gray, high-necked gowns, reminded Lillian of doves. They had long necks, narrow faces, gray hair pulled up in buns, and large bosoms.

The aunts giggled again and then said in unison, "We are twins."

"Ah," her father said. "I knew there was something similar in your looks." Then he winked. Father could be quite the charmer with the ladies when he wished to be. The wink, of course, caused the ladies to giggle even more and her grace to sigh. Out of the corner of her eye, she could see Simon rolling his eyes. He too had heard many such compliments from their father before.

"Finally, I would like to introduce two of my school chums," the duke said. "This is Valentine Montgomery, Viscount Hartley." He waved his hand toward a man who was slightly thinner but about the same height. He had short, dark blond hair and fashionable sideburns. His looks might be considered classically handsome as opposed to the next man to whom the duke brought their attention. "And this is Mr. Davis Rigsby." Mr. Rigsby was nearly a head shorter than his two friends and stockier in build. His dark hair was very curly and his features were strong. His eyes sparkled when he grinned. Both men bowed to the company in turn. All three friends were of a similar age, in the early half of their second decade.

From behind them someone called out, "You have forgotten an introduction, Cousin."

Their small party turned slightly to include the newcomer. "This," the duke announced, "is my cousin, Mr. Howard Ramsay."

"And your heir." The man smirked, then gave a flowery bow to the group that included several turns of his wrist.

The duchess waved her arm to the opposite settee and chairs. "Please will you all sit down? We should be called to dinner soon, but first we can get to know each other better. "Lady Lillian, I understand you have recently returned from —what was it, finishing school?"

"Yes, your grace," Lillian said as she arranged her gown around the chair she had chosen.

"Did you enjoy attending school?" the duchess asked.

Lillian looked up with a smile. "Yes, your grace. So much so I did not wish to come home."

"Lillian!" her mother admonished.

Ignoring her mother, she pulled on her gloves to ensure they were in place and changed the subject. "You must be very pleased to have your son returned to you after such a lengthy absence, your grace."

"Oh, yes indeed. I missed him dreadfully. A house is very lonely when one is separated from all her family," the duchess said with sadness in her eyes. "It has been four years, but I do not know when the ache of losing my husband and Wyvern's twin will go away."

"I am very sorry for your loss, your grace," Lillian said. She looked up to the duke, who was now standing near her shoulder. She had not noticed him move to her side. "Twin?" she asked.

The world tilted. She thought of a smiling man with twinkling blue eyes, so like this man, but not quite. An unbelievable idea came to her. Perhaps the duke's double she had met truly was his twin. Was that possible? He could not be dead and living in the countryside at the same time.

"I apologize, Lady Lillian," the duke said. "Did I not tell you my brother was a twin?"

She met his eyes. "No, you left out that detail."

"London must have been nothing but a trail of broken hearts with two such handsome men about, Theodora," her mother gushed from her chair.

"Oh, you have no idea," the duchess said dryly, then turned to the duke. "Wyvern pour us all a drink would you? Perhaps some ratafia for the young ladies?"

"Yes, Mother." The duke crossed the room to do as he was asked and Simon sauntered over to assist.

"If my son misbehaves in any way, Lady Lillian, you have my permission to swat him with your fan," the duchess said with a mischievous smile.

"Thank you, your grace. I shall keep that in mind," Lillian said, although she did not mention that she had chosen not to bring a fan that evening. Even though they were considered more an ornamentation than anything, perhaps she should start carrying one everywhere to use as a weapon, as the duchess had suggested. It would be a wonderful way to keep people at a distance.

"I shall be happy to take Wyvern's place and keep you company," Mr. Ramsay said as he slid into the place next to her chair. His movement was so sudden it made her jump. "Oh, do forgive me, I did not mean to startle you." His tone was that of a man who was trying to seem concerned but with no true sincerity.

"You only surprised me is all," Lillian said.

The duke came forward with a glass for her and somehow managed to edge Mr. Ramsay slightly away. She never really cared for the sickly-sweet flavor of the liqueur, so she simply let the glass sit in her hand.

Anne then came over and engaged the duke in conversation. "Your grace, I would like to hear more about your travels abroad."

He had begun talking about a visit to Spain when Pennywhistle announced from the doorway, "Your grace, dinner is served."

"Since this is an informal evening," the duke called out, "Howard, if you would escort Aunt Gemma; Lord Simon, if you would take Aunt Gertrude. Lord Wentworth, if you would offer an arm to my mother and Lady Wentworth, then the two of us gentlemen will be privileged to have not one, but two lovely ladies on our arms." This pronouncement caused all the ladies to titter or giggle, with the exception of Lillian and the duchess. The latter had a look of fond exasperation on her face. Mr. Ramsay put on a lackluster smile that made it clear he thought he had gotten the worst of the bargain.

"What ho, Gabe! You have left us poor gentlemen in the cold," Mr. Rigsby said of himself and Viscount Hartley.

"And I doubt either of you are used to it," the duke said with a grin. "You have plenty of women who trail after you. Let the rest of us have a chance this evening."

Mr. Rigsby bowed. "I concede the field, as I assume I will have at least one lovely dinner partner."

Viscount Hartley stood silently as if indifferent to the outcome of who he might or might not take in to dinner, but when Mr. Rigsby placed his arm through his as if he were a lady, Lillian saw the viscount's eyes roll. He was apparently used to his friends' antics.

"I shall just have to escort the lovely Hartley instead," Mr. Rigsby said in a falsetto voice, followed by a wink.

With an indulgent sigh at the behavior of the young gentleman, the duchess led the little group out of the room and finally on to dinner.

So far, so good, Lillian thought to herself. She had had no incidents, but she wondered how long that would last. Constantly protecting herself during social affairs was a strain.

For the hundredth time, Lillian wished she had not been forced to come.

Gabriel first led Miss Hargraves to her seat between Davis and Lord Simon. Then he continued down the table and helped Lady Lillian to the honored place at his right. His mother had placed her there in hopes they could get to know each other better. He had to admit she looked lovely tonight in a color that made her skin glow. So much for avoiding distractions.

The first course of turtle soup was served. As those around the table began to eat and converse, he saw Davis on his left was enjoying a lively discussion with Miss Hargraves. He turned to Lady Lillian. "I do hope you made it to your meeting on time."

"I did indeed, and I thank you for it," she said with a smile.

"Did you find the meeting to be beneficial?" he asked.

Her spoon paused in midair and she cleared her throat. "I beg your pardon?"

"You did say you enjoyed the meetings for the conversation and the problem solving, did you not? Did you clear up any of your issues?"

"It was a pleasant evening, thank you."

It appeared he was going to receive no more information about this mysterious meeting from her. "Besides the usual pursuits of ladies, how is it you enjoy spending your time?" He took a sip of his wine.

"I enjoy studying the medicinal qualities of plants from around the world."

His eyebrows rose in surprise. "That is a rare endeavor. How did you become interested in the topic?"

"There were many students from overseas at the school I attended. On more than one occasion, their knowledge of herbs passed down in their families assisted to improve the health of other students." Her brown eyes sparkled with excitement. "I was fascinated by the power these plants held to heal the body, so I began collecting recipes and treatises on the subject—first from the students, then later I broadened my search to those who are experts. I often used the information to treat my fellow students when they were ill."

"That is impressive," he said and took a spoonful of the soup. It was quite good.

At all the social gatherings he had been to, he had yet to meet a lady who compiled knowledge on any topic other than fashion. Those who did follow more academic pursuits were called bluestockings and considered to be unfashionable. He had never heard such a label given to Lady Lillian. Then again, why bother calling her that when she already had the worse name of Leprous Lillian? Society could be so cruel, and he wanted to know the real reason why they had targeted this lady.

"Did you find many opportunities to solve any mysteries while you were abroad, your grace?" Lady Lillian asked.

"Yes. I spent many an hour on those sorts of tasks," he said. "Do you not find all the puzzles life has to offer vastly intriguing?"

"Hmm." She delicately wiped her mouth and searched for words. "I would not say that to be true for myself as you have stated it. However, I do enjoy learning the secrets nature holds such as the healing properties of plants or the patterns in the positions of the stars. There is so much we do not know about the world we live in."

"I could not agree more. Speaking of something I wish to know more about …" Gabriel leaned in and asked what he had been dying to know since Tuesday night, "The episode you had at the ball—is that something that occurs often?"

Her eyes flicked upward as if surprised at the question. "More often than I would like."

"I am sorry to hear it. Are the rumors that you do not like to be touched true?"

"Not here, please, your grace," Lady Lillian said in a quiet voice. "I would not like my parents to overhear me explaining it to you."

Gabriel locked gazes with her. He wanted to push further—to find out why touch was a problem for this woman, if it was indeed a problem. She was not a shrinking violet. She did not fit the persona of someone who had an aversion to or fear of physical contact. He was intrigued by her story and he wanted to know more. "Later then," he promised and sat back, turning his attention to the food in front of him.

Davis broke the tension of their conversation. "Would you not agree, Gabriel, that saying someone has the fashion sense of a horse is not truly an insult, since horses would never be so undignified as to wear anything that was not at the highest level of fashion?"

"Whatever are you on about, Davis?" Gabriel asked, amused. He saw Lady Lillian hold a napkin to her lips to stifle her laughter.

"I am talking about horses and their superior knowledge of fashion," Davis said. "I believe if they had the choice they would wear a prettily trimmed straw bonnet over one of those ten-inch affairs covered in flowers and fruit."

"You are utterly ridiculous," Gabriel shook his head and grinned.

No longer able to contain her laughter, Lady Lillian burst out, "Oh no, horses would definitely prefer the latter so they could stop and have a midday snack." She had to stop to catch her breath after every few words. The rest of them at their end of the table chuckled, even Hartley.

This was the second time he had seen her laugh, and it transformed her into quite a beautiful woman.

"What is it you find so entertaining, Gabriel?" Her grace called from the other end of the table.

He let his laughter die down. "Nothing really, Mother. I was merely telling about the time Michael and I accidentally got locked in the cellar and thought for certain it was haunted, only to later find out the sounds were coming from the water pipes.”

“Humph. You two always were up to one lark or another. How I kept up with you without going gray, I shall never know,” the duchess said with a fond smile.

“If you have lost any beauty due to your sons, your grace,” Lady Lillian said, “you must have been extraordinarily beautiful to begin with.”

“Thank you, my dear. You are very sweet to say so,” his mother’s eyes twinkled.

The room went back to several quiet conversations while the soup was removed and the fish course laid out.

Gabriel surreptitiously studied Lady Lillian while she ate. Any woman who was so kind to his mother was someone worth a more careful examination. Perhaps he might just have to consider additional outings after all.

TWELVE

From below the table, Lillian felt a squeeze of her hand which caused her to freeze. She was not sure which was worse—the unexpected touch or the fear of what it could bring. She paused, waiting for a physical reaction, but once again none came.

The duke leaned in and whispered, "Thank you for your kindness toward my mother. Since losing my father and brother it has been very difficult for her."

Lillian quickly moved her hand out of reach. "I was merely truthful. She is indeed very beautiful."

He looked down the table at his mother. "Yes, she is. Plus, she has been a wonderful mother. She is not the sort who leaves her children in the nursery only to bring them out a few times a week to show off to guests. We spent much of our childhood on family picnics and outings, and she visited the schoolroom often to observe our lessons." His mother must have felt his gaze, for she looked up and raised a brow in question. He winked and then looked at Lillian. "No mother could be better."

"You are very fortunate. There are many who could not say the same."

"Are you not fortunate in your family?" he asked.

"Oh! I did not mean to imply that I have suffered from a lack of motherly affection," Lillian rushed to explain. "My mother has always been supportive. She has had to deal with much in the raising of me. I often forget that."

She looked at her mother, who was currently conversing with Mr. Ramsay. No matter how driven her mother was to make her into a normal young lady and to marry her off, Lillian could not forget all she had had to put up with because of her daughter's curse. There were many parents who would have sent her to an asylum or worse instead of allowing her to thrive at a special school like Silvano's.

"You seem to imply that you were a beast of a child no mother could love," the duke teased.

"I did not intend that either, your grace." Lillian lifted her fork and took a bite of something to keep her mouth busy so she would stop sounding like an idiot. This man did not need to know her life story.

She found the morsel to be very tasty. Was it trout? She never could tell the difference between the different types of fish.

"You were not a beast of a child?" he asked.

Now she wanted to roll her eyes. "Of course not. How absurd you are." She was not used to men bantering with her in this manner. Usually they took her closed-off demeanor as a sign to take themselves off and find a more willing lady with whom to converse. Pointing to the plate with her fork, she said, "Your cook is very good."

"Chef," Gabriel corrected. "Monsieur Brisson would give birth to a litter of kittens if he were to hear you call him a mere cook."

Lillian laughed at the comment, then looked around the table. She and the duke had been talking so exclusively she had nearly forgotten about the rest of the party. Her mother and brother were now enjoying a lively discussion with the duchess. Anne was smiling at Aunt Gertrude, who was speaking to her. This left Mr. Ramsay to the mercy of Aunt Gemma. He had a bored look on his face.

Several delicious courses followed, one after another, ending with a lovely lemon cheesecake and fresh fruit. At the end of the meal, the duchess stood and invited the ladies to the drawing room. "We will leave you gentlemen to your port," she announced.

"I believe, Mother, since this is such a small party, the men would not mind having a glass of port in the drawing room instead of remaining here," the duke said. "That is, if the ladies have no objection?"

Aunt Gemma tittered. "Of course not, dear boy. I think I speak for all the ladies when I say we will be all the better for the male company."

Viscount Hartley, who had been a silent dinner partner to Lillian's right, held out his elbow. "May I escort you, my lady?"

Lillian cautiously placed her hand on his sleeve. "Thank you, my lord."

"Do you not agree, dear," Aunt Gertrude said from Lillian's other side as they walked down the hallway, "that the usual separating of the men and women after dinner is such a shame? I much prefer to look at all the handsome gentlemen than listen to the ladies gossip." She sighed dreamily.

"Yes, Aunt Gertrude. I quite agree." Lillian truly had no opinion on the matter, but the aunts were young at heart and such enjoyable company.

Later, the tea cart was brought into the drawing room and Lillian relaxed as she inhaled the steam rising from her cup. While the tea was served, she enjoyed time conversing with the aunts in turn and said a few words to the duchess regarding the recent wedding of Princess Charlotte.

Lillian was turning to seek out her cousin when Mr. Ramsay broadsided her. She inwardly cringed when he stood too closely. "Lady Lillian, I hope I am not being too presumptuous by asking, but would you do me the honor of taking a walk in the park with me tomorrow afternoon?"

"Oh, I do beg your pardon, Mr. Ramsay, but tomorrow I have an engagement with friends." It was not a lie precisely.

She did plan to spend time with Sarah and Anne at some point.

"Perhaps the next day?" he persisted.

"That is a shame, Howard," the duke said unexpectedly from her side. "Lady Lillian has promised to stroll with me that day. She has a very full schedule like most ladies of the *ton* as you can imagine."

Perhaps acknowledging defeat, Mr. Ramsay gave a sickly smile, bowed, and backed away.

Music began to fill the room. After her mother's boasts to the duchess of Anne's superiority at the piano forte, it was decided she should play. Lillian was never so grateful for her own mediocre talent as she was now. The last thing she ever wanted was to be put on show.

She turned more fully toward the duke and said in a whisper, "You just lied."

The duke raised his eyebrows and grinned. "Tomorrow you will have to tell your friends what a practiced liar I am."

Lillian felt the heat of a blush rising up her neck and covering her cheeks. She had been caught.

His grace chuckled. "I will simply have to take you on a stroll in truth."

"And I will spend time with my friends," she said.

"Let us take a turn about the room, shall we? Then we may continue to talk without interruption."

She gave a slight nod and joined in step with him.

A burst of laughter came from Mr. Rigsby, who was seated next to Aunt Gemma across the room. He seemed to be enjoying himself.

"Your mother's boast was not empty," the duke said. "Your cousin is very talented. Has she been out in society long?"

"We both came out together this season,"

"Has she done well?" he asked. "Have the gentlemen taken a liking to her?"

"Oh, yes. She is liked by everyone. She has such an easy and friendly personality. It is very difficult not to like her."

The duke nodded. "She should have her choosing of any husband."

"I agree."

She looked off into the distance and thought about her own situation. She had done her best tonight to behave as if it were just an ordinary outing, but nothing had magically changed. As always, she shied away from every possible touch. She felt out of place, as if she were trying to put on someone else's skin and it did not fit.

They listened in silence to the pleasant music for a few moments before Lillian said, "On the subject of matchmaking, your grace, I understand our mothers have been conspiring on our behalf."

There was a slight falter in the duke's step. "I would not say they have been conspiring, rather they have made a suggestion on our behalf. Whether we choose to take that suggestion is another thing entirely."

"You might be able to say that, but it is not so simple for me. Young ladies of the *ton* must marry as their families dictate. However, that is not the main issue in my case."

The duke frowned. "What is?"

Lillian decided she must go a step further to get out of this match her mother had her heart set on. If the duke saw her as a good prospect for marriage, she would be doomed to a course of action she had not chosen. She must take a risk, tell him about her curse, and change his mind.

She took in a breath and let it out slowly. "Your grace, you asked me at dinner about the public incidents which have resulted in a certain reputation."

"Indeed." He nodded. "I have heard you have an aversion to touch."

Lillian gave a tight-lipped smile. "It is far more than an aversion. No one in society, other than my own family, understands the truth of it."

They had reached the end of the drawing room and, in unspoken accord, turned to cross it in the other direction. Aunt Gertrude had taken Anne's place at the piano forte and was playing a beautiful ballad. Anne was surrounded by the duke's two friends and his cousin—like moths to a flame.

"Will you tell me more about it?" the duke asked.

"Yes, I think you should know what you would be getting if you were stuck with me," Lillian said with a grimace. "My reluctance to be touched has nothing to do with the touch itself, but rather the consequences of it." She stopped to take another full breath. She squeezed her hands into fists, then released them. She was not used to speaking so plainly of this side of herself. "I know this is unbelievable, but when I come in contact with certain people, I see images, visions, of their past. Usually, it is the worst parts of their past, their evil deeds and inclinations. I become so overwhelmed it causes me to have what looks like a fit. When I was young, I was sent away to a special school—"

Lillian squeaked as the duke abruptly grabbed her elbow and steered her toward the doorway.

"Lady Lillian and I shall not be but a moment," he said to the duchess as they passed where she was seated. "I would like to show her the portrait of Grandfather in the study."

The duchess raised her eyebrows but did not say a word.

"Your grace, what ever are you doing?" Lillian hissed once they were alone in the marbled hallway.

"I believe we should speak about this matter in private," he said without apology. No more words were spoken as he rushed her up the main staircase to the first floor and down the hallway until they reached what Lillian assumed to be the aforementioned study. "Wait here a moment."

He grabbed a candle from the wall sconce and entered the room. When he returned, he opened the door more widely and invited her into the now well-lit room. He closed it completely behind her.

The room was what she would expect from a man's domain—dark, heavy furniture, shelves lining the walls, and an absence of the adornments one might find in a woman's sitting room.

"We should not be in a room together with the door closed,"

Lillian protested. "I shall end up being compromised." The last thing she wanted was to be forced into marriage with him after going to all this effort to repel him.

"If we are quick about it, no harm will come to you," he said as he moved toward the fireplace where two wing-backed chairs were placed. "Come, sit down, and let us discuss this further. I thought it best that no one overhear what you had to say."

Lillian frowned as she sat across from the duke. "What else is there to say?" Was what she had told him not enough to send the man running? She was absolutely stunned by his reaction.

"I want to better understand your situation. I assure you, Lady Lillian, I have an interest in all the sciences. I have read of such gifts before but have never encountered anyone who claims to have one. I will not dismiss this as youthful silliness or insanity without further information." The duke leaned back in his chair as if preparing to stay a while.

Lillian wanted to run. Not once had she ever considered telling her story outside her family or the Society, both because she knew the shame it would bring to her and her family and because of the real possibility that she might end up at an insane asylum. In the duke's case, she hoped that what little she had already told him would turn him away so he could set his sights on some other lady. She had hoped for her freedom. Instead she had only served to intrigue the dratted man.

The duke continued to wait patiently for her to speak while she inwardly squirmed. The more she confided, the greater the risk to herself. Should she trust this man, a near stranger, with all her secrets?

"Perhaps you can start by telling me about this school you attended," he said, breaking the silence. "What was its purpose?"

That much was easy. "While it was located in the country, Silvano's School for Exceptional Children served no other purpose than to hide misfits like myself away and to lighten the burden upon our families," she said with cynicism lacing her voice.

The duke frowned. "I do not understand. Why hide away?"

Lillian gave a harsh laugh. "Can you imagine what would happen to us if the world knew of what we could do? The answers range from being locked away as if we were deranged to being used as slaves to serve the purpose of those in power. You have seen a glimpse of how difficult it can be for one such as me." She clasped her hands tightly together in her lap. "I may look like a lady, but my reputation is that of one who is far from normal. Have you not heard the name I am called in society—Leprous Lillian?" She looked away toward the cold fireplace, swallowing hard. "It is a wonder my family still receives invitations."

The duke's gaze softened. "I apologize. I had not considered how difficult this must be for you. Your gift of the sight is real?"

Lillian returned her gaze to the duke. "It is not a gift of the sight. That gift is the ability to see the future. My gift— or curse as I call it—is the ability to see into the past."

The duke grinned. "Why that is wonderful! There is so much you could do with such a gift."

Lillian gasped. Was the man insane? He had no idea what it was like to see the visions of horror in people's heads.

"You do not understand. What I see are some of the worst atrocities man can commit. They haunt my dreams. What use could that be to anyone?"

"You could help catch criminals." His eyes shone with an excited brilliance.

She snorted. How ludicrous. "Who would believe me if I went to a constable and said, 'Hello, sir. I think you should arrest Lord Railing, who murdered his kitchen maid. I saw him do it in my head.' "

The duke leaned forward. "Did he truly?"

"Did who truly what?" she asked, brows drawn down in confusion.

"Did Lord Railing truly murder his kitchen maid?"

Lillian waved the question away. "That is not the point. Who would listen to such an account?"

"I am listening." His midnight blue eyes looked intently at her.

Lillian jumped up and paced to the mahogany desk. She leaned back against it and hunched forward with her arms crossed over her belly. This was crazy thinking. She could not expose her secret in such a way. Regardless of what the duke thought, she had experienced how people treated her when they suspected what she could do, and it was not pleasant.

The duke came up and leaned against the desk next to her. "No one can force you to do it if it is not something you wish, but imagine all the guilty people you could help bring to justice."

Lillian rocked back and forth. He was implying what had already been on her mind—the possibility of controlling her ability. But what if she failed?

"I am not in command of the ability," she said now, looking at the floor beneath her silk slippers. "You saw the consequences of that at the ball."

"Ah." There was a pause and then he asked, "but could you learn to be?"

"Possibly," she said. "But do I want to? That is the better question. I had plans to never marry, live secluded in the country, and support myself with books I will write, starting with the one I am working to complete as soon as possible. I do not wish to be a burden on my family or a freak in society."

"This is your plan?" the duke said as he shifted to look more fully at her. "You will bury yourself somewhere away from the world, never having a family or children of your own? Alone and without purpose?"

She looked up, feeling the overpowering weight of despair and sobbed out, "How can I do anything else? Do you not see how impossible it would be?" The tears she so rarely allowed free began to trickle down her face.

The duke pulled a handkerchief from his pocket and dabbed at her cheeks. "Please do not cry, Lady Lillian. I understand this feeling of helplessness."

She grabbed the linen from his hand and wiped her own eyes. "How could you? You are a duke. You can have anything you want," she said sullenly.

He gave a bitter smile. "Not everything. I cannot have my missing family back, and I have yet to find my father's killer. I feel helpless every day the man walks free." He pulled away. "Come, let us sit down again."

Reluctantly she followed him back to the chairs. "I did not know your father was murdered."

He nodded. "We have kept the particulars of his death a secret, but we can speak more on that later." He sat in silence for a moment, his hands steepled together, elbows on the chair arms, as if he were thinking. Finally, he said, "I understand you wish to avoid marriage so you can live a life of obscurity and keep hidden the gift you find such a burden. However, both of our mothers wish to see us well settled for our futures. Currently, I have no desire to woo and win a lady with the aim toward marriage, as it takes my attention away from my pursuit of a murderer. Perhaps we can assist each other."

"How so?" she asked skeptically.

"Let us enter into a false betrothal. For all appearances, it will be quite real, but the end result will be that after a certain time, you will cry off. This will serve several purposes. It will keep our mothers appeased, at least until you end the engagement, and if I am correct, you will no longer need to appear at so many social events. I will be free to continue my investigation, while you will be free to finish this book you mentioned."

The idea was mad. Once Lillian's mother had snared a duke for her daughter, she would never let him out of her clutches. "It will never work. Our mothers will have the wedding planned, the banns called, and the two of us at the altar before we can blink."

He smiled. "Ah, but it is going to be a long engagement, since you are young yet. Seventeen, are you not?"

She nodded. "I will not turn eighteen until next February."

"Excellent. A late spring wedding will do nicely, yes? During that time, much can happen."

Lillian thought it over. If she were engaged to the duke, her mother would no longer be pushing her on other men. She could beg off from social events and stay home to work on her herbal. Given enough time, surely she could show her family that she was capable of independence and did not need a husband.

"There is something I would like in return, however," the duke said, interrupting her thoughts.

"Yes?"

"I would like your help to catch a killer."

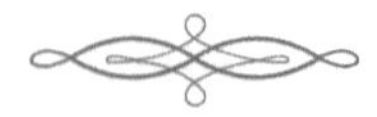

Gabriel watched multiple reactions flit across Lady Lillian's face—first surprise, then confusion, and finally anger as what he was asking finally settled upon her.

"You want me to use my ability?" she asked, nostrils flared. He saw she had curled her hands into fists.

He had spoken truly when he had told her of the accounts he had read of people like her who could do extraordinary things. As soon as she had begun to tell her tale, he had wanted to know more. He had already known he needed to try something different to catch his prey, and if she was telling the truth, this advantage could tip the scales in his investigation in his favor. For this to work, however, Lady Lillian had to see how this bargain would be of benefit to her.

"I am suggesting a mutually beneficial arrangement," he explained. "I will buy you the time you need and in return you will assist in my investigation."

Lady Lillian laughed bitterly. "You make it sound so easy, your grace. At present I have no control over the ability. It is likely that every person I come into contact with will cause me to have a horrible event. Will that do your search any good?"

"You said you could learn how to control it, did you not?"

After a lengthy pause, the lady sighed. "I have made one attempt at it, but I have yet to decide if the potential gain will outweigh the risk."

"Then let this be your training ground," he said, arms spreading wide. "What will it hurt? Your parents will believe you are on outings with me as your fiancé, as will anyone else we encounter. If you do have a fit, it will be of no account. No one would believe I have affianced myself to you if you are somehow defective." He raised an eyebrow, daring her to contradict him.

Lady Lillian bit her lower lip and worried it between her teeth, then clenched and unclenched her fists several times. Finally, she said, "Fine, but I want your assurance that if this becomes too much for me, you will not force me to continue. I need to know there will not be any pressure to use my ability if I cannot learn to control it."

Gabriel felt the rush of triumph, but he smiled genially. He was at such a point of desperation he would have told her anything to get an agreement. "You have my assurance." He stood and held out his elbow. "We have been here quite long enough to cause some concern. Shall we go down and announce our engagement?"

"Now?" Lady Lillian asked in alarm, her brown eyes widening.

"There is no time like the present, is there?" he asked.

"I suppose not." She stood and lightly touched her fingers to his arm. "In for a penny in for a pound," she muttered under her breath.

They retraced their steps down to the drawing room. Upon entering, Gabriel saw the company at their ease, chatting in groups, just as when they had left the room. Aunt Gertrude continued to play gentle music. He paused inside the doorway and cleared his throat loudly. All noise ceased immediately.

He gave a wide smile and looked pointedly at the settee where the mothers were perched. "I would like to impart the best of news. Lady Lillian has just made me the happiest of men and has agreed to be my wife." Several gasps popped through the air at his announcement.

Now let the show begin.

Gabriel could not wait to find out exactly what Lady Lillian could do, and he planned to put her to the test as soon as he could arrange it.

THIRTEEN

Dear Lord, what had she gotten herself into? Lillian trudged wearily up the stairs to her bedroom. Forget the fact that she had endured an entire social evening, and then push aside how her mother was now in a frenzy of high emotions, having snagged herself a duke. That left her with the fact she had not only agreed to enter into a false betrothal with Wyvern but had agreed to practice her ability in order to help him. What had she been thinking?

The truth was she had been tempted by the freedom the bargain had offered.

During the entire carriage ride home her mother had gushed and preened and had driven Lillian near to complete madness. Her father had smiled and her brother, as usual, had smirked.

"A duke! A duke! Oh Walter, a duke for our very own daughter!" Her mother had said this while grabbing at her father's sleeve. "I could not be more pleased or more proud."

Then her mother had begun a recitation of the entire evening from beginning to end as if none of the occupants of the carriage had been there. Anne had squeezed her hand, while all Lillian could do was sit back and rub her aching temples.

She was very much afraid that her plan to avoid marriage was a dream of the past. From this moment forward, she would be swept along on the tide of her mother's endeavors to create The Wedding of The Season—all in capital letters. If she were to be completely truthful with herself, there was going to be no getting out of it.

And she had no one but herself to blame.

Upon Lillian's entrance, Sarah put down the book she had been reading and got up. "How was the evening?"

"You do not want to know," Lillian said morosely. "I have sent down for some hot chocolate. Help me get out of these wretched clothes, please. I feel like I cannot breathe." She held her hands flat against her stomach and closed her eyes.

Sarah silently went to work unhooking buttons and unlacing laces. Lillian took in a refreshing gulp of air as soon as the corset came off. Her friend had just placed a nightgown over her head when there was a quiet rap on the door. Sarah quickly crossed the room to answer it.

Anne came inside dressed for the night—wrapped in her dressing gown, blonde hair braided. She carried a tray. "I came upon the maid bringing this to you and offered to bring it in myself." She placed it on the table by Lillian's elbow.

"Thank you." Lillian took the cup of chocolate from the

tray and took a sip, then crossed to sit at the dressing table.

"Lillian, what in the world happened tonight?" Anne asked. "You had every intention of avoiding any connection with the duke and the next thing I know he is announcing your engagement. Did he force you into it?"

Sarah gasped at the news.

Lillian scowled, then sighed. "Come sit down and I shall tell you." She patted the empty space on the bench next to her and handed the hairbrush to Sarah. "Please get started on my hair, Sarah, while I talk. It might help ease the growing ache in my head."

"Let me do it," Anne said, grabbing the brush instead.

Lillian closed her eyes as the hairpins were removed and her cousin began to stroke down the long, dark tresses. She sighed in bliss.

The soothing motion stopped. "Now talk, or I will not keep doing this," Anne said in a teasing tone.

"Blackmailer," she grumbled. "Fine, but what I am going to tell you must stay among just the three of us." The brushing began again and she closed her eyes once more. "I decided the best way to get the Duke of Wyvern to run away from me faster than the wind could carry him was to tell him about my ability."

Anne gasped. "Did you? Truly?"

"I did," she continued, "but the telling did not turn out as I had planned. The minute the words were out of my mouth, he whisked me up the stairs to his study and pressed me to tell him more. 'I have an open mind about scientific ideas,' he says. 'I have heard of such things before,' he says." Her tone was laced with disgust. "Instead of turning him away, I caused him to become more interested."

"Then what happened?" Sarah asked. She had taken the open spot on the bench.

"I told him I have no plans to marry and hope to live far away in the country," she said. "He told me he currently has no time to court a woman since he is looking for his father's murderer."

"Searching for who killed his father? I do not understand," Anne said. "If I remember correctly, he died in a hunting accident."

"I do not know the whole of it, but apparently that is not the truth," Lillian said, "and the duke is quite dedicated to the task of finding the culprit. To that end, he proposed a bargain: that we would pretend to be engaged so I could finish my herbal and continue my plan toward independence, while he would continue his quest. But there is more." She paused.

Anne tugged at her hair. "Do not dare stop now, you wretch. Tell the rest."

Lillian swallowed hard. "He said that in exchange for the freedom of the pretend betrothal, he wants me to use my ability to help him catch the killer."

The brush stopped and the air was silent for several long moments before Sarah said, "Well, this could be interesting."

She looked at her friend out of the corner of her eye. "What do you mean by that?"

"You were just recently discussing the possibility of learning to control your ability and needing people to practice on," Sarah said. "You must admit this could be the perfect opportunity to see what is possible."

"Oh, I see what you mean," Anne said.

Lillian threw up her hands. "What if I cannot learn to control it and I have an episode every time? It will have been time wasted and nothing but more embarrassment and distress for me."

Anne yanked on her hair again.

"Ow! That hurt," she said, rubbing the sore spot on the back of her head.

"I think it is time you stop thinking so negatively," Anne said. "If you expect the worst in every situation, the worst is what you will get. You need to change your expectations. This might turn out better than you could ever imagine, and you might end up with far more in the end."

"Like what?" Lillian asked.

"Like a normal life, you ninny. If you could control your gift, you could have everything we know you deserve—a husband, a home and a family of your own, a place in society," Anne said. "I know you are different from me and have no desire to spend all your time surrounded by crowds of people at balls and parties, but can you honestly say your heart's greatest desire is to go away to the country alone, and never to be seen again?"

Lillian swallowed hard into the silence that followed Anne's scolding. She could not help but agree with how her cousin had summed everything up. These were some of the things she might allow herself to want if she thought she could have them.

Maybe it was time to stop thinking life was nothing but a series of challenges she could never overcome.

"You both think I should embrace this … this …" She struggled to find the right word. "This chance that things might be different?"

"I do indeed," Anne said as she braided her hair for the night.

"Sarah?" she asked.

"I do too, Lillian. I have seen how long and hard you have struggled. I would give anything to see you in charge of your life instead of it being in charge of you."

"What an interesting way of putting it," Lillian said, "but you are right. I have never felt in control of my choices and I want that for myself."

She sat quietly as she thought over what her friends had said about the opportunity this bargain could bring to her life. She swiveled on the bench so she could look at both of them. "I am so blessed to have you as my friends. It always help me understand my feelings better when I can ask for your advice." She nodded once. "I will give this a chance and see how I can gain from it. If I think about it, there truly is nothing to lose."

Anne broke out in a wide grin. "Precisely. If it works, think of all that you will gain." She paused. "And I do believe it will work."

Lillian returned the grin. "However, if the duke does not like Prince Albert, all bets are off."

All three women laughed.

"Changing the topic of conversation, but what do you honestly think of the duke?" Anne asked.

"I am not going to marry him, if that is what you are thinking," Lillian said in a rush.

"Stop being such a peagoose," Anne said. "I am not asking you to design your wedding gown. I simply wish to know what you think of him as a person."

"Fine," Lillian said. "He is intelligent, commanding, and cares about his mother. That is really all I know about him at this point." She paused. "Oh, and I can touch his gloved hand without incident. Now that is all I know."

"You must admit he is handsome," Anne said.

Lillian shrugged as if she had not noticed, although she had. "I suppose."

"And he certainly seems to enjoy your company," Anne said.

"I doubt it. He has only spent time with me because our mothers were attempting to make a pair of us."

"Hmm," Anne said. "We shall see."

There was a knock on the door. Sarah jumped up to open it and allowed a frowning Lady Wentworth to enter.

"I saw the light under your door and heard voices as I passed by. It is late, girls. You should go to bed and get your beauty rest."

"Yes, Aunt," Anne said. She kissed Lillian on the cheek and pecked her aunt's as she breezed by. "Goodnight, Lillian.

We can talk more about it tomorrow."

After she left, Lillian said to Sarah, "You can turn in for the night. I need to speak to my mother alone."

Sarah curtsied and left.

Lillian stood and faced her mother. Now was a good time to start taking advantage of the opportunity before her, and she could begin by doing more for those who had taken such good care of her. "Mother, a great many things will change in the coming months as I prepare to become a duchess."

"I know, dearest. There will be wedding plans to make, a new wardrobe to order, a betrothal ball to—"

"Yes, Mother," she interrupted. "It will all get done by the wedding next spring, and preferably one thing at a time."

"I still do not see why we cannot have the wedding at the end of this summer," her mother said with a pout.

"Because Wyvern and I both wish to wait until I am a little bit older. I have barely just turned seventeen. Besides," she went on before her mother could start an argument, "think how impressive it will be to start next season with the one event everyone will wish to attend." She knew the prospect of preparing the largest, most lavish, and most well-attended wedding of the season would keep her mother happy for months.

"It will be talked about for years to come," her mother said, mollified.

"Yes," she said, crossing her arms. "As I was trying to say earlier, I also need to prepare for the future, and with that in mind, I wish to promote Sarah to the role of my companion." She hurried on before her mother could cut in. "I know you have rejected the idea in the past, but as a duchess, I will need a secretary and no one is better suited than Sarah. She will need time to adjust to a role in which she is more often by my side outside of this bedroom."

"Sarah is merely the daughter of a tenant farmer," her mother said with a superior air. "That does not make her suitable as a companion or a personal secretary."

"She was educated alongside me from the moment I was sent to Silvano's and has spent years mingling with other ladies of our class at the school. Above all, she is someone I can trust. Trust cannot be taught. It has to be earned. Sarah has far exceeded any expectations on that score."

She saw her mother would dearly love to argue, her mouth opening and closing again without a word. But now that Lillian could insert her betrothal into her reasoning, her mother could not so very well object.

"Fine," her mother finally said. "We will need plenty of help getting ready for the wedding. I will be able to put her to good use."

Lillian wanted to sigh. Sarah was her companion, not her mother's, but she was not about to start a new quarrel after she had just gotten something she wanted.

After her mother left, Lillian slid into bed, blew out the remaining candle, and lay back on her pillow. Prince Albert scampered up the side of the bed and settled against her. The evening's events swirled around her head like a violent storm. She doubted she would be able to sleep with dual thoughts fighting each other in her head. On the one hand she had just committed to the very thing she had been adamantly against from the beginning and it could turn out very badly, but on the other hand she might end up with far more than she could ever have dreamed. Time would tell which side would win.

Before the last dinner guests departed, Gabriel took Davis and Hartley aside and asked them to stay behind for an impromptu meeting. He had a new strategy and there was no time like the present to start making the most of it. He wanted every trusted man available to assist.

After bowing to the Hargraves family and seeing them out the door, he had to do some maneuvering to get Howard to go away. If his cousin had had his way, he would have lingered to rub elbows with Gabriel and his friends.

"You will excuse us will you not, Howard?" he said as he approached his cousin in the drawing room. The man was slumped in a chair near the fireplace, nursing a brandy. "My friends and I need to depart for a meeting, club business."

"Club business?" Howard perked up and sat straighter in his chair. "If that's the case, then should I not be in the meeting? The club is run by the Ramsay family, and I am your heir after all."

Not in this lifetime, Gabriel thought. If ever there was a man he did not trust with responsibility, it was his cousin, and it looked like that fact had not changed one bit since they were children. Howard was the oldest of the cousins, older than himself by a year, but none of them had ever looked up to him. He was always the one who bullied those weaker than himself or of lower social status. He was the sort who let others to take the blame for his poor actions.

His father would turn over in his grave if his son allowed Howard to be a part of anything that had to do with the Network.

Gabriel tamped down his desire to sneer in Howard's face and took in a slow, calming breath. He pasted on a congenial smile. "Being a Ramsay is not what matters the most at the club. It is about who has earned trust and worked their way up the hierarchy. You are new to the club, Howard. You have yet to take steps that would allow you into the inner circle." *And you never will.*

Gabriel saw Howard's left hand tighten into a fist before he let it go. He gave a pouty smile and stood. Placing his drink on the side table, he straightened his coat. "Fine. I will just be off to the club to have a drink with some of the men then, shall I?"

That was not what Gabriel wanted either, but at least it would get the man out of his hair for a while. That did not mean the problem of his cousin would go away. He still had Howard's debts to address. He stopped his cousin from leaving. "Hold there, Howard. Perhaps you would care to join me at my fencing salon tomorrow for a short bout? Shall we say nine of the clock? I prefer to exercise early in the day."

Howard stood taller with a smug expression. "I believe I can fit that into my schedule."

"Tomorrow then." He turned to his friends. "Go up to the study and pour yourselves a drink. I will be up in a minute." He knew his mother would want to speak to him first.

"We will be off to bed if you will give me your arm and help me to stand, Nephew," Aunt Gemma said.

He took her hand, steadied her below the elbow, and guided her forward. He did the same for her twin.

"Your girl is a lovely lady," Aunt Gertrude said with a pat to his cheek. "Fine choice, my boy. Fine choice."

"I agree," Aunt Gemma said as they drifted slowly out of the room. "She will make a fine addition to the family."

Gabriel turned to his mother who immediately raised one dark eyebrow and pierced him with knowing eyes. "What was that all about?"

"What was what all about?" he asked, all innocence.

"You know my exact meaning, Son. You spirited Lady Lillian away and then returned and announced your engagement with no warning to any of us."

He shrugged casually. "You know me, Mother. When I know what I want, I go after it. There was no point in delaying."

"You have decided you want Lady Lillian?" The skeptical eyebrow rose again.

"Indeed," he said, holding her brown-eyed gaze.

She cupped Gabriel's left cheek in her hand. "I am not sure what you are up to, young man, but as long as it ends in a wedding, I will be pleased."

"That is my intention." He gave her a boyish grin and kissed her on the cheek. "I must be off to join my friends. I will speak to you in the morning about what plans you may wish to make regarding the betrothal."

"Fine, Gabriel, but I am warning you now, I do not trust you an inch." Under her breath, but loudly enough that Gabriel could hear it, she muttered, "Club business indeed."

Right before he left the room, she called out, "Gabriel."

He turned his head to look over his shoulder. "Yes, Mother?"

"You know I do truly trust you, do you not? You are a fine duke and a better man."

Gabriel felt his chest tighten and his throat clog with emotion. He nodded. "Thank you, Mother."

He had not lied to her. Gabriel had every intention of marrying Lillian when this was all over, but no one needed to know that yet, least of all the lady herself. Not only did he like Lillian, she and her friends would be incredible assets for the Network. No other woman could be a better choice.

When he had his mind set on a course, he never wavered from it, but he knew it was going to take some fancy maneuvering to get Lady Lillian to see things his way.

His friends were waiting in the chairs placed before his study desk, drinks in hand. As usual, Davis was doing all the talking. On the way up, he had asked a footman to find Jersey. He closed the door and went to the decanters on the sideboard. He splashed some brandy in a glass and went to sit down behind the desk. Davis broke off his conversation about racing horses.

"I will get right to the point, gentlemen. First, I need your assurance that what I am about to tell you will not leave this room. It not only involves Network business, but the privacy and safety of a lady."

"Of course," Davis said.

Hartley nodded.

He swirled his brandy, then took a sip. There was a knock on the door. He called out, "Enter," and Jersey came inside.

"You summoned me, Oh Masterful One?" he asked.

"Do you have a report on Lady Lillian and the Benevolence Society I wanted you to look into?" Gabriel asked.

"Indeed I do, sir. I have it right here in my pocket." Jersey patted himself in several places as if looking for the object in question.

Gabriel wanted to groan, but he knew it would just urge his valet to continue the theatrics.

Finally, Jersey pulled a paper out of his breast pocket, then pulled his spectacles out of the same pocket. He sat silently as if waiting for permission to begin.

"Well, go on." Gabriel waved a hand at the man.

"I was just waiting to see if you were truly interested."

Gabriel gritted his teeth. "Read the damned report if you please."

"Lady Lillian Ruth Hargraves, age seventeen, was born to the Earl—"

"You can skip the begats," Gabriel said.

"Do you want to hear the report or not?" Jersey asked mulishly. He took great pride in his work.

Gabriel looked up at the ceiling and gathered all of his patience. "Yes, I would like to hear the report. Please continue."

From his seat, Davis smirked.

"Well, now I have to start all over." Jersey straightened both arms, holding the paper out as if to see it better, and tilted his head. Gabriel knew he was being punished for his interruption. He remained quiet so the whole process would not be repeated all over again.

Finally, Jersey cleared his throat. "Lady Lillian Ruth Hargraves, age seventeen, was born to the Earl and Countess of Wentworth at their country seat in Norfolk. She has one brother, Lord Simon, but no other siblings. Her cousin Anne Hargraves, a year older and daughter of her father's younger brother, lost both her parents at a very young age and came to live with the family when Lady Lillian was six. I understand they get on well.

"There are rumors of some odd goings on with Lady Lillian—I am sure you already know the rumors going about town—but her family's staff in town is very loyal and wouldn't say anything against her."

Gabriel nodded. "I do."

"Some think she is mad, others think she is a witch. Whatever her problem is, when Lady Lillian got a little older and was out of the schoolroom more often, neighbors started to see signs of it, so at the age of nine, she was sent to some sort of special school. Sarah Duggins, now her maid, was sent along. She recently returned from this school a few weeks ago." He lowered the paper and looked at Gabriel. "There hasn't been enough time to send a man to where the school is located to ask around for information, but I recently learned it burned to the ground a few weeks back anyway."

Gabriel raised his eyebrows in surprise. This was news to him.

"Now this is where it gets interesting. I looked into the Benevolence Society as you requested. The building where it is housed has been rented by one Mr. Giuseppe Silvano— the same man who was said to run the school Lady Lillian attended."

Gabriel sat up and leaned forward. This was indeed interesting. "Have they moved this mysterious school to London, then?"

"Could be, Commander. There are boarders who live at the place as well as Silvano himself and a few servants."

"I would really like to know more about this school or

society or whatever it is now. Lady Lillian said it was a place for people like her," he said.

"I could try to get a man inside if you want," Jersey said.

Gabriel got up and splashed more brandy into his glass before answering. He held up the decanter in question to his friends. They both shook their heads. He sat back down. "Yes, let us see what we can learn about the place. The information might be of use to us."

"Consider it done," Jersey said. "Is there anything else?"

"No. Thank you for the report, Jersey."

With a rare show of deference, his valet bowed before taking a seat at his own desk.

"I can see something interesting is afoot," Davis said. "I hope you plan to put us out of our misery and tell us what it is."

"Your misery," Hartley said.

"What?" Davis asked, turning to their friend.

"You said 'our misery,' but it is your misery. I am not feeling the least bit miserable," Hartley said in his matter-of-fact way.

Davis grinned. "Fine, put me out of *my* misery then. Hartley here appears to care less if you tell us anything."

Gabriel leaned forward, his elbows on the desk. "I wished to tell you the real reason why I announced my engagement to Lady Lillian tonight."

"What ho! Machinations upon machinations. That's our Gabriel!" Davis said.

"In an attempt to stave off a possible betrothal arranged by our mothers," Gabriel continued, "Lady Lillian took a risk and told me tonight the truth behind the rumors about her."

Hartley sat up straighter. He may not have been miserable, but he was interested.

"We have all heard of people who have the second sight and of other such supernatural phenomena," Gabriel said.

Both his friends nodded.

"It appears Lady Lillian has such a gift, but instead of seeing the future, she sees the past, and it happens when she touches people."

"Which is why she has the fits which have earned her the name Leprous Lillian," Hartley said.

Jersey whistled. "That is a big something to wrap my head around. She said there's a whole school full of people just like her with these magical gifts?"

"Not magic, Jersey," Gabriel said. "They simply have God-given abilities others do not."

"What, I got left off the special list when God was giving them out?" he said in feigned shock and surprise.

"Imagine what can be done with such a gift," Davis said.

"Precisely," Gabriel agreed, "and I have convinced Lady Lillian to enter into a false betrothal while she assists my investigation. I am going to need your help to pull this all together successfully."

Davis put his glass on the desk. "You know we will do anything you need, Gabe."

"Thank you," Gabriel said, feeling warmed by the show of support. "I plan to have Lady Lillian begin meeting suspects as soon as possible. I will speak to you again when I know more."

If he could convince the lady to join him, he already had plans to attend a garden party the very next day. Gabriel leaned his head back and felt a rush of relief. Yesterday, success felt unattainable, but now the possibilities were endless.

FOURTEEN

Signor Silvano's Sayings Number 14
To be in control, you need to make life happen.
Do not wait for life to happen to you.

Lillian found a note beside her plate when she sat down at the breakfast table in the morning. She frowned, wondering who could have sent it, but from the end of the table, her mother piped up with a cat-that-got-the-cream smile: "It is from the duke. It has his seal."

She was afraid of what such a letter might contain. She chose to ignore it in favor of buttering a piece of toast and taking her first sip of nice hot tea, but her mother was not going to allow it.

"Well, go on." She gestured at the folded paper. "Open it and see what he says."

Beside her, Anne gave her a sympathetic smile.

Lillian sighed inwardly. She would have preferred to sigh out loud, but her mother would scold. When she had agreed to this plan of the duke's, she had not thought through all the details. She had not thought of all the ways it might cause her more stress rather than less—for example, her mother's constant pecking.

When her mother made a tsking noise, she knew she had procrastinated long enough. She peeled back the red wax seal, imprinted with a dragon whose wings encircled a W, and unfolded the note.

Never the patient one, her mother immediately prompted, "Well, what does he say?"

Lillian refolded the paper and looked up. "He wishes to escort me to the Bridges' garden party this afternoon." She shrugged as if it were of no importance, but her head was spinning with a million thoughts. The note implied this would be the first attempt on the duke's part to use her to find his father's killer. She had not expected this to happen so quickly. She had rather hoped she would have time to prepare herself—perhaps to begin learning how to control her ability before trying to use it in a public setting.

Her mother clapped her hands together several times in excitement and beamed. "What an attentive gentleman, and ready to show you off to the world. I knew it would be like this."

"Knew what would be like what?" her father asked as he entered the room and took his usual seat at the opposite end from her mother.

It was a well-known fact that if anyone had something to say to her father, they had better say it before the morning paper was unfolded and in front of his face.

Her mother hurried to tell him: "I knew that the Duke of

Wyvern would be quite taken with our daughter and wish to squire her about town on his arm." With a conspiratorial smile, she added, "He has already invited her to a garden party this afternoon."

"Of course he has," her father said with a gentle smile, just before the now unfolded paper went up, cutting off all future communication. It appeared that was all he had to say on the matter.

"I do wish we had time to go to the modiste before your outing," her mother said. "You will need some new gowns."

"Whyever for?" she asked. "I just had a whole new wardrobe made only a few weeks ago."

"Yes, but you were not the fiancée of a duke at that time," her mother said. "You will need more lavish ball gowns and maybe something with more color, and I am sure you do not have enough accessories."

This really had to stop. If Lady Wentworth had her way, her daughter would be trussed up like a Christmas goose, so overloaded with lace and flounces and accessories she would not even be able to move.

"Thank you, Mother," she said, "but my gowns are quite adequate to the task of being out in society. Besides, I do not believe his grace will even notice what I am wearing."

"Ah, but my dear Theodora will," her mother said. "It will not do to look shabby."

Lillian nearly snorted into her tea. She had no idea what her mother meant by shabby when every single piece of her cloth-

ing was of the finest quality, from the fabric to the workman-
ship. "Mother, the duchess seemed to think I was good enough
for her son before today. I do not see why anything needs to
change to impress her at this point. You both already have
what you want."

"What ever could you mean?" her mother asked, all innocence.

"What ever indeed," Lillian muttered. She wiped her mouth
and stood. Her appetite had fled the minute she had opened
the note. "If you all will excuse me, I have several things I need
to accomplish including replying to Wyvern's invitation."

Anne stood as well. "I will come with you." Her cousin
linked arms with her in the hallway and gave a wide grin. "You
know your mother is going to drive you crazy constantly
now, do you not? I must admit you may have traded one trial
for another."

"I was thinking the very same thing, Anne, but I am determined to make the best of it now that I have chosen this
course of action." Her attention was distracted by a tumble
of fur speeding toward them. "Ah, there you are Prince Albert. I noticed you had gotten away this morning." She let
go of Anne to reach down and scoop the ferret up, cradling
him in her arms. He closed his round little eyes and sighed
into a relaxed pose on his back.

"I wish I could be so comfortable," Lillian muttered.

"Will you attend the garden party?" Anne asked as they
started up the main staircase.

"I would rather wait a little before beginning this new adventure, but I suppose I must. A bargain is a bargain," she said. "You will come with me I hope."

"Of course I will, if you wish it," Anne said.

"He has asked me to begin using my ability today, and having you by my side will make it easier. I am terribly afraid of what might happen, as I do not feel ready to try this new method in earnest."

"You must simply take care," Anne said. "If it becomes too much, you must tell the duke so. There is no point in making yourself ill."

"Or further embarrassing myself," Lillian said.

"Or that," Anne agreed. "Besides sending a reply to the duke, what else do you need to do this morning?"

"Something you can help with, actually. I convinced Mother last night to allow me to promote Sarah to my companion."

Anne gasped. "Why, that is wonderful!"

Lillian smiled broadly. "It is indeed, and exactly what I have wanted for some time. This betrothal to a duke situation does have its advantages."

"What do you need my help with?" Anne asked.

"I need to go through Sarah's wardrobe and make certain she has enough gowns suitable to wear in company. You are far better with fashion and knowing what is suitable than I."

"Say no more," Anne said. She clapped her hands in glee. "Oh, this shall be such fun! I imagine you can persuade your mother to buy a few new gowns for Sarah now that you will be the bride of a duke."

Anne and Lillian looked at each other with conspiratorial smiles.

"Yes," Lillian said. "Yes, I imagine I can."

The air was quite cold for a late May morning, but Gabriel took little notice. His heart beat rapidly at the thought of the new strategy he would put into play this afternoon. Add to that, he was about to wipe the floor clean with his cousin. Perhaps while he was at it he could get the man to take some responsibility for himself.

When his carriage arrived at the fencing salon, Gabriel hopped down, allowing Jersey to follow with all that would be needed for his little adventure. Once inside, the salon's attendant greeted them. "Good morning and welcome, your grace." He bowed low. "A Mr. Ramsay is waiting for you in the blue room. He said you have an appointment?" The last was said with a raised eyebrow and a skeptical look.

"We do indeed have an appointment. Thank you," Gabriel said. "If you will send him up to the dressing room, I would be much obliged."

"Of course, your grace." The man bowed again and went to his duties.

He bounded up the stairs, leaving Jersey puffing hard behind. "Your grace, what's the hurry, eh?"

At the top of the stairs, Gabriel looked down and smiled. "No hurry, Jersey. I am merely pleased."

"It's that lady, isn't it?"

"Lady?" Gabriel asked, perplexed.

"Yeah. The lady who you have just recently got yourself engaged to for your own purposes."

Gabriel made a gesture for silence by slicing a finger across his neck. "Hush. No one need know our business. No, it is not about the lady. Now come along. We have other things to get to today." Gabriel continued down the hallway.

Not long after, Howard sauntered into the dressing room. "Cousin! I see you are ahead of me in dressing."

"Quite sorry about that, Howard. There is someone I wish to speak to before we begin." He pointed to Jersey. "I believe you have yet to meet my new valet, Jersey. He will help you suit up and make certain you have any gear you may require. I shall meet you in the red salon in—shall we say a quarter of an hour?"

Howard did not answer at first, as he was still staring up at Jersey. Gabriel's valet really was an intimidating sight at six feet four inches of solid muscle. His panting and wheezing on the stairway had been one of Jersey's usual absurd shows. He could have been up and down those stairs before Gabriel could run up them once.

"What? Oh, yes." Howard shook his head as if to clear it. "That will be fine."

Gabriel did not truly have anyone he wished to speak to. The fact of the matter was he never could stand to be in a room with Howard for any length of time. He headed for the red salon with his épée in hand. The room was aptly named, as the walls were painted crimson and the benches and chairs along the perimeter were covered in varying shades of red fabric. It was a large open room with a polished wooden floor, where men could practice or put on displays of their abilities for a small audience.

Gabriel began a few warmup stretches and lunges. Mr. Salazar, the salon owner, a Spanish man with a thin mustache, interrupted. "Your grace." He bowed low. "It is a pleasure to have you return to my establishment after so much time."

Gabriel walked over, holding out his hand. "There was a time, Salazar, when you merely shook my hand." The thin man gripped it with a smile.

"Indeed, your grace. Much has changed in four years. I understand you have brought a guest in today?"

Gabriel lowered his voice. "Yes, my cousin, and this is not a situation that will be repeated. I do not wish him to feel he can take advantage of your hospitality based on my name alone. I hate to speak ill of my own kin, but he does rather lower the tone of an establishment."

"Ah, *bueno*. I do understand completely, and I thank you for the warning between friends."

Gabriel smiled and backed up a step. "Indeed. I owe you much for your years of training, my friend."

Howard swaggered into the room, as if he were the master and not the student.

"Salazar, would you like to observe our practice and see if I am in need of any tutoring?" Gabriel winked at the owner.

"I would be honored, your grace. Shall I play judge?"

"Yes, thank you, Salazar." Gabriel intentionally did not introduce the two men. He did not wish Howard to think he was to be on friendly terms with the owner of the salon. "Howard, are you ready?"

Howard inexpertly swished his épée in the air several times. "As ready as ever."

Seeing the incompetent form his cousin was already displaying, Gabriel wanted to snort. Howard would be easy prey today.

The two men saluted each other and walked toward the center of the room.

Salazar called out "*En Garde*" and each man pushed down his mask to cover the face. Next he asked "*Prêts?*" and when both men saluted him, he called out a final "*Allez!*"

Gabriel had known before coming today that Howard would not be up to his caliber and had decided to go easy on him. The man was spoiled and soft. He realized from the very first lunge he had made the right decision. Howard was slow to react and barely brought his blade up in time to parry the coming blow. From the corner of his eye, Gabriel could see

Salazar's amusement over the mismatch.

This clumsy play went on for nearly a quarter of an hour when Gabriel decided he had better get on with why he had come today before he completely wore the man out. "I have heard you have been quite the man about town in my absence."

Out of breath, Howard panted out, "I am a duke's heir. It is expected that I be seen in society."

"True. Have you thought of getting married and settling down?"

Howard lunged forward, and Gabriel had to pull back quickly to keep from jabbing him in the chest.

"You have snagged the only interesting woman I have met." Howard brought his attention back to the play and thrust his épée forward again. "She is only an earl's daughter. As a duke you could reach as high as you wish."

Gabriel parried. "Yes, but I consider her character to be more important than her social standing."

Howard backed away to rest his arm. Gabriel allowed it. How his cousin was still standing was a mystery to him.

Howard stepped forward and Gabriel circled his opponent. "I have heard a rumor that you have acquired quite a bit of debt in the past four years," Gabriel challenged. "How did that come about?"

"A wager here, a tailor's bill there," Howard said with a careless air as he followed Gabriel's movements. "It all begins to add up. These people do not expect a gentleman to pay them in a timely manner. It will all come to rights." He lunged forward and Gabriel easily met the blows that followed with his épée.

Gabriel's jaw clenched and he swung repeatedly. Howard could barely keep up and eventually stepped back for another breather. Gabriel hated such a cavalier attitude as this, which many men of the *ton* had toward paying their bills. Tradesmen had to eat too. "A few bills is one thing, Howard, but more than ten thousand pounds is not. How do you expect to ever pay back such a sum?"

"As I said," Howard said breathlessly, "it will come to rights before you know it." When he leaned forward to put his hands on his knees and catch his breath, Salazar called out *"Arrêt!"*

"I think we have had enough practice for today, Salazar. Thank you for your time," Gabriel said to his friend.

The man nodded at him with a wink and left the room.

Gabriel picked up a towel off the bench at the side of the room and wiped the sweat off his neck. "You do understand the dukedom will not assume these debts on your behalf, do you not?" he asked. "For one, you have an adequate allowance. For another, necessities are one thing, but gambling debts and extravagances are something else altogether."

Howard sneered at this. "You think the pitiful allowance I receive is enough to keep me in the lifestyle I deserve as the grandson of a duke? The estate—no, the estates—are worth far more than enough to do better by me. Grandfather would have given me far more."

The truth was Grandfather would have given Howard less. He had never been able to abide those who gambled and threw money away on a lavish lifestyle, but Gabriel had no wish to argue with his cousin over that point. Instead, he said, "Howard, you have no occupation, you oversee no estates, you simply gad about town all day, every day. I see no reason to increase an allowance you neither need nor deserve."

"You never did believe I deserved to be the heir did you?" Howard's face screwed up in anger. "Yet if my father had been born two years earlier, I would be the duke right now. It is only a matter of chance that you are the duke and not me."

"There is nothing to be done about the succession, Howard," Gabriel said calmly, although his blood was quickly heating up. "I did not make the rules of inheritance, but because of them, I am the one who works hard to care for all the estates and holdings of the dukedom that provide your allowance."

"Is that what this is all about?" he asked. "You are sick of providing my allowance? Not only do I not receive the respect I deserve in society as a duke's heir because of the way you ignore me, you now no longer wish to provide for me?"

Gabriel reached up to rub the back of his neck. His head was starting to ache. "That is not what I meant at all, Howard. My point is you do nothing to earn the allowance you do receive; therefore, I would like you to give more consideration on how you spend your money and the consequences of your actions."

"Consequences?" Howard asked, eyebrows raised.

"Yes. When people do not pay their debts, there are consequences. Debtors' prison being one of them. Not to mention you have borrowed from money lenders, and they do not tend to take kindly to those who do not pay them what they are owed in a timely manner."

Howard gave him an incredulous look. "You would allow me, your heir, to be thrown into prison for a few measly debts?"

"Your debts are not measly, Howard. You have more debt than most people earn in a lifetime." He squared off, fully facing his cousin and looking straight into his shifty eyes. "Do you truly think I will allow you to live such a dissipated lifestyle paid for by the dukedom? You need to understand that these debts are yours and yours alone. Find a way to cover them using the monies you already receive or sell off some of your newly acquired and expensive toys. I care not how you do it, but any bill collectors who come to me with their hands out will be sent to your lodgings, Howard. Are we clear?" His cousin opened his mouth as if to argue once more, but Gabriel was finished with this conversation. "Are we clear?"

Howard clamped his mouth shut into a thin line. He nodded once jerkily.

"Good." He gave his cousin a jovial pat on the shoulder. "Any time you would care for a bit of swordplay, let me know."

He did not wait for a reply, but left the room without a backward glance. It was time for his cousin to grow up. Michael and he had had to do so four years ago and Howard did not deserve any more time. Not on his watch.

Later in the carriage, he turned to his valet. "Jersey, I want you to have my man of business to start buying up Howard's debts anonymously. I think it is time we start making my cousin feel a little nervous. Let us make him sweat. He who holds the debts holds the power over him."

Jersey gave him a wolfish grin and saluted. "Aye, Your Lordship. Consider it done."

"Now, let us get back to the townhouse. I need to clean up before my outing."

"Like I said, it's the lady," Jersey said with a grin.

Gabriel rubbed his temples to ease away the stress of going toe to toe with his cousin. He was learning not to argue with his valet. It was a battle he could never win.

Lillian usually knew what to expect at social events—they were all essentially the same. The women gossiped and the men chatted about horses, crops, and politics. All this while everyone compared their level of superiority to those around them. Why Anne enjoyed such outings she would never understand. She would have preferred to stay home with a good book.

Today was different, though. Today she would be focused on using her ability rather than avoiding it.

In front of Lord and Lady Bridges' lavish Richmond home, she exited the carriage behind her cousin and smoothed out the skirts of her dove-gray walking dress. She had chosen to wear more subdued colors today, including a blue-gray parasol and a plain straw bonnet adorned with nothing more than blue ribbon. She hoped the simple outfit would help her blend into the background.

"Come along, dear cousin," Anne said softly. "The only way to know how this day will go is to march right on into it."

"I am so pleased you were willing to accompany me today." After a pause she added, "And doubly pleased Mother had another obligation."

Anne smiled. "I could just imagine how it might have turned out if she were by your side this day." She pulled gently on her arm. "There is the duke. Let us go and greet him."

Lillian took a deep breath and let it out slowly. *I can do this, I can do this, I can do this*. The old familiar song played in her head.

Wyvern had been waiting for them in the forecourt. Once they reached the duke, he bowed and greeted them. "Hello ladies. How lovely to see you on this fine day. I am grateful you were able to come on such short notice."

They curtsied in return. Looking around briefly first to ensure they would not be overheard, Lillian said, "Perhaps you would like to tell us what our goal is here today, your grace?"

The duke tilted his head pointedly toward Anne.

"As to that," Lillian said, "Anne and my companion Sarah are the two people in the world I trust with all my secrets. You may speak freely in front of either one of them and expect complete discretion."

He nodded. "Very good. I imagine it is helpful for you to have some allies."

"Indeed."

"Perhaps now that we are betrothed, in the eyes of society at least, it would make more sense to use our given names? I am Gabriel or Wyvern if you must."

"If you wish," Lillian agreed. "I suppose it would be much better than constantly your-gracing you."

"And I am Anne," her cousin said.

He smiled. "Excellent. I specifically wanted you to attend this party today because of who is in attendance," he explained, "but let us not stand here or we may be interrupted. Let us stroll toward the pond beyond the back gardens."

Gabriel held out an elbow for each of them. Lillian lightly placed her hand on his sleeve and they began walking.

"I have told you almost nothing of my investigation, but I will do so now," Gabriel said. "Four years ago, at a house party that took place at my family estate in Kent, my father was shot and killed while in his study. We kept this fact a secret to prevent scandal. It is assumed the murderer was someone he knew well, since he was a cautious man and not likely to allow someone unknown to him get so close as to shoot him from point-blank range." He stopped walking and looked at Anne and then at her. "I apologize, are these details too distressing for you?"

Lillian snorted. "I have seen horrors I do not believe even you have encountered." She looked at her cousin. "How about you, Anne?"

Anne waved the idea away. "I am not naïve. I know that all sorts of wickedness occurs in our world. Thank you for your concern."

"Let us walk on, then." Gabriel said. "The killer did not stop with my father. He later made several attempts on my life as well as my brother's."

"Yet you could not find him," Anne stated.

Gabriel shook his head. "There were dozens of people at that house party. Every one of them, excluding a few family members and some of my friends, could have been the culprit, and most of them my father had known for years or even decades. Over the past four years I have endeavored to have each person investigated in hopes of finding the killer, but to no avail. Now that I have returned, I have visited several of them."

"With what purpose?" Lillian asked.

"I know it seems futile, but I have exhausted every avenue of inquiry and I am at a dead end," he said, his shoulders drooping a little. "I do not have your abilities. It is not like I can look them in the eyes and see their guilt, but with every encounter, I desperately hope for something, anything—maybe words they say or an action—that will give them away."

"Now you wish for me to meet these dozens of guests," Lillian stated.

"I hope it will not come to that. My desire is for a quick resolution, for both our sakes. To that end, I have prioritized my list in order of those I think most likely to have done the deed. Two of those men are here today with their families."

They had reached the edge of the pond. He stopped and turned slightly toward Lillian. "Are you up to the task? You did say you might not be able to control your gift and it will cause you distress."

Lillian swallowed past the lump in her throat. No, she did not think she could handle this. "I know not what will happen, but I am willing to try."

He nodded. "That is all I ask. Let me scan the area and find our first quarry." He shaded his eyes with a hand and looked about the grounds.

The lush green lawn surrounding the pond was quite expansive. The guests who were not loitering on the terrace next to the house were strolling about the garden and the lawn in small groups. There were a great many in attendance today.

"There he is," Gabriel said, pointing his head in the direction of a gentleman walking with two ladies. "Lord Alston." He began leading them toward the man in question. "Both he and his wife are on the list."

"Why is he at the top of your list, if I may ask?" Anne asked.

"His lordship owed my father a great deal of money," he said.

"What is it they say?" Anne asked. "Most crimes can be attributed to motivations of power, passion, and money."

Lillian looked at her cousin in surprise. Where had she learned such a thing?

Anne saw her look and blushed. "I read a great deal, Cousin."

"Not the sorts of things I read apparently," Lillian said, amused.

Lord Alston was a gentleman with salt and pepper hair, who might be in his fifth decade. Next to him stood a lady of the same age, who was likely his wife, and a younger, pretty young lady with blonde ringlets. His lordship smiled at the duke as they approached.

"Lord Alston, well met," Gabriel said with an outstretched hand. Lord Alston shook it. "Although cool, it is such a lovely day for a garden party, would you not agree?"

"Indeed, indeed," Lord Alston said genially.

"May I make known to you my betrothed, Lady Lillian Hargraves, and her cousin, Miss Hargraves? Lillian, Anne, Lord and Lady Alston and their daughter, Lady Mariah."

Lillian knew what she was supposed to do, but it was difficult to make herself do it. After several heartbeats, she put out a hand to greet Lord Alston, while repeating in her head: *Take his hand and pull away. Take his hand and pull away.* She could not get caught up in the visions or once again she would lose control. Lord Alston hesitated—perhaps he had heard the rumors about her—but he had no choice other than to take what was offered. She curtsied as his fingers closed about hers. The world about them changed.

FIFTEEN

Signor Silvano's Sayings Number 15
When you are required to do something
you would rather not, put on a smile
and pretend you are enjoying it.
Perhaps you will soon believe the lie.

"That will fetch us a pretty price, my dear."

Lillian saw a vision of Lord Alston in a lavish bedroom talking over a jeweled snuffbox with Lady Alston.

"It was just lying there in the drawing room," the lady said. "It is not really stealing if they cannot keep track of their own possessions, now is it?" She giggled.

Lillian abruptly pulled her hand back. She wanted to sag in relief that she had been able to prevent an episode by keeping herself present and aware, just as Christopher had suggested, but she was too overwhelmed by this new direction her ability had just taken.

She did not have time to think about it, as Lord Alston was giving her an odd look. She must have hesitated too long with her hand in the air. She placed a shaking hand over her queasy stomach and pasted on a large social smile. "It is lovely to meet you, my lord, my lady, Lady Mariah." She gave another small curtsy.

"Your betrothed, did you say?" Lady Alston asked. "Well, this is news. I have not seen the announcement in any of the papers."

"The best sort of news," Gabriel agreed jovially. Apparently he could put on quite a facade when the occasion warranted. "The announcement will appear in tomorrow morning's papers, as we only informed the family last night."

"Jolly good!" Lord Alston said with a hearty laugh. "Every man is better for having a good lady by his side." He patted his wife's hand which was laying on his arm.

Lady Alston beamed up at her husband. "I could not agree more."

"If you will excuse us," Gabriel said, "I would like to introduce Lady Lillian and her cousin around.

"Of course, of course," Lord Alston said. "Off you young people go." He gave a small flick of his hand.

When they were far enough away not to be overheard, Anne said quietly, "He certainly does not seem like the sort to commit murder."

"He is not," Lillian said absently, "but he is a thief."

Gabriel abruptly stopped walking. "Explain yourself please."

Lillian stood there for several minutes replaying in her mind what had just happened with her ability. Was this change a result of the new practice? In the past, random visions had come unbidden. This time, she had set an intention of going back to the time of the murder, and it worked. Best of all, she had chosen when to end the vision. She had been in complete control of the entire session. Warmth filled her chest at the thought.

She felt a tug at her sleeve. "Lillian, what is the matter?" Anne asked. "You have been silent too long."

She brought herself back to the here and now. "I do apologize. Something strange occurred while I was greeting his lordship." She frowned in concentration. "Not only was I able to control the period in time I wished to see, but I also felt like I was drawing information from Lady Alston in addition to what I saw from Lord Alston. It is not something I can easily explain except to say I now know things about her I did not previously."

"You have never experienced this before?" Gabriel asked.

She shook her head. "No, this is a completely new facet of my ability, but now is not the time to explore it." She turned to look at Gabriel, letting her arm fall to her side. "I am not surprised Lord Alston owed your father money. He has no head for managing his finances, so he and Lady Alston support their lifestyle by stealing small valuables while they are at house parties and the like."

Gabriel's lips thinned and he slowly shook his head. "Unbelievable. You got all that merely from touching his hand?"

There was nothing 'mere' about it in her opinion, but she nodded.

Gabriel's eyes held a faraway look now as he scanned the distance. "I can see there are two sides to your ability. On the one hand, you have been able to eliminate someone from the list of suspects and I am overjoyed, but on the other hand, hard truths have come to light." He grimaced. "I have known Lord and Lady Alston since I was a boy."

"I believe there are many things better left unknown," she said in a quiet voice.

He returned his gaze to her with a brief smile. "I am willing to risk it. I must say, your gift is remarkable, and I am confident it will enable me to bring this search to a close at last."

Anne interrupted with a gasp. "Wait. You had a vision, but did not black out or have a fit! That is wonderful. Does this mean the new method is working?"

"All I can say is this one felt unlike other visions. I had a shorter glimpse into his memories, but more understanding of the facts surrounding them. Perhaps making a choice to see the past has a different effect on me than when I am forced to see something or when I avoid seeing it," she said. "Do not get too excited yet. This was a very tame vision compared to many I have seen in the past. It is possible the intensity of the vision makes a difference."

"Would you not agree this is a step in the right direction though?" her cousin asked, hopeful.

Lillian shrugged. "Perhaps, but it is difficult to say after only two trials." She remembered something Gabriel had said. "Will our betrothal truly be announced in tomorrow's papers?"

He nodded. "My mother said this morning that she would work out the details with Lady Wentworth this afternoon."

"Nothing good can come of those two with their heads together, I think," Anne said with an amused smile.

"Indeed not," Lillian agreed. She had to breathe through the panic that was rising in her chest before she could speak again. "This all feels so permanent. To the rest of the world our betrothal will be real, and I fear I will be forced to hold to it regardless of what I want."

Gabriel took her hand and let his midnight blue eyes meet hers. "I made an agreement with you and I will not renege on it. You must trust me on that."

She pulled her hand away and crossed her arms, hugging them against her chest. "You do not know my mother. Once she has her teeth into something, it is hard to pry it loose." She looked away across the lawn, not really seeing anything, and swallowed hard.

"You do not know *me* well enough yet," Gabriel said. "I never waver from my resolve." He held out his arm. "Shall we move on?"

Lillian was pushing herself far out of her usual state of comfort, but if she had learned one thing from Signor Silvano, it was how to put on a good face. She straightened her spine and took Gabriel's arm. "Yes. Who is next on the list?" she asked as they began their walk back toward the refreshment tent.

Gabriel was elated. He had come to this party with the high hope of eliminating a couple of suspects from his list. Seeing Lillian's gift in action had given him a thrill of excitement as he imagined all the possibilities. His father's killer did not stand a chance.

Lillian. Every moment he spent with her gave him a new glimpse into her extraordinary character. He had not lied to her. If she still wished to be set free after getting to know him better, he would hold to their bargain, but he had every hope that she would change her mind.

"Lord Jolley is next," he said now in answer to her question. "From what I understand from my mother, he and my father had a falling out shortly before the house party, although she did not know the cause of it. Father did not tell her before his passing. In light of this fact, I am surprised his lordship attended that party." He pointed his head in their direction. "He is with his niece, just over there."

Lillian nodded once.

If Gabriel had had his way, he would have found out where the next six people on his list were today and dragged Lillian to meet all of them. He was eager to bring his mission to a conclusion. Unfortunately, he had promised her he would not push her past what she could handle, and he must honor that.

He brought himself back to attention as they were just now approaching his father's friend. Lord Jolley had always been a reserved, but a kind and gentle man. He was beginning to show signs of age, with thinning blond hair and deepening creases about the eyes.

"Good day to you, Lord Jolley, Miss Thompson," he said with an easy smile. "How are you on this fine day? May I introduce you to my betrothed, Lady Lillian Hargraves, and her cousin, Miss Hargraves? Lord Jolley and his niece, Miss Thompson, Lillian."

"My wife's niece, actually," Lord Jolley said.

"How do you do, my lord? Miss Thompson?" Lillian said.

He once again watched in anticipation as she reached out a hand. The man took it as she curtsied, then hung on to him for a fraction past what would have been considered proper when greeting a new acquaintance. But before it could become too awkward, she let go and stepped back.

Anne immediately covered the strange silence with a question. "Are you out for the season, Miss Thompson?"

The young lady's face lit up. "Oh, yes. This is my second season. It has been ever so nice going to balls and parties and meeting so many new people."

"You must have a great many beaux," Anne said.

"I do not know about that," the young lady said, blushing.

Lord Jolley patted his niece's hand, which was in the crook of his elbow. "Cordelia's just being modest. She has had plenty of young bucks chasing after her since the start of the season. She will have her pick, mark my words."

Gabriel was relieved when Anne said, "Perhaps we will see you at some of the events in the coming weeks, Miss Thompson," as it gave him the perfect opportunity to pull away from the conversation.

"It was good to see you, Jolley, but I need to take my companions about for more introductions."

"Very good, Wyvern. Always good to see the son of my old friend. I will need to pop by and pay my respects to your mother some time. It has been an age."

Gabriel nodded and led the ladies back across the lawn. He wanted a chance to find out what Lillian had learned without being overheard. When they were far enough away from the other guests, he asked, "Well?"

Lillian shook her head. "He is not your man. However, I can tell you what the falling out between him and your father was all about. Four years ago, he wished to marry his wife's niece soon after he was widowed, and your father was adamantly against it."

"I do not see what the problem is. It is his wife's niece, after all, and no relation to him," Anne said with a frown.

"She was only fifteen at the time," Lillian said flatly.

Anne gasped. "He has to easily be in his forties. Ew!"

"May-September weddings happen all the time," Gabriel said. "Why is this so different?"

Lillian turned to face him. "Matching a young lady who is out in society, perhaps seventeen or eighteen years old, with a much older man is acceptable in the *ton*, although it is not usually desired by the young lady. That is one thing, but matching with a lady who is not yet out of the schoolroom is another thing. She would still be considered a child. Although it is perfectly legal, it is frowned upon for ladies to be married off before the age of seventeen."

Gabriel brows drew together. "Not being a lady, I know little of such things. Two years makes that much of a difference?"

"Indeed," Lillian said. "Were you the same person at eighteen as you were at twenty?"

He did not think long on that question. Of course he was not. At eighteen, he had lost his father and his brother. He had been angry, brash, inexperienced in the ways of the world, and still impetuous. After two years of working for the government overseas during the war, he had quickly grown up and matured. He could honestly say he went from being a boy to a man during that time.

"I see your point," he said. "I suppose my father understood such things well, which is why he advised his friend against the match."

"If it is any consolation, it appears Lord Jolley ended up taking your father's counsel and allowed Miss Thompson to grow up free from the bonds of marriage," Lillian said.

"I wonder if he still has designs on her," Anne said.

Lillian shrugged. "I could not say, as the vision I saw was of the past, not the present. I imagine there is little we could do about it regardless." She tilted her head. "That is three suspects crossed off of your list. How many more are there?"

Gabriel rubbed the back of his neck with one hand, feeling uneasy. "There were a total of twenty-eight guests, not counting the immediate family."

Lillian pursed her lips. "That means there are twenty-five more people to meet and touch. Even if we were able to do this two or three at a time such as today, that would be at least a dozen more events."

He huffed out a breath. "I wish there were an easier method. If I had my way, we could simply recreate the house party, but—"

"Why could you not?" Lillian interrupted.

His eyes flicked to Lillian. "People would find it strange, would they not, if I invited only those who were there at my father's murder to the country?"

"Men have no imagination," Anne chimed in, glancing heavenward. "You simply tell them you wish to honor your father's memory by asking those who were well known to him to gather for an event at which to celebrate his life. You can say you had no chance before while you were out of the country but wish to do so now. You can invite additional guests. Mark my words, no one will question it or even give it a second thought."

The idea was preposterous, and yet as Anne had said, no one would dare question it. Except perhaps the killer himself. "What if some of them do not come?" he asked.

"I believe most of them will, which means it will be a more efficient use of our time," Lillian said. "I for one am in favor of the idea. Gather everyone in one place and get the deed done, so to speak, as quickly as possible."

He frowned. "Is this truly so distressing for you?"

Lillian's jaw tightened. "You saw one result of my ability at the ball. How could you think any of that was not distressing for me?" she snapped.

He put up his hands in conciliation. "I apologize. I truly had no idea."

Lillian's face fell. "No, it is I who must apologize for being so waspish. This is all new to me, and I will admit I am tired."

"I understand," Gabriel said. "Since we have done what we had come to accomplish, if you wish to depart, I can have your carriage brought around."

"That would be nice," Lillian said. "I would like to go home and rest." She smiled. "Besides, you now have a house party to plan."

"The mothers will be in raptures about it," Anne said.

"The mothers," Lillian groaned out.

"Do not worry," he said. "I will handle them." *Famous last words,* he thought to himself. When had he ever handled his mother?

Gabriel tugged the bell pull in his study immediately upon returning. When Pennywhistle arrived, he called for Jersey as well as requesting a pot of strong coffee. He needed fortification. He flopped into the leather chair at his desk and pinched the bridge of his nose. Nothing Lillian had revealed was truly shocking, but it was a lot to take in.

Jersey soon entered the room, bearing the coffee tray laden with tea cakes and sandwiches. "I brought you an extra nice snack," he said.

"Since when do you do me any favors?" Gabriel asked in a skeptical tone.

Jersey looked at him sheepishly. "Since I might feel slightly bad about how I behaved this morning, ribbing you about the young lady."

Gabriel did not believe him for a moment, but he said, "It is nice to see you have a conscience, Jersey. Pour us each a cup and then we can discuss a few things."

"Such as, your grace?" his valet said as he poured the black liquid.

"I need to give you new information I gathered today."

Jersey handed a cup to Gabriel. "I am all ears."

Gabriel took a sip of the coffee and began to relax. He placed the cup on his desk. "Now—" A knock on the door interrupted him. "Come," he said with a frown. He was not interested in distractions today.

Pennywhistle popped his head in. "Begging your pardon, your grace, but Viscount Hartley is here and says he has some urgent information to impart."

"Very good. Show him in."

Within seconds, Hartley strode into the room. His keen green eyes took in everything, including Jersey, but stopped at the coffee service. "Is that coffee?"

"You know it is," Gabriel said. He turned to Jersey. "Bring another cup please." To Hartley he said, "Have a seat and tell me what you have."

"It is about Gemini."

This made Gabriel sit up and place his forearms on the desk for support. "What about him?"

"We have finally received word from Eagle. It seems that Gemini has gone to ground in Scotland in the company of his keeper. Eagle would not divulge anything more specific. He says Gemini had been hiding from some enemies on his trail, which is why he went deep."

Thank God he is safe. Gabriel took a deep breath of relief before asking, "Did Eagle say anything more?"

Hartley waited to answer as Jersey returned. He poured the man a cup of coffee, then stood off to the side. His friend took several gulps of the strong brew, and looked at Jersey. "Thank you. I needed that."

He turned back to Gabriel. "To answer your question, Eagle did not share any additional information except to say he was able to meet with Gemini for a short time near the border and Gemini will stay hidden until such a time as the problem is solved. Eagle said he is safe and well."

"Good, that relieves my mind, and your timing today is perfect," Gabriel said. "We have something new to put into action and I will need your assistance."

"Give me more of that coffee and I shall do just about anything," Hartley said.

Gabriel recognized that, for his friend, this was an attempt at humor. Hartley was learning.

"Does your cook not know how to make it?" Gabriel asked with an amused smile.

Hartley shook his head. "She has yet to master it and I believe Monsieur Brisson's brew is worthy of the gods."

Gabriel laughed, then sobered. "Back to the subject at hand—you might not credit it, but Lady Lillian's ability was able to eliminate three of the suspects on my list today."

Hartley sat forward with interest in his gaze. "That is incredible. I can only imagine how much help she could be to us in the future."

"I agree," Gabriel said, "but she has not yet learned how to harness the power of the gift, and it takes a lot out of her. Because of this, she has come up with a plan which I wish I had thought of much sooner." He sat back in his chair and rubbed his chin.

Over a coffee pot and a plate of tea cakes, Gabriel told Hartley all he had learned today.

"Seeing Lady Lillian's ability firsthand made me a true believer in the existence of such gifts," he leaned forward and clasped his hands, "and since I have been told there are others like her, there is every reason to find out if we can make use of them in some way for the good of the country."

"With or without their consent?" Hartley asked with a raised eyebrow.

"With, of course," Gabriel said defensively. "I am not that heartless."

Jersey raised an eyebrow as if to say, 'Are you not?'

He scowled at the valet. "Now is not the time to debate this at any rate, and we will not know more about these others until Jersey's man inside the Benevolence Society gives us a report. Right now it is more important to put this murderer to bed. Will you help me set up this house party, Hartley?"

"Of course. I will do whatever you need."

"Good. I will want Davis there too. I think the more hands on deck we have, the better our chance of success. Let us meet in a couple of days to hammer out details about security. If we are going to invite a murderer to dinner, we had better make sure we have our backs covered."

Hartley nodded once. "I agree."

"Now, tell me how things are going at the club."

Hartley placed his cup on the desk and leaned forward. "I wonder at the wisdom of admitting non-Network members. Does it not leave us vulnerable to attack from the inside? Would it not be better to keep the club only for the Network?"

"I had this conversation with my father long ago," Gabriel said. "The point was to keep the club from being a conspicuous target that says, 'All men within these walls are spies.' By mixing in some everyday gentlemen, we are essentially hiding in plain sight."

"Perhaps you need to improve the caliber of the membership. These young men with little sense are going to become liabilities at some point rather than assets."

Gabriel chuckled. "Says the man who is only twenty-three years old."

"I feel old compared to some of these gentlemen who have nothing better to do all day than spend their fathers' money and hang about the club," Hartley said.

"I imagine you already have a list of the harebrained twits for me?" At Hartley's nod, he said, "Then let us cut some of them loose and find gents who will better fill their shoes." He turned to Jersey. "Start a list of men who would fit our requirements."

"Yes sir, Captain. I'll need a little time if you want some variety."

He waved the issue away. "Take the time you need. It is not our highest priority. If we are a few members short for a time, it will not be the end of the world."

"Right you are, then," Jersey said.

"Good. We are set on that issue for now so we can concentrate on what is most important," he said.

"Now that you have Lady Lillian as a secret weapon, so to speak, you have a high chance of tracking this man down," Hartley said with a gleam in his eyes.

"Not just a chance," he said. "I have every expectation of doing so. It is time to finally let my father's ghost rest."

"And bring your brother home," Hartley said.

"Yes." He felt a tightness in his chest. He had ached for his twin every day of the last four years. "It will be time to bring Gemini home."

SIXTEEN

Signor Silvano's Sayings Number 16
Life can be agonizing at times.
Do not allow yourself to be tortured by it.
Instead, go shopping!

For once, Lillian was glad to have the distraction of shopping to keep her mind off the whirlwind of change in which she now found herself.

Her mother made good on her threat to completely outfit her daughter from head to toe with all new additions to her wardrobe now that she was betrothed to a duke. Lillian tried once more to insist that she most certainly did not need any new clothes, but her mother had defeated her, again.

"Look at this beautiful amethyst watered silk." Anne held up a portion of the fabric to Lillian's face. "You would surely dazzle the duke if you wore a ball gown made of this." She gave her a cheeky grin.

Lillian wanted to cover the growing heat in her cheeks. She had no idea where it was coming from.

"Ah, *oui*, mademoiselle, this color would be perfect for you," Madame Favre, their dressmaker, said as she took the bolt of fabric from Anne and went to place it on the growing stack that would be used for the new dresses.

To cover her embarrassment, Lillian raised her voice and said, "Look at this beautiful icy blue watered silk. Would it not make the most beautiful ball gown for my cousin, Madame?"

"*Oui*, my lady. This would be the very thing for the young miss," she agreed.

While she had momentum, she added, "And over here, I saw a lovely yellow silk that might suit my companion?" Sarah needed to be brightened up. All she had were drab browns and grays.

Madame Favre did not concur on this, however. "No, my lady. Bright yellow would not look well on the miss, with her dark blonde hair. It would make her look sallow." Her eyes lit up. "But perhaps over here. I have a pretty sage green. Come look."

Lillian fingered the light-green cotton, while Sarah looked over her shoulder. She had to admit the modiste was right. "With embroidered flowers, this would look amazing, do you not agree, Sarah?"

"It is quite lovely, I admit, but I have no need for anything so fine," Sarah said quietly.

"Of course you do. Let us not forget you are now my companion. Besides, you deserve better and everything you own is out of date and out of fashion." She held the fabric up to

Sarah's face to see how it would look and lowered her voice to a whisper. "The best time to presume on my mother's goodwill and acquire some new clothing is while she is on a shopping spree."

Sarah snorted out a laugh. "Fine, fine. I will not argue with you while you are being assertive. Just do not attempt to turn me into something I am not."

"You give yourself far too little credit," Lillian said. She then turned to Madame Favre. "This will do very nicely, perhaps with some embroidered flowers at the hem and sleeves, and we shall need additional day dresses for my companion in any colors you feel are suitable. We have only just come to town and her wardrobe needs to be updated."

Shopping and dress fittings were going to keep them busy for days. Perhaps Lillian could use it as an excuse not to attend any more social events for a while. 'I am sorry, Mother. I simply cannot attend the ball tomorrow evening. My new gowns fit for a duke will not be ready in time,' she could say.

She smiled to herself at the thought now as she removed her bonnet and cloak in the entryway of their home and gave them to Sarah to put away. Higgins stepped forward and presented a silver salver with a letter laying on top.

"For me?" she asked.

"Yes, my lady."

Lillian took the letter and turned it over. She immediately recognized the seal of the Duke of Wyvern. Feeling a rush of emotions, she headed to the stairs.

Sarah kept pace behind her. "Is it from Francesca?"

"Sadly, no," Lillian said over her shoulder.

When they reached her room, she flopped down backward onto the bed and broke the seal. She immediately scanned to the bottom and saw it was not from Gabriel, but his mother.

"The Duchess of Wyvern has invited us to tea on Thursday." Lillian laid the letter down and closed her eyes. She really was quite tired after visiting so many shops.

"All the ladies of the house?" Sarah asked.

"Yes, we are to plan this celebratory house party together. It seems the duke has told his mother it will be both in honor of our betrothal and a memorial to his father."

Lillian listened to the normal sounds of Sarah bustling around the dressing room, putting things away and generally keeping everything tidy. Lillian was fortunate. Without her friend, she would likely live as a slob.

"Sarah, I believe I shall stay in this evening. Between the challenges at the garden party Saturday and all this shopping, I need time to refresh my spirits. Let us camp out in front of the fire and make cheesy toast like when we were girls."

Sarah smiled. "As delightful as that sounds, I doubt we could get away with it."

Lillian wrestled herself into an improper sitting position with her legs splayed wide and her shoulder slumped. "What is there to get away with? I may do as I please in my own room, and one of the benefits of being my companion is you get to partake in all of my adventures, just like at Silvano's, with no one raising an eyebrow."

"I do like that idea, but we shall see how long your mother tolerates it."

Ever practical was her Sarah.

"As long as I am engaged to the duke, I believe my mother will tolerate anything. It is what will happen once I break off the engagement that I have no wish to contemplate." She shooed her friend away with mock sternness. "Now off with you. We are in desperate need of provisions for our little party."

"Yes, your highness." Sarah gave a cheeky curtsey and departed.

"Oh, there you are Prince Albert." The ferret had slithered up the bed and was now curling in her lap. She stroked his fur from head to tail. "I wish life could be as simple for me as it is for you—nothing but eating and sleeping, not a care in the world, you silly pet."

Being a lady was a lot of work. Whoever thought otherwise had no idea. The multiple changes of clothing a day took up several hours alone. She mentally ticked off the fingers of her hand. Then there were the balls and parties, the visitations, the letter-writing, the shopping to keep up one's appearance, the study of the rules of society—the list could go on for forever. If she knew being a lady was difficult, she could only imagine what it might be like for a duchess. No thank you very much.

The next day was finally Wednesday again, and Lillian eagerly returned to the weekly Society meeting, ready to tell of her recent progress and to hear what Signor Silvano thought of this new way of dealing with their gifts.

Today she was running late due to an extra fitting with Madame Favre that had taken longer than expected. An all new wardrobe was not a simple business.

When she arrived, the meeting room was already full.

"Fran is not here," Sarah remarked.

Lillian scanned the room thoroughly, but did not see a tall girl with noticeable red hair. After her betrothal announcement appeared in the papers, she had expected a visit from Fran who would rib her mercilessly, but she had not heard from her friend since the last meeting.

She frowned. "I have never gone so long without hearing from her." Lillian saw Turpentine's lanky form and made a straight line for him. He was turned away talking to Samuel. She yanked lightly on his sleeve causing him to jump and spin around.

"What? Oh hello, Lil."

"Good evening, Turpentine. Have you seen Francesca?"

"Nope. Rumor is she has gone to the country for an extended holiday," he said.

"She told me at the last meeting that she was considering it, but why did she not send me a note?" Lillian asked. "How very odd."

Turpentine shrugged. "Who knows? Women can be odd creatures." Lillian glared at the comment. He grinned with no remorse.

Their conversation was cut short when Signor Silvano entered the room and called everyone to attention. "Hear ye, hear ye! Gather around all who will listen." Today he was wearing a lavender suit with gold embroidery that looked like it had come from the previous century. It was if he was still on a stage from decades ago.

Lillian took her regular seat, eyeing the empty place beside her. Why would Francesca miss a weekly meeting?

Silvano made eye contact with each student across the room as he spoke. "In the past, I have taught you strategies to use to diminish the effects of your gifts in hopes they would be less troublesome. However, a week ago the problem was raised that for many of you, there is no possibility of keeping your gifts from spontaneously appearing. For some of you, the gifts have grown stronger. Perhaps due to our move to London. I would not know. Christopher proposed a new strategy we might try of intentionally using your gifts to gain practice in control."

He paused and moved to the side of the podium, one hand on top, one behind his back. "I have thought long and hard on this idea as a new way of working going forward and have talked to Christopher at length about the technique he uses. I believe this might succeed, but it is risky. I have no idea how it might affect you physically or mentally, but I will leave it up to you if you feel the risk is worth the outcome. I understand some of you have been practicing the new strategy, and I would love to hear of your results. If someone wishes to volunteer, we shall begin with you." He waited until a hand rose. It was Turpentine.

"I have a pretty good handle on my ability, but I already practice it all the time unlike many of you." He looked around the room smugly.

"Excellent. Come up here, Master Walker, and let us demonstrate this new strategy."

Turpentine strutted to the front of the room like a preening peacock. Once there, he held his coat by the lapels and rocked back and forth lightly on his feet.

"What are you waiting for? Proceed!" Silvano barked out.

Startled by Signor Silvano's command, Turpentine jumped and dropped his arms. In the blink of an eye, an object materialized in his hands.

"Ayeeee!" Luciana yelled from across the room while clutching her head. A small flame shot into the air. "Return that to me!" The girl had a terrible time controlling her ability at the best of times, but when she was upset it was worse.

Turpentine held up his prize for all to see—Luciana's hair comb. A few in the room gave approving 'oohs.'

Silvano only sighed. "You are showing off again, Master Walker. This is obviously too easy for you. Show us something more difficult."

Turpentine scrunched up his face. "Such as what?"

Silvano looked around the room. "Try to lift a chair." Turpentine smiled as if the task was also too easy. "While someone is sitting in the chair," Silvano added.

Turpentine's smile dropped. He reached out his left hand, and the sound of wood vibrating against wood filled the air. Lillian turned her head and saw that Samuel's eyes had widened. He clutched the sides of the chair to hold on as it ever so slowly rose from the ground until it was a few feet above the floor.

"Enough!" Silvano commanded, and the chair dropped with a thump. "It is obvious you have been working on your skill, but not challenging yourself." When Lillian turned back to the front of the room, she could see that Turpentine was breathing hard. "Thank you Master Walker for your excellent demonstration. You may be seated." He looked around the room again, person by person. "Who is next?" His eyes landed on her. "Lillian, come! I understand you have been working with this new strategy."

Lillian walked slowly to the front of the room, licking dry lips. "Yes, I have made some progress since last week's meeting, signore."

"Very good. Tell us about it."

She stood now before her mentor in front of the room and told him, "After Christopher's advice to give in to the visions rather than try to run away from them, I have practiced a few times."

"How was it?" Silvano asked.

"It was not a wonderful experience by any means, and still made me feel quite ill, but I was able to stay alert and listen to the visions until they went away. I did not black out. I also had command of which memories I wished to see."

He clapped his hands together twice. "Good! This is excellent and shows us that what Christopher has suggested could work for all of you. Now, give us a demonstration."

Lillian wanted to protest violently. She had no wish to see into the mind of someone she admired so greatly. What if she saw a vision of something that might change her opinion of him? But how could she explain why she did not wish to do what would be expected of anyone else in the room? She looked down at his hands and saw that he was not wearing gloves. "If you would please take my hands, Signor Silvano." Lillian held out her gloved hands, palm up. She could sense he was surprised at this boldness. She never offered to touch another.

He placed his hands in hers and she grasped them lightly, closing her eyes.

She concentrated on the man in front of her. When she realized she was not feeling anything, she decided to be brave and changed tactics. Without a word, she slowly removed her gloves one finger at a time. She heard a few gasps from the audience. A fleeting thought crossed her mind that Fran was not here to witness this momentous event. She laid the gloves on top of Silvano's podium. "Once more, please." They resumed their former stance. This time she was hit instantly with visions.

"Do not run from the vision, Lillian," Silvano said in a low tone. "Listen to it. Let it tell you what it wants you to know."

Lillian's breath was coming fast and shallow as she began to shake.

"Remember to breathe, Lillian, as I have taught you."

She deepened the rhythm to calm herself. *Breathe in, breathe out. Breathe in, breathe out.* She listened to the sound of her own breath.

Signor Silvano was in the woods speaking to a large man in rough clothing, who looked like his nose had been broken more than once.

"Their lordships want their money back, and you'll give it to 'em iffen ya know what's good for ya," the man said.

"I do not know what you are talking about," Silvano said, hands on his hips. "You obviously have the wrong man."

The larger man snorted. "They's been lookin' for ya a good long while, that interested in gettin' their revenge they are. There's no mistake that you be Jack Seaton. Now, as I sees it, ya gots two choices. Give 'em back the money ya stole or they's gonna make you pay. Take the one ya likes best."

Lillian could see Silvano's eyes shift nervously back and forth several times before he collected himself and looked the man in the eyes. "You are wrong. My name is Giuseppe Silvano, and as far as I know it, I do not owe anyone anything."

In the blink of an eye, the large man grabbed Silvano by the shirt front, hoisted him in the air, and slammed him against a tree. "I'm not here to play games with ya, and it won't go well with ya if you don't come up with the money. Ya got one week until I come back. Iffen you don't hand over what ya owe, I gets to take it out of yer hide." He pulled Silvano forward and slammed him against the tree again. "And there might not be anything left of ya when I'm done."

The scene changed.

Silvano was in his office at the school speaking to Halvar. "I need to make contingency plans in case something happens to me. I want the school to continue on whether I am here to oversee it or not."

"Don't be daft. Nothin's going to happen to you," Halvar said genially.

Silvano went to the locked cabinet where he kept his spirits and poured a few inches of something into a glass. He swallowed it down in one gulp and refilled the glass before turning back to Halvar. "Look, I do not want to embroil you in all this, but when I started this school ten years ago, I used money I acquired by less than honest means. Although I will say I can fully justify the way I went about it." He walked to his desk and sat down. "The people I got the money from want it back."

"That's easy enough," Halvar said. "Pay them back in installments."

"You do not understand." Silvano took a sip of his drink. "Everything I have was put into this school for the students. We take on every charity pupil who applies. There is nothing left over. These are the kind of men who would kill someone *over this and I do not want the children to be forced to go on without some sort of leadership if I end up dead."*

"How could you put these kids at risk like this?" Halvar asked with a scowl.

Silvano sighed. "How could I not? It has been a far better life for all of them, even with the threat of discovery hanging over my head." He pinched the bridge of his nose. "I do not know yet what I am going to do."

Halvar slammed his fist on the table. "It is your responsibility to keep these children safe, so you best figure it out fast." He rose swiftly from his chair, knocking it backward onto the floor, and left.

Before Lillian could learn any more, Silvano yanked his hands back and turned away. She gasped and fell back a step.

When her mentor turned around again, he wore a strained smile. "Very good. This is the best work you have ever done."

With shaking hands, Lillian took her gloves from the podium. "Indeed, signore. I will try again, but it is very exhausting."

He looked at her with a softened gaze. "Yes, exhausting now, but perhaps with time, you will learn how to master it even more. All these years, I thought it was better for you to hide away and never see another vision again. I now know I have been teaching you the wrong strategy, because if you continue this way, who is in control? You or the visions?"

She did not answer his rhetorical question and donned her gloves once again. She still felt like the world was her enemy without them.

She returned to her seat.

Silvano stood behind the podium once more. "Today has been an excellent example of what we should be spending our time working on going forward. I know many of you have already made attempts, and I recommend the rest of you do likewise. For those of you unable to practice your gifts here at the school, I will consider each of your situations. You must do this over and over again until you have the highest level of control. Control is everything!" He slammed his palm on the wood of the podium in his typical dramatic fashion, then moved to the side and bowed. "I thank you, Christopher for your great insight. You are correct. I have been working all this time to help you diminish your gifts when in fact you should expand them to control them. It does not make sense at first, and yet it does."

Back in her bedroom, Lillian had much to think about. She sat on the seat below her window and looked outside, not really seeing anything. The revelations from Silvano's past had raised so many questions for her. The students had been told the school had been burned down by locals who were afraid of the students, but what if that had not been the case? What if Silvano's money problems were the real cause? And if so, should she tell anyone else about it? They had always taken everything Silvano said on faith. Now she wondered if it that faith had been misplaced.

Sarah interrupted her swirling thoughts. "Are you well, Lillian? Your practice with Silvano today was amazing."

She turned to her friend. "I am well, simply a little tired after seeing another vision. Why do you think Francesca would go to the country without any word to me? Today was indeed a very important moment. I controlled another vision and I regret she was not there to see it."

"Perhaps she did not have time to write before she departed. You could always send her a letter."

"Hmm. It is unlikely she could not pause long enough to send me even a short note," she said, "but you are correct that I should write to her as soon as possible."

Lillian closed her eyes, trying not to think about dukes, revealing visions, absent friends, or shopping. That left Prince Albert. She smiled as she thought about her pet's recent foray into Simon's room. He had managed to chew one slipper to pieces and make good progress on a Hessian boot. Good ferret.

"A nap before dinner would make you feel better," Sarah said.

Lillian shook her head. "No, I have neglected my writing for too long. I need to work on my manuscript if I am to ever finish it."

Sarah was silent so long Lillian opened her eyes to see her friend watching her. "Is it still your plan then to write the book and go away? I do not see why you cannot just go through with the marriage. He seems like a decent man and I doubt you could do better."

Lillian sighed. "But *he* could. I have made progress this week, which is wonderful, but it must be acknowledged that my ability will never go away. What kind of duchess will I be with it always looming over our heads?" Not to mention she had no desire to be married to a man who only wanted her for her ability. She closed her eyes again and leaned her head on the window frame. "No, I have a plan, and as always, I will stick to it."

SEVENTEEN

Signor Silvano's Sayings Number 17
When all else fails, throw a party!

It was a rare fine day for London. The sun was not precisely shining, but it was peeking out now and then. The birds were singing outside his window and Jersey had done a splendid job as valet. Gabriel was dressed smartly with a nice smooth shave to match. He rolled his shoulders to break up any knots.

Today he would have tea with his mother and Lillian to plan how they would bring down a killer. Of course his mother did not know that, but Lillian did. Lillian. He had wondered more than once these past several days how she was holding up after using her gift on his behalf. He hoped he had not pressed her to a point she could not bear, as that would not help their cause.

He threaded his onyx cravat pin in place and took one more look in the mirror to be certain he was presentable. He nodded at himself, feeling fine and full of hope.

Impatient to greet his guests and move this investigation forward, Gabriel nearly bounced down the stairs, greeted Pennywhistle at the bottom, and headed for the drawing room. He opened the doors wide and strode in. His eyes immediately went to Lillian who stood in front of the fireplace, her back to him. Today, her dark brown hair was done up in ringlets that cascaded past her shoulders. She wore a sky-blue gown with dark blue gloves.

His perusal was short lived however as she turned toward him. She curtsied, low and formally. "Good day, your grace."

"It's Gabriel, remember." He came closer. "How are you faring today?" He scanned her face for any signs of distress. "Are you recovered from Saturday's outing?"

"I am well, your gr—Gabriel. I admit to some fatigue, but nothing sleep could not cure."

"Good. I hope you will be well rested before our journey to the country. I can only imagine what toll that event will take on you."

"No, I do not believe you can imagine it," Lillian said softly. "This is not child's play for me."

Gabriel grimaced inwardly. He had stuck his foot into his mouth. "I did not mean to insinuate it was. Please accept my apologies. I believe I had an unrealistic understanding of your gift and will fully admit I have much to learn. I will do my best in future to have a greater respect for how difficult this is for you."

"Thank you," she said. "I appreciate your consideration."

"Ah, there you two are!" His mother's cheerful voice broke the tension of the room.

"Your grace." Lillian curtsied deeply and smiled smile. "How pleasant it is to see you again. Thank you for the lovely invitation to tea."

The duchess waved away the compliment, then frowned. "Where are the other ladies? Do not tell me they misunderstood the invitation."

"No indeed," Lillian said. "They should be here shortly. I had an appointment at the modiste's for a fitting and came straight here afterward. My companion, Sarah Duggins, has joined me. She will be able to take notes."

For the first time, Gabriel noticed a dark-blonde-haired woman near the window facing the street. She looked very young to be a companion. Miss Duggins turned and curtsied.

Gabriel saw a twinkle in his mother's eyes. "How well thought of you, Lady Lillian! I shall gladly accept the help. Come, Miss Duggins, and join us. Let us take a seat and talk pleasantries before the tea arrives.

Gabriel allowed the ladies to take their place on the settee before sitting in the chair next to it. Miss Duggins sat across from her mistress.

"How is it you became Lady Lillian's companion?" his mother asked.

The girl looked uncertainly at Lillian, but at her nod, she began to explain. "I grew up on the Wentworth estate in Norfolk and became Lady Lillian's companion as a girl when she went away to school."

The duchess' eyebrows rose. "That is unusual to send a young girl off to school, is it not?"

Lillian shrugged. "My father has a progressive view on girls' education. The school I attended teaches all manner of subjects usually reserved for boys, including Latin."

His mother began to reply, but was stopped by the entrance of Pennywhistle, who carried the tea tray and headed a stately parade of two maids, Lady Wentworth, and Anne Hargraves. The butler bowed after placing the tray on the table. "Lady Wentworth has arrived."

"Oh good!" the duchess said in delight, patting the place on the side not occupied by Lillian. "Come sit here, Lavinia, and we will have a delightful time planning this event."

Anne took the remaining chair next to him while the three servants laid out a vast array of sandwiches and pastries before bowing themselves out of the room.

The duchess reached toward the tea pot. "How do you take your tea, Lillian? My I call you Lillian, since it will not be long before you may call me Mother?"

"Yes, please do," Lillian agreed. "And I take it with milk and sugar."

His mother poured the tea while Lady Wentworth offered a plate of tea cakes with elaborate decorative icing to each of them. Gabriel put several cakes on a small plate for himself and ate like a man starved.

Just as he was about to stuff another in his mouth, his mother hissed, "Gabriel. Manners, if you please!"

He looked at the cake in his hand as if completely unaware of what he had been doing. He placed it back on the plate and said sheepishly, "Sorry. I have missed English tea time."

Lillian laughed lightly and said to the duchess, "No one should get between a duke and his sweets, your grace."

"Quite right," he grumbled.

The duchess clucked her tongue, then turned to Lillian. "Now, let us take care of the business at hand. I am more pleased than I can say that Gabriel wishes to host a grand house party that serves the dual function of celebrating your betrothal and my dear husband's life. There is no reason we cannot do both." She turned to Lady Wentworth. "Would you not agree that house parties can drag on into tedium, but with two celebrations it will keep things interesting?"

"Indeed, Theodora," she said with a gleam in her eye. Gabriel imagined she was more excited about the betrothal celebration than honoring his father.

"Now, first we must compile a more complete guest list," the duchess said. "Nothing too large, but with a variety of guests to keep things lively. Do you not agree, Gabriel?"

He had been about to pick up the abandoned cake again, but sat up straight at her question. "Exactly, Mother. Let us start with the list I gave you of a few of Father's old cronies and their families, some of my friends, then add whomever you and Lady Wentworth wish to invite."

"Lady Francesca Grantham, daughter of the Marquess of Effingham, my dear friend, is the only person whom I must have on the list," Lillian said.

His mother nodded. "I know the Granthams." She turned to Lady Lillian's companion. "Miss Duggins, start a list of names as we think of them."

Gabriel caught Lillian's eye and flashed a mischievous smile at her, snatched up the desired treat from his plate before he could be told to put it down again, and crammed the whole thing into his mouth.

He saw the laugh threatening to burst from her, but she was quickly distracted by the duchess, who was talking again.

"I know it is the middle of the social season, but I believe we will still have a good turn out, being that you are a duke and all, Gabriel," his mother said. "Hmm. Since today is Thursday, I believe it will be just enough notice for a party to begin next Friday, do you think?"

"Normally I would agree with you, Mother," he said, "but because we want many of Father's friends to attend, and they may be all over the country, we had best give them more than a few days' notice. It could take several days for an invitation to reach them."

"You are correct," the duchess said, "and it is not as if we are in a hurry. What is another week to us?" She took a sip of her tea, then said, "What shall we plan for the activities?" She directed the question at Gabriel who had just stuffed another entire biscuit into his mouth.

He felt the heat creep up his cheeks and blushed. He put his fist against his lips in an attempt to hide his overfull mouth.

Lillian did laugh this time, and Anne giggled. Even Lady Wentworth's lips twitched.

The duchess sighed. "As a little boy, he could never get enough sweets." She shook her head. "It is a wonder he never grew as large as a house!"

After washing his biscuit down with a gulp of tea, Gabriel cleared his throat as if nothing had happened. "Other than an evening to celebrate Father, with perhaps everyone gathered around to tell fond memories, I have nothing set in mind. Do we really need to have it all planned ahead of time?"

"Men," his mother said in exasperation. "Of course we need to have it planned in advance. An event with no organization is doomed to certain failure. We do not want our guests to become bored." She waved absently in the air. "Never mind, we ladies will sort that out. Now, let us make the guest list at least before this afternoon is over. The rest we can decide upon later." She clasped her hands in front of her bosom. "I have not had any entertainment in an age. Oh, this is going to be so much fun!"

Gabriel was glad his mother thought so. He had only one objective for the party, and it was hardly a matter of 'fun.' Having finished his tea, he stood. "Mother, you now know my thoughts on this matter, so I will make my bow and leave you ladies to it." He turned to Lillian. "Perhaps you will do me the honor of joining me for a visit to Kew Gardens in Richmond tomorrow? Since you have a keen interest in herbs, you might be interested in their collection."

Lillian looked startled. "Oh, yes I am. I would very much like to see the gardens, as I have never had the chance before."

"Good. Shall we leave in the early afternoon, perhaps one of the clock?"

Lillian looked to her mother in question. At the lady's nod she said with a smile, "Yes, that will do very well. Thank you."

He bowed to the occupants of the room and left, his mother's animated voice trailing behind him. She was rarely this exuberant over anything. His heart expanded at seeing her happy once again. He mentally rubbed his hands in exhilaration that in two weeks' time, he would have a chance to add to her joy when they finally accomplished what he had not been able to in the past four years.

That evening, Lillian struggled to find a sense of peace. She was becoming increasingly worried about Fran. Something had to be wrong. Her friend had not replied to any of her notes. and the footman she had sent over could get no information from the Marquess of Effingham's servants. She would not wait another day to find out what was going on.

She begged off from that evening's ball in preparation. As she had hoped, her mother was happy to excuse her, since she had already attended the tea with the duke and duchess today.

Once darkness had descended and the hour grew late, she sent Sarah to discreetly discover if anyone was present at the Effingham home. If Fran was still in residence, she would find a way to sneak in to see her. Hiding away from all who held her dear was not the right answer to her friend's problems. Lillian paced as she waited impatiently for Sarah's return. She snorted to herself at her thoughts. Who was she to judge another like her for wanting to live as a recluse?

Sensing her agitation, Prince Albert stopped in front of her on the floor and stood on his hind legs. This was his signal that he wished to be picked up.

"Hello, you," she said as she scooped up her pet and draped him over her shoulder. He stretched up to lick her cheek several times with his tiny rough tongue before settling back down. She stroked his fur and began to pace more slowly.

Finally, after what felt like hours, Sarah returned. "I have interesting news," she said breathlessly after closing the door, her skirts swishing.

Lillian stopped pacing in the middle of the room. "Tell me."

"It seems that Fran's ability took a turn for the worse," Sarah said in a rush. "Unfortunately, during a dinner party hosted by her family, she called out at the table that she was 'tired of all the damn voices in her head.' "

"Oh dear," Lillian said, shoulders slumping.

Sarah nodded. "That is not the whole of it. She put her hands over ears when she said that, and when they came away, there was blood on her gloves."

Lillian gasped. "Her ears were bleeding?"

"Yes," Sarah said. "When she saw the blood, she fell over in a dead faint. Her ladyship called in a doctor right away, but he could find no reason for the bleeding, which had stopped by then anyway." Sarah leaned in as if to share a juicy secret. "The doctor told her ladyship that Fran was suffering from female hysteria and suggested laudanum to keep her calm."

Lillian could feel the blood rise up to her face as her anger grew. Female hysteria indeed! She ran her hands up and down Prince Albert's back to soothe him. Her anger had made him fidgety.

"That is not the worst of it," Sarah said.

"How could it get any worse?"

"It can. According to Mildred, the second upstairs maid, Fran's parents have gone to a place in the country to consult with a specialist in this 'female hysteria business.' " Tears welled in her friend's eyes. "But Mildred said, and I am agreeing with her, that she thinks the place is a madhouse and they plan to have Francesca a-a-admitted." Sarah broke down and cried on her final word.

"Over my dead body, Sarah." Lillian growled. "Fran has been there for all of us at one time or another and we shall not stand by and let this happen to her." Lillian found the handkerchief in her pocket and handed it to her friend. "Is Fran still being kept at home?"

Sarah nodded.

"Was anyone else in the family there when you visited?" she asked.

"No," Sarah said in a nasal tone as she wiped her nose. "Lord and Lady Effingham are still out of town."

"Then there may be just enough time to save her. Come, Sarah. Let us hurry to Effingham House to see what can be done."

Her companion rushed to leave the room to retrieve their cloaks and bonnets, but Lillian stopped her. "Sarah, wait. It is not safe to walk in the dark, and we cannot use one of our own coaches or my parents will know we have left the house. Can you bribe a footman to hire a hackney coach for us and keep the fact to himself?"

"Of course I can. I will return shortly."

Efficient as always, Sarah returned in only a few minutes and instructed Lillian to follow her.

The two of them snuck out a side door and followed the alley to the waiting vehicle out front. Lillian's foot was on the bottom step when she noticed a bearded gentleman, dressed all in black, across the street, watching her. She was suddenly wracked with shivers. She entered the coach and closed them safely inside. But whoever the man was, he was quickly left behind and out of her mind.

Fran's room was completely shrouded in darkness. No candles burned. No windows had been opened to allow in fresh air, and the room was indeed in need of fresh air.

Why is there no servant here? There should have been at least one person nearby to attend to her.

It had been a breeze sneaking up to the room. With the lord and lady out of town, the servants were all down in the kitchens enjoying their time off, and Lillian knew of a side door. Fran had shown it to her long ago when they were younger, during one of their rare visits to town, along with where the key was hidden.

Now, her eyes immediately flew to Fran's bed. Her friend lay as if lifeless under a pile of blankets—her face so pale it was like a beacon in the gloom.

"Fran?" she whispered. She received no response. Lillian stepped up to the bed. "Fran," she said again, a little bit louder. The girl did not move.

"Sarah, light a candle and bring it here please," she said over her shoulder.

Once lit, Sarah handed Lillian the candle. She took in the surroundings, including the bedside table. A tray lay there with a glass of water and a small brown glass bottle. Nothing else. She leaned toward the table and took up the bottle for a closer look. Laudanum. It was a potent sedative used to mask pain and help people sleep, but if given in too high a dose or too often, it could be dangerous.

Lillian slammed the container of medicine down, handed the candle back to Sarah, and sat on the bed. Taking both her friend's shoulders in her gloved hands, she vigorously shook her. "Franny, wake up! You must wake up now." The girl's head merely lolled to the side with no response.

"She is out cold," Sarah said in a whisper.

"Yes. They must have given her a great deal of laudanum for this strong an effect." Lillian took her friend's hand. "Oh Fran. What has happened to you?" Fran had always been the strongest of all the children at the school. No matter what difficulties came her way, she would stand tall and face them down like a warrior queen. Seeing her like this was devastating. Lillian only hoped she could find a way to help her.

"What can we do, Lillian?" Sarah asked. "We could not carry her out ourselves even if we should try."

They needed a plan. Lillian closed her eyes in concentration, quickly thinking through many possible ideas. After several minutes, she opened them again and asked, "Sarah, who on the staff would work against us if we should find a way to get Fran away from here?"

Sarah sniffed back tears before answering, "Mrs. Pettibone for sure." Just the name of Fran's evil housekeeper made Lillian shudder. Fran had told her many stories about the woman. "And Lady Effingham's maid, but she is traveling with her ladyship at the moment. Hopewell could be paid to make certain no one else interferes."

Lillian nodded. "Very good. Now, who do we know who can help us?" She squeezed her free hand into a fist, then let it loose. "Simon would only give us a lecture. No use asking him. My parents would be completely sympathetic, but I could hear my mother now: 'Dearest, we should not interfere with someone else's private business.' "

"You sounded just like her," Sarah giggled, breaking the tension in the room.

"Who do we know who would be willing to be sneaky and a little bit devious?"

"Signor Silvano?" Sarah suggested.

"I think we best not drag him into this. He has had enough to deal with moving the school recently to London, and we would not wish to draw attention to the Society."

She squeezed her hand again, the sound of the creaking leather filling the silence. "Wait. I think turnabout is fair play." Lillian jumped to her feet and rushed to Fran's writing desk with a swish of her skirts.

"What is it?" Sarah asked, following behind.

Lillian held up her finger to forestall her questions while she sat down at the desk, then pulled out paper from the drawer. She dipped the quill into the ink and wrote hastily. When she was finished, she sprinkled sand on the letter then blew it off. "I am not sure of anything yet, Sarah, but who can we entrust this note to for immediate delivery to Wyvern?"

"The Effingham's footman, Thomas, will do it." Sarah said.

"Excellent." She folded the note. "Give this to Thomas and this." She pulled a small coin from her pocket. "Tell Thomas to give the note to the duke and no one else."

"Yes, Lillian." Her companion reached for the letter, but Lillian pulled it back.

"No one else, Sarah. No matter what it takes, Thomas must put this directly into Wyvern's hands himself and wait for a reply."

Sarah put one hand on her hip and held the other out. "I understand."

Lillian gave her the note and prayed that relying on Gabriel for help was the right thing.

Sarah took a few more steps toward the door before Lillian called out again. "Sarah."

"Yes?"

"Do not get caught."

Sarah turned with a mischievous smile and said, "Never, my lady," before she crept out the door.

EIGHTEEN

Signor Silvano's Sayings Number 18
Friends can be difficult to come by.
Take care of the ones you have.

After hours of making his own plans for the house party down to the most minute detail, Gabriel was ready for a break. "You know what needs to be done to strengthen security, Jersey. Get started while I pen a note or two."

Jersey's reply was interrupted by a knock on the door.

"Enter," Gabriel called out.

Pennywhistle took two steps inside, his head high. Keeping his gaze over Gabriel's left shoulder, he said, "Begging your pardon, your grace, but a footman has come with a message and express instructions to hand it to you himself. I attempted to bring it with all assurances of its safety, but he would have none of it."

"Send the man up, Pennywhistle. We have concluded our business here for now."

Pennywhistle bowed and left the room.

Gabriel lifted an eyebrow. "I wonder what news this could be?"

"Perhaps I should stay a spell until you know for sure, Your Highlyness," Jersey said.

"Jersey, that is not even a word. You are slipping," Gabriel said in an amused tone. "But yes, you should stay."

The door was opened again by Pennywhistle with a young footman trailing behind. "He would not give his name, your grace."

"That is fine, Pennywhistle. You can leave us now, thank you." As Pennywhistle bowed himself out of the room, Gabriel eyed the footman. He was not familiar with the livery. The young man looked decidedly nervous, shifting from one foot to another. Gabriel held out his hand. "You have a missive for me, lad?"

"Y-yes, your grace." Instead of handing it over, the footman bowed and then repeated the action.

"None of that, young man. What is your name?"

"Thomas, your grace," he said, standing upright again.

"You have something for me?"

Finally remembering his mission, he pulled a letter from his coat pocket. "Yes, your grace. I was told to put this in your hands directly. No one else is to touch it, you see."

"I understand, Thomas." He took the letter and quickly scanned to the bottom to see the note was from … Lillian? He went back to the top and read.

Gabriel,

A dire situation has presented itself concerning my dear friend Lady F, whom I have mentioned. I would like to presume upon our friendship and ask your immediate help in this matter. Her parents have listened to the advice of a quack doctor who believes Lady F is not of sound mind. They have dosed her heavily with laudanum and even now are procuring a place for her at an asylum. They could return as quickly as tomorrow. I am waiting by her bedside in hopes you will come through for us.

Will you help me to take her to a safe place away from London? It bears repeating that time is of the essence. The footman who has brought this letter to you will wait for a reply. If you are able to assist, I shall forever be in your debt.

L

"Jersey, put everything else aside for the moment. We have something more immediate to see to," Gabriel said. He turned to Thomas before Jersey could ask any questions. "Wait please and I will pen a reply." He took up a piece of paper from his desk and began at once to write to Lillian. When finished, he melted wax onto the edge of the folded note and pushed his seal into it.

"The same instructions apply, Thomas. You are to see this letter into the lady's hands and no other, understand?"

The young man bobbed his head and then bowed. "Yes, your grace." He took the letter, preparing to leave.

"One moment," Gabriel called out. He pulled a shilling from his waistcoat and gave it to Thomas.

The lad bobbed several times. "Thank you, your grace."

"Yes, yes." Gabriel waved him away. "Hurry now, there is no time to waste."

With one more bow, the footman was out the door.

"What is afoot, Your Greatness?" Jersey asked.

"The unexpected, that is for sure. I am going to need some of your special skills for this job, and I will need the location of the Marquess of Effingham's town home."

"Right you are. I'm on it."

He hated to feel a thrill at the expense of Lady Francesca Grantham, but this was what he loved to do: make plans and thwart villains. If it helped Lillian out at the same time, he could not help but think it might go a small way toward gaining her forgiveness for the pressure he had placed on her to use her ability. Perhaps it was time to even the scales more fully between them.

Thomas returned more quickly than Lillian had expected, which eased some of her anxiety. Time was not on their side. He gave the reply to Sarah through the door, and she brought it to Lillian. Fran's condition was unchanged. She looked to be barely breathing she was so deeply in an unnatural sleep.

Lillian quickly broke the seal and read.

L,

I gratefully accept the task you have set before me. However, I will need additional information in order to enact a successful plan. I will come for you at Lady F's home immediately following this missive. Look for a plain black carriage two doors down from the house.

G

Lillian turned to Sarah and said, "He will do it! Oh, I cannot tell you how relieved I am."

"I as well."

She wanted to take a moment to cry in relief, but there was no time. "I must hurry. He needs more information to do what is needed and is most likely already waiting for me outside. You will stay and watch over Fran, will you not?"

"Of course I will," Sarah said, her head up like a lioness ready to protect her cubs.

Lillian squeezed her sleeping friend's hand one more time before getting off the bed. "Keep alert for any sounds of Mrs. Pettibone returning, Sarah, until I reappear. If she comes, you must hide until she leaves again. We cannot be caught out before we have the chance to get Fran away."

"Yes, Lillian. All will be well. You go and see your duke."

"He is not my duke, Sarah," she grumbled. "Not really."

Sarah chuckled lightly, which gave Lillian the feeling she was purposely poking at her.

After she rushed down the stairs, she passed Hopewell at the front door, saying breathlessly as she went, "You did not see me, Hopewell, and no doubt will not see me when I return in the next quarter hour."

She did not wait for an answer, but hurried outside to the waiting carriage. A large man sat on the driver's seat. She opened the door herself, as no footman was present. Gabriel held out his hand to assist her inside.

"Hello again, Lillian," he said. "I am sorry it was these circumstances that has brought us back together so soon."

"Thank you, Gabriel," she said, working to catch her breath. "I am only glad you are willing and able to assist us." She settled in the seat as the team of horses moved the carriage forward. "Before you commit to helping us, in the interest of full disclosure, I must tell you the reason why Lady Francesca has found herself in this position."

"The reason is not important right now," Gabriel said with the wave of a hand.

"I need you to understand," she went on. "Fran is one of the students from Silvano's School."

The air in the carriage was charged with silence while Gabriel absorbed the information. "She has a gift."

Lillian nodded. "Yes. She can hear others' thoughts and she may be in some distress because of it. She recently told me the ability was getting stronger."

Gabriel blew air out from pursed lips. "That is quite a skill." He held up one finger to pause the conversation. "Give me a moment." He sat silently in thought.

Was Gabriel now repelled by the idea of what her friend could do?

After an anxious stretch of time, he spoke again. "I apologize for what may seem like reticence on my part. I need to explain something, and after you have entrusted me with your deepest held secret, I know I can trust your discretion."

"Of course you can," Lillian said.

"I have mentioned to you that I often solve little puzzles for members of society as a sort of hobby, but it is far more than that." He paused in thought. "How best to explain it to you quickly? This is somewhat of a family business going back several generations. My father taught it to Michael and me, his father taught it to him, and so on. Each man may have held a slightly different position, but the job was basically the same."

"What job is that?" Lillian asked.

"It has many different titles, but essentially, I am in charge of a network of men who work undercover for the good of the country and on behalf of the government."

Lillian's eyes widened. "Do you mean you are spies?"

Gabriel chuckled softly. "That is one such name we are given. When my father died, his role as head of the operation was turned over to me. I was trained for it my entire life, you see." He draped his left arm across the back of the seat. "You may wonder why I have brought this up at a time like this."

"Yes, I do," Lillian said.

"I am concerned that the secrets of my network may become vulnerable if Lady Francesca is exposed to the thoughts of my men during her rescue."

Lillian inwardly breathed a sigh of relief. This was easy to address. "First, you must understand that Fran has been privy to the thoughts of some of the highest members of society during the season. She both cannot control what she hears and has no desire whatsoever to use this information for any purpose. I know without a doubt that you can trust her. Besides," she added, "she is so heavily dosed with laudanum she will not hear a thing for some time."

Gabriel nodded once. "Your assurances put my mind at ease." He drummed his fingers quickly on the leather. "Let us talk about how my men and I may get your friend to safety." He leaned forward. "This is what we are going to do."

Lillian could not help pacing her room the next morning in restless anticipation. She had to put her trust in Gabriel's plan, but now she could do nothing but anxiously await the news that her friend was safely away.

Once she and Sarah had helped Mildred pack Fran's things for her journey last night, they had gone home. There was no other way to be of help, and they would have run the risk of discovery if they had stayed any longer. They had nearly been found out as it was when they left Fran's room for the night. Thank goodness Mrs. Pettibone's rattling keys had given them enough warning so they could duck inside Fran's dressing room until the way was clear again.

What would happen when Fran awoke from her drug-induced state in a strange place? Lillian had sent a letter to be given to Fran when she woke up, but would it be enough?

Gabriel was sending Fran to his estate in Kent. It was a large home where no one would notice her presence, and Lillian would be able to reunite with her friend and help her make further plans for the future during the house party. It was a good arrangement.

Lillian crossed the room once again. Prince Albert scuttled ahead of her and turned in a circle.

Not only did she have her friend to worry about, but now she had swirling thoughts of what Gabriel had told her earlier. He was a spy? Not just any spy, but the head of an organization of government agents.

She stopped and tried to take a deep calming breath, but she could not settle.

"I am going to take Prince Albert with me to Kew Gardens today," she said to Sarah, who was embroidering a handkerchief. "He could use the fresh air, and I could use his calming presence."

Her friend's eyes widened, eyebrows raised. "Do you think that a good idea, Lillian? There is no telling what manner of havoc he could wreak." She paused a heartbeat before adding, "And are these not royal gardens?"

Lillian shrugged. "I will put him on the leash so he cannot run off. He will enjoy the outing."

"If you say so," Sarah mumbled. Then more loudly said, "It will be your funeral if he misbehaves, and he always misbehaves."

Lillian chuckled. "He is a ferret. He cannot help himself."

An hour later, Gabriel called as promised to take her to Kew Gardens. She assumed, by the discreet nod he had given her when he entered the drawing room, that the job had at least been successful. Now she wanted details.

As soon as Gabriel slapped the reins and the horses pulled the curricle away from the front of her home, Lillian burst out, "How is Francesca? Tell me everything, please."

"Last night at approximately two o'clock in the morning," Gabriel began, "I and two others were able to enter the side door as you prearranged with the maid. We had no difficulty carrying Lady Francesca and her things out without detection. She remained unconscious for the duration. She is currently in the care of Viscount Hartley on their way to Kent and I would expect the drug to wear off some time today or tomorrow at the latest. She may have ill effects from such a high dose, however."

Squeezing her hands together in front of her chest, almost as if making a plea, Lillian said, "I want to leave for Kent as soon as possible. Francesca should not go through this alone."

Gabriel's midnight blue eyes locked on hers briefly in silence. She waited patiently for his answer. He shook his head. "I am sorry, but I see no way to convince the mothers to depart any earlier than a few days before the party. I know this must be hard for you, but you will need to trust that I have placed your friend in good hands and that she will receive all the care she needs."

Lillian was about to argue further, but Gabriel added, "Besides, it would look suspicious if your friend disappears at the same time you take an expected jaunt to the country." He shook his head. "No, it is best all around if you wait. Lady Francesca is in the care of her maid and footman. She will not be alone."

Lillian sat back, exasperated, but he was right, drat him. Fran's parents might be cruel, but they were not stupid people. It was possible she might be the first person they asked to find out what had happened to their daughter. It would be better if she could stay behind and act shocked that Fran had disappeared.

It was time to stop fretting. Fran was safe, and she needed to be grateful. "I thank you for your reassurances of her well-being, Gabriel. I could spend hours telling you how common it is for people like Fran and I to be mistreated—most undeservedly I might add."

"I cannot imagine what it must be like to live with such a heavy responsibility as these gifts," Gabriel said. "You have given me clues about its effects, but perhaps you would be willing to share more with me about your story. About when your ability started and how you have dealt with it, I mean. Perhaps it will help me better understand your experiences."

Lillian thought for a while before she decided to speak. She took a deep breath. "My ability first became evident to me at the age of five. I had no idea what was happening at first. I simply thought I was falling asleep and having nightmares. When I touched someone or they touched me with bare hands, I could see not only visions of their past, but I got a sense of who they were as a person. When I am touched, I appear to faint, but I am not unconscious. I am listening and experiencing the other person's thoughts and feelings as I see living pictures of their former days. The episode I had at the Grantley ball?" She looked to Gabriel in question.

He nodded.

"This is what happened. That man touched me and I saw into him—not just the visions of evil things he has done, but the essential darkness of who he is. Now, that essence clings to me and I cannot shake it off. I truly wish I could." Lillian swallowed hard and looked away. This was the worst part of her gift. Once she viewed someone's evil so personally, she could never remove it from her head.

"At the garden party, you did not have a fit like before," Gabriel stated.

"Yes, with this new practice I am learning to choose to see the vision rather than run away from it. It is beginning to make a difference."

"I am glad to hear it. What occurs when you touch people who are not full of evil thoughts, such as a child or your cousin Anne for instance?" Gabriel asked.

"Most everyone has bad thoughts at some time or another—not just their own horrible deeds, but also what has been done to them." Lillian turned back to look at him. "But your question is a good one. Once I discovered what was happening to me, I had little desire to test a theory to see how many people I could touch without any negative effects."

"That is understandable," he said. "What happened to you after you discovered this gift?"

She tapped her lips with her forefinger, thinking about where to begin this part of her history. "Thankfully, I had unusually understanding parents. I told them what was happening, and they believed me. Besides family and servants, others were not so kind about my strange behavior, so I stayed at home most of the time. Two people came into my life when I was still quite young who made a profound difference to my comfort. One was my cousin Anne and the other was my companion Sarah."

Lillian had met Sarah by chance when she was eight. She had snuck out to play alone in the woods of her family's estate and had instead found company in a kind little girl who took her by the hand and showed her many of the forest's secrets. Lillian asked her mother about the girl who she could touch without having a fit. Her mother was so thrilled about this fact she made inquiries, and after hearing she was the child of a farmer on their estate, she paid the man to have Sarah come play with Lillian every day. It was not long before Sarah's duties turned into those of caretaker as well.

She was distracted as Gabriel navigated the horses around a knot of produce carts.

"As all little girls do," she continued, "I grew older and became bolder with age. I attempted to sneak out to have adventures in the village. This did not go well for me. The villagers became suspicious after I had several episodes." Lillian paused to backtrack. "You must understand also, my parents did all in their power to find help for my problem. In the beginning, they brought in doctors, but many of these so called doctors made the suggestion to lock me away in an insane asylum." Gabriel let out a curse. "I quite agree," Lillian said. "As did my father. He began to write instead to men of science, those supposedly well versed in unexplained phenomena. Unfortunately, most were more interested in studying me rather than offering help.

"No help came from that quarter, but one day a strange letter arrived from a Signor Silvano. He claimed to not only understand the needs of people with unusual abilities such as mine but that he had a school expressly for the purpose of helping them learn how to get along in society as well as how to control their abilities. My father immediately wrote for more information. To make a long story short, at the age of nine, I was sent to Silvano's School for Exceptional Children with Sarah by my side."

"You were very young," Gabriel said. "Did you find relief at this school?"

Lillian looked off into the distance and thought about how to answer that question. It was certainly complicated. "Not so much relief, but understanding. There were others there with gifts more difficult to handle than mine, all of whom had been ostracized from society. Some had been abandoned by their families. Others endured worse. I felt very grateful to have parents who loved me enough to accept me as I am. Perhaps accept is not the best word, but they certainly tolerated me."

"After all these years, you are just now learning to control your gift," Gabriel stated.

"This is unfortunately true for most of us, yes."

After finishing the ride in silence, Gabriel pulled the horses through a gate onto a drive with an expanse of green lawn all around them. "Here we are," he said. "I sent a note around that we would like to view the herbarium. Someone should be available to give us a tour."

Lillian looked forward to the day ahead and the chance of learning about some herbs she may not have encountered before. They would make nice additions to her book.

Once the horses stopped, she stood and picked up the bag which contained Prince Albert, but he became very wriggly.

"Here, let me take that and I will help you down," Gabriel said from the ground below. Without waiting for an answer, he took the writhing object from her hand. He nearly dropped it but caught it in time and held it at arms-length. "What the deuce is in here?" He eyed the object suspiciously.

She made her own way down from the vehicle, using the front wheel as steps, took her bag back, and opened it to reveal Prince Albert who immediately shot out and perched on her shoulder. She grabbed the leash before it could become tangled.

"Gabriel, may I introduce you to my pet, Prince Albert?"

He grinned and shook his head. "Why am I not surprised you own a ferret? Is he friendly?"

"He is. If you would like to scratch behind his ears, he will be your friend for life."

Gabriel did just that, and she could feel Prince relax into it. He chuckled. "I see he likes that and I see you have him on a leash, which is a wise idea. There is no telling how many plants here may be poisonous to one such as this little animal."

"Yes, he knows to stay on my shoulder while on a short leash," she said. "I hope you do not mind my bringing him."

Gabriel shook his head. "Of course not."

Lillian smiled to herself. Gabriel had saved her friend, was helping her expand her knowledge of herbs, and had been kind to Prince Albert. She had to admit that she was beginning to see him in a whole new light.

NINETEEN

The herbarium was a sprawling brown-brick building with three stories. Lillian had had no idea before coming how large it was. Her heart sped up in anticipation.

When they walked inside the door, a man rushed up and bowed low. "Good day to you, your grace, my lady." He bowed again to each of them. "I am Dr. Vishna, and I am pleased to welcome you to the herbarium. I am a specialist in herbs which I understand is your interest." Like her friend Neera, Dr. Vishna was from India, with light brown skin, dark hair, and the familiar rhythmic accent of their country.

Lillian was about to reply when her pet sprang without warning onto the floor, scampered up the doctor's leg and settled on his shoulder.

"Prince, no!" She still had a hold of the leash, which she had had to slacken lest she strangle the animal, but she could not very well yank him back now. "I am so sorry, Dr. Vishna. Prince Albert has never done that before."

The doctor chuckled and tickled Prince under the chin and then behind the ears. "It is no problem. I have a ferret at home too. Perhaps he smells my Rani on my clothing." He took the leash from her and coiled it around his hand. "He will do very well where he is."

Lillian smiled and let out a sigh of relief. Sarah had not exaggerated when she had said Prince Albert always found a way to misbehave.

Dr. Vishna turned and entered a doorway to a large open room lined with rows of cabinets. "Let me show you what you have come to see."

Their guide walked toward the first row of cabinets, which had tables interspersed between. "The building is separated by which areas of the world the plants have come from," he said. "The cabinets are labeled by country and in each cabinet you will find different collections." He turned back toward her. "Is there a particular country where you wish to begin?"

Lillian wanted to see all the plants they had, but the building was enormous and it would have taken weeks to accomplish it. "I would very much like to take advantage of your expertise, Dr. Vishna. Perhaps you would be willing to share some of the plants with which you are most familiar?"

The man's eyes lit up. "Of course. Please come this way. I will show you the newest collection I recently brought from Africa."

"Africa," she breathed. "I have no knowledge of plants from there. This will be very enlightening."

After two hours of engrossed listening and note-taking, she realized that Gabriel had been patiently attending alongside her the entire time. She doubted the lecture could be as interesting for him as it was for her. Although she would have spent as much time as she could soaking up more information, if she had had her way, it was not fair to her companion.

While the doctor was putting away the most recent case they had reviewed, she thought it would be a good time to stop for the day.

"Dr. Vishna," she said. "This has been incredibly instructive, and I would love to know more. However, I believe it is time to return home. Would it be presumptuous of me to ask if I may return again to learn more with you as my guide?"

He gave a broad, white-toothed smile. "Oh, yes. I would be very pleased to teach you more about the plants I have discovered and their medicinal qualities. It is not every day I find such an attentive pupil."

Lillian replaced the notebook in her bag and stood up from the table, rolling her neck a few times. She had been so engrossed in learning she had not noticed how tense her body had become from sitting in the same position.

"Perhaps a short walk before I return you home will restore your stiff muscles," Gabriel suggested.

She nodded. "Yes, thank you."

They followed the doctor to the door and she took the now sleeping Prince Albert from him. He lay like a limp rag in her hand, which made her smile. "When he sleeps, he really sleeps," she said.

Dr. Vishna chuckled. "It is the way of the ferrets." He bowed low to them. "I look forward to your return."

"Thank you for everything," she said, donning her bonnet and tying the ribbons. "I will send a note around to see if you are available when I can make time in my schedule."

She had to blink several times when they went back outdoors to adjust her eyes to the difference in the light. Although it was overcast, it was still brighter than inside the building. She took Gabriel's arm and allowed him to lead her down the stone-lined pathway that ran through the garden grounds. Kew Gardens was an extensive property with miles of greenery and gardens surrounding Kew Palace and beyond. Lillian took a moment to drink in the lush view.

Gabriel really had been very kind, thinking of her interest in herbs and planning an excursion, which would allow her to collect more information for her herbal. That was not something he had had to do. When they had first made their bargain, she had expected to have little to do with him other than visiting the people on his list to see if one of them was the murderer. Now, they had had two outings, their families had dined together, and they were in the midst of arranging a house party at his country seat. This whole situation was turning into something she had never planned on. What she still had yet to decide was whether this was a good thing or a very bad one.

"It was incredibly kind of you to bring me here today, Gabriel. What made you think of it?"

Gabriel had no immediate answer to Lillian's question. He had heard about the herbarium from a passing comment made by a member of the club, and he had thought she might like to see some of the collections. It was not usual for him to do something simply for someone else's benefit without gain for himself. It felt good seeing how much Lillian was enjoying herself.

He shrugged. "I thought you might enjoy the outing, and it seems I was correct."

"Oh yes," Lillian breathed. "I could spend entire days here without losing interest, and Dr. Vishna is ever so knowledgeable." She chuckled lightly and patted her comatose pet. "However, it seems Prince Albert was not so sanguine as I."

He smiled. "How did you come to own a ferret, may I ask?"

"That is an interesting story," Lillian said. "Traveling gypsies, or the Roma as they call themselves, often came to stay on the lands where Silvano's School was located. Their presence was a wonderful chance for the students to interact with people who would not judge us." She stopped to take the sleeping pet from her shoulder and place him in the bag she carried. "He will be more comfortable inside here."

They began walking again. "One day we went out to visit the Roma. Some students liked to buy their wares, but I liked talking to the healers about their remedies."

"Of course you would," Gabriel said with a grin.

"One of the young men had a ferret he was teasing with something he had fashioned from a stick and some string. I was amused and stopped to watch. After a few minutes, the animal stopped its play, noticed me, and scampered over. He stood up on his back legs and stared at me. 'He wishes you to pick him up,' the young man had said. I did so, and he settled onto my shoulder. The man told me to scratch the ferret behind the ears and he would be my friend for life."

Gabriel nodded at a gentleman who passed them on the pathway.

Lillian continued. "When it came time to go back to the school, I tried to give the ferret back to the man, but Prince Albert would not leave me. I put him on the ground and he scrambled back up my skirts. I tried to hand him over, but he turned back around and climbed up my arm." She laughed at the memory. "We were drawing a crowd at this point and one of the elders of the group came forward. He said, 'An animal chooses who he wishes to be with and this one chooses you. Take him with our blessing.' "

She turned her head to look at him. "I tried to refuse. I mean, what was I to do with a ferret? I had never had so much as a cat or a dog as a pet, but I eventually caved, as I did not wish to offend the people who had been so kind to us. That is how I acquired Prince Albert."

Gabriel gave a bark of laughter. "That is quite a tale. Did you name him or was that what the Roma called him?"

"You may not believe me, but he named himself."

He cleared his throat and raised an eyebrow. "Truly?"

"Yes. One of the other students at Silvano's has the ability to speak to animals and she told me that he wished to be called Prince Albert."

He stopped abruptly. He did not know why he was surprised. She had told him the school they attended was for people with unusual gifts. "There is a person who can speak to animals?"

"Yes. She is from India, like Dr. Vishna."

He nodded. "That is extraordinary though." Then he huffed out a laugh. "What kind of ferret wants to be known as Prince Albert? What an odd creature."

Lillian laughed alongside him at the thought.

As the stone path took them through a thick stand of trees, they walked in silence, and he imagined again the endless possibilities of having access to these students with such incredible powers.

Lillian turned at the sound of pounding feet and saw her friend running toward them. "Turpentine, what on earth are you doing here?"

"Catriona sent me," he said breathlessly, "and there is little time." He bent over taking several gasps of air.

"What is it?" she rapped out.

"Catriona said there would be a man here today who would shoot the duke. We need to get you out of here." Turpentine quickly scanned the area. No one was visible. "Now." He grabbed her sleeve.

"Does she know who this man is?" Gabriel demanded from over her shoulder.

Turpentine shook his head. "No. Most times she only knows about the event itself and very little of the details."

"If what you say is true, this is most likely a man I have been searching for over the past four years, and I need to capture him," Gabriel said tightly.

Lillian turned and grasped Gabriel's coat lapels desperately. "No. It is not safe for you. We are out in the open with no way to see who could be hiding among the trees. Let us leave as Turpentine suggested."

What happened next went by so fast it was if Lillian experienced only a fraction of a second of each event as one rolled into the next.

Turpentine called out, "I see him. Get down!"

He ran off toward the trees to their right.

A loud boom rent the air, causing terror to fill her chest.

Lillian felt a push at her back that caused her to knock hard into the duke.

His back slammed into the ground.

She landed on top of him with an 'oof!' as the wind was knocked out of her.

She struggled to breathe.

It was an eternity before Lillian's lungs began working again, and she was able to heave in great gulps of air. She looked down at Gabriel, whom she was sprawled over. His eyes were closed. "Gabriel, are you hurt?" she gasped out.

He blinked his eyes several times as if attempting to come to his senses. Lillian shook his sleeve. "Gabriel! Speak to me please."

He lifted his head slightly. "You do not need to shout. I can hear you from here. Why did you knock me to the ground?"

"That was Turpentine. Did you not hear the gunshot?"

"What?" he blinked his eyes, once again attempting to lift his head. Something was not right with him.

Dread clawed at Lillian's stomach. "Gabriel, are you hurt?" She was afraid to get up until she heard from Turpentine, but she knew time could be of the essence if Gabriel had been shot. She looked as far as she could down both ends of the pathway and into the trees, seeing no one. Surely the man trying to kill him would have run away by now. Lillian had to take the risk. She wrestled with her walking dress and got up on her knees in order to see more of her companion.

She hesitated before touching him. *Come on, Lillian. This is no time to let your old fears get in the way.* She straightened her shoulders and let her training as a healer take over. She ran a trembling hand across one arm, then the next.

"What are you doing?" Gabriel asked, his voice sounding groggy.

"I am looking for a bullet wound. Do you feel pain anywhere?"

"Devil of a headache."

"Anywhere else?" He did not answer. She worked to push down the growing panic. He should have been more responsive than this. "Can you sit up?" She attempted to pull at him, but he was too heavy and was of no help at all. She looked around wildly. Seeing Turpentine striding back toward them, she called out, "Hurry, I need your help."

He ran the remainder of the way, then crouched down by Gabriel. "The shooter got away," he said breathlessly. "Was the duke hit?"

"I cannot tell, but something is wrong. Help me get him upright." Turpentine did as she asked. They both stared down at the trembling hand he had used to push the duke upward. It was covered in blood.

Turpentine looked up, his wide brown eyes meeting hers. "The bastard got him, that's for sure."

Lillian cursed and scanned the area again. "Are you certain he is gone?"

He ran his clean hand through his hair. "Yes. He got away on horseback. 'Sides, Catriona said he was only after the duke."

"All right. Help me take his coat off, quickly." She concentrated on removing Gabriel's neckcloth while Turpentine wrestled with the coat.

"What happened?" Gabriel lifted his right hand and unsteadily put it to the back of his head. He let out a hiss and brought his hand back in front, staring at it.

Lillian looked down and cursed again when she saw more blood. "You have been shot," she answered in a wavering voice. She explored the back of his head and found a large lump. "And you have hit your head on the pavement, which means we have double the trouble." She looked up bleakly at her friend.

"Nah," Turpentine said, running a hand through his hair again. "He probably will not even need stitches for that." He finally got the coat free and immediately found the location of the wound. Blood was spreading from his left shoulder. "He got shot in just the right place for a speedy recovery."

"How would you know?" Lillian snapped.

Brown eyes flicking back and forth met hers. She had seen this before in a panicked gaze. "I am just trying to say the sorts of things you told Tommy when he got bit by that mean old dog back at school."

Lillian took a deep breath and ran a trembling arm across her perspiring forehead. Her ill temper would do none of them any good. "I apologize, Turpentine. I have no experience with gunshot wounds."

"I imagine it is no different from any other injury you have dealt with before. Tell me what you want me to do."

She got up and motioned Turpentine out of the way. "I need you to find transportation while I hold this neckcloth against the wound." She went through ideas in her head of how they were to get him home. The park was still deserted. "We came in his curricle, but it is too far back to where it is parked in front of the herbarium to carry him there."

He got up to do as asked. "I will figure it out."

"Please hurry, Turpentine," Lillian urged, "and be careful."

He gave a quick nod and took off at a run back down the path.

She pressed the cloth hard into Gabriel's shoulder, causing him to wince. It was awkward attempting to hold the large man upright while pressing on the wound, all while kneeling. She imagined there would be bruises all around in the morning. "You are going to be fine," she said, more to reassure herself.

She let go of Gabriel's back, awkwardly using her knee as a brace, and opened her bag to check on Prince Albert. The ferret was sleeping the day away as if nothing had happened, his breathing deep and even. That was one less worry.

She did not have to wait long before the curricle came rolling down the narrow pathway with Turpentine at the reins, a brown horse tied to the back.

He jumped down. "I am going to have to do some fancy

driving, Lil, with me standing on the footboard, but I think we can have him home in no time. First, we need to get him into the seat." He pulled on Gabriel's arm. "Here we go, Duke!" he grunted. "Can you stand?" With her help, they got his dead weight into a clumsy standing position. She wrapped his injured arm around her shoulder. "Now here is the tough part, Duke," Turpentine said. "You must climb into your vehicle there."

The two of them supported him while Gabriel slowly and shakily put one foot in front of another. Turpentine had to give more than one strong push to help the duke into the seat. He slumped there while Lillian scrambled up and then helped Gabriel to get more comfortable by leaning him against her shoulder. She pressed on his wound again, but his confusion and inability to move well made her more worried about the head injury now.

Lillian handed the reins to Turpentine, who held them while standing in front of Gabriel. They were like a circus show event. She only prayed they would make it to the duke's home in time. It would take at least an hour to travel the eight miles through London traffic.

She was unable to keep from continually scanning along the road for the shooter, returning to finish Gabriel off. "Did you see the man with the gun?" she asked her friend.

"He was too far off by the time I got there to get a good look."

"Did you see anything?"

"Brown horse, rifle, clean shaven man with a dark cap pulled low and a dark coat. That's all."

It was very little to go on.

By the time they arrived at Wyvern House, Lillian was exhausted from holding it together emotionally and keeping Gabriel upright.

The front door opened, and the butler stepped out. "Pennywhistle," Lillian called, "Wyvern has been injured. We need help to get him inside and please send for a doctor and a constable immediately!"

"Yes, my lady." Pennywhistle disappeared behind the door.

Turpentine jumped down from the curricle and handed the reins off to a footman. "Shall I heave him down?" he asked.

"No!" Lillian nearly yelled. "Let his servants manage it. I do not want to cause further injury."

The front door opened again, with a bang this time, and a gigantic man strode out like an earthquake. "What's happened then?"

"He has been shot in the left shoulder and got a knock in the head when he fell," Lillian explained.

The man cursed, and in one fell swoop, he had Gabriel over his shoulder and was heading into the house. Lillian had hoped for the duke to be handled more delicately. She scrambled down to follow, but remembered her friend who was now untying the horse from the back of the curricle. "Turpentine, thank you for what you did."

"I did not really do anything, now did I?" he asked in

self-disgust. "I was supposed to keep the duke from getting shot and I botched it."

"It was not your fault. You made every attempt to make us leave. Besides, I believe you knocked us down in time." The push that had put Lillian and Gabriel on the ground had not come from any hand. "It could have been worse."

"Yeah, I suppose." He shrugged and looked down at the ground.

"I am very grateful you were there. It is because of you we were able to get the duke home so very quickly."

Turpentine blushed. "I shall just be on my way, yeah?"

"I need to go look after the duke. I will speak to you later."

Turpentine saluted, mounted his horse and rode down the street.

When Lillian turned back around, Pennywhistle was at the door. "My lady, perhaps I can call Mrs. Cartwright to help you." He eyed the blood on her gloves and pelisse.

"None of it is my blood. I am quite well. I need to stay with the duke until the doctor comes. Take me to him."

"I get nothing but bossy women in this house," Lillian heard him mutter as he led her up the stairs to the duke's suite.

"That reminds me, do you think the duchess should be summoned?" Lillian asked.

"Her grace is shopping," he said over his shoulder, "and should return shortly. I shall apprise her of the events as soon as she walks over the threshold."

"How long before the doctor comes?" she asked anxiously.

"I sent our fastest groom after Dr. Collins the moment you arrived," he said. "It should not be long, but for now, Jersey, his grace's valet, has some basic medical training and can take care of him."

Lillian was relieved by this news. She picked up her pace, nearly running into Pennywhistle's back. The man only seemed to have one speed, and it was not fast enough.

When they reached the duke's room, Lillian burst in and saw that behemoth of a man bent over Gabriel, who lay on a large bed with heavy dark red curtains.

"How is he?" she asked urgently.

Jersey looked at Pennywhistle. "What's she doing here? No place for a lady."

Pennywhistle bowed. "Forgive me, Oh Great and Powerful One, but she insisted and now that I have done my duty, she is in your hands."

"Fine," the valet said gruffly. "You stay over there near the door then and tell me what happened."

The butler started to leave, but the valet's voice stopped him.

"Pennywhistle, get a message to Raven. Tell him Lion's down for the unforeseeable future and he's in charge. Tell him to start searching for the bastard who did this."

"Of course," the butler said before he left, closing the door.

What an odd assortment of menservants Gabriel employs, she briefly thought.

"Now, start talking," Jersey said to Lillian.

She worried her skirts, clutching them and letting them go. "I hardly know what happened. We were walking on one of the pathways of Kew Gardens." Lillian took a deep breath to gather herself, then continued, "We had just stopped to talk to a friend of mine and were preparing to leave when a shot rang out. My friend pushed us to the ground and ran in the direction of the shot to see if he could find the culprit. When I felt it was safe, I assessed Wyvern's wounds and my friend and I brought him home."

"Did anyone see the man with the gun?" Jersey asked.

"My friend, but he said he did not get a very good look at him—not enough to identify him at least."

The valet had a cloth in his hand. He put it in a basin of water on the table beside him, then wrung it out. Lillian watched as the water turned to blood. Her stomach lurched. He went back to wiping Gabriel's wound, she assumed, as she could not see around his broad back.

"Is he conscious?" she asked, noticing a small quaver in her voice.

Jersey poked at Gabriel's other shoulder. "Are you awake, Duke?"

She heard a slap, likely Gabriel batting the hand away. "Stop that," Gabriel whispered hoarsely.

"Yeah, he's awake," Jersey said. "Just been through an ordeal is all. He'll be fine once he is patched up and gets some rest. Now tell me about this friend of yours. What's his name?"

Lillian cleared her throat and began tapping her foot. *When is the doctor coming?* "Um. I call him Turpentine, but his real name is Jack Walker. I have no idea where he lives. He is a good kid." She was babbling. She never babbled. She finally took the initiative to walk around the bed to see Gabriel's condition for herself.

She gasped at the hole just below his left shoulder.

"I told you this wasn't a place for a lady," Jersey growled. To Gabriel he said, "You sure know how to pick them, mister!"

Lillian leaned over the bed, trying to ignore the fact that Jersey had removed the duke's shirt. "Gabriel." When he did not respond, she said his name again a little louder, "Gabriel!"

He blinked his eyes a few times and said, "What?"

"You are going to be just fine. I have heard that your valet knows a thing or two about patching up a person." She tried to put a smile in her voice. She reached out and squeezed his hand. He squeezed back, but not as strongly as Lillian would have liked.

"I know." He opened his eyes and turned his head to look at her. His eyes widened. "Jersey, tend to Lillian first," he slurred. "She is bleeding."

Lillian shook his hand slightly. "No, Gabriel. None of this is my blood. It is all yours."

"Promise?"

"Yes. I promise." She tried to make a joke of it. "You bled like a stuck pig! I bet your mother is going to be quite upset about the ruined linens."

He chuckled lightly as she hoped. "My mother is going to be upset about something."

A knock on the door interrupted their conversation. When Jersey called out, "Come," a man carrying a black bag entered. At the sight of the doctor, her stomach loosened, but only the tiniest bit.

"Now is the time for you to leave the room, my lady. No arguing," Jersey said sternly.

She nodded, too tired to quarrel.

She squeezed Gabriel's hand one more time. "I will not be far away." She tried to let go, but he held fast to her hand. Then he tugged slightly. She moved closer. "What? What is it?"

"I am sorry."

"For what?" she asked, confused.

Gabriel's eyes were closed, and for a moment she thought he had finally slipped into unconsciousness, but then he continued, "You told me to leave and I would not. I thought I could finally get the bastard who was after me. Please forgive me."

She leaned in even closer and said, "I am unhurt, Gabriel."

"I put you in danger."

"Let us not trade in what ifs," she said softly. "Nothing happened to me that a good wash with water and soap will not cure. You mark my words," she shook his hand once for emphasis, "we will get the man who is responsible for this."

He nodded almost imperceptibly, as if he had no more strength.

Lillian left the room and quietly closed the door. She leaned back against it. Today had felt similar to experiencing one of her visions where she was nothing but a helpless observer, but this time it was someone she knew who had been hurt. God, she never wanted to go through this again.

From out of nowhere, Pennywhistle appeared. "Come this way, my lady and Mrs. Cartwright will help you to refresh yourself and bring you some tea."

"Thank you, Pennywhistle."

With a trembling hand, Lillian brushed aside several wisps of hair from her face, then pushed away from the door. She had just made a promise to Gabriel that they would get the man responsible for today's attempt on his life. She had already agreed to that when she accepted his bargain, but now it was personal.

The killer had made a crucial error today. Now, Lillian was more determined than ever to expose him.

TWENTY

Signor Silvano's Sayings Number 20
When you do what you must
in order to survive—feel guilty or not,
but never apologize.

Francesca jolted awake. She was not certain what had woken her, but she was groggy and disoriented. Her mouth felt as if it had been stuffed with cotton, and her vision was hazy. She blinked several times to clear her eyes before looking around, only to realize she was not at home in her bed, but in a moving coach with a gentleman sitting on the opposite seat, reading a book.

Panic gripped her. She scrabbled for the door handle, hoping she could fling herself out of the carriage to safety.

"You should not do that," the man said pragmatically. "This coach is drawn by four horses, which means we are going fast enough that if you open that door and attempt to get out, you will likely break your neck."

Francesca looked again at the man who was calmly observing her with his piercing green eyes. He might have been a lying fiend, but he was right about one thing. It would be better in the long run if she sat back and made a plan while her captors were lulled into believing she would follow along meekly like a lamb to slaughter.

She refused to be forced into an insane asylum.

She slumped back and turned to look at the space beside her. How had Francesca not noticed the other woman? "Mildred? How could you?" She never would have thought Mildred would go along with a scheme to have her locked up.

"Everything is right and tight, my lady," the maid soothed. "We are rescuing you, aren't we?"

"Rescuing?" Francesca had never felt so lost in her life.

Holding a folded paper out toward her, the man spoke again, "Lady Lillian has sent this note to be given to you upon your wakening. It explains the situation. She did not wish for you to have any concerns."

"More like a bloody fright," the maid grumbled under her breath.

Francesca snatched the note from the man's hand. She could not tell if he was a villain or if he spoke the truth. Her mind was still so cloudy her ability was not working.

A brief glance at the contents told her it certainly was from Lillian. Francesca knew her handwriting well.

Dear Fran,

I was concerned that you would wake, startled to be in a carriage with a stranger, so I put it upon myself to explain the situation in its entirety.

Yesterday, I visited your home to find out what had happened to you—it is unlike you to ignore me for so long. I shall be forever grateful I did. I found you lying in a drugged state, unable to be awakened even by the most vigorous of shaking.

Sarah had learned of your parents' plans to send you to an asylum to be cured of female hysteria. I am angry from simply writing those words. You are the least hysterical person I know!

Instantly, I knew I must find a way to rescue you. For this, I begged the Duke of Wyvern for assistance—the only one I could think of who might have the resources to render such aid—and, blessedly, assist us he did.

As discreetly as possible, we packed your things, as many items as we could in the time we had. Then in the dead of the night, Wyvern—and I do not know who else—were let into the house by Thomas and Mildred, and spirited you and your trunks away to the carriage in which you are currently riding. It is owned by Viscount Hartley, who will accompany you, Mildred, and Thomas to the duke's home in Kent until such a time as you recover from the laudanum and further plans can be made.

Mildred and Thomas are now in the duke's employ since they had no wish to stay in your former home after they saw the state your parents and Mrs. Pettibone had put you.

I shall see you in less than a fortnight when we arrive in Kent and will fill in the remaining details. In the meantime, know that you can have complete confidence in the integrity of Viscount Hartley, who will see you safe and well to Ramsay Hall.

With all my heart,
Lil

Francesca's hands were shaking by the time she finished reading. She was not sure whether it was from the effects of the laudanum or from the sheer relief of being rescued. Because of her ability, she had known for some time that her parents were considering this action against her, but she always hoped their desire for the good opinion of society would force them to put up with her. The incident at dinner must have tipped the scales toward the asylum.

She took a deep breath to calm her nerves before speaking. "Thank you." The words came out at less than half strength. She cleared her throat and tried again. "Thank you both for what you are doing for me." She looked at Mildred, then at the viscount. "My mind still feels like it is filled with a thick fog, so I do not fully understand all that has happened, but I do understand the gravity of the situation I was in."

Mildred patted her arm and said, "Thomas is up with the driver. He and I will take good care of you, my lady, at least until you might decide you don't need us."

Francesca smiled. She had always liked Mildred and her forthright manner. She was a few years older than Francesca, short and sturdily built, with dark brown hair—such a contrast from her own tall frame and flaming red hair.

She had never been assigned her own maid, as her mother preferred to have Mrs. Pettibone to attend to her needs—the better to keep her under the family thumb, Francesca knew.

"I believe we shall do very well together, Mildred. You understand my needs better than anyone in the household ever did. I would very much appreciate if you would take on the duties of my lady's maid." There were few in the Effingham household who knew about Francesca's odd ability and even fewer who did not judge her for it. Mildred was one of them.

The woman's face grew into one huge smile. "Oh, thank you, my lady!"

The viscount shifted positions across the carriage. This entire time he had been completely silent. How refreshing. She took a moment now to appraise him. He was a fairly young man, not much older than her nearly eighteen years, although the sideburns made him look more mature. He had dark blond hair that was short and straight and a reserved air.

"I do not believe we have been introduced in town, my lord," Francesca said. "Why is that? I thought my mother had introduced me to every eligible young man in all Christendom."

"Perhaps, my lady, it is because I specifically do not attend *ton* events for that very reason. I prefer not to know every giggling young lady fresh from the schoolroom." The man did not smile in that false way many young gentlemen of society did. In fact, he did not smile at all.

"I do not giggle," Francesca grumbled.

"I beg your pardon. I did not mean to lump you into that group. I merely meant I choose to avoid young ladies altogether." He gave a bow—the best he could while sitting in the confines of the carriage. "Valentine Montgomery, Viscount Hartley, at your service—and before you say it, I know." He grimaced. "My mother was cruel to give me such a romanticized name."

"Especially since you are a man who prefers to avoid the sort of young ladies who would find it charming," Francesca smirked. She then bowed her head slightly and said, "Lady Francesca Grantham, daughter of a Lord and Lady Effingham who are better left unmentioned at present."

The viscount scowled. "I completely agree on that last point. It is a pleasure to meet you, although the circumstances are less than auspicious."

Francesca smiled slightly, then sagged against the seat, allowing the full feeling of freedom to cascade over her. Not only had she escaped her parents' hateful plans for her, but she would never have to deal with them again. Thank the almighty, everlasting, merciful God.

She watched the trees go by through the window and enjoyed the quiet inside the carriage.

It was such a welcome change from the constant cacophony of voices that lived in her head.

Her eyes snapped up and she looked wildly at the other two occupants as she realized it was *too* quiet in here. She concentrated first on Mildred, then on the viscount, but heard nothing.

Francesca's first thought was to panic. She had never been without the extra sense, and its sudden absence left her shocked. Then she realized that the excess of laudanum likely had dulled all her senses including her ability to hear the voices. She decided to wait to see if they returned or if she would need to learn to adjust to a new way of life. She was getting a new life of sorts as it was.

The viscount broke the silence. "You have slept through what was left of the night and into the morning. We have changed horses once already, but kept your servants hidden away during the change. We do not want anyone associating this carriage with them, since they will be suspiciously absent from your household. We have no way of knowing if your parents will send out people looking for you, but we cannot take any chances."

Francesca nodded her understanding of the facts.

"We have been traveling at a slower pace to allow you to rest, but I am sure you will very soon need a chance to stretch your legs and use the convenience. We shall be stopping at an out of the way inn a couple of miles ahead where you can do so." He looked at her gravely. "It is very important that you and your maid stay completely covered by your cloaks the entire time, speak to no one, and return to the carriage in—shall we say five minutes?" He pulled out his pocket watch to check the time. "I shall do all the talking and will order enough food for the remainder of the journey. I imagine you are hungry."

This man was very business-like, but Francesca was relieved to know that he was in command enough to handle the particulars of a rescue. "I had not thought about food yet, my lord, but thank you."

He gave a short nod.

She closed her eyes to rest a bit more, but the sensory deprivation she was experiencing was disorienting. She could not decide which was better—the familiar noise or the alarming silence.

Several minutes later, like a faint light at the end of a long tunnel, she heard it: Mildred's voice whispered in her head. "Got to write my sister. Will need to be fast at the inn. No time to dillydally."

The maid's voice had always been quieter than most and everything was stated in a list. She tried once again to hear the man across from her, but it was like a great void—not even a small buzz or whisper. After several minutes, she could stand it no longer.

"What are you thinking of, my lord?" From the corner of Francesca's eye she could see the maid give her an odd look.

The viscount, who had been staring as if at an unseen

distance, focused his eyes on her. "I was thinking through every step of our journey and creating strategies for keeping you safe." He paused. "Why do you ask?"

Francesca shrugged as if it did not truly matter, but her heart was pounding in her chest. All that had been going through his head and she was unable to hear a word of it? What could it mean?

She did not have long to ponder it, as the carriage soon pulled into an innyard. When it stopped, the viscount said, "Wait here," and hopped out before the steps could be put down.

Francesca put a shaky hand to cover her eyes and let out a big sigh. "Mildred," she asked uncertainly, "am I dreaming? None of this feels quite real."

The maid patted Francesca's other hand resting on her lap. "Everything will be just fine, you'll see. It's that nasty laudanum what's made your head a bit muddled. His lordship is to take us somewhere safe where you can rest."

Francesca nodded behind her hand. There was little else to be said.

They would not allow her to see Gabriel. Lillian had tried again that morning, but had been turned away at the door—Pennywhistle not even allowing her into the entrance hall of Wyvern House. She was pacing her room madly now, although she had other things she should be doing. *How is he faring?* She kept imagining the worst, but surely if he had died since Friday, they would have told her; the door of his home would have been draped in black.

"You are going to wear a hole in the carpet if you keep that up."

Lillian stopped at Anne's words. "What?" She was so caught up in her own worries she had not noticed her friends were in the room. Anne and Sarah gave her mirrored looks of concern.

"Wearing yourself out like that is doing the duke no good," Sarah said. "You should work on your herbal or go take a walk. Anything is better than this."

Lillian paced to the bench beneath her bedroom window and sank into it. "It has been two full days and a half now since the shooting, and I have had no word regarding his health or the state of the investigation. I cannot sit here and do nothing. Perhaps you, Sarah, or one of the footmen can go to Wyvern's and find out what is happening? No one will tell me anything."

Anne came and sat beside her. "It will be all right. You said yourself it was just a flesh wound."

"People die of putrid flesh wounds all the time!" she wailed.

Sarah gave her an indulgent look as she took the remaining place next to Lillian. "With the high level of care he is receiving, I highly doubt that will occur, but I will tell you what I can do." She patted Lillian's knee. "I shall pop around to the kitchens at his house and see what I can learn. Will that put you at ease?"

Lillian worried her bottom lip with her teeth. She was too anxious to sit here and wait for her friend's return. It would drive her just as crazy. "No, I am coming with you."

Sarah cleared her throat. "Will it not look odd when you, a lady, show up at the kitchen door?"

She bit her lip again, thinking. What reason could she give to appear once more at the Gabriel's house? She had been turned away twice before. Then an idea came to her. "I know. I will mix together some herbs to make a strengthening tonic. Since they would not allow me in the front door, I will have no choice but to bring it to the back." She jumped up and hurried to the table on which her herbal case sat. "Go retrieve our outdoor things, Sarah. I will only be but a moment."

Once she had an envelope prepared with the medicinal, she sealed it, said goodbye to Anne and met Sarah downstairs in the front hallway. "Let us walk. We could be there by the time a carriage is prepared, and I need to walk off some of my anxiety."

As the crows flew, she only lived two blocks away from Grosvenor Square, but by the time they walked down a few streets, it was closer to half a mile. When they reached Wyvern House, they descended the back stairs that led to the servant's entrance and knocked.

A young maid who looked to be barely more than fourteen years old answered. "Yes?" she asked.

"I am Lady Lillian, the duke's betrothed. I am hoping you can tell me how he fares? Pennywhistle would not let me in the front door, which was most preposterous of him, I must say, so I have been forced to seek information here."

The maid stared at her, goggle-eyed.

Lillian cleared her throat loudly. "What is your name?"

That got the girl's attention. "Jenny, my lady." She spoke with a slight Scottish accent.

"Good. Jenny, can you tell me how his grace is recovering from his injury?"

The maid frowned. "From what I've heard in the kitchens, my lady, he took a fever in the night. They have sent someone to fetch the family doctor."

Lillian pushed past the girl. "Show me how to get to his room from here." Under her breath she said to herself, "The doctor may know how to stitch up a bullet wound, but I am certain he will attempt to bleed the infection out of him. It is one of the most ignorant common practices of those from the medical profession." Without waiting for direction or her companion, she stormed through the kitchen.

She could hear Jenny behind her saying, "My lady, you can't go up there. It isn't proper."

"Show me the way, Jenny, or I will find him myself if I must look in every room in this house," she called over her shoulder. "I am certain there is a servants' stairway somewhere nearby."

The maid caught up to her and said in a more subdued voice, "This way, my lady." She brought them to a door that revealed a staircase when opened. They ascended one flight of stairs. At the top, Jenny stopped. "I shouldn't be on this floor without permission, my lady, but if you go down this hallway to where it ends, go to the right and it will be the last door at the end."

Lillian slipped her hand into the reticule hanging from her wrist and gave the girl a coin. "Thank you, Jenny. I will not tell a soul that you helped me."

She began marching down the hall as fast as her skirts would allow.

"This is madness, Lillian," Sarah said breathlessly from behind her. "What are you doing?"

"I need to hurry and reach Wyvern before the doctor does," she said. "If they attempt to bleed him, he will take longer to recover—if he does at all."

"I know your negative view on bloodletting, but surely this situation would not require such a course of action," Sarah said.

Lillian stopped in her tracks, causing her companion to bump into her. "Doctors use bloodletting and leeches to treat even the slightest of fevers, and I have seen their negative effects." Lillian sneered in contempt. "If he has a fever, he almost certainly has an infection. It has to be treated properly immediately. Many people have gone from an infected wound to death in a matter of only a few days." She began walking again.

She knocked sharply at the door they were instructed to find.

The door was opened and held by a surprised Jersey. He recovered quickly and asked with a scowl, "What're you doing here?"

She was determined in her mission and walked under Jersey's arm, through the door, before he could realize what she had done.

"Here now," he said. "There's no call for that."

She ignored him. "Your name is Jersey, is it not?" she asked absently. "Has the doctor arrived yet?" She looked around the room, and finding what she wanted, crossed to the wash basin. Since she did not trust the cleanliness of the water it already contained, she carried it to the window, put it down on the ledge while holding it in place with her hip, opened the window and sloshed the contents to the ground below. She returned and poured in fresh water.

She realized Jersey had not answered and turned in his direction. He stood in the middle of the room with his arms crossed over his chest like a huge stone statue.

Whatever his problem was, she did not have time for it. She made a sound of exasperation, removed her gloves, briskly washed her hands, and then dried them. She hurried over to the bed and felt Gabriel's forehead. He was very hot indeed. His cheeks were flushed red and his skin was dry. She pulled the bedclothes down slightly and noticed his chest was naked. She fought a blush and got back to work, pulling at the bandage on his shoulder.

"Here now!" Jersey stepped toward her and protested, "You can't be doing that."

"I can, and I am," she said. "Have you changed this bandage since Friday?"

"Of course I have," he said mulishly.

She looked around and spotted her companion. "Sarah, please find a basin in which to put these used linens."

She finally wrestled the rest of the bandage loose and bared the wound. The area around the stitches was red and swollen. "It could be worse," she said to herself. "At least the odor of the wound is only slight and the swelling has not spread."

Sarah handed her a basin, and she dropped the old bandage into it. "I am going to need my case of herbs, some fresh honey, and clean linens. Go to the house for my case please and I am sure we can find the other items here."

"I will be back in a trice," her companion said.

Jersey came closer and sighed loudly. "His nibs is not going to like this one bit."

She glared at him. "I rather think he will not mind at all if I help save his life."

"That's what the doctor is for!" Jersey roared.

"Yelling at me will not help your master. If your family doctor has some incredible remedy that will cure this infection, I will bow to his superior knowledge. However, I have seen from the many times doctors have visited ill students at my school, that they always try to bleed the patient before trying any other remedy, and this causes them to grow weaker." She straightened up, turned, and fully faced the block of a man before her, standing nearly toe to toe with him. "I have knowledge of healing herbs and experience with nursing the ill that may make the difference in whether Gabriel recovers or not." Her voice hitched at the end of her sentence and she had to swallow down the lump in her throat. "Can you think of one good reason I should not stay and help?"

"I'm sorry, did you just call that man my master?" He slowly crossed his arms over his chest once again. "Like I'm a slave or something?"

Lillian blinked. Of all the possible parts of her lecture he could have latched on to, she had not expected it to be this. He really was an unusual valet for a duke. From his conversation with Pennywhistle the other day, she had assumed he assisted Gabriel with his endeavors as head of a spy organization. She could see how having a man the size and build of a bull by his side probably afforded a great deal of protection.

She cleared her throat. "It was merely a figure of speech. Now, may I get on with it or must we have a tussle here by Wyvern's bedside?"

Jersey smiled mischievously. "Oh, I wouldn't mind a little tussle with you. I believe you would be up for the challenge, but I don't think his loftiness would like it." He uncrossed his arms and relaxed his posture. "Now tell me what you need, since it appears you won't take no for an answer."

She did not wait for the man to change his mind. "I need fresh honey, clean linen, and hot water to start. Oh, and I will need a tea tray sent up, but just boiling water in the pot. I am going to make an herbal tea."

Jersey saluted. "Right you are, lass."

Lillian took the time alone in the room to study Gabriel. At least he was sleeping peacefully and his breathing was stable. In his relaxed state, his face was softer somehow. More approachable. She absently pushed back a lock of dark, curly hair that had fallen onto his forehead.

She yanked her hand back and looked at it as if it had been burned. When had she removed her gloves? Her heart began to pound and her breath stuttered.

Breathe in. Breathe out. Repeat.

She was not going to die because her hands were uncovered, and so far she had had no visions from touching Gabriel.

She took another deep breath and readjusted the covers. There was nothing else she could do except cool his brow until the supplies arrived. She refreshed the water in the basin once more and soaked one of the cloths from the washstand into it. She laid it over his burning forehead.

Lillian looked down at her hands again. Each day, circumstances were pushing her further toward what one might consider a normal life. It felt like she was being swept away by a tide of change. She only hoped she could keep her head above water. She brushed the idea to the side. Her problems could wait.

Right now she needed to concentrate on Gabriel's recovery and how she was going to convince the doctor to let her treat him.

TWENTY-ONE

Jersey burst into Gabriel's room with an entire entourage behind him—maids carrying supplies, Sarah, and Dr. Collins, a middle-aged gentleman with dark hair, graying at the temples. Lillian would have rushed over to retrieve her case, but she did not wish to allow the doctor free access to Gabriel.

"If you will allow me, I would like to examine the patient," Dr. Collins said, having come up beside her.

"She won't budge, Doctor," Jersey said with a grin from the other side of the bed, clearly enjoying the scene. "She's like a guardian angel brandishing a sword."

Lillian lifted her chin defiantly. "I will not let you bleed him."

Dr. Collins smiled kindly. "I am glad to hear it, for I have never agreed with the practice."

From just inside the doorway, Sarah said, "I have your case, my lady."

The doctor raised his eyebrows. "What have we here?"

He nodded toward the leather bag in her companion's hands.

"My herbs. I have some remedies that will be of great benefit," she said in a tone that dared him to argue.

He did not. Instead he moved forward, forcing Lillian to take a step back or be pushed over, and examined the injury. "Yes, I see. Wyvern has a bit of an infection in the wound." Still leaning over, he turned his head toward her. "What are these remedies you wish to recommend?"

Lillian was so surprised by the question, she hesitated before answering. "I would try an application of honey first, since his case does not appear dire, along with some willow bark tea for the fever. If the honey does not begin to work, I can make a poultice of crushed garlic and mustard. If I had some fresh yarrow, I would use that instead, but I do not suppose it is found in great quantities in London." She finally wound down and took a breath.

Dr. Collins looked thoughtful for a moment and then said, "I agree with your choice of remedies. I do know an herbalist here in town who might have some yarrow if you would care to send someone around to her shop." He reached into his bag and rummaged around until he came out with a small pad of paper and a pencil. He scribbled something on it. "However, if the infection has gone too deep, you will need something more aggressive." He tore off the top paper and handed it to her. "Here is the name of the herbalist."

"Thank you," she said quietly. She had expected a fight.

He turned to Jersey and said, "It appears her ladyship has

all in hand. There is nothing more I would do in a situation like this unless it becomes far worse." He turned back to Lillian. "If it further swells, changes colors, or he has trouble breathing, you must send for me at once."

"Of course," she said.

The doctor smiled. "I can see Wyvern is fortunate in his choice of a future bride. I doubt he could find finer care in all England."

She returned the smile. "I know you exaggerate, but I thank you for the compliment and your expertise today."

He nodded, collected his bag, and left.

Lillian breathed a sigh of relief that she had won that battle.

She could now get on with what she had come to do in the first place: save Gabriel's life. She looked at the trays brought up by the maids. One had the teapot full of steaming water and another held the honey jar and cloths. She went to her case which Sarah had placed on a table and found the jar of willow bark. She sprinkled some in a teacup and poured the hot water over it to steep.

She handed the name of the herbalist to Jersey and said, "Can you send someone to this address and find out if they have any yarrow? I need the leaves, and they must be fresh. Dried will not suffice. This is very important."

"Your wish is my command, Magnificent One," Jersey said with an exaggerated bow. "You won over that doctor like a mesmerist."

"Ha!" she barked. "Hardly,"

He raised one silent eyebrow in argument, then left the room.

Lillian inwardly smiled at the valet's recognition and got to work. She replaced the water in the basin with some of the fresh hot water, took it to the bed, and cleaned the wound so it would be ready for the application of honey. She patted the area dry with a fresh cloth.

"Sarah, can you bring the honey? I am ready to make use of it."

She took the honey from her companion and the spoon she held out. She drizzled it over the wound, then spread it lightly and evenly with her fingers.

She briskly wiped her hands clean. "That is all that can be done for the outside. Now I will see if I can get him to drink some tea." She looked up at Jersey, now returned, who stood quietly on the other side of the bed, merely watching. "When was the last time he took anything to drink?"

Jersey scratched his chin, thinking, then said, "Yesterday evening after I changed his bandage. He hasn't been awake yet today.

Lillian tsked. "That is not good." She went to the tea tray and strained the well-steeped willow bark tea into another cup and picked up a fresh spoon. She quickly realized she would have little success spooning the liquid into Gabriel's mouth without him choking on it. "Mr. Jersey, perhaps you can put another pillow behind Wyvern and lean him up a little higher?"

"That I can do," he said. He went to the dressing room

and returned with another pillow.

Once Gabriel was better positioned, she brought the spoon to his lips, but nothing happened. She had no idea what she had been thinking—that she would put the spoon before him and his lips would magically open?

"Here, this is what you need to do," Jersey said. He reached over, cupped one great hand around Gabriel's chin, and squeezed his cheeks until the lips made an O.

She inwardly shrugged. It would do. She carefully dribbled some of the liquid inside. After about a full spoonful, she saw his throat swallow. Her shoulders slumped in relief.

Once she had managed to get about a fourth of the cup into Gabriel, she cleared everything away and straightened the bedcovers once more.

"Now all we can do is wait and keep his brow cool," she announced to the room.

Jersey nodded. "I can do that if you would like to go home now." He gestured toward the door.

She snorted. "I thank you for the offer, but after all that, I am not going to leave him now. Besides, he may need additional care at some point."

Jersey smiled and shrugged. "I thought I would at least try."

Lillian shook her head at his attempts to get rid of her. She refreshed the cloth over Gabriel's forehead and resolved to search for a chair. Her back was beginning to ache from bending forward at such an odd angle for too long, but as soon as she turned to move, Jersey appeared with a plush wing-backed chair.

"Here you are," he said.

"Thank you, Jersey. It is exactly what I needed." She also needed a cup of tea and a good book to read, but she was not going to say that. Lillian sat down and looked up at the valet who was now on the other side of the bed. "Jersey, can you tell me what has been done to find the man who shot Wyvern?"

He folded his arms over his chest. "Well, I already spoke to your friend, Jack. He is an odd duck, that one."

Lillian smiled. She and all her friends could easily be described in that manner.

"Unfortunately, as you said, he didn't get a good look at the villain," he continued. "Our men scoured Kew Gardens for any clues, but found nothing. There were no other witnesses, and he left nothing behind."

"Which means we are no closer to finding him than we were before, and nothing but a bullet wound to show for it," she said, feeling deflated. "I am assuming this is the same man who killed his father?"

"Yep. That is the way of it on all counts." He tapped the side of his nose. "But I have a good feeling you are going to find him out soon, with this fancy gift of yours." He turned and went into the dressing room.

That confirmed Jersey was in Gabriel's highest confidence if he knew what she could do, as she did not believe the duke to be the kind of man who betrayed secrets.

She looked at him and saw he was resting comfortably. Time would tell if her remedies had worked. She reflected on the pride she felt when Dr. Collins had acknowledged her abilities in herbal healing and how Jersey had been impressed by it. Outside of Silvano's, she had never been recognized for anything other than her standing as a lady in society. It did feel good to be more than just a woman living in a constant state of anxiety and fear. Anne would be pleased to hear her say that.

Thoughts of her cousin made her realize that she had no idea what time it was and it would not be long before her mother discovered her missing. She closed her eyes and breathed in and out slowly several times as she had learned to do at school when under stress. "Gabriel will be fine. Everything will work itself out in time," she whispered to herself. She must believe it. She opened her eyes to discuss her latest problem with Sarah when the door opened and the duchess rushed in. Lillian had not once considered Gabriel's mother today until now.

"What is going on here?" the duchess asked, distress in her voice, as she hurried to the bed with Aunt Gemma and Aunt Gertrude trailing behind. "I understand Gabriel has taken a turn for the worse?"

Lillian nodded. "His wound is slightly infected and he has a fever. The doctor was here and agreed to my treatment. It will be a while yet before we know if he improves."

"You are treating him?" the duchess asked incredulously. "My dear, that will never do. You are an unmarried lady in a bachelor's bedroom. If word of this should get out ..." her words trailed off. She did not need to complete the sentence for everyone in the room to comprehend her meaning.

Lillian held her ground. "I understand, your grace, but if he should worsen, I have the necessary knowledge and experience to help him."

"I have heard you know something about healing plants, but that does not mean you are qualified as a doctor." She turned to Jersey. "Why did Dr. Collins not stay to watch over my son?"

Jersey shrugged. "He left her ladyship in charge."

"Left her in—" She broke off. "This is not acceptable. I must have Pennywhistle send for another doctor at once." Her voice began to tremble. "I have suffered enough loss in my family."

"I empathize with your concerns, your grace," Lillian stood, squeezing her hands together, "but if you call another doctor, he will merely want to bleed Gabriel, which will do far more harm than good by making him weaker than he already is." She desperately needed the duchess to agree with her. "I know it is unconventional to allow me to stay and nurse your son, but I ask you to give me a chance to make him well. I have cared for many of the students at my school during illnesses, and I promised Dr. Collins we would call for his return if Gabriel should worsen. I do not believe he would have left me in charge if he did not trust in my abilities." She paused and said solemnly. "I promise you that my knowledge of herbal remedies is truly his best chance at recovering from this infection."

"Theodora, dear," Aunt Gemma said softly, "I believe Lillian's suggestion is a sound one."

"Indeed," Aunt Gertrude said. "Give me a woman who knows how to properly apply medicinal plants over a male doctor with a lancet any day of the week."

The room was silent for several heartbeats before the duchess collected herself and let out a breath of resignation. "This is highly irregular, but I want Gabriel to get well, and if it is as you say, then I should allow you to continue." She turned to the valet. "Jersey, I need a chair, a tea tray, and a maid carrying my writing desk in that order, if you please. If this is the strategy we must employ for Gabriel's health, let us do it correctly." She sat primly across the bed from Lillian when the chair appeared. "Now, let me tell you what we are going to do to prevent any damaging gossip."

The plan was simple, and it amazed Lillian what a duchess could get away with. If she had tried to tell her parents that she was needed to assist another lady with some party planning and must therefore spend the night, they would have smelled the lie a mile away. A short note from her grace and the matter was settled. Her mother was probably dancing about her sitting room in raptures at the thought of her daughter being the personal guest of the duchess.

"Brilliant idea," Aunt Gertrude said sweetly. "Gemma and I will go back downstairs and get out of your way, but please ring if you need us to take turns watching over our dear Gabriel."

Lillian sank back into the plush chair and took a sip of the tea that Sarah had brought to her. It was nice to finally have a moment to rest and think. In the past fortnight, her life had been filled with one dramatic event after another. She was used to drama at school, but this was different.

The more she used her ability and became embroiled in Gabriel's schemes, the more she wondered if perhaps she had been wrong all this time about what she wanted. Life in the country, with nothing more than her correspondence and book-writing to keep her company, was beginning to seem dull compared to these recent experiences.

She took another sip of the warm, comforting drink and closed her eyes. She need not sort out her entire life today, which was good because the duchess was speaking to her.

"Tell me, how did my son propose to you?"

Contemplating the rest of her life suddenly seemed easier than finding an answer to this question. She took a deep breath, gathered all her courage, and lied.

Gabriel was becoming the worst kind of patient. He knew it, as did every one of his household staff. He did not like being confined to bed, and besides, he felt fine. Truly. But his mother was adamant that because of the head injury—which was very slight, in Gabriel's estimation—and the infection he had suffered, he should remain abed until it was time to leave for the house party. He growled under his breath. He could not recall the last time he had stayed in bed for more than a day and he had been stuck here for more than ten.

To top everything off, Jersey was doing all in his power to make him miserable. He refused to let him out of bed even to sit by the window and he kept up a continuous threat of withholding the news sheets if his master did not obey—those were his exact words. To further annoy him, his valet spoke with the most execrable accent more than half the time and butchered French the other half. He knew Hartley would be doing a fine job in charge of the Network, but Jersey refused to relay updates unless they were of the utmost importance. "Wouldn't want to worsen that knock in the brain box you took, would we?" he had claimed. The man knew his head was fine.

Worst of all, he would not give him any updates on Lillian. "She's shopping," was the only news Gabriel could get out of him. From what he had been told, she had stayed to nurse him until his fever broke a week ago Monday. How extraordinary—not only that she had done so, but that his mother had allowed it. More and more, Lillian was turning out to be everything he could hope for in a wife. When the worst had happened, she had faced it down like a true Amazon. He could not wait to see her again and find out how she fared after the ordeal.

Today was the last day he would be cowed into staying in bed. Tomorrow, there was work to be caught up on, a journey to prepare for, visits to make, and real food to eat, by God.

His mother breezed into the room and began fluffing the pillows behind his head. "You will be pleased to know," she announced, "we have everything in readiness for our trip to the country in two days' time." She bent her knees to look him in the eyes. "Do you believe you will be up for it by then?"

Gabriel hid his smile of glee and instead looked exasperated. "Mother, I have been ready to get out of this bed for a lifetime. I most certainly will be able." He stretched out his arm and bent it at the elbow several times. He kept the wince he wanted to make to himself so the duchess would not see it. "See, I am fit as a fiddle and ready for anything."

"I thought you would say so." She eyed him critically. "However, I might recommend you have that man of yours clean you up as soon as possible. You look like a pirate."

He chuckled. "If you would give him leave to do so, I might make some headway, but he has refused to so much as shave me until I have permission to get out of bed."

The duchess clucked her tongue and shook her head. "That man is a menace."

"I agree, but he is very good at what I employ him for," Gabriel said.

His mother scowled. "Every part except finding the man responsible for attempting to kill you once again."

"Mother, that is not fair and you know it. Jersey is doing all in his power to find the villain's trail. We will get him this time." Gabriel knew his mother was scared that the killer would succeed again as he had with his father, but he was not going to let it happen.

She nodded once. "Good. Now, send your man to my sitting room and I will inform him you are no longer on bed rest."

Gabriel grinned. Oh how he would love to be a fly on the wall during that conversation. He was elated that his jail sentence had been lifted and that he would be seeing Lillian in two days' time. Then at last the plan to bring down the bastard who had killed his father would begin.

Things were looking good. Very good indeed.

Lillian was sitting in her heavy wool nightgown in bed. As spring turned into summer, the temperatures did not appear to be rising much. After the stressful couple of weeks she had had, she had decided to relax with a good book and a tea tray by her side. The peace and quiet by herself would refresh her spirits.

Her mother was not pleased she would miss another night's worth of social events, but acceded due to the fact that Gabriel was recovering from his illness—this was what the duchess had told everyone—and she therefore could not be seen with him.

She was grateful he had turned the corner and now appeared to be on the mend. When the honey had not acted fast enough, several hours later, she had wiped the application away and applied the crushed yarrow leaves, which the herbalist had indeed had in stock. Yarrow was miraculous for wounds if one had it at hand.

Lillian was contemplating if she could find a way to grow

the plant indoors when Sarah interrupted her thoughts. "A maid just brought up a letter for you that got misplaced in the foyer and has just been found by Higgins." She handed her the missive.

Lillian broke the seal and read.

My Dearest Lillian,

I wanted to make you aware of a little uninvited guest who was recently discovered in our midst. As you know, it takes very little time before one of our Society members detects such people. Most interesting, which is why I write to you today, this person was sent here by the Duke of Wyvern to work as a maid, so she could gather information about us. Note to self: We must choose staff more carefully in the future. Perhaps, Lillian, you can speak to your duke and ask him never to do that again? I would consider myself grateful.

With all affection,
Silvano

Lillian gasped. He would not have dared! She read the note again. Apparently he would. So much for mutual trust.

"What is it?" Sarah asked.

Lillian was so livid she could not tell her friend. Instead, she jumped up out of bed, causing Prince Albert to tumble along with her, and handed the paper to her companion.

"What?" Sarah asked incredulously after reading. "Why would he do that?"

Lillian began to pace. "I have no idea, except he has mentioned how much our abilities could help 'catch enemies of England,' which is apparently the business he is in." She stopped to take a deep breath to calm herself. "But why he did not simply ask me for more information I do not understand." Prince Albert began to jump about the room, spinning and rolling.

"From what you have told me about his clandestine activities," Sarah said, "perhaps it is the only way he knows how to gather information and he is not used to asking directly for it."

Lillian whirled around to look at her friend. "Why must you always come up with a rational explanation for everything? Can you not simply allow me to be angry?"

"Oh, I am angry too," Sarah said. "Do not mistake me about that. This was not well done of him. If he is going to use your ability for his own aims, the least he could do is show you a little bit of respect."

"I thought you were in agreement with the bargain I made with Wyvern," Lillian said.

"I still am, but your duke needs to learn a thing or two about how to properly treat a lady and this," Sarah held the letter up in front of her, "is not how you treat a lady."

"For the thousandth time, he is not my duke," Lillian ground out.

Sarah shrugged. "For all intents and purposes, at the moment he is."

"Well, I will tell you one thing," she said. "Even if it is meant to buy my freedom, this betrothal will not continue if Gabriel cannot learn to ask me when he wants to know something. All this skulking about is ridiculous." She went to the cupboard which housed Prince Albert's toys and retrieved a stick with a string and a yellow feather on the end. She wiggled it in the air. "Here, Prince, play with me." She needed to work off some steam.

Prince Albert scuttled across the room and batted at the feather. She yanked it away before he could reach it.

"I think that is a very good idea," Sarah said.

"What?" Lillian looked up. "That I play with the little prince?"

Sarah smiled in amusement. "No, that you set some boundaries in your relationship with the duke. If he wants the benefit of your abilities, he must comply with your wishes."

"I agree." Prince Albert caught the feather this time and shook it wildly in his mouth. It looked like she would need to replace yet another one. "I will speak to him as soon as he is up from his sick bed and make certain we reach an understanding." She did not know what she would do if Gabriel did not listen. She had every intention of finding who shot him and killed his father, but their bargain had to continue for her to do so.

TWENTY-TWO

Signor Silvano's Sayings Number 22
If you cannot be safe in your own home
it is time to change your address.

Gabriel was more than pleased to be out of the house for the first time in days. At the earliest hour possible for a morning call, he took the opportunity to visit Lillian to see how she fared and to thank her for her care. As soon as he entered the sitting room, Lady Wentworth sailed in, Lillian not far behind.

"Wyvern! How good of you to come, and how glad I am to see you feeling well again after your illness." Lady Wentworth curtsied low. Grasping his arm, she steered him toward the settee. "Will you come in and sit down? There is a seat available right here." If she had had the strength, he thought, she might have pushed him down. As it was, he was intelligent enough to know a losing battle when he saw one, so he sat.

"Allow me to have tea brought in," she said. "I recall you are very fond of sweets. I shall be sure to have plenty sent up."

He drank the tea he did not truly want and carried on a polite conversation, biding his time until he could have a private word with Lillian.

After a considerate amount of time, he decided to take the situation in hand.

He stood up abruptly. "Lillian, it looks like it may rain; however, I believe we can enjoy a few moments outdoors before it does so. Would you care to accompany me for a short walk in your gardens?"

She nodded. "Yes, thank you."

The Wentworth town home could not boast a very large garden, but it was enough to have more than one path lined with beautiful roses and ornamental shrubbery.

"Gabriel—"

"Lillian—"

Both began at the same time. "Ladies first," he said with a small bow of his head. This reminded him of their promenade at the ball—neither looking at each other, tension between them. He wondered why.

"I was only going to say first, that you are looking well and second, I apologize for my mother's manhandling," she said stiffly. "I hope she did not reinjure your wound."

Gabriel chuckled. "Yes, I have never been manhandled in quite that way before. Not even by my own mother." He paused to think. "Well, perhaps by my mother, when I was very young and very naughty."

That had not gotten the laughing response Gabriel had expected. They had walked far enough away from the house now for privacy. He turned to look at her. The golden flecks in her brown eyes flashed brightly like reflections of the sun.

His perusal was short lived however. Lillian's nostrils flared as she spoke tightly. "I endured quite a shock last evening when I received a note from Signor Silvano informing me that you had placed a maid in the Benevolence Society for the purpose of uncovering information about us."

Damn. Gabriel shifted his stance uncomfortably.

Lillian took a step closer. "When I entered into this betrothal agreement with you, it was with the understanding that there would be mutual respect and trust between us. However, it appears you—" She took another step forward so she could poke her finger at his chest. "You," she repeated, "did not have the same understanding. Now, I would like to know what you are going to do about it." Before Gabriel could begin to speak, she added, "And you owe me an apology." Lillian's chest was rising and falling rapidly now.

He wanted to smile and laugh at her fierceness, but he did not believe she would take it as intended. Instead, he made his expression grave as he answered. "For more than four years, my family has been plagued by someone who wishes us dead. This was the entire reason I left the country for as long as I did. With my father dead and repeated attempts on both my life and my twin's, I felt the safest thing to do was for us both to get out of harm's way while my team flushed the man out. You were witness to the latest attempt."

"What has any of this to do with your betrayal of my trust?" Lillian asked.

He cleared his throat. "I want you to understand why I am so desperate to find out who is behind all this, which means I will use any resource at my disposal."

"You are still missing the point," Lillian said. "This was my family you went behind my back to spy on. If you wanted information, you should have asked me."

Gabriel put one hand on his hip and rubbed the back of his neck with the other. He knew he was in deep waters here, but it was difficult to make another person understand the depths he would go to in order to achieve his aims, and why he would never apologize for it. He blew out a breath. "I am used to gaining information by indirect means. I rarely simply ask for it as it is rarely simply given."

"I believe you must understand what trust means, Gabriel. The fact that you are willing to expect I am telling the truth about the visions I receive means you have a great deal of faith in my integrity. Why trust me with this, but not in all things?" Lillian paused, placed her hands on her hips, and let out a breath. "If this is going to work between us, you need to believe I will either give you the knowledge you seek or tell you that you cannot have it. Then you must respect that boundary." Her gaze paused on his eyes before she asked, "Can you do that?"

Could he?

Gabriel thought over her words. In his line of business,

he had learned to trust his own men, but rarely anyone else. Lillian was now not only on par with his men in this investigation, he expected her to become his wife.

"Yes, I can do that," he said. "I will endeavor to do better."

"Thank you," Lillian said softly as she took a step back. After a pause, she shook her head in confusion. "Wait. You said, 'Get us both out of harm's way.' I thought your brother was dead."

Gabriel's lips thinned. "Ah, yes. That was a lie we put about so Michael could safely go into hiding as he has done these past four years." He felt his jaw clench at what his brother had had to sacrifice. "Until I catch the man responsible, the world must continue to think him dead."

Lillian burst out, "Your twin! It must have been your twin who helped rescue me from being stranded outside London, several weeks past." She quickly told him the full story.

"I daresay it was Michael. When we first met and you said we had met before, I wondered if you had encountered my brother, but I could not understand what he would be doing in so public an inn."

"I have no idea what he was doing there."

"Hmm. Someday, when we are reunited, I must ask him about that. For a man in hiding, he was not doing it very well."

"Gabriel and Michael?" Lillian mused. "Was your mother living with the hope that by naming you after angels, you would behave as such?"

Gabriel chuckled. "That is what she said, but I do not think it worked as she planned." He sobered. "I miss him more than I can say."

Lillian reached out and softly touched his arm. "I am so sorry for all you must have suffered because of one person's evil."

"Thank you," he said, putting his hand over hers. He turned them back toward the house. "Now, shall we discuss the final details for our departure on the morrow?"

Wednesday was overcast, but thankfully no rain hindered their travel. Lillian had begged to ride beside Gabriel on the journey since she had had little opportunity for any lengthy rides since coming to London. They had an entire procession, with Gabriel, Jersey and Lillian riding out front, six carriages following, and six outriders interspersed among the group. First in line was Wyvern's personal coach, which held the duchess and her parents. Anne and Sarah were in the second vehicle with the two great aunts, and the remaining carriages were full of servants and luggage. Jersey rode several paces ahead.

Lillian wished they could have moved at a brisker pace, as she was anxious to reach her friend, but she was grateful not to be closed in and confined inside one of the coaches.

She took a breath of the cool, fresh air. Today she wore one of her new riding habits. It was navy blue with long sleeves and a high neckline, keeping her warm enough for now. She hoped the sun would appear later. Prince Albert sat alert on her lap so he could look at everything that passed by, although there was little more than a view of dirt and trees.

Gabriel broke a long stretch of silence. "Lillian, I have not yet had the chance to adequately express my gratitude to you for seeing me home so quickly after the shooting so I could receive care, and then using your skills to heal the wound when it became infected."

She waved the praise away, although inwardly it pleased her. "I did what anyone would do under the circumstances."

Gabriel snorted. "I do not know of any other lady who would have taken charge of the situation rather than faint dead on the spot. Plus, you thwarted my mother's attempts to send you away. You are indeed formidable." He gave her a wide grin.

She shrugged casually. She had never before thought of herself as a strong woman; she had always needed to spend all her energy hiding away from society. A new Lillian was beginning to emerge and take shape. She was not yet certain how she felt about that.

"How is your injury this morning?" she asked.

Gabriel rolled his shoulder a few times and winced. "It is still sore, but nothing I cannot live with, I assure you."

"I am glad to hear it."

His face turned grave. "I also wish to apologize again for my reckless behavior. There was every possibility the shooter could have targeted you as well that day. I put you in danger without a second thought and I will admit to being ashamed of it.”

“You have already apologized,” Lillian answered, “and to be perfectly honest, I do not know what I would have done if I had been in your boots and I had had a chance of getting my hands on the villain. I am only sorry he got away.”

“That is very understanding of you.” After several moments, his face broke into a boyish grin. “Ever since our betrothal, my mother pauses to give me an odd look every now and then. She knows we are up to something but has no idea what it is.”

Lillian laughed lightly. “Yes. It is always a delight to put one’s parents in a state of confusion.”

“May I ask you a personal question?”

“Certainly. I do not believe I have any secrets remaining,” Lillian said.

“How have your parents dealt with your gift? I mean, you already told me they sought help for you, but what about on a personal level?”

Lillian did not think long on her answer. “My parents have been very good to me. Although my mother has an excitable nature and a great desire that I fit in well with society, she also has a spine of steel, especially when she makes up her mind on a matter. From the beginning, she did not try to shame me, but firmly decided to improve my life. My father did the same.”

"I imagine many would not be as fortunate to be treated so well by their families under the circumstances, as in Lady Francesca's case," Gabriel said.

"Indeed," Lillian said. "What was your father like?"

"My father was a very influential figure. He was both a hard man and a kind one. He liked to take charge of everything and everyone because he believed he always knew what was best." Gabriel reminisced as the sound of hooves clopping on the dirt echoed from the trees. "But he was fair. If you could prove you had a better idea than he, my father would concede."

"You miss him," Lillian stated.

"Yes, I miss him very much. As does my mother. They were an amazing pair. It saddens me to see her forced to live without him."

Jersey was in his element as he galloped ahead of the entourage only to return a few moments later at the same speed.

Gabriel shook his head at the man's antics. "One might think he is not watching out for us, as is his job, but Jersey is sharp as a tack and is able to do ten things at once—all of them exceedingly well."

"How ever did you acquire such an unusual servant?" Lillian asked.

Gabriel chuckled. "Now that is an interesting tale."

When he did not begin, Lillian prompted, "Are you going to tell it? You have me waiting in suspense."

"You are so impatient," he teased. "I met Jersey not long after I left the country four years ago. Our ship had stopped in Spain to pick up cargo, and I disembarked to stretch my legs and look around a bit. The war was in full session at the time, so I could not go far. On my return, I heard shouting in the town square, where a small mob was forming. As I passed by, I saw a man with his hands manacled, standing against a stone wall, facing a line of men with rifles, about to be executed."

Lillian gasped. "How horrible."

"I thought so too, and not wanting to get caught up in the violence of the event, I quickly made my way back to the ship, which was soon out on the open seas again." He paused, then turned his head toward her and smiled. "This is where the story gets good. That night, I retired to my cabin after dinner to prepare for bed and what a shock I received to find a man—unknown to me—lying in my bunk. A man with manacled hands."

Lillian drew in a sharp breath. "How?" The story was too unbelievable.

"To this day, I do not know, although I have asked. My first inclination upon seeing him was to grab up my pistol from the wall cabinet to protect myself. I pointed it in his direction and asked, "What do you want?"

" 'Well, Your Honor, it's like this,' he answered in an accent that told me he was an Englishman. 'I need passage away from that stink hole and I would greatly appreciate assistance with the removal of these.' He held up his wrists.

" 'Why should I not simply call for help and have you thrown in the brig?' I asked the man, who was not the least bit intimidated by my pistol. Why should he be? He had obviously just escaped half a dozen or so armed men.

" 'Well, Your Highness, it's like this,' he repeated. 'I think you could use a man like me in your employ. This ship is bound for a new land isn't it? I am a man who knows his way around.' He inspected his nails like he had no cares in the world. 'You could have me locked up as a stowaway, but most likely the captain will have me working the deck in the blink of an eye. A ship is always one man short, it seems like.' He held up his wrists again. 'It's up to you what you want with me.'

"I stood there, incredulous for some time. The audacity of this man who had just escaped certain death for a crime—well, he could have been a murderer for all I knew, or worse, and I a duke. But there was something about him. Something that made my intuition scream, 'This man could change your life.' I put the pistol down and set about getting his manacles off. That was the easiest part of getting to know Jersey. He still remains quite the mystery to me, but he has taught me a great deal that has benefited me in my role as head of the Network."

Lillian chuckled, amused by the story. "I am the last person who might judge having such a man in one's employ. I have a large variety of unusual friends."

"Oh, Jersey is most certainly not my friend," Gabriel protested, "and he refuses to even call me by the correct title."

She smiled fondly. "That is part of his charm, I think."

"Charm?" Gabriel gave her an incredulous look.

"In his own way, yes, and I would argue that he is indeed your friend, whether you wish to agree or not."

Gabriel merely grunted, then asked, "Are you willing to tell me more about this school of yours and those who attend? You did say I should simply ask."

She stroked a hand down Prince Albert's back and smiled. "Yes, I did. There are students from all over the world at Silvano's, who are as young as six and the eldest is in his late twenties."

"What is the most unusual gift you have seen?" Gabriel asked.

Lillian had to think about that for a minute. They were all unusual or all normal depending on which way you looked at it. "That is difficult to say," she finally said, "but I think it would probably be the boy who can change his appearance to look like anyone he wishes. It can be quite unnerving when he pops up beside me in someone else's body but speaking in his own voice."

Jersey was just rounding the bend ahead to return, when a muffled scream rent the air behind them. Gabriel had his horse turned before Lillian could react. By the time she wheeled her own horse about and started to ride back toward the carriages, Jersey and Gabriel had already reached them.

A great cacophony rose, with more screaming, while someone thumped against the inside of the main coach. The two men had jumped off their horses and wrenched open the coach door before it came to a full stop. A flurry of ladies emerged, one practically on top of the other. Her mother and the duchess were each breathing hard and talking at the same time. The one word Lillian recognized as she reached the coach was "ssssnake," which shakily came from her grace, who was being ineffectually fanned by Lady Wentworth's hand.

The chaos caused Lillian's pulse to speed up. What was happening?

Her father had not come out of the coach. She peered over Gabriel's shoulder as he assessed the situation. Prince Albert, who was now perched on her shoulder, rose up to look as well. Her father was frozen in place, with sweat dripping down his face, his breath ragged. She had never seen him in such a state before, but the reason why was now clear. A large, variegated brown snake, with what looked like a wide veil coming from around its head, stood upright in front of him.

"Cobra," Gabriel said to Jersey, while never taking his eye off the enormous snake standing tall from the carriage floor.

Next to her, Jersey foully cursed at the word.

This could not be good.

"Wentworth," Gabriel spoke in a slow, soothing voice, eyes still on the snake. "As long as you remain calm, you will be perfectly fine. Everything is going to be just fine."

"What do you have for me, Jersey?" he asked.

"Canvas bag, Your Greatness."

Lillian had no idea where the bag had appeared from, but she glanced his way briefly, and saw he was holding it up in his hands.

"Do you have your knife ready?" Gabriel asked.

"Sure enough," Jersey answered.

Lillian wanted more than anything to soothe her father, whose face had bleached of all color and who was now breathing in a very shallow manner, but Prince Albert, having seen the snake, began screeching in her ear and shaking. She feared he would agitate the cobra and make the situation worse, so she took several steps away to watch the two men working in tandem to dispatch the snake. She cradled the ferret against her chest and stroked his fur, both to soothe him and herself.

Gabriel slowly put one hand out behind himself, and Jersey handed him the bag. He continued to croon to her father in reassurance. She was not sure if the words were for him or the snake. Maybe both. "All is well. You are safe. Deep breaths now. Nice and slow. That is the way."

From beside her, Jersey said in a low and quiet voice, "You can do it, sir. Quick as a blink and I'll do the rest."

Lillian had no idea what they were talking about, but she saw the knife in Jersey's hand for the first time. It was no small knife one might keep in a boot or up a sleeve. The blade was at least a foot long and three inches wide. Lillian blinked several times, wondering where such a knife might have materialized from. The man was like a magician—conjuring items out of thin air.

The ladies behind her had stepped off the road into a grassy meadow. Lillian could hear them still whimpering and panicking, but it was much quieter than it had been at first. Sarah, Anne, and the great aunts had now joined them.

Gabriel continued to speak into the carriage, while Jersey stood by. What happened next was so fast it was a blur. Gabriel whipped around holding the end of the canvas bag closed around the body of the snake—which was so long its tail thumped on the edge of the carriage door on the way out. He continued twisting until he was in a crouched position with the snake on the ground.

Jersey crushed his boot onto what Lillian assumed was the snake's head and in one quick motion, sliced downwards, making a loud *thwack*. Blood pooled over the sack. Gabriel, who still held the bag closed, did not let go of the body of the snake. The tail continued to twitch.

"It's good and dead, Captain," Jersey reassured him. "You know they move like that for a good while after you do them in."

Gabriel let go of the creature and wiped his hands against each other as if to clean them. He stood up and backed away, leaving the mess to Jersey, who grabbed the sack at the end and picked it up, blood dripping.

Lillian did not know whether to feel fascinated or nauseous at the sight, but thankfully, she remembered her father's dilemma and went to assist.

"Papa," she called softly into the carriage. "Papa, the snake is gone. Let me help you out of the carriage now."

Her father did not answer. He was frozen in place, his eyes wide in fear. Lillian called over her shoulder, "Wyvern, I need assistance, please."

Gabriel was breathing rapidly, not at all unaffected by what he had just accomplished. He leaned into the open carriage door. "What is this then, Wentworth? Surely, you wish to vacate this carriage while my men look it over thoroughly to be sure there are no more surprises waiting?" He asked this in a pleasant tone, as if a venomous snake had not just been lurking inside. At least Lillian assumed it was venomous considering how seriously Gabriel and Jersey had dealt with the matter.

This got her father's attention. "More?" he asked in a tremulous voice.

"It is not outside the realm of possibility, sir." Gabriel reached in to take her father's arm. "Come now, let us get you outside into the fresh air. No snakes will be found out here, I promise you."

Gabriel pulled on her father to propel him forward until he stood on shaky legs at the doorway. Lillian took his other arm, patting it. "Come, Papa. We shall have a nice rest out here. It truly is a pleasant day." He allowed them to pull him slowly to the grass and ease him down onto a small boulder. As soon as he was seated, Lillian went to work removing his cravat.

"How brave you were, Papa, to face that monster down, and not a scratch to show for it."

She had just removed his neckcloth when her mother hurried over and spoke in a highly dramatic fashion. "Oh,

Walter!" she said as she sat next to her husband. "I ran like a frightened ninny and left you behind." She pulled his head down to her bosom and rocked slightly from side to side. "I am so sorry to have abandoned you, but all is well now."

Lillian's father, apparently receiving the attention needed, said on a sob, "Oh, Lavinia. I hate snakes."

"I know, I know," her mother patted the side of his head.

Feeling like an intruder, Lillian backed away and motioned for Gabriel to do the same. She wanted to have a few words with the man.

Once they reached the other side of the carriage, out of view, Lillian said in a fierce whisper, "Even I, who know little about creatures of the earth, know that was no ordinary snake or you would not have gone to such lengths to dispatch the thing. What was it doing in your carriage?"

Gabriel grimaced. "I have no idea where it could have come from, since it is not native to England, and I have no idea how it could have hidden so long without detection."

"That does not answer the question, as you well know," Lillian said in clipped tones. The shock had worn off and left her feeling fierce. Prince Albert, who had calmed down, now began to bob up and down and chirp loudly in her ear. She reached up and gently stroked his head.

Putting his hand behind his neck, Gabriel rubbed it and sighed. "I cannot say for sure. I can only suspect the same person who has been attempting to kill me has tried again." He shook his head in disbelief. "This was a clumsy effort. There is no predicting a snake's movements. It could have struck one of the servants who was loading the carriage or any one of the occupants, and as was the case, it completely missed me." He looked off into the distance, thinking. "I always took the murderer to be a cunning man. Now, I begin to wonder."

"Perhaps he has merely grown desperate and took an opportunity that presented itself," she said.

Gabriel took her left hand, rubbing his thumb lightly across the back. "It could be as you say. I know this was a frightening incident, but soon we will have the man responsible brought to justice, thanks to you."

Lillian swallowed hard and said nearly in a whisper, "I have never been so frightened in my life, Gabriel. Not just because of the snake itself, but because I watched you put yourself in danger to confront it. I think I stopped breathing for several minutes at least."

He chuckled, not in true humor, but to lighten the mood. "I am fairly certain I stopped breathing as well." He continued to slowly run his thumb over and over across her gloved hand. "I have killed snakes before. Different snakes in different parts of the world, but none quite as formidable as a cobra. I am grateful at a time like this to have someone like Jersey at my side."

"What an interesting life you must have led during your time overseas," she said.

"Indeed." Gabriel gave her hand one last squeeze, then dropped it. "Perhaps it is time to begin herding everyone back into the now inspected and clean-of-snakes carriages so we can be on our way. I would like to reach Kent before nightfall. We will be safer there than if we spent the night on the road."

"Yes, of course, but I shall leave it to you to find a way to get my father back in there because I do not see how it is going to happen. You charmed a snake to its doom. I put my faith in you that you can charm my father into continuing the journey."

TWENTY-THREE

Signor Silvano's Sayings Number 23
The saying goes: Do not put off until
tomorrow what can be done today.
I say, take the day off.

In the end, Lord Wentworth had to be given a dose of laudanum to help him relax enough to return to the carriage, as he was far too shaken to consider riding in the saddle outside with the others. Once they were on their way, the journey thankfully continued with no further incidents.

As they moved along at what felt like a snail's pace, Gabriel had time to reflect on how Lillian had kept a cool head during the entire snake incident, and once the serpent had been dispatched, she had been the one to calmly assist her father. Any other society lady would have been fainting or shrieking—even his mother had done the latter. Such a levelheaded woman would make a formidable duchess.

His thoughts turned toward their coming venture. Although he was confident Lillian would be able to vet all twenty-eight of their suspects, he knew it was going to be an arduous endeavor on her part. He wondered if a better way existed. *If only I had an entire team of people with similar gifts.*

He did not. But Lillian did.

They had ridden without speaking for some time, perhaps the shock of today's events having dampened their spirits. He broke the silence now. "Lillian, I would like to ask you for a favor."

"I owe you more than I could ever repay," she said, "both for my father's life and that of Francesca's. What favor would you ask?"

Gabriel huffed out a laugh. "We could go back and forth on how much we each owe the other. I owe you my life after the shooting." He cleared his throat. "I have been riding along considering ways to be more efficient in scrutinizing all the suspects on my list. Having to make contact with nearly thirty people is going to take a considerable amount of time, and I assume, a great deal of energy on your part." He looked at her in question.

"It will likely drain me very quickly and I will need to nap often, yes," she said.

He rolled his shoulders, attempting to relieve the tension and the throbbing pain of his wound. It had already been a deuced difficult day and it was still only morning.

"Do you never take a day away for simple pleasure?" Lillian surprised him by asking. "Or is work all you have?"

Gabriel grimaced. "I am afraid to say there is no such thing as a true holiday in my line of work."

"Perhaps after this house party you will find the time for one," she said. "You had a favor to ask of me?"

"Yes, as to that." Gabriel paused and shifted uneasily in his saddle. "As I said, I would like to flush out the killer as quickly as possible with as little effort on your part as necessary. Would it be possible to call on some of your friends to assist in the endeavor? Lady Francesca will already be on location, so it would only be a matter of a moment for her to attend. As to any others, we could quickly have them transported to Ramsay Hall from London."

Lillian wanted to be angry at the request. Students from Silvano's kept their abilities a secret to avoid being used in precisely this way. The only reason she had originally agreed to help him was because of what she was receiving in return. Her friends would have no such incentive. It did not matter that the cause was a just one, it was simply asking too much of them.

Before she could answer, Gabriel rushed to add, "I know I am asking a lot, but I believe you understand my desperation to take care of this once and for all. I cannot endure another failure."

Yes, she did understand, and she felt the weight of what she now owed this man—but that did not mean she wanted to offer up her friends as a sacrifice to his investigation.

"Many of the students at Silvano's face the same difficulty as me—they do not have control over their abilities," she finally said.

Gabriel nodded. "I could see how that would be a problem, but would it hurt to ask a few of those who do have control?"

Would it hurt?

She thought of Fran's bleeding ears. Did she have the right to make the decision to say no on everyone's behalf though? No, she did not. "I will speak to Francesca on the matter and see what she thinks. I cannot promise any more than that."

"Thank you," Gabriel breathed.

After they rode again for some time to nothing but the sound of horse's hooves and carriage wheels, Gabriel spoke again. "Your friend Turpentine said he had been sent to Kew Gardens that day by Catriona. What did he mean?"

Lillian gave him a sardonic smile. "I see you are making good on your promise to ask me directly for information."

Gabriel shrugged. "I thought I would make the attempt and see what results it yielded. So far I am pleased with the experiment."

"You asked, so I shall tell you," she said. "Catriona has the second sight, as many call it. I learned more from her during last week's meeting about the vision she had before the shooting. Although she knew very few details, she had sent Turpentine to assist us."

"He was there to warn us to leave?" Gabriel asked.

She shook her head. "Not exactly. Turpentine has the ability to move things with his mind."

Gabriel let out a small whistle, impressed.

"I believe Catriona thought he could do more than simply sound the alarm," she said. "As it turned out, this was indeed the case. When you fell to the ground, I did not push you as you believed. Turpentine did that from a good distance away."

"That is extraordinary," Gabriel said. "It sounds as if those two have some mastery of their gifts."

She shook her head. "Visions come to Catriona at random. She cannot choose what futures to see, and although Turpentine is better able to use his gift than many of us, at sixteen years old he is still a novice."

"I happily concede that I made an incorrect assumption that having an ability meant that the possessor naturally knew how to command it," Gabriel said.

"I do wish it were that simple," Lillian said with a sigh.

The remainder of the journey they discussed more mundane topics such as the weather and their differing thoughts on women's right to vote. Gabriel was not adamantly opposed, he simply had no strong opinion on the matter. Lillian endeavored to change his mind while she attempted not to worry about what he had asked of her friends.

When they finally arrived at the long drive of Ramsay Hall, Lillian could see one of the turrets in the distance. She had already known it had to be a very grand estate as the ducal seat, but she had seen little of places away from home in her lifetime. She was intrigued to see where Gabriel had grown up.

It was some time before she had a glimpse of it again, as the drive took them around a bend which seemed miles long, and a wall of trees obstructed the scene. At last, they turned again and were presented with a view of the sprawling manor in all its glory, surrounded by the glow of the setting sun. More than one architectural style was present, as seen in the two-story white stone turrets standing tall at each end of the building and portions of a castle wall. The largest middle section had A-line roofs and third-story attic rooms. Ahead of them, she could see a fountain in the middle of the wide carriage drive and beyond that a wide pillared portico fronting the home.

"The newer part was built in the early eighteenth century in the Palladian style by the Earl of Kirkenwell," Gabriel began. "However, after being caught in acts of treason, the king seized the earl's properties and a decade later gave this estate to the Earl of Haversham along with the title of first Duke of Wyvern."

"I imagine it is an extensive property," Lillian said as she took in every aspect of the manor including the lush surroundings.

Gabriel nodded. "It is comprised of over twelve hundred acres, including extensive woods, a lake, a succession house, farmland, and gardens. The manor itself boasts one hundred and twelve rooms as well as indoor plumbing. You will have the privilege of opening a tap for hot water in the bathing rooms while you are here." He grinned.

"My, that is a luxury," Lillian breathed. She was too much in awe to say more. She had never had aspirations of owning a great home or wealth, but Ramsay Hall was—well, the only word she could think of was breathtaking. It was a shame she would never become its lady.

When they reached the forecourt, Lillian draped the now sleeping Prince Albert over the horse's neck, removed her foot from the stirrup, and waited for someone to assist her down. It was Gabriel who appeared.

He reached up his arms and said, "Allow me." He wrapped his hands around her waist and slowly lowered her to the ground. Lillian's breath caught at how close he was. They stood, gazing at each other, for several heartbeats. This was different than the first time he had helped her down at the park. Then she had been afraid of him. Now she knew differently.

The spell was broken by the crunching of carriage wheels on the drive. There was no lazy retreat from the first carriage, but more of a tumbling out as if the occupants had been anticipating the moment the conveyance would stop. Lillian was not surprised. She would not have wished to remain inside any longer than necessary either.

Her father was looking better but still groggy and in need of proper sleep. This gave Lillian the opportunity she had hoped for.

"Mother," she said when they met under the portico, "why do you not take Father upstairs for a nap? I am certain we could all use one before dinner." She turned to Gabriel. "Oh, I did not think. Do you keep country hours and host an early dinner?"

The duchess answered from behind. "My dear, after the day we have had, I proclaim we shall all rest for the remainder of the day. We shall push dinner to eight o'clock." She stood as tall as possible in her drooping frame. "We have an excellent staff prepared for any kind of change in the schedule." With a nod, she disappeared up the stairs and inside.

Servants were swarming around them like ants, taking the horses to the stables and unloading the luggage. Her father was led up the stairs with her mother on one side and Anne on the other, the great aunts trailing behind, keeping up a constant flow of chatter. Sarah was walking toward her with the herbal case in hand. Now that everyone was occupied, she would be left to her own devices, which was exactly what she wanted.

She eased over to Gabriel, who was conferring with Jersey. "Excuse me," she interrupted quietly, "but I believe this would be an excellent time for me to visit your guest?" She tilted her head up at him in question.

"Ah, yes. Let me take you up." He held out an elbow. "And just to let you know, Jersey has footmen assigned to search the luggage for any more surprises as well."

She feigned a serious gasp. "You mean they will be rifling through our undergarments?"

Gabriel chuckled. "It cannot be helped, but if it makes you feel better, they will be supervised by the maids."

"No, that does not make it any less distressing." She gave

him a teasing smile, then a more serious look. "I am sorry it must be done, however."

They started up the front steps. Once inside, she was much too anxious to see Fran to study her surroundings. She knew Sarah would also want to visit their friend. She looked over her shoulder. "Do you want to hand that over to a footman to be brought up and come with us?"

Sarah shook her head. "I would never let someone else handle your case. It is not too heavy. I shall take it with me."

Gabriel led them on a complicated path up one staircase after another, winding around the home. By the time they had reached the highest floor, she was quite out of breath. "You are keeping her in the attics like a lunatic?" she gasped out.

"I assure you this is the quietest and safest place for her," Gabriel said. "Only once in a blue moon does anyone come to this part of the house."

Gabriel knocked on the door twice. Waited. Then knocked two more times.

A whispered voice startled Lillian, as there had been no sound of footsteps. "Who is it?"

"Wyvern and Lady Lillian."

The door was opened just a crack at first then all the way as Mildred, the former Effingham maid, allowed them in.

"How is she?" Lillian whispered as she entered.

"She can hear you," a voice from across the room called. Lillian smiled. Her friend was in fighting form once again. She rushed over to the divan where Fran was lounging, propped up with pillows, a book in her hand. She wore a dressing gown, and her red hair was up in a loose bun.

Lillian took her other hand and squeezed. "Oh, Fran, how are you faring?"

Sarah bent down and kissed her cheek.

"I am better. Much better now that I am away from the whirl of society and the machinations of my parents. I slept most of the way here and have been well cared for by Mildred and Thomas since arriving. As I understand it, none of the staff but the housekeeper knows we are here."

"She is very discreet, so you should have no worries on that score." Gabriel's voice startled Lillian. She had thought he would leave without coming inside the room.

Gabriel bowed to Francesca. "I have already heard from Lord Hartley that your journey was without incident. I expect you will want to rest here a while, especially while Lillian is my guest, before you decide what you wish to do next. I assume you have no desire to live in my attics for the remainder of your life?" He grinned.

Fran gave a low chuckle. "Tempting, but no, your grace."

Lillian waved her hand at Gabriel in a shooing motion. "Go away, if you please. We ladies would like to chat in private."

"Your wish is my command, my lady." Gabriel gave another short bow, turned, and left.

Fran smiled in amusement. "You have that man eating out of the palm of your hand."

"No I do not, nor do I wish to," Lillian said.

"Yes, she does," Sarah argued.

Without being asked, Thomas brought chairs over for Lillian and Sarah. She sat gratefully, placed her sleeping pet in her lap and said, "Thank you, Thomas." Sarah finally placed the herbal case on the floor.

"What pleases him," Fran said, "is to please you. Remember, I can hear a thing or two about what people are thinking."

Lillian quickly put her hands over her ears. "Do not dare tell me. I have no wish to know."

Fran's smile grew large at her friend's antics. "It will be just as you wish. I shall tell you no more. I shall start instead by saying how very lucky I am to have a friend like you. If you had not orchestrated my escape, I would most likely be in that asylum as we speak."

"Let us not think upon such things," Lillian said gravely. "What is done is done and what was to come has not passed. You are safe, and that is all that matters now."

"Too true." Fran sat back, putting the book on the window ledge to her left. "I could not be more pleased with the solitude I have had, and the quiet has been delicious." She smiled and stretched her arms above her head like a contented cat.

"You do have Mildred and Thomas with you all day, do you not?" Lillian asked.

"Yes, but they are quiet creatures and when they do speak —or do not speak, as is more often the case—they are quite reserved about it. Nothing like my screeching mother or the hundreds of voices in a crowded ballroom. It is a refreshing change." She paused and leaned in, whispering, "Do you want to know something very interesting?"

"Yes, I do," Lillian whispered back.

"I cannot hear Viscount Hartley."

"At all?" Lillian asked.

Fran flapped her hands. "Oh, I do not mean when he is speaking, but the other … you know."

Lillian, who had leaned forward to listen, sat back, astonished—nearly speechless. But she quickly regained her wits. "Has this ever happened before?"

Fran shook her head. "Not that I have ever noticed. It is possible it has occurred with others, but I could not tell due to the sheer number of voices in the room."

"What does it mean?" Sarah asked from beside her.

"I have no idea, but it was a most unusual carriage ride with him and Mildred being my only companions. It is no wonder I was able to sleep most of the way."

The ladies were silent for a moment, digesting this interesting tidbit, until Lillian began to laugh.

"What?" Fran asked

"Did you really announce to the entirety of your mother's dinner guests that you were tired of the damn voices in your head?"

Her friend slowly smiled until all her teeth showed. A very satisfied smile. "Oh, yes I did. At the time it was an act of desperation, but when I think back on it, I believe it was a fine way to have my final say. Let my mother live that incident down!"

The ladies all laughed joyfully at the idea. "Oh, stop," Lillian finally said, her hand over her stomach. "I must catch my breath!"

Mildred appeared like a ghost with a tea tray from one side of Lillian, and Thomas came from the other with a small table. Mildred placed the tray atop it and poured the tea. Once it was served, the two servants faded away again.

"I never realized how quiet they could be," Lillian whispered.

Fran nodded. "Which makes them perfect for me."

Lillian inhaled the steam rising from her cup. Tea was exactly what she needed after the day she had had. She sat up straighter. "Oh! I must tell you about the incident that occurred on our journey here." She proceeded to recount every detail of what she would always refer to as the 'snake incident,' including how Gabriel mesmerized the snake and trapped it, and how Jersey cut off its head.

Fran was properly astonished. "You, my friend, have been very busy since we last had a proper talk."

"This was actually only one such unsettling event since meeting Gabriel. I never thought, after making his acquaintance at the ball, that I would ever see him again. It turns out he is not like other men I have encountered in society. He speaks to me like an equal and does not shame me for my gift." Lillian placed her now empty cup back on the tea tray.

Fran leaned forward. "I read of your betrothal in the papers. I thought you were quite opposed to marriage. Has that changed?"

"The betrothal is not real," Lillian said and explained the bargain she had made with Gabriel and the shooting that soon followed.

Fran shook her head. "My goodness. Is this my quiet Lillian telling of all these larks?"

"I would not call attempted murder—twice—a lark."

"However, pretending to be engaged to a duke to catch a killer is. This is more in line with something I would do." Fran eyed her critically. "Yes, I can see you have already changed much since I last saw you, and for the better I think." Fran put down her teacup. "Now that you have had a chance to practice being in a close relationship, do you think there is any possibility it could become real?"

Lillian shrugged. "I have never dared to hope or even consider it. I have always thought it would be simpler to just fade away into the country."

"You just told me that the duke has no difficulties accepting your gift," Fran said. "What would be the harm in marrying him and living an ordinary life as you deserve?"

"Can you imagine if we wanted to have children, Fran? What if one of them turns out just like me? Or all of them?" She shuddered. "It frightens me."

"If it so happened your children had your gift, you would already know how to handle it. And if the duke does not judge you harshly, why would he judge his own children?"

"What kind of reputation would that be for a duke?" Lillian asked. "To have a family of oddities such as myself?"

"My dear, you are simply making excuses and you need to stop. You must follow your heart in this matter, and that is all there is to it. It sounds as if he is an extraordinary person and I believe you would find it difficult to discover his equal."

Lillian sighed. "I have had little time to consider how I feel about him, but that is the least of my problems. At present, I am afraid he only sees me as someone to further his cause."

"What ever do you mean?" Fran asked.

"The only reason he is betrothed to me is so he might use my ability for his own purposes."

Fran smiled. "Oh, I think I could argue there are more reasons than that, but you have already said you have no wish to hear his private thoughts, so I will keep that to myself."

"That is for the best," Lillian said. "Let us speak no more about this today. It has been a very long journey and I will need to dress for dinner. Do you wish me to check in on you before I retire for the night?"

"No, no. Tomorrow will be soon enough."

Lillian stood, bending over her friend, and bussed her cheek. "I shall see you on the morrow then and I shall bring Sarah along again as well. She will have more freedom than I to visit you on a regular basis."

In turn, Sarah bent and kissed their friend on the cheek.

"That sounds lovely," Fran said. "For now, I shall finish this fascinating horrid novel. The behavior of the characters truly is atrocious. My mother would faint if she knew I was reading it." She winked. "Which means I must find another when I reach the end of this one."

"Where did you find such a thing?" Lillian asked, amused.

"The duchess has quite an interesting collection of books in her personal library."

Lillian shook her head. "Just when you think you are starting to know a person …" She trailed off. "Have a wonderful night, dear friend. May your dreams be sweet."

Fran, already absorbed in her book once again, merely lifted her hand in farewell.

Lillian stepped lightly as she left the room, in much better spirits than when she had entered. She was so uplifted, she and Sarah were halfway down the first staircase before she realized she had no idea where to go. As she turned on the landing to go down the next flight of stairs, she ran into Gabriel's valet who had been walking up. "Mr. Jersey!"

He nodded. "My lady. You must be lost."

"What makes you say that?"

"For one thing, you are near the family's quarters," Jersey raised an eyebrow. "Unless you were looking to visit His Excellency's room?"

Lillian was scandalized. "I most certainly was not," she huffed. "I was visiting my friend, but I have no idea now where my room would be."

Jersey rolled his eyes and sighed. "There's nothing for it then but that I help you, being a lady in distress and all."

Lillian smiled at the man's irreverence. "That would be very much appreciated." He turned on the stair and they followed him down.

For the entire journey through the house, she thought of what lay ahead for her in the coming days. Lillian felt like she was embarking on a brand-new life, completely foreign to her. She had to admit to being not just apprehensive but downright afraid. Because if this did not turn out well, any hopes for a different future would be snuffed out permanently.

TWENTY-FOUR

Signor Silvano's Sayings Number 24
You of all people should know
things are not always what they seem.
Keep an open mind.

From the window of her bedroom, facing the back of the house, Lillian could see mist falling like a sheer carpet on the wide expanse of lawn. Although this year had been colder than usual, as May was about to turn to June, Lillian longed to wear short-sleeve dresses, but it was only a dream. The fear of being touched still consumed her. Sarah had dressed her this morning in a long-sleeved pale turquoise morning gown and a pair of tan leather gloves. She was not yet ready to break the habit of keeping her hands well covered.

Prince Albert was frisky and chasing a small ball of yarn —one of his favorite playthings—about the room. She smiled at the sight, glad that he had no trouble adjusting to different living quarters.

Quickly the reality of why they were at this house party hit her once again. She was here to touch more than two dozen people to ascertain if they were guilty. There was no doubt they were all guilty of something, but whether they were murderers was another matter.

Lillian gave her ferret a pat on the head and a stroke down his fur before heading downstairs for the morning. She expected the breakfast room to be empty at eight o'clock, but either everyone had gone to bed early as well or they were habitual early risers. Today, she might have been considered late. Her entire family, the duke, duchess, and the great aunts, as well as Viscount Hartley were accounted for. The gentlemen all stood as she entered, and Gabriel pulled out an empty chair to his left.

As she walked past, she stopped before the duchess and curtsied. "Good morning, your grace. I trust you had a pleasant night?"

The duchess delicately wiped the corners of her mouth before speaking. "Yes, thank you for asking." She leaned in to whisper, "All the better for having taken a sleeping powder.

"I believe there was an outbreak of insomnia in the house last night, causing a great need for sleeping powders, your grace," Lillian said with a wry smile. "Perhaps it signals a change of weather?"

The duchess chuckled lightly. "Perhaps so."

Lillian proceeded down the table and sat in the offered chair. She was grateful for the cup of tea that immediately appeared in front of her. She took a sip, then looked around the table. Anne was to her left, and the viscount sat to the duke's right.

"Did you sleep well," Anne asked quietly.

"Very well, thank you," she said.

For the first time, she noticed a footman in the now-familiar red and silver Wyvern livery standing at her side. "Oh. I would like coddled eggs and toast, if you please." The man bowed and went to the sideboard to fill a plate for her. Lillian took another sip of tea and turned back to her cousin. "How was your slumber?"

Anne visibly shuddered. "Honestly, after the incident yesterday, I was too frightened to go to sleep, although I did not ride in the carriage with the beast."

"I do not blame you in the least," Lillian said. She squeezed her cousin's arm lightly.

Anne began to giggle and quickly put her hand over her mouth to stifle it. She leaned in and whispered, "Your poor father. I had no idea he was so afraid of snakes. Did you?"

Lillian shook her head with a fond smile. "I do not know whether to laugh or cry over it all, but thankfully it is behind us now."

Their conversation was interrupted by the footman placing a steaming plate in front of her. At the same time, the duke finished his conversation with the viscount and turned to Lillian. "What is on the agenda today, your grace?" she asked him.

"Since we are all at sixes and sevens, Mother and I discussed it and we have decided to have an easy day of it so those who traveled in the coach may recover."

"That sounds very wise," she said.

"Gabriel," he said.

"Hmm?" Lillian asked absently.

The duke leaned forward and said quietly, "You seem to have forgotten my name is Gabriel." He straightened. "Guests are not expected to start arriving until later this afternoon. If you are up for it, after all the time in the saddle yesterday, I would like to take a group for a tour of the grounds. Those who have no wish to ride may remain in the parlor with the duchess."

"I enjoy riding very much, but the weather is somewhat dreary," Lillian said.

"True, but I do not think it is so bad as to stop us from going outdoors," Gabriel countered.

"You may count me as a part of your group, then," Lillian said, then looked to Anne. "How about you, Cousin? On such a day would you like to spend some time outdoors?"

"Oh, yes," Anne readily agreed. "A morning ride is exactly what I need to restore myself after yesterday's journey."

Lillian turned back to Gabriel. "There you have it. Two ladies ready to join your party."

"Excellent." He pulled out his pocket watch and checked the time. "Shall we say in three quarters of an hour's time?"

Lillian nodded and took another bite of eggs.

Gabriel leaned in so only she could hear. "I am sure Hartley will be pleased to tell you more about his journey during our ride."

"And I shall be very pleased to hear of it." Lillian smiled.

"How is the manuscript coming?" he asked.

Lillian was startled by the reminder of why she had agreed to their betrothal in the first place. "I still have several chapters remaining before it is complete. There has been little time to work on it as of late."

"I can imagine," Gabriel said with a gentle smile. "Hopefully you will find time at the end of this house party to finish it. I know it is important to you."

"Yes it is, but it can wait a few more days." Currently, finding the late duke's killer was much higher on her priority list. She knew Gabriel would not be safe until the villain was apprehended.

Her hand, which held a forkful of eggs halfway to her mouth, began to tremble. She quickly put the food in her mouth to cover any emotion on her face. She had agreed to this bargain with Gabriel, expecting there to be an even exchange, and for them to part ways at the end of it. But she was finding herself growing more fond of him than she had foreseen.

The eggs turned to sawdust in her mouth. She stood abruptly. "I think I should go up to dress for our ride." Without waiting for a reply, she headed toward the door.

"I will join you," she heard Anne say from behind her.

Once in the hallway, Anne said in a rush, "What is it, Lillian? Why are you so upset?"

She felt a flood of fondness for her cousin, but what could she say when she did not fully understand how she was feeling, let alone well enough to explain it to someone else? She settled on, "I am merely tired after the long journey yesterday is all."

Anne hummed her disbelief. "There is more to it than that. I can tell."

Lillian hugged her cousin's arm as they started up the stairway. "You are sweet to care so well for me. I will admit I am a bit overwhelmed by all the changes happening in my life. If you had asked me a few weeks ago if I could see myself where I am right now, I would have called you insane."

"I cannot begin to imagine all that you are going through," Anne said, "but you are handling it very well. I know you have always shied away from what you called a normal life, but do you feel like that aversion has changed?"

"I could not say." Lillian swallowed hard. "I am afraid to allow myself to want something only to have it dashed to pieces."

"Did you never dream as a girl about marrying a handsome gentleman and living happily ever after?"

That was an unexpected question, but Lillian knew the answer. "Perhaps when I was very young. But then I quickly saw how my ability kept me apart from anyone who was not part of the school. There are only so many times a girl can attempt to connect with people and have it fail miserably before she decides never to try again."

They had reached the floor where the guest rooms were located, and Anne stopped. "Yes, I understand and I think you are very brave. Please do not lose hope. Not for anyone else's sake but your own, will you please keep trying?"

She thought for several heartbeats before saying, "Yes, I will keep trying."

Anne gave her a bright smile. "Good. Now, we must hurry and change our clothing if we are to be on time."

When she entered her room, Lillian whispered herself, "Yes, I will keep trying," because she truly did want to believe in happily ever after.

Anne and Lillian arrived at the forecourt, where everyone was waiting, within the expected time. Lillian had only brought the one riding habit, so she was dressed the same as the day before, although her outfit had been cleaned and pressed and no longer bore the dust of the road. The garment had been fashioned with a split skirt and she wore breeches underneath. She preferred this style since she more often rode astride at home on their estate as well as at the school. It allowed more freedom of movement than the typical habit with a long train, although she would be riding sidesaddle today. Anne wore a jewel-green habit. The color made her skin glow with health.

Gabriel, Viscount Hartley, and a young lady unknown to her were standing near the horses which several grooms were holding in place. The girl wore a dark green riding habit with a matching cap that covered very little of her golden curls, brighter than Hartley's blond coloring. The outfit made her look quite mature, but Lillian guessed her to be no more than fifteen or sixteen years old.

One of the horses, a dappled gray mare, must have decided she had been standing too long. She quickly pulled her head up, wrenching the reins from the groom, and took several short hops to the side. The young lady screeched and jumped into Lord Hartley's arms.

All was put quickly to rights by the groom, who got the horse under control, and the Viscount patted the young lady awkwardly in consolation.

As Anne and Lillian came up to the group, the groom turned and winked at her. She blinked slowly several times to be certain her eyes were not playing tricks on her. It was Turpentine! What was he doing at Gabriel's estate? She would have given anything to ask him that very question right then, but it would have to wait until she could talk to him in private.

"We are a rather small party today, are we not?" Anne asked.

Viscount Hartley stepped forward. "Small parties are often the best kind. Lady Lillian, Miss Hargraves, may I introduce you to my sister," he gestured with his hand to the young lady on his right, "the Honorable Elizabeth Montgomery? She arrived early this morning from our family's estate not far from Ramsay Hall."

"Also known as Lizzie to my friends." The girl leaned forward to speak across her brother with a bright, friendly smile. "It is very nice to meet you, Lady Lillian. We are Gabriel's neighbors to the east. I understand you will soon be our neighbor as well?"

The thought gave Lillian a start. She once again wondered briefly what it would be like to call this estate her home. "I am pleased to make your acquaintance, Lizzie. You may call me Lillian if you wish, and yes, Wyvern and I recently became betrothed." The lie was getting harder to repeat.

The sun had begun to peek through breaks in the clouds which was a good sign for their ride.

Lillian moved toward the high-spirited gray and slowly reached out her hand to stroke the mare's nose. "You are a beauty, are you not?"

Gabriel came up behind her. "I chose this mount especially for you. She has plenty of heart for an experienced rider like yourself. I know you brought your own horse but thought perhaps she needed a rest."

"That was very thoughtful of you. What is her name?"

He patted the horse's neck. "This is Grizzie, short for Grizelda." The mare took a step back then forward again. "It looks like she is eager to get started."

Lillian laughed at the frisky horse. "Perhaps we should begin our outing then?"

Gabriel cupped his hands for Lillian's foot to help her into the sidesaddle while the groom—no, Turpentine—held the reins. As he handed her the leather straps, she gave him a narrowed-eyed look that promised a reckoning.

The horse sidestepped again, commanding her attention. Lillian spent several minutes working to take charge and steady her before turning toward the group. Everyone else had mounted and was waiting for her to join them. She grinned as she trotted up. "This little beauty is eager for a ride! Shall we?" Without waiting for an answer, Lillian turned and let the horse gallop for a bit to get some of the extra steam out. Then she slowed her pace to allow the others to catch up, although it was evident Grizzie was reluctant to comply.

"Lillian," Gabriel said in an amused tone as he came up beside her, "Grizzie knows these lands very well, but do you have any idea where you are going?"

"Not a one," she said with a delighted smile.

They both laughed. It felt so good to be out in the open, nothing but miles of land before her. There were no worries of who she might accidentally touch or what decisions for her future might lay ahead.

Viscount Hartley flanked her on the right side. "My lord," she said. "I have not yet had a chance to thank you for the assistance you gave to my friend. She told me the journey here was quite uneventful."

"It was indeed, and it was my pleasure," he said. "It was easily achieved and no trouble, as it allowed me to spend more time with my family at home before the house party."

"Regardless, we will forever be in your debt, and I can nearly go so far as to say you saved her life."

"She deserved better," he said simply.

Lizzie rode up on her other side and Viscount Hartley pulled his horse back, apparently finished with the conversation.

"Are you looking forward to the house party?" Lillian asked.

Lizzie pouted. "Sadly, my brother has given me only a short list of activities I am allowed to attend, since I have not yet had my come out. It is very difficult when a young lady knows a party is taking place next door but that she cannot attend the whole of it."

Lillian smiled kindly at the girl. "You will have many years ahead of you to enjoy parties and balls. I know it may seem like you are missing out, but attending many events one after another can become quite tedious and exhausting."

"That is one opinion," Anne said as she rode up on Lillian's other side with a wide smile. "However, there are many, such as myself, who believe there can never be such a thing as an overfull social calendar."

"Each to her own, dear cousin. We shall agree to disagree." Lillian turned back to Lizzie. "However, I think the waiting will make you enjoy it all the more, and before you know it, you will meet more gentlemen than you know what to do with and they will surround you like bees to a flower." All three ladies laughed. "Do you like to gallop, Lizzie? I believe my horse is not interested in walking at all today."

"Yes, shall we?" Lizzie answered breathlessly. "How about if we race to that large oak and back." She pointed to a tree in the distance. Before waiting for an answer, the girl was off like a shot. Lillian reacted quickly to the challenge, squeezed her left leg as she tapped Grizzie on the right side with her crop, and followed on the girl's tail.

Lillian exhilarated in the freedom of the flying horse. She had not been able to go at a pace faster than a trot since joining the season in London. Lizzie was ahead by two lengths, but Lillian was determined to catch her. Although she was hampered by the confinement of the sidesaddle, she leaned forward and allowed the horse to take the reins. Could Grizzie ever run! She imagined she could easily win top prize in any race.

It did not take long before Lillian blew past her opponent and drew ever closer to the finish. She looked quickly over her shoulder and saw that she had gained several lengths on Lizzie. Her problem now was how to wheel the powerful horse about after she had put on so much speed. Just beyond the oak was the beginning of a forest. Lillian was running out of room.

Hoping Grizzie was well trained, she pulled the reins to the left to change their course as she approached the great oak. When they reached the tree, she pulled harder left, stayed in the forward seated position, and clamped hard onto the pommel with her right leg. The mare's hooves pounded the earth as she turned sharply around the tree, barely slowing down in the process. Once they made it all the way around, Lillian loosened everything enough to let the horse run again. When she neared the group of riders, she gradually pulled back on the reins, slowing the mare. Her breath was coming in pants from the hard ride, and she worked to slow that as well.

She looked over her shoulder again to see that Lizzie had veered off to the left of the tree to slow down and was now leisurely walking her horse back to the group. Lillian had unmistakably won the race.

"Lady Lillian," Viscount Hartley called out as she approached, "where did you learn to ride like that?"

Lillian answered between still-choppy breaths. "I had quite a lot of free time on my hands while at school. Riding was one of my daily pleasures."

"I was quite unsettled as you approached the oak at such a high speed, worrying that you would be injured, I must admit," Hartley said with a concerned look on his face.

Lillian blew off his worry with the wave of her hand. Over his left shoulder, she saw Gabriel, who looked … angry? She had not thought whether he might be concerned over the safety of his horse while she made the risky maneuver.

When he and Anne reached her, Lillian made to turn her horse to the same direction as the others, but Gabriel grabbed her arm in a firm grip, holding her in place.

"I would like a word with you, Lillian." The words came out clipped, and she saw his jaw was tight.

"Of course." She lowered her head in contrition.

Anne and the viscount had passed out of earshot. Gabriel jumped down from his horse and reached for Lillian. Without a care, he hauled her from her seat. She had to work to remove her left foot from the stirrup as he pulled.

"Gabriel!" she exclaimed as her feet touched the ground. "I was attached to that horse. Literally."

He let go of her abruptly as if he had been burned. "I apologize. I often forget about your aversion to touch."

She looked back up and into his eyes. "As of yet, I have had no problem with you."

"I still should have had a care." He stood close and towered over her. His nostrils flared and his face set as if it were made of stone. For several minutes he stood there and breathed hard as if too angry to speak. Lillian held his gaze at first, but quickly gave in and lowered her head. Was what she had done so bad?

"Do you have any idea," he finally spoke with a quiet intensity, "how frightened I was watching you run full speed into that turn? How helpless I was, knowing there was no way on this earth I could catch up to you in time to do any good? I had to sit back and watch that scene unfold—the entire time praying you did not end up dead." His voice rose in volume. "Any small miscalculation and the mare would have stumbled, which would have broken her leg and snapped your neck!" He reached out as if to grab her arms for a good shake, but abruptly lowered his hands. "I could shake you for the fear you just put me through."

"I apologize," Lillian said in a small voice, "but once I neared the tree, I had no idea how else to round it in the space

I had remaining, so I had to commit to the sharp turn. I took a risk with your horse that I know I should not have."

"My *horse*?" Gabriel shouted. From the corner of her eye, Lillian could see the others watching them with looks of concern on their faces. "I do not give a damn about my horse!"

Lillian brought her eyes fully back to him, more confused than ever.

Not saying anything more, Gabriel stalked away and re-mounted his bay gelding. Without a backward glance he rode to join the group, now waiting beneath the oak, and left her standing alone. Lillian was wracked with guilt. She had treated his horse as if it were her own and she had taken a terrible risk, not knowing what the mare could or could not do. Tears pooled in her eyes, but she was determined not to cry in front of the others.

Thankfully, she had learned at the school how to pull herself up to the saddle, even if it was not considered lady-like. Once she was settled astride, using her thighs to hold on since she had only one stirrup, she grabbed the reins and galloped back to the stable.

She had had enough riding for the day. Perhaps enough for a lifetime.

TWENTY-FIVE

Signor Silvano's Sayings Number 25
When there is a party, I say
the more the merrier!
It makes it easier to hide in plain sight.

After leaving Grizzie in the care of the stable hands, Lillian wanted to fly up the stairs to her room, but upon her return it was Turpentine who appeared to help her dismount.

Not in the best of humors, she hissed, "What in the world are you doing here?"

Her friend shrugged casually as if there was nothing unusual in his presence at Gabriel's estate. "After the shooting, I received a visit from that behemoth who works for your duke."

"Jersey?" she asked in surprise.

"Aye. He knocked on the front door of my home like he was making a social call."

"Did he? What did he want?"

"He cordially invited me to have a little chat with the duke."

He lowered his voice so only Lillian could hear when another groom passed by. "Your duke wanted to say thank you in person and asked if I might be willing to use my skills as a—" He broke off and coughed into his hand. "Use my skills as a Society member, as it were, to assist in this little venture you've got going. He said I might come in handy if anyone needs a little extra protection." Turpentine grinned. "He even offered to pay me."

Lillian could not decide how she felt about Gabriel asking for her friend's help, or Turpentine accepting. Then she realized what he had said. "Wait one minute. I only told him yesterday about your ability. How did he know?"

Her friend looked sheepishly up at the sky.

"Turpentine." She drew out the name.

He looked at her and said, "I might have told him after he mentioned he knew I was a chum of yours from the school."

A huff of air escaped from her lips. She was not sure if she was angrier at Turpentine for telling his secret or Gabriel for acting yesterday as if he had known nothing about her friend's abilities. What was all that about then, asking for a favor during their ride in hopes she would convince other Society members to help him as well? He had already spoken to at least one of them and received an agreement. How many more secrets was Gabriel keeping from her, and how many lies would he use to cover them up?

Finally she hissed, "Please refrain from doing anything stupid, Turpentine. If you are found out, we could all be at risk."

Her friend looked hurt. "I know better than to get caught, Lil." Then he gave her one of his charming, boyish smiles. " 'Sides, I am only here as backup, so to speak, in case I am needed, and to nose about a little bit. That is all."

"Fine," she grumbled. "See that you take care." With that she stomped off to the house, emotion threatening to burst forth like a volcano.

Once inside her bedroom, she locked the door and flung herself down on the bed. Thankfully, Sarah was currently off somewhere else, so she could have an improper fit of crying. She shoved her face into a pillow and let out heart wrenching sobs. Every emotion one could possess choked her. The old feelings of letting everyone down rose up, along with the fear and frustration her ability brought, while anger at this man she was starting to think of as a good friend became mixed in. She had allowed herself freedom today that she had not had since leaving Silvano's and he had yelled at her for it. He had lied to her about Turpentine.

When there were no more tears left, she wiped her eyes and lay there on her side in a stupor, wallowing in her distress. Lillian briefly considered finding a way to go back home and avoid the party altogether. Maybe if she feigned a violent illness, her parents would whisk her away.

Prince Albert hopped up in front of her on the bed and licked her face. She absently stroked his back as he cuddled beside her.

Calm began to reassert itself and she remembered all the

reasons she had come here in the first place. She had made a bargain with Gabriel, and she had a friend living in the attics who needed her. She could not let Fran down. Besides, she was now determined to catch this villain who not only killed once before, but had nearly killed Gabriel and her own father.

She sat up and rubbed her eyes. She knew what she needed to do: go talk to Fran. Her friend would understand her feelings and would help her turn the world upright again.

Lillian went to the washstand, poured some water into the basin and splashed her face several times. After drying it with a cloth, she looked in the small mirror on the back of the stand. She let out an exasperated sound of dismay at what she saw. Her eyes were red and puffy, but there was no time to make it better.

Before she ascended the staircase to the final floor, she looked about to be certain no one watched. She remembered the way to the attic room, as Jersey had shown her the evening before. At the door, she gave a double knock and waited just as Gabriel had done last night. Mildred cautiously opened it a crack and, seeing who it was, opened it wide and motioned for Lillian to enter.

When she noticed the state of distress she was in, the maid cried, "Oh, my lady, look at you!" She closed the door. "Shall I bring up a tea tray?"

"Yes, Mildred. That is the very thing that is needed. Thank you." She spoke again, stopping the maid. "And perhaps some cakes?"

She nodded and left.

Lillian walked briskly to her friend, who had her hands outstretched and said, "Tell me everything."

She briefly squeezed the offered hands, then sat in the chair Thomas had brought as soon as she entered the room. She began to cry again. She felt like such a ninny!

"You are not a ninny, my love," Fran said. "You are a normal female, and like the rest of us, sometimes your emotions get the better of you." She pulled a handkerchief from her sleeve and held it out. "It is clean, I promise," she said with a laughing smile when Lillian looked at it skeptically.

Lillian wiped her eyes with the linen. As best she could, while trying to hold back even more tears, she told the story in its entirety to her friend—her discussion with Gabriel about trust, Turpentine's appearance, and the entire horse incident.

"Goodness! It sounds like your life has turned into an entire series of adventures recently!" Fran said. "As someone with a gift different from yours, I must offer another perspective. I know you are afraid of trusting the duke, but I believe you can." When Lillian began to protest, Fran held up a hand to stop her. "It is true, he is single-minded in his objective of finding his father's murderer and will do anything to meet his goal, but I also believe he would not purposely do anything to hurt you or any of us."

"That does not mean he will not inadvertently hurt us as a consequence of his actions," Lillian said sullenly.

"Yes, but Lillian, I think all of us from Silvano's School

have been cosseted for far too long, to the point where we no longer make our own decisions. Maybe it is time we stop treating each other as fragile objects. If your duke wants to ask us to help him, that should be our choice to make. No one should need to protect us from ourselves."

Lillian felt contrite. Fran was right. They had been secluded together at the school for so many years they seemed to think as one, in an attempt to protect themselves, rather than as individuals. The truth was, it did not protect them.

"I cannot lie and say it does not scare me to attempt to use my gift in the same manner as you have," Fran said, "but I also owe your duke a great deal for saving me from a fate worse than death." She took a deep breath and let it out slowly. "I will consider assisting if I can. Now," Fran said brightly, "I was not there when your duke yelled at you, but I suspect more was going on than you think. Did it not once occur to you that he was not truly angry at you, but rather afraid for you?"

"No," Lillian said mulishly, wiping her eyes as fresh tears flowed. All this weeping was not like her.

"If I were the duke and I cared for you, as I believe he does—" Lillian started to interrupt with a denial, but Fran stopped the words with a stern green-eyed look. "As I was saying, if I cared for you and something happened that could have harmed you or even killed you and all I could do was to sit back and watch it happen, yes, I believe I would feel very angry. Not at you, but at the situation and at myself."

"Why should he be angry at himself?" Lillian asked. "That

does not make any sense."

"Because he could not do a single thing to help you. You must remember, I have been in the minds of many men and I know better than most how they think. Most men are protective and want to feel in control. When they cannot or are not, they get angry." She paused as Mildred brought the tea tray and poured both ladies a cup. When the maid went away again, Fran took a sip, then continued. "Women cry. Men get angry. This is one reason they spend so much time fencing, riding, boxing, that sort of thing. They have all this pent up anger and frustration that vigorous activity helps them to alleviate."

Lillian sat forward to take a pink-iced tea cake from the tray and looked at her friend in astonishment. "The things you know could fill a book." She smiled. "Actually, I have always thought you should write books. You of all people can observe the world as it truly is. If you wrote it all down, I believe it would be very popular. Salacious perhaps, but all the more popular for it."

Fran laughed, not at all pleasantly. "No, my dear. Many of the things in my head would not be fit reading material for any-one. The world is often a dark and disgusting place, as you know." She took another sip of her tea. "But this conversation is not about me. It is about you. I am sorry you felt you had to leave and miss what could have been such an enjoyable outing."

"No matter," Lillian said with a casual shrug. "It was ru-ined for me at that point."

"Yes, I suppose so, but I do feel you need to speak to the duke again and clear the air."

"Oh, Fran. I do not know if I can face him ever again."
Lillian felt like she would burst into tears once more. All this
emotion was getting ridiculous. She bit into the cake to keep
herself busy, but it felt like dirt in her mouth. It was not what
she needed. She took several sips of tea to wash it down.

Lillian jumped, splashing tea on herself when she heard:
"I figured this is where you had gone off to." The man was
stealthier then a cat on the hunt.

She did not turn around or look up. Instead she concentrated on wiping at her bodice with a napkin, as if this was
the world's largest problem.

"My lady." Gabriel bowed to Francesca. "How do you
fare today?"

"Quite well, thank you, your grace. I am much improved
with each day that passes thanks to you and your friends,"
she paused and looked at Lillian, "and thanks to mine."

"I am glad to hear it," Gabriel said. "I wonder if I might
borrow your friend for a short time?"

"Of course, your grace. You know I can refuse you nothing. However, you must promise to be gentle and kind or I
shall keep my friend firmly under the protection of my wing
and refuse to relinquish her." Fran smiled playfully.

Gabriel bowed again. "Your wish is my wish as well, so
an easy promise to make."

He turned to Lillian and held out his arm. "Lillian, will
you do me the honor of taking a turn about the portrait gallery
with me?"

She did not want to confront Gabriel, but putting it off would serve no one. Fran winked at her in encouragement. She stiffened her spine and stood, taking Gabriel's arm. "Of course," she said. She let him lead her out of the room.

Gabriel wore a passive look as they walked in silence down the stairs to the floor below. Lillian could not read his face, and she certainly did not have Fran's gift. What was he going to say? She bit her bottom lip.

They turned onto a side corridor, which was indeed a gallery lined with portraits of dukes and their families from across the centuries. Rather than continuing to stroll, they stopped beside a cushioned bench between two tall windows. Lillian sat down and stared at her shoes. She had been taught well how to hide in plain sight, but not how to face down a vexed duke.

Gabriel broke the silence that hung heavily between them. "There is not much time before our guests are expected to begin arriving, but I wanted to clarify some things as soon as possible." He paused, working to find the words that would make her understand his feelings when he himself did not fully comprehend them. She continued to look at the floor as he spoke. "I am sorry for yelling at you, Lillian. I imagine I did not express myself well out there, but under the circumstances, I hope you will forgive me for such brutish behavior."

Lillian started to speak, but he put up a hand to stop her. "Let me finish, then you can have your say." He took one of her gloved hands in his. "I have not grown up with sisters and have been much in the company of men. When it comes to explaining how I feel, I am very much afraid I do it badly." He paused again, taking a deep breath. "When I saw the danger you were in on that horse, I was angry at what I saw as your lack of care for your own safety. I was afraid for you—for your life, so utterly afraid that it made me feel helpless. There were one hundred and one ways in which the entire scenario out there could have gone horribly wrong. I wish I could have taken the time to appreciate your incredible horsemanship, but instead all I could think of were the possibilities in which you ended up dead." He squeezed her hand. "I care about your well-being. I want you to know and understand that."

Lillian appeared to be on the verge of tears, when she finally looked up. "I apologize for leaving the group and returning to the house as I did. I felt as if I had used your horse badly and that it was best to return her to the stables for the day."

"You foolish, foolish girl," he said and pulled her closer. Without thinking, he wrapped his right arm around her, laying her head against his chest. He chuckled. She sat up straight again looking at him in question. "Grizelda probably had the time of her life out there today. I do not know the last time she had such a ride."

Lillian gave a wobbly smile, but it quickly turned to a frown. "I have a bone to pick with you while we are being honest with each other. You lied to me."

He raised an eyebrow at the accusation.

"I spoke to Turpentine and he told me you had already asked him to come to Kent so you could use his ability." She gathered her breath. "But on the trip yesterday, you acted so surprised when I told you about him and then you went so far as to ask my permission to involve any of the Society members when you already had. Why bother asking?"

Gabriel ran his hand through his hair. What could he say? The recitation of events was accurate. He blew out a breath. "I know I can tend to trample over people in order to meet an objective, and unfortunately I have been taught not to apologize for it. I am accustomed to acting first and asking for forgiveness later. As to Turpentine, again, I share secrets with very few people in my life," he pointed back and forth between the two of them, "and I am not yet in the habit of sharing my business with you."

Lillian clenched her jaw. "Turpentine was my business first. He is like a member of my family."

"Yes, and I know I have disappointed you again." He lowered his eyes to the ground. "I was hoping I might redeem myself in your eyes when I asked if you would consider contacting other members of your Society, rather than forging ahead." He looked up again and spread his hands wide. "I can only say I will try to do better in the future."

"You have said that once before, Gabriel. I do not know how many chances I should give you."

"In my defense, I have had only two days to practice

changing my ways. I would ask that you help remind me of my faults in the coming days. I will do my best to—" His heart leapt as voices drifted along the corridor.

He stood and held out an arm. "Shall we go greet our guests? I believe some of them are arriving."

Lillian placed her hand in the crook of his elbow. "Gabriel, I am still in my riding habit and my hair could use some attention."

"It is nothing," he said with a twinkle in his eye. "I am still in my riding gear and my hair is decidedly windblown, as it would be if I had just come in from riding. Besides, I am a duke. I may greet guests in any state of dishevelment or shevelment that I choose."

Lillian laughed. "Indeed."

They went down the main staircase to greet the newcomers. Gabriel was not certain they had resolved their problems, but the possibility of finding his father's killer tonight had driven any further thoughts of the matter from his mind. His veins were thrumming in anticipation of justice for his family.

The small party they had originally planned had quickly turned into a list of nearly fifty people. Lillian plastered a cheerful social smile on her face as she assisted Gabriel and his mother to greet the guests who streamed through the Ramsay Hall foyer. It was a wide, ornate entrance with a red carpet which led to two staircases on opposite sides.

Before long, Lillian's cheeks had begun to hurt.

Gabriel whispered tidbits in her ear about each new member to their party as they passed by on the way to their rooms. She had no plans of touching anyone yet, as she first wanted to get an initial impression about each person.

Some of the new arrivals included Lord and Lady Truellan and their two daughters—Lord Truellan being a former military officer—Lord and Lady Archly and their two children Minerva and Archibald—Archie Archly, such an unfortunate name—Colonel Olmstead, Miss Isabelle Meadows, who arrived with her bosom friend Lady Evangeline Murray, the two lords she had already met at the garden party and their families, and a large handful of others whose names Lillian had already forgotten. Gabriel's friend Mr. Davis Rigsby entered the foyer and gave him a hearty handshake and a bruising pat on the back. She saw Gabriel grimace and she cringed at the pain the gesture had likely caused his wound.

Several more guests were to arrive the following morning, including the locals.

A familiar face made an entrance. "Simon," Lillian said, "I was not aware you would be able to make it to the party."

Her brother attended to removing his outerwear, including his hat and gloves, and handed them to Pennywhistle. "Yes, well," he said, neither smiling nor frowning, "I concluded my estate business much more quickly than expected and decided to travel down here after all."

He bowed to the duke and then the duchess with a "Your

grace." He looked around. "Where are Father and Mother?"

"They are resting in their rooms before tea," she said. Simon raised his eyebrows at this. "I know, I know. Mother would usually much prefer to be in the thick of things like the social butterfly she is, but we had a difficult journey here and they have not yet fully recovered."

"A difficult journey? Recovered?" Simon asked in some surprise. "What the devil happened?"

"You need to ask Mother about it," Lillian said. "She was in the coach, while I chose to ride Mirabelle. I am sure Mother will be pleased to have another sympathetic ear to listen to the tale."

Simon grimaced.

"It truly was a dramatic incident," the duchess said with a smile, "but I shall not take away Lavinia's delight in telling you."

"Oh, joy," Simon muttered.

"Tea will be served in the drawing room in half an hour," Lillian said. "Mother will expect you to be present when she hears you have arrived."

"Yes, yes. I will look forward to catching up on all the news," he said vaguely as he followed a footman carrying his trunk up the stairs.

Gabriel turned to her. "I am really quite surprised that not only has my cousin failed to appear, but that he was not the first to arrive."

"Why do you say that?" Lillian asked.

"Lately he has been acting quite sullen that he has not

been given more social prominence as my cousin and heir to the dukedom," he said.

Lillian leaned in and whispered. "He does not know then that Michael still lives and he is in truth *not* your heir?"

"Good God, no," Gabriel said. "The man cannot keep a secret to save his life."

"What a shock he will have when he learns the truth then," she said.

"Not to mention he has been living on credit given to him because of his supposed position and has accumulated debts he cannot pay."

As if on cue, the man nearly stumbled through the doorway, held open by the butler. He looked flustered, dusty, and wind-blown.

Gabriel kept his hands behind his back and did not offer one to his cousin. "We had begun to despair of you ever appearing, Howard, but here you are just in time to add your number to our little party."

Mr. Ramsay ran a shaky hand through his hair. "I had a spot of trouble along the way. One of the carriage horses threw a shoe not five miles outside of London. Had to ride at a snail's pace to the next village, don't you know." The man swept his hands down his coat sleeves, sending a cloud of dust puffing into the air. Gabriel grimaced. The duchess frowned, but said nothing. "When we arrived in the village, I was told it would be a day before someone would be available to reshoe the beast. There was nothing for hire other than a finicky nag," Mr. Ramsay grumbled. He swatted his hat at his grimy pant legs. Lillian, Gabriel, and the duchess backed up a step as a second cloud of dust wafted in their direction.

"I imagine you could use some refreshment after your ride," the duchess said politely. Mr. Ramsay nodded and began to speak, but she overrode him. "However, perhaps a bath is in order first?" She quirked an eyebrow. The man looked down at himself and nodded again. "Very good. I shall have a tea tray sent up to your room. You will wish to rest and refresh your spirits after such a trying journey, I am sure."

Howard walked toward the left staircase to the family wing, but Gabriel stopped him. "Sorry, old chap. I forgot to tell you. We are renovating the guest rooms where you usually stay, but we have a nice room ready for you in the guest wing." It was a lie, Lillian knew. Gabriel had purposely placed all the people from the original house party four years ago together in the same wing of the house.

"Fine," Howard bit out and stomped toward the right staircase, leaving a trail of dust in his wake.

Gabriel clapped his hands together and turned to the duchess with a grin. "Well, Mother. That is everyone for today, I believe. Shall we begin the festivities?"

"It is a house party, not a village fête, Gabriel." She frowned at her son. "People come to get away from the rush of town life. Therefore, we shall begin with a sedate cup of tea and quiet conversation in the drawing room. You may escort me there."

Gabriel offered his arm to his mother, who took it. "Of course, Mother. You are quite correct. We shall all be dull as mud and enjoy ourselves tremendously at it." He turned his head to Lillian and winked. "If we hear of anyone attempting to turn their stay here into one of frivolity, we shall squash the attempt immediately."

"If I had a fan, I would rap your knuckles for such impertinence! The very idea," the duchess said sternly, but Lillian saw a smile play across her lips. "Are you coming, Lillian?"

"Yes, your grace. I am right behind you."

The entire way to the drawing room, Lillian thought to herself, *Yes, this house party promises to be everything but dull. But will we survive it?*

TWENTY-SIX

Signor Silvano's Sayings Number 26
If you have an impressive skill, use it.
You might earn the respect of your peers
and draw attention away from
those things you wish to remain hidden.

The hum of conversation was intertwined with the clinking of silver on china that evening as the party enjoyed pleasant company and a lavish dinner befitting a duke. Lillian had been seated to Gabriel's left at the long formal table as his betrothed. Viscount Hartley had been placed to her left. He was such a quiet man, observing more often than talking during conversations. She wondered if he was socially awkward or merely did not enjoy the company of others.

She heard a throat clearing and realized the viscount had been speaking to her while she had been contemplating his personality. "I do beg your pardon, my lord. I went wool-gathering," she said.

He smiled briefly. "I saw that, my lady. Your eyes glazed over and you simply disappeared."

"I apologize again. I am afraid it is a common occurrence on my part and not at all a reflection of the good company."

"I shall not take it personally then," he said matter-of-factly but without a smile. He took a sip of wine from his glass before continuing in a lowered voice, "I understand you will begin your work on behalf of Wyvern tomorrow."

"I will indeed," she said. "Perhaps he will be able to bring his search to a conclusion very soon." Lillian sat back and allowed a footman to remove her plate and serve the dessert. Small platters of cheese, fruits, and nuts had also been placed along the table. She took a small bite of the strawberry trifle.

"For Wyvern's sake, I am pleased to hear it."

"I imagine the two of you have been good friends for a long time," she said.

"His entire life, since I am a year older." Hartley reached for a pear and began to peel it. "He was there for me when my father died when I was only fifteen."

"And you have returned the favor," she said.

"Yes," was his only response, but it was full of heavy meaning. Lillian imagined he would do anything for his friend.

There was a lengthy silence before Mr. Rigsby piped up with a grin from down the table, "I am sure the duchess will have all sorts of exciting plans for our day tomorrow. It promises to be another fine one. The only question is whether we shall all be together as a large party or whether the men will take off for more manly pursuits while the ladies simper about the lawns." The guests laughed at his dramatic imitation of manly men versus simpering women.

Barely raising his voice, Gabriel called to his mother

down the long expanse of the table and like magic the room quickly fell silent. "Your grace," he said with a please-forgive-me smile, "what say you? Will it be naught but strolling about for the ladies, or do you believe they are made of sterner stuff?" He sat back in his chair, allowing his mother to have the party's full attention.

The duchess looked at Mr. Rigsby and harrumphed. "Strolling about all day—indeed not!" She put her spoon down and looked about the room to gather everyone in. "The early morning will be reserved for those who wish for a bit of riding before breakfast." She looked at her son. "Wyvern, I shall expect you to lead a party about the grounds." He nodded. "Very good. After breakfast, there are to be competitions in archery for the ladies and shooting for the gentlemen. With very nice prizes to sweeten the fun of course." Oohs and ahs erupted across the table. The duchess continued, "Then, once we have enjoyed a fine picnic at the folly by the lake, there will be a choice between taking boats out or lawn games. I for one am looking forward to a lively game of croquet. I was quite the champion in my day." The duchess smiled at this reminiscence. She brought herself back to her discourse. "Now let me see, where was I? Oh, yes. In the evenings there will be parlor games of course, but we also have something special planned. Wyvern, would you care to explain it?"

"Of course, Mother. We plan to put on a small theatrical performance in a few days' time using the folly as a stage.

Tomorrow, Lady Lillian will begin organizing the production and shall assign parts and discuss costumes and such. Everyone," he looked at each person in turn with a genial smile, "and I do mean everyone, will be expected to participate in some capacity."

"If we are all to be in this play, your grace, who will be the audience?" Lord Archly piped up with a jovial chuckle.

"An excellent question. An invitation will be put about the village for any and all to come view a spectacular spectacle," Gabriel said.

One of the younger ladies—Lady Viola, Lillian believed it was—giggled and said, "Oh what a delight! I have never performed for peasants before." Lady Evangeline, seated to her right, quickly hushed her.

"I would hardly call the hard-working and honored members of our community peasants, Lady Verbena," Gabriel said with a hard-eyed gaze.

Verbena. That was the silly girl's name. The lady lowered her head with a mumbled apology. Goodness. Lillian wondered if she had ever behaved so foolishly, even when she was younger.

"Ladies," the Duchess broke in as she stood, "this would be an excellent time to leave the men to their port while we retire to the drawing room. Perhaps we can begin discussions about what is needed for the performance. I believe Lady Lillian has more particulars." The gentlemen rose as the ladies left their seats.

"Indeed I do, your grace," Lillian answered as she stood. Her mother and the duchess had decided during their planning for the house party that putting on a play would be an enjoyable way to bring everyone together for a shared amusement.

Lillian nodded in farewell to both of her dining companions. As she passed down the long table, she was stopped in her tracks by a sense of strong darkness emanating from someone. She reached out gently, but could not locate its origin. She shuddered in revulsion and hurried to join the mass exodus from the room.

The following morning, Lillian allowed Sarah to help her dress for the new day. Today she would use her ability in earnest, and she could only hope she continued to stay in control. She had tossed and turned all night worrying, knowing that one of the guests was a murderer. She yawned loudly as Sarah brushed out her hair.

"Lillian, you need to wake up if you are to be of any use today," her friend said. "You have made a promise to the duke, and he will expect you to fulfill it. You are already running late."

"I know," she said with another yawn. "I simply could not sleep last night out of dread for today."

"What is there to dread? Nothing will happen today that has not occurred before, will it?"

Lillian shrugged. "Perhaps I am merely picking up one of the guest's strong emotions, or else the heavy expectation is causing me stress. Who knows?"

"I am sorry you are struggling so and I am doubly sorry that you could not go riding with the duke this morning on account of sleeping in so late."

Lillian waved the thought away. "The last time we went riding did not go so well. Besides, I can ride with him another day."

"I suppose so," Sarah said, "but since it is a mock betrothal, you still need to bring him to a real proposal if that is what you decide you want after all."

Lillian met her friend's eyes in the mirror. "I have not yet decided what I want. Besides, there is no time for courting at the moment."

"Well if you should decide in favor of the duke, it does not look as if there is any competition for his attention here. Most of the ladies at this party are too young and silly. The rest are too old or already married."

Life felt too precarious today to be making such heavy decisions. She changed the subject. "You will have plenty to keep you busy this morning sorting out costumes and scenery for the play we are to enact. You should have no problem staying out of trouble."

Sarah snorted. "When do I ever get myself into trouble? You are mistaking me for Fran." She quickly braided Lillian's hair, coiled it atop her head, and added pins. Lillian yawned again and took a sip of the now cooled tea from her cup on the dressing table. "You had better wake up quickly, Lillian. You have an archery tournament at which to make a good showing."

Lillian turned her head to look up at her companion. "You know I am only mediocre at archery. How do you expect me to make a good showing, as you say?"

Sarah made a sound in the back of her throat. "I bet most of these young ladies have more hair than talent other than at the most feminine of pursuits. I think you may have a chance to win this thing if you can simply wake up!" She shook Lillian's shoulders.

Lillian scrunched up her nose at her friend. She removed her dressing gloves and exchanged them for the dark pink gloves that matched her burgundy walking dress. She stared at her hands. Would there ever be a time when she could stop wearing gloves every hour of the day? Could the new practice make it possible?

She stood and turned in a circle. "Now, do I look presentable for company?"

"Presentable enough, if you do not count those dark circles under your eyes," Sarah said with a wink.

"Oh, do stop. No one can see them beneath the rice powder you convinced me to use." She snatched up her bonnet and headed toward the door. "A lovely day to you, Sarah," she said with a smile.

"And to you. I will be going up to see Fran by the by."

"That is an excellent idea," she said, then departed.

The day was sunny and fine, with large puffy white clouds providing some shade—perfect for a day of outdoor activity. By the time Lillian had reached the back lawn where the archery was to be set up, it looked like the whole party was already accounted for except her.

Gabriel spotted her and sauntered over. "I had begun to fear you were not coming."

"I apologize," she said. "I had difficulty sleeping last night."

"I am sorry to hear it," he said sympathetically. "I do hope the strain of what I have asked you to do is not becoming too much."

She shook her head slightly. "I will admit, I have done more these past few weeks than I am used to dealing with. Not only the use of my ability, but it is not every day a friend is shot before one's very eyes, you know." She smiled gently. "But I will manage."

Gabriel shifted uncomfortably, glanced to the side and then back at her. "I should tell you that I spoke to Lady Francesca this morning and she has agreed to attempt to listen to the guests during our gatherings to ascertain if she can gain any information. Perhaps she can further narrow down our list so you will not need to exhaust yourself."

Lillian let out an exasperated sigh. "I do not see why you bothered asking me to speak to her and then ended up doing it yourself. You either need to ask for my help and wait for it or not."

Gabriel grimaced. "I know. As I said, I will do better going forward, but I hope you understand this is too important for me not to use every resource available to me"

Lillian flinched at the words. Was that all she was to him —a resource?

Gabriel offered his arm and led her toward the area where the ladies were choosing their equipment for the competition. He leaned his head slightly toward her. "I assume it will be best if you meet people naturally today as situations present themselves, rather than having me direct you."

"That is sensible," she said. "Do you wish for me to begin at once?"

Gabriel patted her hand on his sleeve. "Yes, if you feel up to it. Perhaps you could greet a guest or two from the list to get things started? I am anxious to see the results of your ability this week."

She nodded.

He flashed a grin at her. "Not to put any pressure on your archery performance this morning, but I have put a hefty wager on you as the winner."

"You did not!" Lillian huffed. "You have no idea of how well I shoot."

"I have it on good authority from your father that you are a fair hand at it, and I cannot imagine you will have much competition here."

"Sarah said much the same," Lillian mumbled to herself. To Gabriel she said, "I can only do my best. I make no promises about the quality of my performance."

They had reached the rest of the ladies. "Ah, Hawkins, I see you are assisting with the bows. Do you have any which will suit Lady Lillian?"

Hawkins—a tall, thin, older man with weathered skin—closed one eye and sized her up. What he could tell by doing this, she had no idea, but it was obvious Gabriel trusted him. "I have the very bow, your grace." He reached behind him, and presented his find to Lillian, then handed her a quiver of arrows. The bow did not look like it had any qualities superior to the others, but she took it graciously with a "thank you."

As they walked to the staging area, Gabriel said, "Hawkins has been a groundsman here since before I was born. He also helps with the outdoor activities during parties. He knows a thing or two."

"If you say so, Gabriel." She noticed some of the ladies were practicing with the targets. Anne was one of them. Lillian watched while her cousin aimed at the target and missed. She smiled fondly. Anne had never been more than competent at archery, but she was always up for trying.

Lillian picked up a leather arm guard from a nearby table. She began to don it, but Gabriel took it from her. "Let me help you with that."

"Thank you," she said as he carefully wrapped the leather around her left arm over the sleeve. The touch gave her shivers, but it was a pleasant sensation.

"Is this high enough on your arm?" he asked, steadily holding her gaze.

Her breath hitched at the intimacy of the connection. She remembered to nod, and he tied the strings to keep it in place. She quickly looked away. She had noticed finger guards were also available, but chose not to use them. The gloves she wore were made of a heavier leather than what ladies usually used for daywear.

"All set," Gabriel said.

She held up the bow and adjusted her grip until it felt right. Then she placed the arrow and pulled back the string without release several times. She took a deep breath and decided she was as ready as she could ever be without more practice.

Behind her, the duchess called out, "Ladies, shall we begin?" Everyone turned in her direction. "I shall have each of you draw a number to determine which order you will play. There will be multiple rounds, eliminating two at a time until the final round. Points will be given for how close to the center each arrow lands. Regardless of the winner, I have a prize for the four best of today's competition." This declaration received quiet applause as well as a few giggles from the younger crowd. "Also, Wyvern and Hartley have agreed to be impartial judges. Now, queue up if you will, ladies, and draw a number."

As Lillian got in the line, she noticed several of the older ladies had chosen to sit on lawn chairs to watch the competition. Many of them were shaded by colorful parasols. The gentlemen were, for the most part, standing about in small clusters. Her brother Simon was in close conversation with Mr. Rigsby.

One gentleman, dressed all in black, whom she had not yet met, was off to the side alone. He must have arrived that morning. He had dark hair and a short beard, accentuated by the dark clothing he wore, a thin nose, and an intense gaze. When he saw her observing him, he gave a short bow. She quickly looked away, her heart pounding, hands trembling. She had seen this man before. The night of Fran's rescue, he had been standing in front of her house, watching. An acute sense of unease built inside her chest. Who was he? He had to be a guest, but why then had he been spying on her?

When Hawkins reached her in the line, she took a deep breath, and put the man out of her mind. She was safe here under Gabriel's eye. She put her hand in the bag and pulled out the number eight. That would place her in the middle out of sixteen ladies.

"If everyone would clear the playing area, we may begin," the duchess called out. "Hawkins will do the yelling from here on out, and I shall take my delight in watching from over there." She smiled genially and pointed to where the other seated ladies had taken their ease.

Four targets were set up a fair distance away in a clearing surrounded by a few large trees. It looked as if nature had formed this area especially for archery. The first four ladies went up to the shooting line in front of a target. Hawkins called, "Shoot when ready, ladies."

At the end of the round, two arrows had missed the target completely and two had made it to the edge. Anne's arrow was one that had made it, but barely. Sarah and Gabriel were correct. It did not appear the competition would be fierce today.

The second set of ladies included Lillian. Before stepping up beside the other three women, she looked around again for the man in black. He was leaning against a tree, arms crossed over his chest, his gaze intently on her. A shudder ran up her spine, but she had no more time to consider him. At Hawkins call, she nocked her arrow, balanced the bow by rocking it up and down gently a few times to get the right feel and then strengthened her stance. She ignored everyone around her, focusing only on the target. When she felt ready, she let the arrow fly with a *zing*. It soared through the air and hit a middle ring. She smiled in satisfaction at her first attempt before looking at the other ladies' results. One young lady was in tears due to the fact that her arrow had not made it even halfway to the target. "Lady Lillian and Lady Truellan will advance to round two," Hawkins called.

Lillian backed away during the applause to let the next ladies have their turn. However, she quickly realized she had backed into someone. She jumped and whirled around. "Oh! I do apologize, sir."

The unknown bearded man bowed stiffly. His piercing gaze took her breath away and set off an alarm inside her head. "Baron Leonides at your service. That was a most excellent showing, Lady Lillian," he said with a slight French accent.

"Thank you, my lord," she said. It came out a little breath-lessly. His was a name she recognized from the list.

He waved his hand across the air. "Please. The French do not stand on such ceremony. A simple 'monsieur' is all that is required."

She curtsied. "I thank you for the instruction."

He leaned in closer, so close she could feel his breath on her cheek, and spoke low. "I expected you would do very well, my lady. I could not imagine any Duke of Wyvern taking a bride who is not far above all the rest in quality."

Lillian took a small step back and her voice came out with a slight quaver. "Thank you for the compliment, monsieur." Her eyes flicked back and forth, looking for anyone who could save her from this encounter. Although she did not understand why, her level of disquiet was increasing, she felt like a trapped hare.

Hawkins called out, "Will the ladies who made it to round two please step forward to choose a number for this round?" and Lillian breathed a sigh of relief.

"Excuse me, monsieur," she said with a short curtsy. She stepped over to where the other round two contestants were waiting, and took several deep breaths to calm her rapidly beating heart. She did not understand why she was so frightened. Was the baron the man who had killed Gabriel's father?

"Are you all right?" A whispered voice came behind her right ear. Gabriel.

Her relief deepened. She whirled around and pasted on her social smile. "Yes, thank you."

He narrowed his eyes at her as if he did not believe a word, but he let the lie stand. Now was not the time to discuss her suspicions with him.

When Hawkins came to her, she pulled number four. She would play in the first set.

By the third round, it was down to Lillian, Lady Truellan—a lady old enough to have a grown daughter and who surprised everyone with her archery skill—Miss Isabella Meadows, and Lady Evangeline Murray, a distant cousin of the duchess. Lillian stood at the mark and waited for the call to begin the final round. All her shots so far had landed in the same spot: right of the center ring. She needed to adjust her stance a little to the left. When the call was given, she prepared as before, but pivoted a fraction to the left. She settled again and let the arrow fly.

It had worked! She hit just outside the center ring. Still not a bullseye, but she had two more arrows in which to get it correct.

Hawkins called out again. Lillian repeated her previous stance and let it go. Her aim was off, and it looked like it would be a poor shot, but at the last minute the arrow suspiciously veered to the left to hit the edge of the center ring. She looked around at the spectators and found who she was expecting to see. Turpentine was casually leaning against a nearby tree. She glared at him and gave a sharp shake of her head in reproach. He grinned in response.

She had one arrow remaining. She aimed a little more to the left this time and let the arrow fly. It hit dead center! She wanted to shout for joy, but settled for a satisfied smile. That smile dimmed slightly when she looked at the other ladies' targets. Although each had done well, Lady Truellan had two arrows dead center. Her third was in the ring to the right. Lady Truellan had won by one arrow. The lady was smiling and a small crowd was forming around her, to give their congratulations.

Gabriel announced to all, "We have conferred and agree that Lady Truellan is the winner."

"Excellent," the duchess called out. "Let us now get on to the business of the shooting competition. Then it will be time for lunch!" This was met with applause.

Lillian took the opportunity to shake Lady Truellan's hand in congratulations. She was also on the list. After a lingering hold, she let go and stepped back. The lady was guilty of nothing but being the victim of a cruel stepmother during her growing years. That was now four people crossed off.

After returning her equipment, she walked over to stand by her mother, where she could survey the scene. She saw footmen were now bringing out a selection of firearms and several tables, already transforming the area into a shooting range.

"Dearest, second place is not shabby. Not shabby at all," her mother said. "Knowing how long it has been since you have used a bow, I know in my heart you could have easily taken first place with a little bit of practice."

"I am quite pleased with the results, Mother. Oh, I see Father is joining the men in shooting."

"Yes, he said no man worth his salt would sit out when he could prove the strength of his skill in front of the ladies." Her mother tittered. Tittered! Like a schoolgirl. It seemed Lady Wentworth was about to be impressed by her husband's shooting regardless of his skill. Her father was a lucky man.

Lillian looked about for a chance to greet one of the other twenty-four suspects. It was the entire reason for her presence at Ramsay Hall after all, was it not? Out of the corner of her eye, she watched Baron Leonides as he prepared to shoot with the others. She must find the courage within herself to greet him as soon as possible. She had a suspicious feeling that he would be the one they were seeking.

TWENTY-SEVEN

Signor Silvano's Sayings Number 27
The greater the risk, the better the reward.

Lillian's father was surprisingly good with a firearm.

While not all the ladies participated in the archery contest, every single man, young or old, stood up to the mark to showcase his skill, including Simon. The targets were covered in some sort of cloth with painted circles to better see the marks from the bullets.

Hawkins likewise kept points during this competition to determine the top four of the six who would advance to the next round. Each man was allowed two shots. After each round, the cloths on the targets were exchanged for fresh ones.

Gabriel's cousin, Howard Ramsay was sent out of the competition in the first round. He stalked off to sit by himself against a tree to sulk. She had a very difficult time believing the man was from the same family as the duke. Mr. Ramsay behaved like a wayward child.

Her father made it to round three, as did Mr. Rigsby, Viscount Hartley, Gabriel, Lord Truellan—a well matched couple there—and Baron Leonides. Her mother was beside herself in anticipation as Lillian's father shot and advanced in each round. She plied her ivory fan vigorously. "Oh, I cannot take the suspense, Lillian, but I cannot keep from watching either."

Lillian laughed. "I know exactly what you mean, Mother. Not long now and it shall all be over."

Once the second to last round had been completed, everyone waited for Hawkins to tally the scores and announce the final players. He called out, "The final round will be played by his grace"—Lillian's heart leapt in excitement for him—"Baron Leonides, Lord Hartley and Mr. Rigsby." She looked to her father to see his reaction, but he was obviously not displeased in the least as he shook each of his opponent's hands and gave them each a hearty pat on the shoulder.

He walked over to her mother and bowed with a large smile on his face. "Well, my dearest. What do you think?"

"Well done, Walter!" her mother gushed. Then her eyebrows drew together. "But I am confused. Were you fifth or sixth place?"

"It does not matter in the least," her father said cheerfully, then turned his attention to the final round.

While the cloths were being changed out and everyone's attention was on the contest, Lillian walked closer to Lord Archly. She wanted to test if she could repeat what had happened with Lady Alston at the garden party. It was possible she had gained information about the lady only due to the close connection to her husband, but Lillian needed to know for certain.

She concentrated on the gentleman, let out all her breath, then pulled it back in slowly, pulling energy with it toward her from Lord Archly. She opened herself to images from his life. When they came, she almost stumbled backward in surprise. She continued to breathe steadily and pulled on each inhale. When she began to shake and feel sweat trickle down her temple, she stopped.

Lillian was shocked. On the one hand, it was incredible that she could now see into people without having to touch them, but on the other hand, did it mean she would no longer be granted the protection of staying out of touching range? Dear God, she feared the implications if that were the case.

This aspect of her ability was no less tiring than the usual visions. She shook her head to clear it.

At least she had eliminated another suspect. She was now up to five.

Hawkins' voice brought her back to the featured activity. "Fire when ready, gentlemen!"

Lillian turned to watch. Gabriel was magnificent as he stood tall—sideways to the target—held the gun in one outstretched hand, and fired. He was so at ease it was as if he were merely taking a walk in the park.

The final round allowed for three shots. Each man reloaded his own gun before firing again. Once all the men took their final shots, Hawkins looked closely at each target, then announced the winners. "In fourth place is Baron Leonides." The crowd applauded politely. "Third Place goes to Mr. Rigsby." More applause. "Second place is awarded to His Grace, the Duke of Wyvern." Lillian's face fell. She truly had hoped he would win. They had both narrowly missed first place today.

The duke's smile did not waver as he turned to the final man to shake his hand and announce jovially, "And the winner is, Hartley! Well done, my friend!"

With the competition over, everyone was directed toward the folly where lunch had been set out.

She helped her mother to gather her things and followed her parents, who were still arguing over the importance of fifth versus sixth place. Lillian rolled her eyes. So much for her mother's excitement over watching her father's manly display.

The back half of the folly abutted a forest and the front half afforded a lovely view of the estate's manmade lake. Lillian turned slowly in a circle, looking at the entire lush landscape. It was very picturesque. Why would she not want to make this enchanting place her home? She sank down next to Anne onto one of the blankets laid out for their al fresco meal and contemplated that question.

After a tasty cold luncheon, tea was made available along with a sumptuous buffet of cakes and biscuits. Gabriel took more than his fair share, piling a plate so high it was all he could do to keep it from toppling.

He was just deciding if he should take a third chocolate eclair when his cousin sidled up to him and asked in a low voice, "Do you have anything stronger than tea and lemonade, old chap? I could use a little something else. Still recovering from the ride here, don't you know."

"I am afraid not," Gabriel said, licking a bit of cream off his thumb. "My mother will not abide the stuff in mixed company." He held his plate out to Howard with a smile. "Here, have a chocolate cake. It will restore you to good humor."

Howard cringed as if he had been offered a plate of worms. "No, thank you. You and your penchant for sweets and drawing room gossip." He shook his head in disgust. "Michael would have snuck off with me to the billiards room for more lively fun."

At the mention of his twin, Gabriel's smile died. "It is unfortunate for us both that Michael is not here. I am afraid you must bear up for the remainder of the house party, since I do not foresee it meeting your expectations." Gabriel picked up his glass of lemonade from the table and took his plunder to more friendly territory.

While striding away, he surreptitiously glanced around the area for Lillian. She was standing at her mother's shoulder; Lady Wentworth was still holding court for anyone willing to listen to her harrowing tale of the cobra incident. Her father was standing across the folly in conversation with a small group of gentlemen. Smart man. He caught Lillian's eye and gave her a brief smile. She rolled her eyes and leaned her head toward her mother. Gabriel could only imagine how many times the tale had already been recounted—and embellished.

He made his way across the lawn to where Hartley and Davis stood together talking—a deadly combination of intelligence and bold action. Add his brother to the mix and the little band would have had double of those traits and more. Gabriel wanted to sigh. He missed his brother so much it hurt. They had been apart for four years. Four excruciatingly long years. Anger toward his prey burned anew.

"Gentlemen," he said with a nod to his friends.

They stopped talking and returned the greeting.

"Wyvern," Hartley said.

"Gabriel," Davis said at the same time.

They both looked at his loaded plate in amusement. Gabriel resisted the urge to hold the plate out of reach like a child hoarding sweets.

"Pennywhistle has finalized security details," he said. "No one will come in or go out of the estate without our knowledge."

"Good," Hartley said.

"Did you have any interesting new developments on our investigation into the lordlings?" he asked before taking a bite of a cherry tart.

"I wish I could say yes," Davis said, "but every time I pursue a new lead, people scurry like rats to their nests. Getting any information has been deuced difficult. I am hoping something will bear fruit before too long." He scowled and took a sip of his drink.

"As do I," Gabriel said. "As do I.

"Speaking of rats," Davis said, "I hear we may have a few in our club."

"Not so much rats as lazy dogs," Gabriel said. "I expect the problem to be taken care of fairly quickly."

"You don't seem to be terribly put out about it." Davis pointed out.

Gabriel shrugged. "I have been gone for too long. It is to be expected that things have become a little bit untidy. When the cat's away and all that."

Davis gave a cheerful laugh. "Rats and cats. We have descended to a level where all men are animals."

"Lady Lillian owns a ferret of all things," Gabriel said, although he had no idea why he needed to add that bit of information. Davis raised an eyebrow. Gabriel cleared his throat and went on. "With what we have seen in our lifetimes, we know how much men—and some women—can behave like animals. It is the nature of the world is it not?"

Davis nodded. "Indeed."

After he had demolished half his plateful, Gabriel realized he had finally reached his limit of sweets. He held his plate out to his friends. "Biscuit?" They both shook their heads. Not knowing what else to do with it, he looked around, and seeing a passing servant, handed it off.

Gabriel clapped Davis hard on the back of his shoulder to repay him for yesterday's assault on his wound. "While we are on the subject, we have one animal in particular to run to ground." He grinned wolfishly. "It has been a long time in coming."

Davis rubbed his hands together in delight. "This, I am

looking forward to. Do you have a specific plan in place or is it all up to Lady Lillian?”

“As you say, I am trusting her abilities at this point. Once she has identified the culprit, we shall decide what is to be done.” Gabriel looked back across the lawn to check on the lady in question. She was standing exactly where she had been at her mother’s side. Maybe it was time to give her a break. Without taking his eyes off of her he said, “I shall let you know as soon as I have more to share—hopefully by tonight. Jersey should be back soon from his scouting expedition with some new information for us on all fronts.” Without a word of farewell, he began the journey to save his damsel in distress. He felt like he needed a trusty steed to complete the picture.

“Lillian,” he said when he reached her, “would you do me the honor of strolling about the lawn?” He saw the obvious relief in her eyes.

“Please excuse me, Mother,” she said before taking his arm. Lady Wentworth, engrossed in her story, barely noticed her daughter’s parting.

“Thank you,” Lillian breathed once they were out of her mother’s hearing. “If I had had to listen to that story one more time, I believe I might have screamed. You would think she would have told it to every guest in attendance by now.”

Gabriel chuckled. “I figured as much by the look on your face. You must admit, it is a fantastic tale.”

“Yes, perhaps for the first five tellings. After that it rather begins to pale." She smiled up at him.

Gabriel looked around while he spoke, ensuring their privacy. "On a more serious note, have you any updates for me?"

"Yes," she said. "You can cross Lord Archly and Lady Truellan from the list. I greeted Lady Truellan, but you may be interested to note I attempted to recreate the experience I had with Lady Alston during the garden party and found success with Lord Archly. I was able to extract information while only standing nearby, without having to touch him."

Gabriel's eyebrows shot up. "That is astonishing! Does it mean you may have an easier means of learning the information we seek?"

Lillian shook her head. "I am afraid not. It is an exhausting way of going about it and for now, I believe the usual way will be simpler."

"I understand," he said.

"I also wanted to point out that something about Baron Leonides makes me very uneasy, and I know he is on your list." Lillian stopped walking and looked more fully at him. "Gabriel, the evening we rescued Fran, the baron was standing in front of my house watching us."

Gabriel drew his eyebrows together. "I do not understand why he would have done that. He was a close friend of my parents, and—" He stopped and shook his head. "I cannot allow that to cloud my judgement. It sounds as if you have not had a chance to touch him. Perhaps you should do so now." He scanned the entire area, but the man was nowhere to be seen. He must have gone inside after eating. "I do not see him. I suppose he will have to wait for a later time. Shall we walk among the guests and see who else we can investigate?" he said, turning them back toward the party. Gabriel would need to speak to the baron later himself and find out what the man was up to.

Lillian inwardly sighed. She knew this is what she had agreed to, but she was growing to hate the idea that she was only at Ramsay Hall as a tool.

With Gabriel by her side, she first greeted Colonel Olmstead, who was a very genial older gentleman, an old crony of Gabriel's father. She was surprised when she took his hand and encountered nothing. It might perhaps have been different if they both were without gloves, but still—this was unexpected. Even with a slight pull on her ability, she came up empty.

Next she spoke to Lord Truellan. When he took her hand, the world shifted around them and she was transported back to the battlefield during the early days of the recently ended war with France. Sounds of gun and cannon fire surrounded her. To the right, a sergeant was yelling at a younger Lord Truellan to take a newly loaded rifle, but he was frozen to the spot in fear. Finally, the sergeant knocked the man down and left him lying on the ground, nearly insensible. Lord Truellan had been the commanding officer of that unit.

When she and Gabriel walked away, she whispered, "The only crime he is guilty of was cowardice during the early days of the war."

That caused Gabriel to raise his eyebrows. "Lord Truellan is a decorated war hero."

She shrugged. "Not everyone starts as a brave soldier, I imagine."

Gabriel examined her face. "Are you well? You look tired and I know you did not get enough sleep last night."

"I am only a little tired as you say," she admitted.

Gabriel continued to look at her, perhaps to see if she spoke the truth. Finally he nodded and took her arm again, steering her to another knot of guests, but her mother intercepted them.

"Lillian, dearest, your father and I are going inside where it is cooler. I know you will want to stay here and enjoy the frivolities with the younger set."

That was actually not true. She did not feel up to enduring an afternoon of frolicking about the lawn today.

"I will come with you, Mother. I would enjoy a little quiet." She turned to Gabriel. "If you will excuse me?"

"Of course." He nodded and leaned his head down to say quietly, "This will be the perfect opportunity for you to take a rest."

"I know you mean well, Gabriel, but I am fine," she whispered. "I will not fall to pieces for lack of a little sleep. Please allow me to fulfill the reason I am here in my own way."

Lillian whirled around and followed her parents into the house while footmen cleared the area and set out lawn games for the guests closer to the back garden. She knew taking a nap would be the smart thing to do, but she wanted to bring the investigation to a quick resolution.

Tea had been served in the drawing room. Lillian poured cups for her parents and herself, then took a seat at the side of the room. She sighed into the comfort of the chair, closing her eyes and allowing the conversation in the room to wash over her.

She must have begun to fall asleep, because she was startled to wakefulness by the voice of Baron Leonides. "You had better not fall asleep with that cup in your hands, Lady Lillian, or you will have a lapful of tea."

"Oh, I was not sleeping, monsieur." Hands trembling, she took a sip of the tea to prove her point. She looked up and saw that he was staring at her again. She had no wish to speak to the baron—something about him put her on edge—but if she did not, she would be unable to accomplish her task.

Placing her teacup on the side table, she said, "Would you care to sit and tell me about yourself, monsieur? I understand you were a dear friend of the late duke's."

The baron nodded and took the chair next to hers. "Yes. My friendship with the duke and duchess goes back many years before his death. I am sorry I was delayed and did not arrive until today, so we were not properly introduced.”

While he talked, Lillian attempted to use the new ability once again to draw information from the gentleman. She got nothing. She tried again, breathing out fully and pulling in more air this time.

Images and voices shot at her from multiple directions all at once, and her heart pounded. The baron, Lady Alston, the maid, others in the room—they all bombarded her. She felt like she was drowning in sensations and pictures of the past. She abruptly stopped pulling and held her breath, cutting off the chaos. Still feeling the buzz of the sensory assault, she slumped back in the chair.

“Lady Lillian, are you unwell?” Baron Leonides asked, alarmed.

She took a cleansing breath. “Yes, monsieur. I believe I need a little fresh air, if you would be so kind as to escort me out the front door?” She needed to get him alone, away from where any other guests might be. It was obvious the new aspect of her ability was disastrous in a roomful of people.

Lillian stood on shaky legs and cautiously took the arm the baron offered. She did not need to fake the weakness she felt. She had already taxed her reserves for the day, but she was determined not to go to bed without knowing if this man was the killer.

“Perhaps you are under too much strain with the pending marriage and now this house party,” the baron said.

"Perhaps," she agreed.

In the hallway, they ran into Gabriel's cousin coming from the direction of the back of the house with Archibald Archly. He bowed indolently. "Ah, Lillian. Baron. Would you care to join us for a spot of billiards?"

"Another time," Leonides said stiffly, and he led her abruptly away. When they had gone several feet he said in a low voice, "I have never liked that young man."

"Which one?" she asked.

"Howard," he spat. "He is one of those young puppies who feels entitled to everything and contributes to nothing." He looked at her with a softened gaze. "Forgive me. It is not my place to speak ill of Gabriel's family."

She did not tell him that likely everyone in Howard's orbit felt the same.

They had reached the door and the footman on duty opened it for them to pass through. Lillian took a deep breath of the late afternoon breeze, fortifying herself. She hoped she had enough energy to try with the baron once more.

Just beyond the forecourt was the fountain in the middle of the carriage drive. In the center was a statue of a rearing horse with a warrior atop, surrounded by lions facing away, and streams of water came from their mouths.

They sat down on the edge of the fountain wall. "We can simply sit here and enjoy the tranquility," the baron said.

"Thank you, monsieur. You are very kind."

Lillian took several minutes to collect herself before she breathed in deeply, and concentrated on the man next to her. Violent scenes came at her, one after another, swirling in her mind. Scenes of war, and sword fights, and gunshots. There was chaos, cunning, and deceit. She struggled to make any sense of it. Finally, she feared she would no longer be able to maintain control and stopped, closing her eyes until most of the shaking now wracking her body had ceased. She had been unable to find the baron's memories from the time surrounding the murder.

No matter how much she felt the need, she could no longer continue Gabriel's search today.

She stood abruptly. "Forgive me, monsieur, but I believe I would prefer to lie down after all."

She allowed Baron Leonides to escort her back inside where she slowly climbed the stairs to her room. She could not decide if this day had been a waste or a triumph. On the one hand, she had practiced the new aspect of her ability somewhat successfully, but on the other hand, she was no closer to finding what Gabriel had brought her here for. If she could not do this one thing, she feared she would be no use to him at all.

TWENTY-EIGHT

Lillian was both pleased with the progress she had made in the last two days as the guests prepared for the coming special performance and frustrated that she was no closer to finding the murderer. She knew Gabriel's frustration was even greater than hers.

So far she had been able to eliminate a total of twelve people from the list. Fran had listened to the thoughts of another four and determined that they were not the murderer. The baron would have made number seventeen, but she had not been able to make sense of his disconnected memories. She and Fran were now more than halfway through the names, but with no result.

Lillian desperately needed time to hide away in her room and avoid being in such close proximity with all the ladies and gentlemen of the party, but she had made a promise to Gabriel and a promise to herself. She was determined to stop the man who continued to threaten Gabriel's life, regardless of the toll it took on her. In a few days' time, they would all be actors on a stage, but today she would have to put on an audience-worthy performance. She would continue on, behaving as if she were truly enjoying the entertainments and as if she did not feel like she was eroding physically and emotionally.

After luncheon, it was decided to forego the afternoon games in favor of preparing for the play, for which the guests showed open enthusiasm. They were to enact *The Count of Sandrio*. A gothic tale full of mischief and mayhem.

The party members met in the ballroom where costumes and backdrops were strewn about—gathered from the attics and who knows where else—to be sorted and distributed. Lillian, assisted by Anne, assigned parts to each guest who would be participating.

Lady Evangeline Murray turned out to be the managing sort. Lillian put her in charge of assigning costumes.

To be contrary, Lillian commanded her brother to decide which backdrops should be used during each act of the play. He grumbled about the chore, but went to work. Small clusters of guests were standing about the room practicing lines, and Lillian was content with how things were beginning to come together.

Anne came up to her with a large grin on her face. "I managed to cajole Mr. Ramsay into playing our villain." She lowered her voice. "I thought it fitting since he is so unlikeable. Is that cruel of me?"

Lillian smiled. "We take our small pleasures where we can find them. I do not begrudge you this one." She turned to survey the room. "Everything is in place, so all we need now is for everyone to learn their lines." Lillian thought through the list of all that needed to be done. "We must rehearse as much as possible tomorrow since the performance will be in two days."

"I suppose it shall not matter if a few miss a line or two since it is all in fun," Anne said.

"Indeed," Lillian agreed.

The play was to have a grand sword-fighting scene, so Gabriel and a few of the gentlemen were on one side of the ballroom working out that part with props in place of real swords.

Lillian could hear Lady Verbena giggle repeatedly in her corner of the room. Thank goodness she had had the forethought to assign the girl only a small part. It appeared even those few lines were going to be a trial for her.

"You look tired, Lillian," Anne said, concern in her eyes. "Have you been pushing yourself too hard these past few days?"

"Probably," she said, "but four days of our fortnight have already passed with no result and I am anxious to be done with this."

"There is no reason to make yourself ill."

"I will be fine," she said absently. "It is nothing a little extra sleep cannot cure, and I can sleep all I wish at the end of next week." She pasted on a smile. "Let us move this little show along, shall we?"

She clapped her hands to get the attention of the room. "Thank you everyone for the enthusiasm you are putting into practicing your parts." Another giggle erupted from Lady Verbena, and Lillian stopped just shy of rolling her eyes. "We shall have a small rehearsal in an hour to run through it together." Lillian smiled. "Keep up the good work."

After rehearsal, they all took tea in the drawing room. It might have been another excellent chance to spend time with some of the older guests and look for her next quarry, but she needed a short break from that duty. She found a seat where she could watch the interplay of the guests.

Gabriel soon took the seat beside hers and smiled fondly. "This reminds me of the first time we met—you sitting like a wallflower, away from the center of activity."

Lillian returned the smile. "It is the way I usually prefer to enjoy a social event—watching rather than participating. I believe I have had more social interaction these past few weeks than I have had in an entire lifetime"

"Has it all been so unbearable then?"

"Oh, I would not choose the word unbearable. If that were the case, I would even now be hiding in my room. However, I will admit it has been taxing." She stood. "There are fourteen more people to sort out and I feel I have rested long enough."

Gabriel stood beside her, his expression turning to concern. "Lillian, although I wish for a speedy resolution, I do not like to see you driving yourself to the point of exhaustion. It will not hurt for you to rest a little longer."

She lifted her chin. "This is the entire reason why I am here at the Hall, is it not? To help find the killer?"

Gabriel took her left hand and held it between both of his. "It is not the only reason. You should know you are more important to me than a means to an end."

Lillian's mouth opened in a soft O. Thrown off guard, she did not know how to respond. She swallowed hard and said quietly, "All right, but I do wish to keep going. I know we are close to the answer." She looked about the room. "Do you have a preference for whom I should spend time with next?"

"Yes, I see two of them speaking together on the other side of the room." Gabriel squeezed her hand and let it go. "Perhaps we could meet in the attics an hour before dinner to discuss how things are proceeding?"

"Yes, if you wish," she said.

The group he led her to consisted of four gentlemen who were deep in a conversation about sports, fencing specifically. Gabriel's cousin sidled up beside her, making her flesh crawl. Although he had never done anything in particular to upset her, she had never been able to like him. Lillian knew the polite thing to do would have been to draw Mr. Ramsay into the conversation, but she did not wish to. Instead, she pretended he was not there. The strategy worked, as he soon wandered away.

"I have always adored fencing," she abruptly declared.

Gabriel turned his head, eyebrows raised. "Really? I thought most ladies preferred quieter and less violent activities."

"That is a myth, Gabriel. Many ladies enjoy sport of all kinds. We merely do not let on about it."

He gave an amused smile. "What sport do you enjoy, Lillian?"

"As I said, I enjoy fencing, but I also enjoy archery and shooting."

His brows rose higher. "With pistols?"

"Yes—"

Lillian was interrupted by Mr. Ramsay, who had now returned. "Aunt asked me to bring you a fresh cup of coffee," he said, offering the cup and saucer to Gabriel. He reached across Lillian, and his arm brushed against hers.

What is this man about?

Her ability screamed at her. Dread and panic welled up from the pit of her stomach. Something was wrong. She narrowed her focus, looking for the cause.

Instinctually, she intercepted the handoff of the coffee, taking it for herself. Her hand shook as soon as the porcelain met her fingers. The cup rattled.

"Lady Lillian," she heard Mr. Ramsay say as he reached out his other hand to grab her by the wrist.

Terror engulfed her.

Gabriel watched in horror as Lillian fell to the carpeted floor and went into convulsions. The cup and saucer had crashed alongside her.

Damn! What have I done?

He had known he might be putting Lillian at risk, but because everything had been going so well, he no longer thought about it.

He knew he needed to get Lillian out of the room as quickly as possible. Without pausing, he put his arms under her and scooped her up and out into the hallway before anyone could wonder at what had just happened. It was more difficult to hold on this time, as her body was wracked with spasms so hard they nearly knocked her out of his arms.

He immediately spied Pennywhistle. "Send for her companion, Miss Duggins," he barked.

Gabriel took the stairs two at a time in hopes of reaching her chamber as quickly as possible.

The guilt had begun to set in. He had done this to her. He had known she had been increasingly drained during the week, but he had not paid enough attention to her care. He mentally kicked himself. He could see what was happening to her now outwardly, but he could only imagine what it might be doing to her inside.

After counting three doors, Gabriel tried using his boot to open the fourth door. It was shut fast. He was contemplating his next move, while trying to keep Lillian still, when the door opened abruptly.

Lillian's companion appeared. "Oh! Your grace. Bring her inside, quickly." Gabriel followed. "Lay her on top of the bed. There is no point in covering her, as she will only get tangled." Miss Duggins went to a chest of drawers across the room, but called over her shoulder, "Do not let go of her just yet please." She rummaged in a drawer and brought what looked like several cravats to the bed.

"What are those for?" He eyed the girl suspiciously.

"I can see this is a bad spell, your grace, and in these cases, we must tie her to the bed. No one is allowed to tend to her except me and Miss Anne, and we are not strong enough to hold her for the length of time one of these episodes lasts."

Gabriel looked at the fabric in her hands, then back at Lillian and made a decision. "I shall hold her. This is my fault. I shall bear the consequences. Quickly—go close the door."

"But your grace—"

"Just do it," he ground out.

As Miss Duggins hurried to do as bid, Gabriel figured out the best way to hold onto Lillian so neither of them would get hurt. He picked her up again and carried her to a wing-backed chair by the fireplace. He placed her across his lap with one arm holding her top half close to his chest, with her head in the crook of his shoulder, and the other arm holding her legs down. It was not the most comfortable position, but it would have to do.

"How long will she be like this?" Gabriel asked.

"It depends on the severity. The previous one, the evening of the ball, lasted about half an hour. This looks to be the worst

I have seen in some time. It could be an hour or more." The companion placed the strips of cloth on the bedside table.

"Is there anything we can do for her?" Gabriel gritted his teeth against a renewed strength in her convulsions, which sent pain into his still-healing shoulder.

Tears pooled in the girl's eyes. "We have yet to find what might be of help to her. As you can imagine, over the years we have tried just about everything."

Gabriel nodded. "All we can do is wait."

"Yes, your grace. Perhaps I should summon her mother? It would not do if you were seen in her bedchamber like this."

"No. Let us not bring in Lady Wentworth just yet. She may bring unwanted attention to the situation. Besides," he tried to smile, "I have no plan to tell anyone I am in here. Do you?"

"Of course not, but were you seen carrying her upstairs?"

Gabriel cursed under his breath. Several people had seen him leave the drawing room with Lillian in his arms. How could they not? Plus, it would be difficult to hide their lengthy absence. He was going to need some help.

"Miss Duggins, I need you to find a footman or a maid who can go down to the drawing room and ask my mother to come upstairs on an urgent matter, please."

The companion curtsied and left the room.

Only a little time passed before his mother entered the room, Miss Duggins in tow. She must have already been on her way up to see what was transpiring when the girl found her. "Gabriel, what has happened?"

"Mother, I cannot fully explain the situation to you, so I must ask you to trust me, but Lillian has taken ill with one of her spells. From what I understand, she will be up and about again before dinner." He looked to the companion for confirmation and at the girl's nod he continued, "But until then, I need you to make some excuse for my absence from the party that does not include my being in her room assisting her."

"Why is Miss Duggins not taking care of Lillian?"

Before he could answer, Lillian was wracked with a fresh wave of powerful convulsions.

"I see," his mother said softly. "I have never seen anything like this. Will she be all right?"

"She will, your grace," Miss Duggins said. "This is an affliction she has had since childhood. It is not dangerous to her health."

Gabriel could have argued that point, but now was not the time.

"Well, as long as Miss Duggins remains with you, I do not see the harm. No one else need know." She patted him on the shoulder. "I will put it about that after assisting Lillian to her room, you were called away on urgent estate business."

"Thank you, Mother." He took in a deep breath of relief.

She left the room and Miss Duggins sat on the window seat, picking up a piece of needlework she must have been engaged with earlier.

Now he would have at least an hour to contemplate his sins. When he had asked Lillian to help him, he had assumed it would be a simple transaction, and that no one would get hurt in the process. How quickly he had forgotten the night they had met.

Never before had he had to consider how his actions affected others as long as the ends always justified the means. He had used Lillian and lied to her repeatedly. He was no better than a scoundrel.

Lillian convulsed again, and he was startled when her ferret jumped up and curled into the small pocket formed between her stomach and his chest. He nestled there as if attempting to comfort Lillian. Gabriel was glad. Someone needed to do a better job at taking care of her than he had.

He had known from the beginning that Lillian would be a good match for him as his wife, but he had had no idea how quickly he would fall in love. *Love?* He tested the word out in his mind. Yes, that was exactly what had happened over the past weeks. He had grown to care deeply for this courageous, strong woman. She had been a constant by his side as he sought to complete this investigation. She had always been a help and never a hindrance, coming up with solutions when he saw no other way. He had been so blinded by his drive to find his father's killer that he had not taken any time to appreciate Lillian beyond what she could do for him.

He cursed. He needed to sort this out soon before he lost her.

While he was kicking himself for causing Lillian's distress, he also had to ask himself how he could move forward from this. He was so close to catching the murderer that he could not stop now. This quest was what had kept him going these past four years. He could not simply let it go.

After some time, Lillian stilled. He loosened his hold and looked down. Her eyes were open.

"Gabriel?" she croaked, eyebrows pulled down in confusion.

"Yes, I am here," he said softly.

"Do not let go of me," she said, golden brown eyes locked with his.

"Never," he promised. "I have you and I will keep you safe."

She closed her eyes and sighed, drifting off to sleep.

He rested his head on the back of the chair. What a mess he had made.

Can I keep her safe?

He was afraid he might have just lied to her once again.

Lillian awoke with a start to a darkened room, Prince Albert snuggled up next to her head on the pillow. It took several minutes to gather her wits. Her head felt cloudy and disoriented. It was a good sign she had had another episode when she could not remember how she ended up in bed. She took several deep breaths, willing her mind to clear. It must be very early or very late. She had no idea.

What happened? She shook her head in an attempt to knock the knowledge loose.

Not having any success, she called out shakily, starting to feel frightened, "Sarah?"

"I am here, Lillian." The voice came from the other side of the bed curtain. "Let me bring a candle."

"What time is it?" she asked.

The curtain parted, and a candle flame flickered in the darkness.

"It is nearly three quarters past five o'clock," Sarah said.

"In the morning?"

"In the evening." Her friend was quiet for a minute then said, "You had another episode. Do you remember?"

"I am having difficulty recalling. I have no idea how I came to be abed."

"What is the last thing you remember?" Sarah asked.

Lillian thought back then asked, "What day is it?"

"Monday. Today you were preparing the guests for the play."

Lillian's eyes widened. She remembered the house party and the particular guests she was supposed to greet. She wiped her hands down her face several times to clear her thoughts.

Air filled her lungs in a rush as she remembered everything—as she recalled every ugly detail of the vision. She put her face into her hands and wept. The scenes and thoughts she had seen and heard were horrifying—the murders, the malevolent thoughts, the insanity. She wept over it all.

How could anyone be so evil and hurt so many people?

After several minutes of allowing the tears to clear her mind, a sudden thought struck her. Gabriel! "Sarah, what time is it?"

Her friend looked at her in confusion. "I just told you, Lillian. It is nearly three quarters past five o'clock. Do I need to summon help?"

"No, no. I am quite fine. I simply need to meet with Wyvern immediately, but there is little time. Take him the message that I am well enough to attend our rendezvous in the attics at six of the clock, then return to help me get changed for dinner." She jumped out of bed. "Hurry!"

Lillian rushed to find the clothing she would need for the evening while she waited for Sarah. Tonight she would wear one of her new dresses—a sky blue, trimmed in navy, with embroidered white daisies across the three flounces. She had to admit it was quite pretty and wondered what Gabriel would think. She shook the thought away. It was more important that she concentrate on the task ahead of her.

When Sarah returned a few minutes later, she went to work unbuttoning and unlacing at full speed. "There is one thing I think you should know," she said. "Wyvern was the one to bring you upstairs alone and held you until the episode stopped. He would not let me tie you down."

"I briefly remember waking with his arms around me. Why would he do that?"

"I do not know, but he did say the whole thing was his fault," Sarah said.

It was Gabriel's fault? Whatever did that mean? He was

not to blame for her situation. Lillian had often blamed the devil, her parents, and even God, but in the end, she recognized that it did no one any good and it would never make her problem go away.

And after tonight's episode, it felt like she would be stuck with the worst manifestation of her problem for all eternity.

The six o'clock hour found Lillian sitting with Fran and Sarah in the attic room, awaiting Gabriel. She was anxious and nervous, and if he did not show up soon, she was going to hunt him down. All this time to think was driving her to madness.

She jumped up and started to pace. She needed to get her mind on something else for a few minutes. "Fran, why must life be so complicated?"

"I have no idea, my dear. However, if we believe the eastern philosophers, then it is because we were very naughty in a previous life." She smiled mischievously.

Lillian stopped and put her hands on her hips. "I know you do not believe that. One life is far more than enough for all of us, thank you very much." She bit her lip. "Every time I think I have things figured out, they become indecipherable again. Gabriel refers to me as one of his resources and yet cared for me so sweetly during my latest episode."

"Can you not be both someone who is cared for and someone who is of help to him?" Sarah asked pragmatically.

Lillian shook her head slowly. "I have been afraid my

entire life of being taken advantage of because of my abilities. It confuses things. In my mind, if he truly cared about me, he would not wish me to use a part of myself that is self-destructive."

"He does not see it that way," Fran said. "Rather, he sees your gift as an amazing part of you—no different than the voice of a talented soprano."

"However he views it, I feel like his kindness toward me comes from guilt rather than any true affection," Lillian said.

Fran softened her gaze and her voice. "You have grown fond of him, have you not?"

Lillian wrapped her arms around her middle. "Yes, but it does not matter how I feel. He had only one reason for this betrothal, which has not changed, and my ability is still like a brick wall between us." Above all, she was very much afraid her love for Gabriel would go unreturned. *Love?* The idea surprised her, as she had never hoped to fall in love with anyone.

Regardless of the emotion in her heart, she feared her love would not be enough to overcome the difficulties they would have to face.

Fran sighed heavily. "Such a weighty topic. For now, let us think about simpler things." She leaned back and smoothed out the skirt of her dress.

Silence reigned. It seemed no one had simpler things to contemplate tonight.

"Your duke is late, by the by," Fran said.

"Yes," she said as she sat back down and restlessly tapped her foot on the hard wooden floor.

A few minutes later, Gabriel finally appeared and bowed. "I apologize for my tardiness," he said a bit breathlessly as if he had been running to make up some of the lost time. "I had a very lengthy report from my man Jersey which needed my full attention." He took the seat next to Lillian which Thomas had brought over earlier and examined her face, worry in his midnight blue eyes. "How are you feeling?"

"I am much better, thank you."

"I am pleased to hear it." He huffed out a breath and pulled out his pocket watch to check the time. "I know we have much to discuss in the next three quarters of an hour, but I am very concerned about you continuing on this quest, Lillian." His face softened. "You said you wanted to stop when it became too much for you and I wonder if you have reached that point."

Lillian held up a hand to stop Gabriel from saying anything more. "That is no longer going to be an issue." She took a deep breath and let it out slowly. "Earlier this afternoon, as you know, there was an incident."

Gabriel had a pained expression on his face.

"I am sorry that yet again you had to go through an experience like that with me," Lillian said. "I wish I could change what happened, but I cannot."

"You have no need to apologize," Gabriel said, "I am just sorry that I pushed you to the degree it has caused you harm."

"That is of little importance at the moment." She waved her hand in the air to push the thought aside. She was getting impatient and must tell Gabriel what she saw. "I need you to understand that I had this vision because your cousin grabbed my wrist to stop me from taking that teacup," Lillian's face clouded in remembrance, "and it caused the worst incident I have had to date in my lifetime."

"Truly?" Gabriel's eyebrows shot up high into his forehead. "I know Howard is an immature scoundrel, but what could have been so awful?"

The weight of the memories from the vision was heavy on Lillian's chest. "The answer to that question, Gabriel, is everything."

TWENTY-NINE

Signor Silvano's Sayings Number 29
Sometimes you must break the rules to win.

Gabriel was confused by Lillian's answer, but anxious to learn more.

"I know you told us your father was murdered, but you put it about that he was killed in a hunting accident," Lillian said. "Can you give me more particulars of when you found him?"

"My father?" Gabriel asked, feeling thrown off course. How had they gone from Howard to his father? An emotion he could not identify was radiating through his chest, threatening to erupt.

At Lillian's nod, he took a deep breath and said, "He was found on the floor of his study, near his desk. The door was locked. Upon closer examination, there was evidence the gun had been muffled through a damaged cushion found near his body." Gabriel felt the choke of emotion rise into his throat. Having to look at his father's body for evidence afterward was not something he could ever forget.

"That is what I expected," Lillian said, her bottom lip trembling. "I saw his murder, and I know who did it."

Gabriel sat forward full of anticipation. This. This is what he had been waiting four years for. "You learned this earlier from the episode with my cousin?"

"Yes," Lillian stopped to lick her lips, "but please bear in mind, I do not know what amount of accuracy my gift offers. I have never sought out facts to corroborate what I have seen. However, what you have just described matches what I saw."

Gabriel nodded, feeling suffocated by the dawning realization of what she was going to say.

"During the vision, I saw Howard Ramsay kill your father."

Lady Francesca gasped.

Gabriel swore viciously. The bastard had been under his nose this entire time. Literally. All that he had been feeling exploded into an anger so strong it took his breath away. He put up a hand. "Give me a moment." He bent forward with his elbows on his thighs and allowed himself to slump. God, he had never expected this. He took several deep breaths to steady himself, then sat back up. He needed to finish this. "Forgive me. Please continue."

Lillian gave him a reassuring smile and went on. "Earlier that day, he snuck into the study and put something in the duke's wine decanter. He knew of your father's habit of drinking wine in the evenings while he worked. The drug made his grace insensible. Then your cousin entered the study through a window he had left unlatched and used a cushion from a chair in the room to silence the gun." Lillian covered her mouth with the back of her hand in horror. "I am sorry," she said as tears fell down her cheeks. "I cannot—"

Gabriel allowed her needs to override the emotions he was having difficulty containing. He grabbed her hand and said, "Do not apologize. I can only imagine what you witnessed. You have said it is as if you are there." He pulled a handkerchief from his coat pocket and handed it to her. She took it, covered her face, and wept. "Shh," he said softly. "You will make yourself ill again."

Transferring her hand to his left, he wrapped his right arm around her shoulders. Feeling this was not enough, he gently pushed her head down onto his chest.

She continued to cry for a while longer until her sobs turned into sniffs, then she dabbed at her cheeks. "I am so sorry to be such a watering pot. Other than at the school, I have never shared my visions with another. Now I see why." She laughed at herself. Then she looked around, noticing her friends, and quickly sat up to make space between the two of them. "I beg your pardon."

Gabriel, however, did not let go of her hand and kept his arm on the back of her chair. She made a small attempt to extricate her hand, but when she saw this would not do the job, she left it.

"I attempted to hear him these past two days—your cousin I mean, since he was on the list—but could get nothing from him but an odd buzzing," Lady Francesca said. "I have heard the sound before from people with confused minds. I think it is a sign of some sort of madness."

"There is no surprise in the idea," Miss Duggins said. "Anyone who plans and commits murder must be somewhat mad."

Silence filled the room for several heartbeats. Then Gabriel spoke up. "Was there more you wished to share with me about my cousin?"

Lillian nodded solemnly. "The reason I took that cup of coffee he attempted to hand to you was because it felt wrong somehow. My intuition was correct. He had laced it with arsenic."

"Howard has indeed grown desperate to kill me if he used such an obvious way to go about it," Gabriel said in disgust. The anger continued to burn in his chest. "If I had gotten sick or died, all would have known who the culprit was."

"Yes. His attempts on your life have become more and more erratic, starting with the previous attacks against you and Michael, up until today. He has such a strong malevolence toward your entire family that his head is full of thoughts of killing you and taking what he believes is his rightful place as duke. It clouds his thinking, and I fear he is now balancing on the edge of insanity."

"I think I have always known my cousin was not normal," he said grimly. "When we were younger, my brother and I always had to keep a close eye on him when he came to visit. He was a kick-the-dog and break-our-toys kind of child. I do not know what went wrong with him. His father—my uncle —was my father's younger brother, and was liked by everyone."

"There is more." Lillian said. Gabriel listened, his heart racing faster with each revelation. "One reason my episode was so strong and prolonged is because when I connected with him, it was as if the floodgates opened wide, telling me fully about his true nature. I do not know if this is because I have strengthened my ability or because so much twisted darkness lived inside of him.

"You need to understand that he is two parts insane and one part like a little child. It is almost as if he is two different people. When you encounter the little child, he is easy to manipulate, but if you should be speaking to him when in the grip of insanity, he can be very cunning and extremely dangerous. You must not underestimate him."

Gabriel slammed his fist against his thigh in frustration. "If he is so cunning, as you say, I do not know how we are to expose him as a killer. The last thing I want is for him to walk away from Ramsay Hall a free man."

"You could have him killed," Lady Francesca offered nonchalantly.

Miss Duggins gasped. "Fran!"

Gabriel ran his hand through his hair. "It is not as though I am not tempted."

"Well, we cannot very well walk up to him and say 'I know what you did' and expect he will confess all," Fran said with sarcasm in her voice.

"Exactly," Lillian said. "I told you his mental stability is shaky at best, and men of his ilk can often hold very tightly to the belief that they are truly innocent of any and all wrong doing."

Gabriel looked at each of them with troubled eyes. "As you said, the man is mad enough to be a genius at times, and he has certainly avoided detection all these years. The rest of the time, he is merely frivolous and immature, which are not crimes, unfortunately. I have no evidence that will convict him."

After all Lillian had seen of Mr. Ramsay's heinous crimes against others, she agreed with Gabriel that he should not be allowed to go free. The spark of a plan began to form in her mind. "If he is on the edge of insanity," she said hesitantly, "perhaps what we need to do then is find a way to give him a little push over that edge. If he surrenders fully to his madness, it should be much easier to get him to incriminate himself. I believe we could have him on his knees begging forgiveness for every single one of his sins starting from the age of three."

Fran grinned. "I like where you are going with this, Lil, but how are we to accomplish it?"

"I think between the two of us, and with a little bit of help, we can make this work," Lillian said, "but I am afraid you will be required to use your ability a great deal, Fran, and I do not know if you are strong enough yet to withstand it."

Gabriel broke in, "I do not wish you to think for even one moment that I am interested in exploiting your talents, but at the same time I am past the point of rational thought about this. Four years of attempting to catch him out have been unfruitful. I would be grateful for any help you could give."

"It is quite all right, your grace," Fran said. "Lillian and I both know your idea is not to use either of us for ill. I for one, owe you a debt I cannot repay and would be happy to help in any capacity." She looked at Lillian. "Tell us all, my dear."

"This is how we are going to do it." Lillian proceeded to lay out her plan.

When she was finished, Fran gave a wide smile. "I must say this is quite ingenious, if a tad dramatic coming from you. I am only surprised I am not the one who thought of it."

"I can come up with grand ideas when I am highly motivated," Lillian said, "and I am currently very highly motivated. I have seen the depths of Mr. Ramsay's depravity."

"One thing you must be concerned about, however," Sarah added, "is how Fran can carry this out without being seen or recognized." She turned toward their friend. "Your height and red hair are very well known traits. "

"I shall have to be disguised obviously, and disguised very well. Hair color can be covered with a wig, but my height, hmm. Let me think about that for a moment." Fran put her hands palm to palm and tapped them against her chin. Then her eyes lit up with excitement. "Oh, I have it, but I am not going to tell you right now until I work out the particulars."

Lillian looked at Gabriel. "I think we can pull off these changes in the two days we have remaining. Do you feel this idea will work or is it too complicated?"

Gabriel gave a feline grin. "I believe it is brilliant. This man who has plagued my family practically since birth will not know what has hit him. He will beg for a nice cozy cell in Newgate prison by the time we are through with him." Gabriel sobered. "Lillian, it is time we went down for dinner. Shall we leave your friend to the design of her disguise while we dine?" Lillian was about to answer when he added, "Lady Francesca, anything you need to make this scheme a success is at your disposal. Anything at all. Spare no cost or detail."

Gabriel wanted to put everything into place right away to take down his cousin, but he was thwarted by his responsibilities as the host. However, he begged off early from the after-dinner port and headed for his study where Jersey would be waiting. He had given Hartley and Davis the signal to follow.

He entered his sanctuary and growled. "Jersey, how many times have I told you, my desk is not here for your pleasure?"

Jersey was sitting in his plush leather chair with a quill

in hand and a pair of small spectacles perched on his nose. He almost looked respectable.

"I apologize, Your Highness. I was just trying to get these messages from the couriers all copied down on paper for you."

"You have a perfectly good table and chair in which to do it." Gabriel pointed to his left. "Right there."

Jersey made a big show of gathering his things and slowly hauling his large body upward. "Your chair is much more comfortable," he grumbled.

"Fine! I shall see about getting you something nicer to sit on, but later. Right now we have two guests arriving and much to discuss. Pour us all a drink." He took his place on the now warm leather seat and rummaged through the top draw for a quill to replace the one Jersey had purloined.

Gabriel looked up from his task when the other two of their party entered the room. "Gentlemen. Thank you for coming." He gestured in front of the desk where leather chairs sat side by side. "Please have a seat and we can get right down to it."

"It is not as if I truly wish to play parlor games with girls nearly half my age. Take your time, Wyvern," Hartley said, easing into his chair.

Davis, who always appeared in good humor, sat and smiled. "You are barely old enough to shave, Hartley. How can these ladies be half your age?"

"Well, I feel old compared to them," Hartley grumbled.

Jersey brought them each a snifter of brandy.

"Have a drink," Gabriel offered. "We are all going to need

it." He took a large sip of his drink, then pinched the bridge of his nose and sighed. His head was aching. After another sip he began. "I have no desire to relay the information I have to share, but I must. As you may have noticed, Lillian had one of her episodes again after being touched by one of the guests. She had not had one for a long time, since she was learning to control her ability, but I believe this time could not be helped because of the powerful nature of the vision." He paused, wiping his hands down his face and back up through his hair. "Lillian was touched by my cousin, Howard, and she confirmed that he is the one who killed my father and has attempted to kill both me and Michael."

Davis sat forward on the edge of his seat. "Bloody hell!"

Hartley's eyebrows shot up. "This was not what I expected."

"Neither did I," Gabriel said solemnly. "I mean, I never liked the man, even as a child, but I did not think he could be capable of cold-blooded murder." He looked at his valet. "Jersey, I would like you to give us a summary of the latest information you have gathered and then I am going to tell you all of the plan we have devised to have Howard arrested."

"Yes, sir." Jersey shuffled the papers around to his satisfaction. "We already know there aren't too many snakes like the variety you encountered to be had in all of England, but one was recently sold to a young gentleman fitting, now not surprisingly, Howard Ramsay's description. He said he wanted to impress his friends."

Davis cursed.

"Indeed," Gabriel said. "Unfortunately—or fortunately, however you want to look at it—the use of this particular weapon was an error in judgement, as he could not ensure it would reach its intended target."

Jersey shook his head back and forth a couple of times. "Your cousin does not have a very bright brain box if he thought that would work. I think we can confidently place the blame for the cobra on him.

"I am pleased we can use these facts against him," Gabriel said. "Now on to other business. Until further notice, I want you to place as many men as you can spare among both the indoor and outdoor servants to keep an eye on things. I do not want any surprises."

"Do you want a tail put on your cousin?" Jersey asked.

Gabriel placed his elbows on the desk and steepled his hands. "Yes, definitely, and now that I think of it, I want someone to keep an eye on Lillian whenever she is not in her room."

"Do you think she is in danger?" Davis asked.

He shook his head. "I have no particular reason to believe so, but from what she has told me, Howard is unstable, which means we should expect the unexpected from him." He looked at his valet. "That is all for now, Jersey, thank you. If you will please get started."

"Immediately, your grace," Jersey said, placing his spectacles on the desk and leaving the room.

"I do believe Jersey has a soft spot for your future duchess," Davis said.

Gabriel rubbed his hands over his face again to relieve some tension. "Why do you say that?"

"Because in the short time I have known him," Davis said, "I have never once heard him call you your grace."

Gabriel let out a small chuckle. It was a good observation. He had grown quite a soft spot for his future duchess as well. Future duchess? What would the future look like if he could not convince her to stay with him? He felt a deep pang of regret that he had not truly made the attempt to court her before everything had turned to chaos.

"Now, what's the plan?" Davis asked, interrupting his thoughts.

Yes, he needed to get back on track. There would be time soon enough to speak to Lillian about their relationship and the possibilities for the future.

Gabriel looked at each of his friends in turn and said, "Gentlemen, now that the murderer has been identified, we have come up with a way to catch him out, and I am going to need your help."

Lillian was jittery and on edge. They had two full days remaining before the play on Wednesday evening, and in the meantime, a murderer was walking among them.

Anne had just come to her room to go with her down to the ballroom for play practice, but Lillian wanted to finish her tea first. She filled her cousin in on all the details that had occurred the previous day regarding Mr. Ramsay and their plan to force him to confess. She jumped at the sound of a spoon clattering on the tea tray.

"I have not seen you this anxious since the day of your presentation at Court," Sarah said, handing her a freshened cup of tea. "What has you so worried?"

Lillian shrugged. "Take your pick: knowing I could be rubbing shoulders with a killer at any moment, using my ability tomorrow night, that this will all end badly. The better question is, what am I *not* worried about?" She squeezed her right hand into a fist, then released it.

Anne reached out and patted her shoulder. "You will not be alone through all this. You have Fran and Sarah and me to help, as well as the duke and his friends."

"I think as usual you are worrying over things that likely may never come to pass," Sarah added.

Lillian took a sip of tea. "I think I recall the last time you said that very thing—it was about how Gabriel would come for a short visit, then go away and never come back. Ha!" She interjected. "Now I am not only betrothed to him, but embroiled in his murder investigation, regularly using an ability I had hoped to never use again."

"I know you have been under a great deal of strain in these past weeks," Anne said, "but I have watched you grow in strength within a very short time." She paused. "I can tell there is more that has you concerned."

Lillian stared into her teacup as if it had all the answers

in the world. "I worry that I am out of time with Gabriel. I have fulfilled my side of the bargain, but I am not ready for this to end. Is that selfish of me?"

Anne gave a happy laugh. "It is not the least bit selfish. You care about him, and I believe he cares about you."

"But if I were to draw him into my world, I would be placing a great burden upon him. He would have to deal with the ramifications of my ability. That is the selfish part." She worried her bottom lip. "I have never wanted to marry, because I never believed any man would want that."

"I think you are underestimating Wyvern," Sarah said. "Talk to him and see how he feels."

"Perhaps." Lillian stood abruptly. She was not ready to face this now. First they needed to get all this ugliness behind them. "Anne, we should go downstairs now and make sure all is proceeding according to plan. Sarah, you were going to go to the folly with those working on the set and ensure all the details are taken care of?"

"Yes. It is pouring down rain, but we will manage."

"Good," she said. "I can only hope it will not rain tomorrow."

As they reached the stairs, Lillian saw Gabriel coming up. Anne held back to allow them some privacy.

"There you are," he said. "I was worried you were still feeling under the weather."

She shook her head as he offered his arm and they descended side by side. "I am well enough. Sarah, Anne, and I were planning some additional details for tomorrow before joining the rest of the party."

"Thank you for going to so much trouble to ensure everything is taken care of," Gabriel said. "All that you are doing, what you have done, truly means a lot to me."

"It is my pleasure," she said, "and as Fran said, she is doubly pleased, as she knows the debt she owes to you."

He waved away the compliment. "It was all easily accomplished and it satisfied me immensely to help her knowing how much it meant to you."

Lillian smiled up at him. "We are all very pleased with each other this morning."

Gabriel chuckled. "Indeed."

With everyone engaged in some activity or preparing for their performance, and an open hour available, Lillian decided to slip upstairs to see how Fran was faring with her role. Inside the attic room she hurried to the divan, but Fran was not there.

"Who are you looking for, my child?" a tremulous voice asked from behind her. Lillian jumped and whirled around.

"What are you doing up here, ma'am?" she asked, fearing for her friend.

The stooped woman was old with a shabby, plain brown wool dress that hung on her too loosely. Her gray hair was stringy and wildly tangled as if it had not been brushed or washed in an age. In all honesty, the woman looked to Lillian like a witch from a fairy tale.

The woman cackled. Then she giggled. Giggled?

"Oh, I had you fooled, did I not?" Fran said in her normal voice.

Lillian put a hand to her heart to slow the frantic beating. She felt the same way every time Samuel popped up in front of her appearing to be someone else, and then she realized it was him. In this case, she was astonished at how her friend's voice could come from this grotesque person.

"Fran, you frightened the life out of me," she grinned, "but what an ingenious costume. Not even your own mother would be able to recognize you." Realizing what she had said, she attempted to apologize, but Fran put up a hand to stop her.

"You are correct. That is partially the point of the disguise, is it not? That my mother could not recognize me?" Fran gave a large smile, that Lillian knew hid the hurt she was feeling. "Shall we go through our parts for tomorrow? This is going to be such fun!"

Fun? Not exactly what Lillian would call it. Frightening was a better word. Outside her family, she had never before confronted someone about what she had seen in her visions. Never had she faced a criminal in person. Now she must put all that she had learned about her ability into practice for the greater good. "Yes, let us practice, Fran," she said. "Otherwise I shall have no idea what we are to say tomorrow."

For the better part of the hour, the two friends set the scene for what promised to be a performance no one would soon forget.

Lillian left Fran with plenty of time to make it back to the ballroom for another run-through of the play. She had only taken three steps away from the door when a hand reached out to take her arm. She shrieked.

"Lillian, it is only me," Gabriel said softly. "I am sorry I frightened you, but you seemed miles away and were about to walk right past me."

"Gabriel," she said breathlessly and put a hand to her heart. "You are forgiven. I am very jumpy today. My mind was on getting back downstairs to the guests in time to start the rehearsal."

"They will not mind if you are a few minutes late," he said, inviting her to a cushioned seat by the wall. There were no windows up in this hallway since it was … What it was Lillian was not quite sure. It was not the servants' quarter. Perhaps storage rooms?

She sat obediently on the seat and slumped her shoulders with a sigh. She had yet to simply sit and relax today. There was too much to do. Gabriel sat next to her, still holding on to her hand.

"Lillian, I need to speak to you on some important matters," Gabriel said gravely.

She looked up at him and waited.

Gabriel squeezed her hand and frowned. "First, I wanted to tell you that I have a growing concern about Howard's hatred for my family, and now that I am more fully aware of what he is capable of, I worry that he may turn his sights on you as my betrothed in order to hurt me."

"You cannot predict how he will behave. So far, his more recent actions have only been directed toward you and your brother."

"This is true," he said, "but still, I would like you to consider going home and forgetting all about this mad scheme. You have already fulfilled your side of our bargain. Orchestrating this trap against my cousin is not worth any harm coming to you. I can find another way."

"No, Gabriel. I admit I desperately wanted to go home as quickly as possible once I arrived, but now that I have seen firsthand the pure evil inside your cousin," Lillian's face grew fierce, "I feel I have a duty to see him removed from society for the good of all." She paused, then said more quietly. "Please, Gabriel. Please trust that I worry more for your safety than for my own. I need to stay."

"Stubborn girl," he said softly. "I cannot like it, but I have already taken precautions against future attacks. I have two servants who will be following you about in turns to keep you safe. Pennywhistle, Hartley, and Davis have also volunteered to look after you and intervene if needed."

Lillian nodded and accepted her protectors. In the past such an action might have irritated her, but in this case, she was grateful for the feeling of security. During her vision, she had seen how far the man was willing to go to get what he wanted. Although she had not lied to Gabriel, Mr. Ramsay could very well hurt her if it helped him achieve his aims.

Gabriel cleared his throat. "I know this is not the best timing, but after tomorrow, we will have fulfilled the main purpose of this house party, and I do not wish you to leave Ramsay Hall next week without the chance to speak to you about our betrothal." He shifted on the seat. "In the beginning, we had a very clear understanding of what each of us wanted out of this betrothal, but as we have worked together over the past weeks, I have come to see what an exceptional woman and what an incredible partner you are. I am not referring just to your gift, but to your intelligence, kindness, bravery, and capability." Gabriel ran his thumb across the back of her hand. "I would like to ask that, when we return to London, you allow me to court you in earnest. It is my greatest wish, after we spend more time together away from all this chaos, that you might allow the betrothal to become real—that you will marry me."

Lillian's mind raced. This was both everything she had feared and all that she had begun to want. But what was she to say? Life never felt that simple for her.

"Gabriel," she said with anguish in her voice. "I have never wanted marriage because of my ability. How could we go on together with it in the way? I feel like it would be impossible."

"How do you know it would be impossible?" Gabriel asked.

Lillian was quiet for a long time before saying, "All I can tell you is that I will consider it. This is too much to take in today with all that is happening." Right now she was too intensely focused on the grand plan before them and there was no room for any other thoughts in her head.

"My timing is terrible, but I want you to understand the depth of my desire for us to stay together." He grimaced and squeezed her hand. "It is not fair to push you right now, and knowing you will think on it will have to be enough. When this is all over we will find time to talk about it again."

Lillian was not ready to follow her dreams. Not only did they go against every plan she had ever made to achieve independence, there was the real possibility the consequences from her ability could fall on Gabriel. She was terribly afraid that if she gave in to his wishes, at least one of them was going to lose.

THIRTY

The morning of the performance, Lillian walked beside Anne and Miss Thompson on their way to the neighboring village of Wattlesford. They had been working so hard for the past few days learning lines and setting scenes that the outing was a welcome break. Several carriages were brought out for the adventure, but most of the young people chose to go on foot. The weather had improved from the day before, and the sun was peeking through the clouds.

She found it very difficult to concentrate on her companions when every word Gabriel had said the night before was echoing in her head. She had never expected any of this. When she had grown old enough to understand how her ability could affect those around her, she had determined not to marry, let alone consider falling in love. She was afraid saying yes to Gabriel would only see him hurt in the end, and that was the last thing she wanted.

Lillian tried to distract herself from her chaotic thoughts by going through the lines she and Fran had discussed the previous night. They had to work together in perfect harmony for the plan to work well. She squeezed her gloved hands tightly into fists and released them. Why had Gabriel chosen to speak of his intentions when he did? Now she could no longer focus.

"You seem far away this morning," Gabriel said.

Lillian jumped. She had no idea when he had come up beside her. "I was thinking of all that needs to be done for the performance," she lied. "There is still much to be managed before tonight." She closed her hands again—slowly— and released them. The leather creaked with each motion.

Gabriel took her left hand, placed it on his arm and covered it. She could feel the warmth through the leather. "Let us fall behind your companions a little," he said, and slowed their pace.

Lillian took a deep breath and let it out. She was afraid talking with the very person she was trying to forget today was going to make things worse.

Gabriel was pleased to have a reason to spend time alone in Lillian's company, although he knew now was not the time to push her into a definite answer to the question he put to her the day before. Emotions were running high in anticipation of tonight's event.

Much of the lane had dried after yesterday's rain, but still had muddy patches. He kept watch, steering Lillian around the worst of them.

"I wanted to reassure you that I spoke to Baron Leonides about why he was found outside your London townhouse," he said. "I cannot give you a full answer, except to relay he said he was there on my mother's behalf."

"The duchess?" Lillian's brows drew together. "Why?"

Gabriel shrugged. "I could not say. I need to speak to her about it, but she has proved elusive these past few days. However, he assured me he means you no harm."

Lillian nodded.

He was not so certain his words would bring her any comfort under the circumstances, but regardless it was time to think of something other than machinations and plots for once.

"Tell me," he said. "If you had one place in all the world you would like to visit, where would it be?"

"Anywhere by the sea," she replied wistfully. "You know, I grew up in Norfolk on an estate only an hour's ride from the ocean. When I went away to school I missed it dearly."

"Ah," Gabriel said. "Although we are a little further away than an hour here, Ramsay Hall is not far from that same sea you grew up along."

Lillian smiled. "Where would you go, Gabriel?"

That was easy. "England. Anywhere in England. I was gone too long as it is and have no wish to leave again for a long time to come."

Colonel Olmstead who was escorting Isabelle Meadows, had caught up to them and heard Gabriel's pronouncement. "Quite right, Wyvern. The war kept me away, but it is high time I enjoy the pleasures of home, what?"

For the next mile they discussed all the pleasures England had to offer.

Gabriel took great pride in escorting Lillian into the shops and introducing her as his future duchess to everyone he met. It was so easy to imagine her by his side forever. She was equally kind and gracious to everyone from the lowliest shop assistant to the gentleman farmer, confirming how worthy she was of their high regard.

For four years he had had only one goal in his life: to bring down the man who killed his father. Now that the journey was coming to an end, he had realized there was more to life than revenge and he wanted—needed—Lillian to be a part of it.

After luncheon and a short respite for a change of clothing, the whole party met in the ballroom. Those who had no acting parts sat in chairs as spectators, facing the 'theater.' This was not where the play was ultimately to be enacted, but an excellent place to practice away from the outdoors, where it was raining once again.

Gabriel directed the men, and Lillian directed the ladies in their parts. There were many stops and starts as players needed reminders of where to stand or prompting of their lines, but the first run-through of the day went very well in Lillian's opinion. But whether the play went perfectly mattered very little to the success of their scheme against Howard Ramsay.

"Shall we go through it one last time before stopping for the afternoon, Gabriel?" Lillian asked.

"I think we had better, my lady. The swordplay scene could use a bit of work." He winked at the men who were in the scene, suggesting it needed no such thing.

"The sense of drama needs to be played up a bit more," the duchess declared from her seat. "Isabelle, it is difficult to tell if you are heartbroken or have a sour stomach." The room laughed as intended. "And Howard, if you are meant to be the evil villain, a more sinister look on your face would not go amiss."

"As you say, Aunt," he answered with in unctuous voice.

The duchess' casual tone led Lillian to believe that Gabriel had not yet told her about Howard. Lillian took a deep breath and blew it out quickly. The poor woman was going to have a shock tonight.

She stepped forward and called out, "Once more, everyone, then we can take a break for tea until five o'clock, when we shall meet at the folly for a full dress rehearsal." She clapped her hands. "Places, everyone! Act One, Scene One."

Lillian was a bundle of nerves, but she was determined to stand strong and play her part well. She took a sip of hot and fortifying tea.

They had gathered in the drawing room for teatime. Some of the younger crowd, as well as a few older, were playing a game of 'I Am Thinking of Something,' in which one player called out something they were thinking of and the other players asked questions until they had enough information to guess the answer. It was a silly game, really, but something to pass the time.

Sarah interrupted the inner turmoil inside her head. "Is there anything else you need me to do for tonight, Lillian?"

Lillian bit her lip. "No. I think all is in place." She lowered her voice. "At this point, the only thing I will need from you is assistance in getting back to my room when this is all over. I have no idea what state I will be in."

"Of course. I will be standing next to that large handsome footman, Rory, in case you have need of him." Sarah winked.

Lillian laughed. "Handsome is not a requirement, Sarah, for a footman to be useful."

"Indeed not, but it helps. I am glad to see you smile."

Lillian sobered. "I look forward to going home when this is all finished. I need rest." She was ready to get this over with and move on, whatever that might mean.

The stage was set, the players costumed, and the lines rehearsed and memorized. Lillian peeked out of the gap in the curtain at the remaining guests and village locals waiting for the performance to start. The duchess and the two great aunts were seated in the first row.

Tall torches set in the ground lined each side of the rows of chairs for the audience's benefit in preparation for when the sun began to set. The folly, which looked like an old Greek temple, was a perfect venue for a theatrical performance. It was completely open, with a colonnade placed in a semi-circle around the outside. The stone floor extended beyond the open portion, which made an excellent stage. The servants had strung heavy cloth between two columns to serve as the curtain. The weather was still cooperating. Now all that remained was for the hour to strike six so they could begin.

The performers were enacting a revised version of *The Count of Sandrio*, an Ann Radcliffe style story complete with damsel in distress, romantic hero and evil villain, but little did they know, in the end, how revised it was going to be. Davis was to play the hero, Lorenzo, teaming up with Isabelle Meadows as the heroine—the fair Sophia. Howard's part as Diego was to attempt every evil deed possible to take Isabelle for himself. The final scene was to be a sword fight between the two men and their comrades, ending with only the two standing against each other. But she and Fran had built in several surprises for the final act.

When the hour to start finally drew near, it was the duchess herself who stood center stage. "I thank you all for attending our little performance. The gentlemen and ladies have worked hard to bring you this entertainment. I hope you will now enjoy our rendition of *The Count of Sandrio*."

The audience clapped while the duchess returned to her seat.

And so it began.

The performance was going well considering how little time the guests had had in which to prepare and learn their lines. These sorts of plays always had such farcical drama about them that a mistake here and there did not distract from the whole. Gabriel was Lorenzo's right hand man, and Lillian could see the true hostility between him and his cousin each time they interacted on stage. The second to last scene involved the kidnapping of the fair Sophia by Diego, who would drag her off to his lair. As the scene began, she quietly slipped away to don her costume for the final act.

Diego had taken Sophia to his hideaway and she was now tied to a chair. In the final act, Lorenzo, with his trusty assistant, was to charge in with his sword in hand, defeat Diego, and rescue Sophia. Howard said his final lines of triumph in his smug voice, leaving a definite chill in the air. The curtain closed, to the applause of the audience, and would soon re-open for the next act. Torch bearers were supposed to be brought on stage for additional light for the final scenes as the sky grew dark, but a change had been made for Lillian and Fran's entrance. Darkness on stage was imperative.

Lillian, dressed similarly to Fran, was at stage left waiting nervously for her part to begin. Gabriel came up beside her and whispered, "We have your back if anything should go wrong. Your safety is more important than anything." Lillian swallowed hard and nodded. "You are an amazing woman. Do not forget that. He leaned down and gave her a kiss on the cheek." Lillian's breath hitched. She put up a gloved hand to cover the place where his lips had touched her, surprised by the sensation. She wanted to explore how she felt about it, but she had to put it out of her mind, needing all her concentration for the play now.

Gabriel squeezed her hand in reassurance. "You will be incredible."

She took one more deep breath.

The curtain opened again to reveal Sophia tied to the chair and Diego, posed with his fist under his chin as if contemplating more evil deeds. Fran entered like a ghost on stage right, while Lillian did the same on the opposite side. Her friend pushed a huge black cauldron before her. It had been placed on wheels, which screeched in the night air. A hush fell over the audience.

From the darkness came Fran's voice as an old crone. "Diego, I know of the evil deeds you have done," she accused. "Nothing has passed by me unseen or unheard."

Howard started at the unexpected voice and looked around in confusion. This was not in the script.

Lillian's voice, also disguised as a crone but not as impressively as Fran, came from her place in the shadows. "I too have seen all you have done, from your earliest misdeed as a youth to the ones you carry out now."

Howard's head swiveled toward the new voice. His eyebrows lowered and his lips thinned in anger as he looked around. He began to improvise, calling out, "Who is there? Who makes such accusations against me, the great Diego, Count of Sandrio?"

Fire and light exploded from the cauldron, illuminating Fran on the stage at the same time a loud boom rent the air. Lillian jumped. The sound of thunder was not part of the plan. Shrieks and exclamations came from the audience.

"I am the one who hears your every thought!" Fran called out fiercely.

"I am the one who knows your every deed!" Lillian echoed.

"Witches?" Howard played along uncertainly.

Fran scoffed. "Indeed not, but perhaps your conscience."

"I was there when you committed your first murder." Lillian advanced a step. "You remember, do you not? The blacksmith's daughter." Howard took a step back in shock and horror. Lillian could see the moment he realized the play had become about him.

"I only meant to push her away," Howard defended himself.

"True," Fran said, "but instead she fell and broke her neck." The audience gasped.

Without thinking, Lillian pulled more facts from the vil-

lain as she spoke. "Instead of confessing your sin to her father," Lillian accused with a finger pointed at him, "what did
you do?"

"I did nothing," Howard said in a shaky voice. "I ran away."

Fran, unseen, threw more chemicals into the cauldron,
causing the fire to shoot into the air with red light. "You lie!
You weighed her down and threw her body into the water
by the mill. Did you not?" When Howard did not answer, she
repeated the question at a screeching yell. "Did you not?"

Howard was visibly shaking at this point. "Yes. No. How
do you know this?"

"I can hear your every thought, you vile coward," Fran
said.

"And I can see into your soul!" Lillian echoed.

"Once you tasted the evil of your first murder you were
not satisfied, were you?" Fran demanded. "You felt the power
it gave you and you wanted more. More of everything! To
get it, you had to commit more sins and more murder!"

The boom came again eliciting more shrieks from the
audience. Lillian's knees were shaking in fear, and she was
finding it difficult to remain standing. She only hoped they
were not causing the same intense reaction in those who
were watching.

"The tavern maid, the gambler, the tailor," Fran said.

"The fellow traveller at the inn, the prostitute, the barkeep.
After so many murders had added up, it was easy to kill
your uncle to steal his power, was it not?" Lillian asked in a

loud voice that carried across the audience. "It was nothing to you!"

"He was nothing to me!" Howard yelled. "And I was nothing to him! I was always treated like a poor relation instead of as the honored heir as I was entitled!"

Fran drew closer to the cauldron, which cast her face in a frightening light. "Ah, but you were not the heir, were you?" She cupped her hand to her ear. "What is that I hear you thinking? You should have been the heir? You were better than all of them?"

Howard stumbled back. "How—how did you hear that?"

"Remember," she answered. "I can hear your every thought."

"And I can see into your soul," Lillian echoed.

Fran threw another vial of chemicals onto the fire, which then turned blue. "Killing your uncle was not enough, was it? To become the true heir, you had two more murders to commit. You succeeded with the first."

Lillian glanced briefly at the audience and saw mixed looks of shock and confusion. The duchess sat with her hand over her mouth, clearly in distress. She could feel the hysteria rising from Howard. The truth of his deeds being laid before him was becoming too much.

He began to back up. "Shut up, damn you! Shut up! You have no idea what you are talking about." He stumbled over a chair on the stage, then righted himself.

"Actually, I do," Fran said. "I can hear your every thought."

"And I can see into your soul," Lillian echoed again.

"You murdered two men for their power, and you still plan to murder the third. Then you will have everything you want."

"I only want what is mine!" Howard yelled frantically.

"What is yours to take?" Fran asked. "You have no rightful claim." She added to the fire, and orange sparks shot out this time. "What makes it yours to take?" she yelled.

"I was born to be a duke!" Howard screamed. "My mother told me as soon as I could walk. She taught me everything I would need to know for the day when I would become the duke."

"Your mother was never quite right in the head though, was she?" Lillian asked, pouring oil onto Howard's anger. "And you turned out to be just like her."

"That is not true! My mother was perfect." He let out a scream and lunged toward Lillian, but an invisible hand pushed him away. He fell heavily and slid across the stage on his back.

Gabriel leapt in front of her, holding out his sword. Howard scrabbled backwards until he located the sword he was to use in the final act—the weapon that was supposed to be merely a prop—but when Howard lunged at Gabriel, the clang of metal sounded. Good Lord! Howard had brought a real sword to the performance. Pulling more information from him, Lillian saw he had meant to use it against Gabriel all along to kill him this night!

"You cannot win," Fran taunted. "Your sins have been found out!"

Another boom filled the air.

Howard was no match for Gabriel's superior sword skills. He slashed wildly at his opponent, who easily met each blow with a well-practiced parry. Gabriel did not advance on his cousin, only defending himself as he hissed, "You killed my father and my brother, but I have no plan to die by your hand as well."

The audience gasped at the words, perhaps the remainder of them realizing for the first time that this was not a regular part of the play.

"You will die!" Howard said. "But first, I shall have you on your knees begging for your life."

"You have become completely insane, have you not?" Fran called out. "You believe your own lies and in the strength of your power, but the truth is, you are weak."

"And a coward," Lillian took up the gauntlet. "A coward who murders the innocent. A coward who hides in the shadows and strikes when his opponent's back is turned. You shot the duke while he was asleep. Like a coward!" She drew out every word of the last part.

Howard began hacking at Gabriel's sword with no finesse or strength. "I am not a coward! I am not weak! I am a duke!" Each statement followed the slap of his sword against Gabriel's.

Gabriel lunged forward to strike a serious blow, but Howard tripped backward, falling. His sword skittered across the stage. He looked about wildly, like a trapped animal. He scuttled across the stone floor, stopping when he reached the back curtain. He pulled a thick, long dagger from his boot and sprang upward. He pointed it at the duke. "Damn you!"

"I think not," Gabriel said with calm resolve, readying his sword in defense. But Howard did not move forward. He threw the dagger at Gabriel, then raced to pick up his sword. He clawed at the curtain until it parted, pulled it aside enough for him to go through, and ran.

The dagger did not hit its intended target, but was halted in midair and dropped, clanking on the stone floor. Lillian looked to the audience, and spotted Turpentine standing along the edge of the chairs.

Gabriel began to follow, but it was too dark to see more than two feet forward. He rushed from the stage, grabbed a torch from one of the torch bearers, then pursued his cousin. Hartley and Davis did the same.

The audience began whispering to each other, confused about what they had seen. Everyone on the stage stood as if frozen in time, waiting. Poor Isabelle had been tied to the chair this entire time.

Fran came center stage rolling the cauldron before her, as if the play continued. Lillian could feel her distress and hear her ragged breathing, but her friend soldiered on, seeming to want to make a dramatic point. It was just like her to get caught up in the moment. "Thus an evil life has been brought low by his own thoughts and deeds. May this be a lesson to all who think that no one sees and no one hears the sins you commit in the dark. You will be found out." She lowered her head.

Thunder rolled and the heavens opened.

The stunned audience, seeing the play was now over and the rain was starting in earnest, quickly scrambled from their seats to find shelter.

Lillian lifted her head to the sky and allowed the cold rain to pour down her face. She had now fulfilled her side of the bargain and had given all of herself in the process.

There was nothing left.

She allowed her shaking legs to finally give way, and she plummeted to the hard, cold, stone floor.

THIRTY-ONE

The cool air felt good on Gabriel's face after the fight against his cousin on the stage. His heart was racing madly as he confronted the man he had been waiting for years to identify.

Howard had not made it far into the dark woods behind the folly before Gabriel and his two colleagues had caught up and surrounded him.

"Throw down the sword and surrender, Howard. You have nowhere to go," he commanded.

"And let you take me to jail? No!" He lunged toward Gabriel with his sword.

Gabriel dropped his torch and easily parried the clumsy blow. "Come peacefully and I will make sure they are lenient toward you as the grandson of a duke."

His cousin was no longer listening and started hacking at

Gabriel like a crazed man. He had no choice but to block blow after blow until he could begin a counterattack, backing Howard up one footstep at a time toward a large oak tree. He hoped to pen him in. Gabriel suddenly slipped on the muddy ground, bringing him to one knee. As Gabriel attempted to steady himself, Howard took advantage, and knocked the sword out of his hand. He lifted his weapon to swing again on his defenseless cousin, but Gabriel pulled a dagger from his boot and rolled to the left, coming up in a crouched position.

Howard started toward him but stopped abruptly when the sword flew out of his hand and landed several feet away in the mud. He stared at his hand for a moment, then the fallen sword, before turning his attention back to Gabriel. His face twisting in rage, he rushed at Gabriel, knocking him and his dagger to the ground, his hands around Gabriel's throat.

Gabriel brought his forearms inside his cousin's soft arms, and easily forced them outward. He put out his palms to push Howard off, but his cousin surged to the side, and snatched up the dagger. Gabriel turned to knock Howard down again, but his cousin was in an insane frenzy. He slammed into Gabriel, and stabbed downward toward his throat. Gabriel pushed Howard's wrist to the right, twisting the knife away from him while at the same time using his full body weight to force his cousin over onto his back. He crashed on top of him.

Howard let out a stifled scream and stopped moving.

Gabriel scrambled back onto his knees and stared at the dagger now sticking out of his cousin's chest.

His head fell forward. Was this perfect justice or just a sad comedy of errors?

His friends closed in, the light from their torches casting eerie shadows.

"Good Lord!" Davis said. "Didn't expect that to happen."

"This will be interesting to explain to the magistrate," Hartley said.

"I am the magistrate," Gabriel reminded them, dully. He felt numb. For so long he had wanted this worm brought to justice and now that it had happened, he did not know what to feel.

Not anger. Not pity. Just numb.

"Please help me," Howard croaked out, opening his eyes to look up at them.

Gabriel jumped in surprise. He had thought the man was already dead.

Hartley crouched down by Howard and examined the knife wound. "You are done for," he said. "I can tell you right now the knife went in too close to your heart. If we remove it, you will bleed out in seconds," he looked at Gabriel, then continued, "and I do not believe you deserve as quick a death as that. We will just wait here until it is over."

"Witches," he rasped. "Damn witches. How did they know about the girl?"

"They told you," Davis answered this time. "They can hear your thoughts and see into your soul. Not witches at all."

"Perhaps avenging angels sent from Heaven?" Hartley added.

Howard gave a gurgling laugh. Gabriel could only imagine the blood coming from his mouth, but he had no desire to look.

"Angels do not look like that," he rasped out. "Do they?"

"Maybe where you are going they do," Davis said.

Gabriel tuned out everything else that was said before his cousin finally breathed his last. He did not want to hear the man's voice ever again. What he wanted to do was run back to Lillian and hold her close, both to reassure himself she was fine and to unburden his own emotions. But as the local magistrate, he waited until the end, then gave orders for the body to be brought to the ice house until his place of burial could be decided—as far away from Ramsay lands as possible.

Although too weak to walk, Lillian was still conscious as Rory carried her upstairs to her room. Sarah took over as soon as the footman left, helping her hobble on jelly-like legs to the dressing room. Her companion turned on the taps to prepare a bath while Lillian removed the costume and threw it in a heap.

"Burn that," she said in a shaky voice.

Sarah helped her into the water once the bath was full.

Lillian was cold, but it was not only that. She had withstood the assault of visions of Ramsay's evil actions while pushing her talent to the limit to draw the thoughts from him. She now regretted it. So many murders. How could one man

be responsible for so much destruction? She had resisted using her ability all these years precisely to avoid seeing these
kinds of horrible images. Increasing her control seemed to
have made the ability grow stronger, and now she no longer
needed to touch someone to receive visions.

Was there a limit to how powerful it could become?

She was wracked with shudders and wrapped her arms
around herself, looking for warmth.

That evening she was brought back to her anxiety from
before the season began—if she did not keep her ability tightly
closed away, it would eventually consume her.

Lillian fought to maintain consciousness as exhaustion
came over her. She briskly scrubbed at her skin with a cloth to
wipe away the feelings of clinging evil. Then she allowed Sarah
to help her get dry and dressed in her nightgown.

Back in her room, she stumbled to the bed and fell upon
it without getting under the covers. She continued to tremble
until darkness enveloped her.

Francesca allowed her maid and footman to help her back to
the attic room where Mildred assisted in removing the costume.

Her ears were ringing loudly enough she felt as though a bell
had taken up permanent residence inside. Mildred helped her
to dress for bed and then brushed out her hair. Her maid tried
to ask her something, but Francesca was unable to make out

the words. She could not remember the last time her ears had done this, but she knew of no way to stop it. "I cannot hear a thing!" she said loudly to Mildred. She might have been shouting, but she had no way of knowing. Even the sound of her own voice was lost to her.

Mildred brought over a bottle of laudanum and showed it to Francesca with raised eyebrows—asking a question.

"Where did you get that?" Francesca yelled although she knew she would not hear the answer. She grabbed the bottle from the maid and threw it against the wall. It shattered silently into a thousand pieces while the liquid oozed into the floorboards.

Never again would she get near that stuff. Never.

She waved Thomas and Mildred away and stumbled into bed. She put a pillow over her head as if it could stop the clanging coming from inside. Then she began to sing, trying to drown out the sound of her own head.

It was after nine o'clock by the time Gabriel had returned to the house. A cold supper had been planned ahead of time, so the guests were well taken care of. Instead of seeking out food, he went to his study and poured a half-full snifter of brandy. He took a large gulp, then fell into his leather chair. The familiar warmth of the spirit spread through his chest. He took another sip, placed his glass on the desk, then sat forward, bracing his elbows on his thighs—allowing his arms to dangle and his head to fall forward. He felt weary to the bone. He had not meant for things to end like this. He had wanted Howard caught and sentenced by the courts, but he had never meant for it to turn into such a violent and deadly public display.

"He is dead, I assume?"

His head snapped up at the sound of his mother's voice. "Yes," he rasped. "He fought me like a madman, tried to kill me, and ended up with my dagger in his chest.

The duchess nodded. "Do you have some of that for me?" she asked, pointing her chin at the brandy.

"Of course," he said and got up slowly to pour her a glass. She sat in one of the chairs in front of the desk, while he took the other.

Her hand shook slightly as she took the snifter. He could see she was working hard to maintain her composure after tonight's revelations. "Perhaps next time you plan such a dramatic demonstration, you will deign to inform me beforehand?" She raised an eyebrow in his direction.

Gabriel let out a laugh, but there was no humor in it. "Yes, Mother. However, I have absolutely no plans for such a demonstration in the future. Nor did I expect this one to end in such a manner."

"Things rarely go the way you expect when dealing with the insane," his mother said, calmly as you please. "I do not believe that boy was ever right in the head."

"No, he was not." He looked at his mother with concern.

"Will you be well?"

"I shall be right as rain as soon as I spend a full night in slumber. This brandy will help speed the way." She held up the glass, then took a sip. "And you? Will all be well with you now?"

"Eventually, yes. There is much to be thought upon and plenty still to be done, but yes. Knowing the running and hiding is over and that Michael can finally come home brings me a great measure of relief."

"Michael." His mother's eyes pooled with tears. "How I miss him. Will you send word to him right away?"

Gabriel had not informed her that Michael had gone underground and that he currently had no idea where his twin was, nor if he was in a position to come home. He had no intention of telling her so now either, so he merely nodded. "Now we can have Father's celebration of life event, knowing the person who took him away from us has paid for his evil actions."

"Indeed. This has been a long time coming." She sighed back into the chair. "I truly had no idea we were harboring such a viper in our midst. After everything we did to care for him, he betrayed our trust." She waved a hand in the air, pushing the negative thoughts away. "That man has taken enough away from us. Now we must look toward a happier future." She was silent for several minutes before saying, "As much as I wanted to discover who killed your father, it has never been an all-consuming passion the way it has been for you.

Now that this is over, what will you do with yourself?"

He sat back and rubbed the side of his hand across his forehead. "I plan to take one day at a time. However, I have a new mission."

She raised her eyebrows and waited.

"I plan to convince Lillian to be my wife."

His mother examined Gabriel's face for a long moment before she broke out in a grin. "Good. I heartily approve." The duchess stood to leave. "I am going to my room to have a good cry, then we must put this all behind us."

Gabriel nodded. "Yes." He stood with a fond smile, leaned forward, and kissed her cheek. "Goodnight, Mother. I love you."

She patted his cheek. "I love you too, my boy. Now, I think you should go to bed as well and get some much-needed sleep."

"Yes, your grace." he bowed with a cheeky grin and watched her leave the room.

Before doing as his mother commanded, Gabriel sat at his desk to write the missive that he hoped would bring his brother home at long last, then tomorrow he would embark on his pursuit of Lillian in earnest.

Soon he would have everything he ever wanted and more.

Lillian awoke with a start to total darkness. She had no idea what time it was, but she felt desperation clawing at her like a feral animal. She needed to leave this place and she needed to do it now.

Lighting a candle on the bedside table, she quickly found her robe and checked the mantle clock. Three in the morning.

She saw Sarah lying in a cot next to her bed, apparently having stayed the night due to last evening's events. Lillian let her sleep on for now. She grabbed the candle, and on silent feet made the journey to the attic room. She knocked on the door, louder than she might usually have done. No one answered, so she knocked again. After several minutes she heard the shuffle of feet coming toward the door.

"Who is it?" Mildred called out.

"It is Lady Lillian."

The maid opened the door. "Is all well? 'Tis the middle of the night, my lady."

"I know and I am sorry for it. I will be leaving at first light and wanted to see if it would be possible to speak to Lady Francesca before I go."

"She is awake, my lady—in that much pain she is—but she can't hear a blessed thing."

Lillian gasped in shock. "What do you mean?"

"I've never seen the like. She came upstairs near to fall on her feet. I could see she had overtaxed herself. When I tried to speak to her, she said she couldn't hear me. The only time I ever heard of such a thing was from my cousin, who was in the war, he was. Got too near a cannon when it went off. Said he was deaf for three days."

Lillian sagged in dismay. She had been worried something like this might happen if Fran used her gift in such a manner.

"Will you tell Lady Francesca I came to visit and tell her I will write as soon as I reach London?"

"Of course I will, my lady," Mildred said.

Lillian turned as the maid closed the door and for the first time noticed a young man huddled on the floor nearby. She peered closer. "Turpentine? Is that you?"

He lifted his head. Bleak eyes met hers. "Aye."

Lillian crouched, put her candle down, and carefully lowered herself next to her friend. "What are you doing up here sitting on the cold hard floor?"

He shrugged. "I thought Fran might need me or something."

Lillian could see it was far more than that. Turpentine usually strutted around with a devil-may-care attitude. She had never seen him like this. "What has happened?"

"He is dead."

Lillian's heart started to pound in her ears. She had not yet found out what had occurred after Gabriel left the stage to chase his cousin. "Who?" she croaked.

"That villain who you were all trying to catch."

"Oh." She sagged in relief. Turpentine was unusually upset over a man he did not know. "Did you—" She cleared her throat. "Did you have to kill him?"

"No," her friend said quietly, "but I helped. He might have killed the duke otherwise." After a pause he added, "I have never seen a dead man before."

Lillian put her arm around Turpentine's bony shoulders. "I am sorry you had to be a part of such ugliness, but I cannot regret what you had to do if it kept the duke safe."

He looked up suddenly, his eyes widened. "Did you just do that?"

Lillian had felt it too. It was as if something had transferred from inside of her to inside of him. She jerked her arm away. "Oh, God, Turpentine. Did I hurt you?"

He shook his head. "No," he breathed. "It was like a warm breeze that filled my chest and made me feel better. I didn't know you could do that."

"Neither did I," she whispered. More loudly, she said in a rush, "Will you be all right? I need to go back to my room."

"Sure thing, Lil. Thanks."

She nearly ran all the way back downstairs. Inside the room, she went to Sarah and briskly shook her shoulder. "Sarah, wake up."

"What is it?" her friend asked groggily.

"I wish to leave immediately and need you to help me pack my things."

Sarah's eyes opened instantly, and she sat up. "What do you mean you wish to leave?"

"I am not going to explain it now," Lillian said in an exasperated tone. "I wish to depart at first light before any of the family gets out of bed.

"Do you think that is such a good idea? The last time we traveled alone did not turn out so well for us," Sarah said.

"We got home eventually, did we not?"

Sarah grumbled something else under her breath Lillian could not hear, moved to the two trunks against the wall, opened them, then walked to the armoire where the dresses hung.

Two hours later, the trunks were packed, Lillian was dressed for travel, Prince Albert was in his favorite travel bag, and they were ready to go. She walked down the stairs, finding the night footman still on duty by the front door.

"Excuse me, but I need the assistance of Pennywhistle, if you would be so good as to fetch him? I also need a footman or two to retrieve the trunks from my room."

The footman bowed. "Of course, my lady. Right away."

Lillian and Sarah sat on the bench in the entryway to wait. Only a short time passed before Pennywhistle appeared.

"How may I be of service to you, my lady?" he asked with a bow.

"I need to leave for London immediately. I have the choice of going into town to find a hired carriage or perhaps Wyvern has a traveling coach he could lend me for the purpose?"

Two footmen came down the stairs with her trunks.

Pennywhistle's eyebrows rose. "Do you plan to travel alone, my lady?"

"With my companion, yes."

Pennywhistle stiffened and said, as if he were a mighty lord, "I do not believe his grace would be pleased to hear of this."

"Be that as it may," Lillian said tightly, "he is not my lord and master yet, and I will be leaving one way or another. The only question is in which equipage I will travel."

The butler was silent, seeming to weigh his options. Lillian had no wish for any servants to face the consequences of her actions, but she was beyond rational thought.

"I will summon his grace's traveling coach for your use, my lady. Do you wish to take breakfast before you go?"

"Thank you, Pennywhistle," Lillian said in relief, "and no breakfast is necessary. We will take tea along the road."

Less than half an hour later, Pennywhistle assisted them into the coach. He handed a basket inside. "I took the liberty of asking the kitchen to prepare some tea for your journey. You can never trust inns to make a proper cup."

"Thank you, Pennywhistle. That is most kind," Lillian said.

The butler bowed and closed the door. Once again, they were on a journey to London.

"Shall I prepare a cup for you, Lillian?" Sarah asked.

Her mind already on other matters, Lillian said vaguely, "Yes, please."

Was she doing the right thing leaving without a word? She desperately needed time away to recuperate and make sense of the chaos her life had become. There was one thing she now knew without a doubt, though. It was not in Gabriel's best interest to pursue her. Her ability was growing out of control, and the consequences would indeed spill over onto him.

Her thoughts were interrupted by an exclamation from Sarah. "There is more than just tea in this basket! We have a full breakfast of sandwiches, fruit, boiled eggs, and pastries. Would you like some?"

"Just the tea, Sarah. I am not hungry," Lillian said wearily.

She must get back to her original plan for her future. In that plan, no one could get hurt because of her abilities. The best thing she could do for all of them—her friends, her family,

Gabriel—was to go away. However, every past attempt to do so had failed. Her manuscript was not finished, and her bargain with Gabriel was at an end. She needed a new plan, one that would be successful this time.

Sarah handed her a cup of tea, which was surprisingly hot. She took a sip and sighed, closing her eyes. She could do with some uninterrupted sleep.

"Do you wish to talk about it?" Sarah asked.

Lillian looked at her friend and the tears she had been pushing down welled up and spilled over, running down her cheeks. She could not speak for several minutes as she swallowed past a lump in her throat. "Do you know, all this time, no one has truly asked me what I want. Everyone has simply told me I must want a husband, a family, a public social life, like all the other ladies newly come out in society—that the herbal is just an excuse to hide."

Sarah lowered her eyes. "It is because we all believe you have never allowed yourself to want all that you could have —all that you deserve."

"What if I do not want more than what I have already planned for?" she asked softly.

Sarah studied her face for a long moment. "Is that truly the case?"

"How am I to know?" She lifted her unoccupied hand, palm up. "I have been told what to think and want for so long, I no longer know what is in my own mind. Right now, I feel I have lost control of everything—my ability, my emotions, my entire life. I must get away and find my own way, without all this pressure to conform to what everyone thinks I should want."

"What about Wyvern?" Sarah asked quietly.

"It is time to let that fairy dream go." She leaned her head back against the leather seat. "He said he wants to marry me in truth, but I do not believe he fully understands what it would mean having to deal with my peculiarities." Another tear trickled down her cheek. "I am the wrong woman for him. In my absence, he will see that."

"You will leave even though you love him?" Sarah asked quietly.

Silence filled the coach for some time before Lillian spoke again. "It is because I love him I will leave. I have no wish to see him hurt."

"Your leaving will hurt him," Sarah said.

Lillian waved the thought away. "Only for a moment, I am certain. I must think of myself right now and how I am to move forward."

Sarah pulled a pastry from the basket and took a bite. After swallowing she said, "I thought this new approach with your gift has been of some help. Am I wrong?"

Lillian shook her head wearily. "The range of my ability continues to widen. Thus, as I gain control, it grows out of my reach again and it frightens me all the more. I have no reassurance that I will ever master it enough to move normally among society."

Lillian took another sip of tea and closed her eyes.

"I know you will not wish to hear this," Sarah said, "but I do not think running away from Wyvern is the answer. He could help you find a way to make this all work if you let him."

More tears spilled down Lillian's cheeks. No. As she had said, she must let him go for his sake alone.

After drinking her tea, Lillian settled back into the seat and eventually fell asleep. This time, their journey by coach was not hampered by disasters.

"Gone? What do you mean she is gone?" Gabriel yelled at his butler. Pennywhistle had knocked on his bedroom door while he was preparing for the day. He had been filled with the anticipation of seeing Lillian this morning.

"She summoned me at first light asking for help in acquiring a conveyance in order to return to London immediately, your grace." His butler recited this, while standing stiffly to attention. "I was made to understand she would take public transportation if none other was made available for her. I sent her in one of your traveling coaches."

"You let her leave alone?" Gabriel growled.

"She is in the company of her companion and one of your footmen is up on the carriage box. She will be safe enough," Pennywhistle said.

He was furious, mostly at himself. Had he pushed her too

hard the last time they spoke in private? "Did she say anything as to why she needed to leave?"

"No, your grace, and I did not feel it was my place to ask. I did mention to her the fact that you would be quite displeased."

"Damn right," Gabriel bit out.

He could race after her on horseback and most likely catch up, but he had this entire mess with Howard still to deal with today as well as his father's celebration and would not be able to give Lillian his full attention.

He let out a frustrated groan, then realized something his butler had said. "She left—what, over two hours ago? And you are just now informing me?"

Pennywhistle gave him a cheeky grin. "I felt it was sporting to give the lady a head start."

Gabriel growled again, more fiercely this time. "I do not pay you to give ladies a head start, Pennywhistle! I pay you to keep me informed of everything that goes on under my roof."

The butler did not look the least bit repentant.

"This will have to wait until later," Gabriel said, pinching the bridge of his nose. "You had better pray not a hair on Lady Lillian's head is harmed or you will wish you had never been born." He stalked back to the mirror and finished tying his neckcloth. "Have breakfast for four sent to my study and summon Hartley and Davis there immediately. We have quite a bit of clean up to do before the day's end. Also, I need you to oversee the setup of the ballroom for tonight's celebration." Gabriel waved the servant away.

"Of course, your grace." Pennywhistle bowed, then left the room.

Jersey whistled. "Looks like you have gotten yourself in a right mess, Your Eminence."

"Oh, shut it, Jersey, and help me with this neckcloth." Gabriel unwound the battered material from his neck and flung it to the floor. He had not been this flustered since his forced bedrest. He had no plans of losing Lillian, and as soon as he could see her again, he had every intention of making sure she understood that fact.

THIRTY-TWO

Signor Silvano's Sayings Number 32
When you fall off the horse, get back on.
Or else you will be stomped to death
and never get up again.

Despite sleeping for a portion of the journey, Lillian was exhausted when they arrived at the Wentworth's London townhouse. She had a light meal brought up, then went straight to bed.

On the way to London, she had had plenty of time to think on how to move into her future. It was time to live wholly on her own terms, but before she could, there were some loose ends that must be tied up.

After her morning cup of tea, she and Sarah left in the family's town carriage for the first destination of the day, taking Prince Albert with them. They arrived in Soho and climbed the steps to the Society building. Sarah knocked and they waited.

Halvar opened the door, and seeing who was standing on the doorstep, gave a huge grin. "Lillian, Sarah! Have you returned from the country then?"

The girls entered. "Yes, Halvar," she said flatly. "I need to speak to Silvano. Is he available?"

Halvar's smile fell. "He will be available for you, lass, but is all well? You look haggard."

"It all depends on your perspective, but yes, I am well in body if not quite in spirit." She lowered her voice to almost a whisper. "This information is for Society ears only. Francesca has left the city and is safe. That is all I can tell you other than that her family may be hunting for her and wishes her harm."

Halvar growled. "We worried that was the case." He laid a hand over his heart. "I will keep her secret close to my chest. Now, let me tell Silvano yer here to see him."

Lillian left the little entryway and entered the large room where their meetings took place. It felt so lifeless with no members to fill it. She and Sarah each sat in one of the chairs and waited.

Halvar returned and told them to meet Silvano in his sitting room. Her mentor stood up from a small writing desk and hurried forward to greet them.

Today he was wearing an atrocious mustard-colored waistcoat paired with matching satin breeches and a sky-blue coat. He grinned. "Dear one! How nice it is to see you returned safely from the country. Tell me, how was your trip?"

Lillian scowled. "I have several bones to pick with you."

Silvano's cheerful expression turned into a rueful one. "Would you care to sit down and tell me what this is all about?"

Lillian and Sarah sat on the settee near the fireplace while he took the chair opposite.

"Yes, Joseph Silver," she put an emphasis on his real name, "perhaps you can start with when you were going to share the truth with the other students as to why our beloved school burned to the ground?"

"Joseph Silver is not so glamorous as Signor Silvano is it?" he said with a self-mocking smile.

Lillian was in no mood for playing his games. She glared at him and waited for answers.

He sat back with a dramatic sigh. "I was worried you had seen something upsetting during our practice session together." He crossed one leg over the other. "I will admit, Lillian, this is one time I am fully ashamed of the outcome of my actions." He held up one finger. "However, I still believe the ends justified the means. I started this school to prevent all of you ending up used or dead like my brother. I have alluded to my personal connection to those with abilities like yours, but I've never told you the full tale. My brother had a gift which allowed him to see the future and our mother exploited it, selling it to the highest bidder. When he could not produce the right answers on demand, they killed him for it." He hit his left fist against his thigh. "I did not want any more people with such gifts to suffer, so you can see why I was willing to go to such lengths to swindle that money out of the very people responsible for his death. My revenge was sweet, but you all have now paid for it, and for that I am sorry."

Lillian was not satisfied. "What is to keep them from burning *this* school to the ground? What is to keep them from killing off my fellow students?"

He waved a hand in the air as if it was of no importance. "The situation has now been handled. Those men will not bother us again, I can assure you."

"How can I trust you ?" she asked. "You lied to us about this and I feel you have been lying to us since the beginning —selling us the idea that we could live normal lives. Only in the past few months have I fully realized what a defective dream that is."

"I have always been honest with all of you, Lillian—that I am no teacher with special skills who could magically help you overcome your abilities. That I am just a man." He spread his arms wide as if presenting himself. "Yes, I suppose I did start this all with the unrealistic hope I could do more for you, then later realized what I was up against. Your gifts usually have minds of their own. However, you must admit, what I have ended up offering has been a far sight better than what children like you have ever had before." He waved his hands around to indicate the Society. "Here you have a safe place to learn about your gifts and to make friends who understand what it is like to live with them."

Prince Albert popped out of his bag. Now awake and seeing Silvano, he scrambled out, raced over to his friend, and stood up on his hind legs expectantly.

"Hello Princey," Silvano said. "I haven't seen you in an age. Up you go." He picked up the ferret and placed him in his lap.

Lillian squeezed her hands tightly together to steady herself, then looked fully at Silvano. "We understood that you were not a magician and could not make our abilities disappear, yes, but we all believed so completely in you regardless. We trusted you could make our lives different, better, but are any of us better? Are any of us living normal lives? I feel as if all these years have been nothing more than smoke and mirrors."

Her mentor leaned forward, causing Prince Albert to jump down. "I want to let you in on a little secret, Lillian. Any good actor brings out what is already inside of their audience. A person cannot cry at a scene if they do not know compassion. A person cannot be angry at a villain if they do not believe in justice. What I did during your years with me was to bring out what was inside of you to begin with.. You became stronger because I showed you that you were already strong."

He sat back again. "Yes, there is no magic elixir that will make your abilities disappear. I am merely an acting instructor who has been teaching you for years how to act on a stage. 'All the world's a stage, and all the men and women merely players,' " he quoted from Shakespeare. "I believe you already know this. You are simply looking for excuses not to take control of your gift. Because if you did, you would have to face the world instead of running away from it. Running is easy.

Standing up for yourself and taking what you want is hard."

Lillian stared at her lap and thought on this for several minutes. All this time, had she been using excuses to keep her life small out of fear? Had she been running away like a coward?

Of course she had; her ability frightened her.

Sarah lightly touched her gloved hands, which she now noticed were clasped tightly enough to cut off the blood from her fingers.

"I do not know what to do," she whispered. Looking at Silvano again she said, "I am currently at what one might call a crossroads. You know I have always wished to stay away from society due to my ability, but my family recently made that impossible. Christopher's new practice was one possibility for controlling the visions, but my ability has only grown stronger since using it. I have come full circle back to wishing for nothing more than quiet and seclusion." Leading a normal life might have been possible, but in all these years she had never even come close.

Silvano eased further into his chair and crossed one leg over the other again. "Lillian, you are a strong woman, but you have never trusted in your strength. I believe if you give it a chance, you *can* control this gift. You can be the master and make it the slave instead of the other way around. To do that, you must trust yourself and work past the fear. You must experiment. If one way does not work, try another. Other students have been successful this way, but they had to face their abilities head on." His gaze locked with hers. "While you are at it, you need to discard this notion of a utopia you call a normal life. It has *never* existed. I believe what you are looking for is peace and happiness intertwined with your gift, and that you *can* find. You have spent enough time running. Now it is time for you to stand and fight."

Lillian felt emotion build in her throat. Deep down she had begun to discover this for herself. She had been letting the problem control her since it first appeared. She had been racing in the wrong direction the entire time: away from it. It was time to change that. It *was* time to stop running.

She nodded and stood abruptly, picking up her pet who had been playing on the floor. "Thank you for speaking to me so frankly and for your advice. I only wish you had given it much sooner."

Silvano shook his head slowly and looked up at her regretfully. "You would not have been ready for it, love. As I said, you are strong, which means strong-willed. If I had told you this before now, you would have claimed I was wrong and retreated further into yourself." His face split into a wide grin. "I am pleased to see you are ready now, and I look forward to seeing the results."

"I will keep you updated," she said. She turned to her friend. "Come, Sarah. We have more visits in town to make today."

"Lillian," Silvano called out softly when she reached the door. She paused, but did not turn around. "It may not always seem like it, but I do truly care about all of you, with all of my heart."

She nodded and they left the Benevolence Society building. Once they were back in the coach, she said, "It will be time for an excursion to Norfolk tomorrow, Sarah. If I am to become stronger, I must do it away from all these social expectations."

Sarah gave a twinkling smile. "I could cheer for you. It is high time you became the powerful woman God created you to be."

Lillian sighed. "I have been rather stubborn all these years, have I not? I suppose I have finally grown tired of myself."

"I am glad to hear it," Sarah said, still smiling. "All of us who love you have been waiting for this day."

Their next stop was Effingham House, the location of Fran's grand rescue. Lillian had not heard from Fran's parents, so she could not be sure if they were even looking for her. At the door, Lillian asked to speak to Lady Effingham. Sarah stayed behind in the coach while she was taken to the drawing room to speak to the lady of the house. She took several deep breaths to gather her courage before entering.

Lady Effingham was what Lillian might have called an overdone lady. She wore a red wig, face powder, and heavy face paint. Her gowns, in fashion decades ago, were bright and gaudy with too much lace and jewels to match. She was like a toad trying to wear the clothing and skin of a princess, but they were all wrong for her.

She curtsied. "Lady Effingham, I appreciate you taking the time to see me." She came closer and sat when the lady waved her hand at a chair. "I am very concerned about Francesca. I have written several missives with no response and have come to your home only to be told she is not receiving. Can you tell me anything about her wellbeing?"

Lady Effingham brought a lace handkerchief to her nose and sniffed as if the room stank of rot. This was a continual habit of hers as well as the frown that came with it. She spoke slowly and as if someone were pinching her nose. "Yes, well. I have not wished to put it about, but I know I can tell you in confidence that Francesca has fallen ill with a case of female hysteria."

Lillian did her best not to react in anger at this ridiculous pronouncement. "Oh dear," she said sympathetically. "I had no idea such a thing was possible for one so young. Can the doctors do anything for her?"

The lady sniffed into her handkerchief again. "They have prescribed complete quiet and bedrest for several months. She is to have no visitors and no excitement."

"Is she still here in town?" Lillian asked, all innocence.

"No, she was sent to our country estate the moment the doctor said it was what was best for her. At present, I have no notion of how long she will remain there."

Lillian pulled slightly on her gift to see what she could learn. She saw a flash of Lord and Lady Grantham discussing how to best find and retrieve their daughter. They were indeed searching for Fran but were not about to let it be known publicly that she was missing.

Lillian stood. "I will not take any more of your time then. I am grieved to hear of Francesca's condition. May I write to her in the country?"

"No excitement, the doctor said."

"Will you let me know when the condition improves, my lady? I will very much miss her company."

Lady Effingham did not answer other than to give a regal nod.

Lillian curtsied then said, "Good day," before leaving.

If she had had any doubts about whether taking Francesca away to the country was what was best for her, she had them no longer. Lady Effingham was a nasty woman and her husband was no better. Their daughter had never been anything more than a commodity to be married off for their convenience and benefit, and now they could not have that, they wanted her imprisoned in an asylum.

Lillian had played her part to make them believe she had no knowledge of what had happened to her friend. After that farce, she was in desperate need of another cup of tea and maybe a scone or two to go with it.

That evening, her family arrived in London in full force. Lillian had known it would happen soon. She wished she did not have to face them, but if there was to be no more running, she must. Her parents did not even wait to wash off the travel dust before calling her into her mother's sitting room.

Tea had been laid out, and although her parents were at ease, her mother looked frazzled and her father exhausted. She did not let that sway her from her new course. Anne was sitting silently off to the side. The tableau was only missing Simon to make it complete. She would have to face him another day.

Her mother started railing at Lillian the moment she saw her daughter. "What were you thinking, taking off like that by yourself and without a by your leave? Not only was it improper, it was rude." She began wringing her handkerchief in her hands. "We had to attempt to explain your absence to the duchess and then to all the guests when you did not appear for the late duke's celebration. We told them you were terribly upset by what happened to Mr. Ramsay, although we still do not fully understand it ourselves." Her mother continued with a cry. "Do you have any idea the embarrassment you caused to our family? To me?"

Still standing, Lillian had her hands clasped behind her back in an effort to hold herself together. "The reason you gave for my leaving was indeed a partial truth. What you do not know is the duke asked me to use my ability to discover who killed his father, and that was accomplished with a great deal of distress for myself."

Her mother placed her handkerchief to her mouth and gasped.

"I will also tell you, things are about to change drastically for me."

"What ever do you mean?" her mother asked.

Lillian thrust her heavily gloved hands forward and presented them, her face tightened in anger. "Do you have any idea what it is like for me to live like this? Have you ever cared?"

Her mother drew in a sharp breath.

Her father scowled. "Here now. That is no way to speak to your mother."

"No!" Lillian said fiercely. "It needs to be said. When I go to sleep at night, this curse will always be with me. If you marry me off—as Simon once said to me—I will become someone else's problem and you will all sleep better at night, but my situation will not change."

She clenched her hands repeatedly into fists and released them. Then she lowered them to her sides. "Can you tell me that when you sent me away to school you did not feel incredible relief? Relief that you would suffer no more embarrassment in front of the neighbors or receive rude comments from society? Can you tell me that when it was time for me to return once again, you did not feel anxiety that all you had kept at bay for years would return?" Her mother opened her mouth to say something, but only a small croak emerged. It was as good as an admission. "Exactly," Lillian said.

Her mother began to weep loudly into a handkerchief her father had produced, but Lillian marched on. "All my life, I have had to live with this … this … problem! Constantly living in fear of what it might do to me and what would happen if others found out. Knowing that I could never live a normal life. Knowing that there was no magic spell that would make it all go away." She pointed a finger at her mother and then her father, whose face had turned a deep red. "All you had to do was find a way to hide me away. Not once have you asked me what I want, what would make me happy. Not once have you taken into account what I need. I talk, but you never listen."

Lord Wentworth had moved closer to his wife and placed a comforting hand on her shoulder. Lillian could not be moved.

"I shall not be marrying the duke or anyone else. If you choose to throw me out on the street for it, so be it. I am quite finished attempting to turn myself into something I am not to suit your desires. There can be no more miserable alternative than that. For at least the rest of the season, I plan to go home where I can find out for myself who I should be."

Having finished with her declaration, she stomped out of the room and up the stairs to her room.

Her things were already packed. Lillian had asked Sarah to gather them earlier in the day. The following morning she planned to travel home to Norfolk—by mail coach, if she had to.

She sank down onto the bed.

"Do you wish me to help you dress for bed, Lillian?" Sarah asked.

"Yes. We should be well rested for our journey tomorrow."

Lillian had risen to start the task when a knock sounded on the door. Sarah answered and she could hear her father's voice across the room. He came inside and Sarah slipped away. Lillian stood tall again. She would not let anyone sway her from her resolve.

"Lillian, I need to speak to you, if I may?" her father asked.

She nodded and walked to the bench seat beneath her window where they sat down.

"I do not know where to begin," her father said gruffly. "Did you know I had an older sister?"

That was an odd question. She shook her head.

"Yes. Her name was Daisy. She died at about the same age as you are now." He stopped to clear his throat. "You see, she was born with an oddity that our parents could not accept." Lillian gasped. "So they brought in doctors—all of them quacks—men of science, and even priests who attempted to call the demons out of her. Nothing worked. They hid her away from society as completely as they could: they locked her away in her room with only an old woman for a companion. I would sneak in to visit her on occasion, and I knew how miserable she was."

Her father shifted uneasily. "This went on for years until my sister was a mere shell of her former self. She had given up begging to be let out of her prison—for a prison is exactly what it was. I had saved up some money so I could help Daisy escape. I was so young then that I had no idea what it would be like for a woman alone in the world." Tears formed in his eyes, but he blinked them away. "One night, when I was home on holiday from school, I stole the keys to the rooms and led my sister away from the house. I gave her all my money. She kissed me on the cheek," he briefly touched his cheek with one hand, "and told me I was the best brother in the world." He cleared his throat again. "Two days later, Daisy was found by some local men, lying broken on the rocks below the cliffs along the coast. It seemed she had no intention of going on with a new life."

"Oh, Father," Lillian breathed.

"I was devastated at the time, but later came to realize Daisy was finally at peace. I never forgave my parents. I left home and never saw them again." He looked fully at his daughter. "You see, I did not want that kind of life for you. I wanted you to have a happy and normal life. I suppose your mother and I pushed you too hard in the opposite direction from my own parents, did we not?"

"Father, no. It is not at all the same. What you and mother have done I know has been done out of love, but yes, you have pushed too hard. You forgot to take what I needed into account. However, I am not Daisy. If you had locked me away, I would have found a way to escape. It is time for me to escape now, Father. Please give me your blessing to go to Norfolk alone for a time until I decide what is best for me."

He pressed his palms against his eyes as if to stop the flow of tears and then ran his fingers upwards through his hair.

"Yes. That is what you shall do. You are a sensible girl and I know you will figure things out. You always do. But if I may give you one piece of advice?"

"Yes, Father?"

"Do not give up on the duke just yet. I can see how much he cares about you, and it is obvious he has accepted your gift. Will you wait to make a decision about your betrothal?"

Lillian wanted to tell him the betrothal had never been real regardless, but she kept that to herself. If her parents were willing to give her the solitude she needed, she would give them this. "Yes, Father. I will wait."

He patted her knee and said, "Good, good. Now tell me, were you truly the one who discovered who killed the late duke by using your gift?"

She looked at him grimly. "There is more to the story, but yes. I promised Gabriel I would do so and I have."

"That took a great deal of bravery, as I know how hard you have worked to avoid your visions altogether."

Lillian cleared her throat. "As to that, in the past few weeks I have been learning how to control my ability. Helping Gabriel was one means to do that."

Her father smiled. "I am proud of you for taking such a step. Only a courageous woman would do so." He stood to leave.

"Father?"

He turned back. "Yes?"

"What was the oddity your sister was born with?"

"Like you, she could see into men's souls and know their past secrets. Scared my father to death, as he was not a good man."

Lillian was shocked. "Why have you never told me this before?"

Her father looked sad. "I know it makes no sense, but because of what happened to Daisy, I was afraid that if you knew about her, you would make the same choice she did. I know now that was a foolish decision." He turned and left the room.

A huge weight had been lifted from Lillian, while another weight remained. If her aunt had had the same affliction, was that proof positive that if she had children they would be just like her?

THIRTY-THREE

Signor Silvano's Sayings Number 33
All's well that ends well.

After tearful goodbyes to her parents and Anne, Lillian left for their country estate—not to hide away, but rather to get to know herself and what she was capable of. Within a couple of days of their arrival, her mother sent a message saying the duke had called, but as Lillian had asked she told him to give her daughter some time alone. This relieved Lillian of one burden, for now at least.

Sarah spent as much time as she could spare with her own family, who she had rarely seen over the years while confined with Lillian at Silvano's. During her companion's time away, Lillian began the task of creating an herb garden next to the kitchen garden. It only made sense to grow as many of the medicinal plants she used for healing as she could.

Less than a fortnight after she arrived home, she received an odd letter from her brother.

Dear Lil,

There is much that needs to be said between us, but I am not ready for that conversation. For now, I wish to say I am proud of what you did for Gabriel. This is a different Lillian from the girl I knew who cowered for years in the country.

When you see Gabriel again, he will likely tell you I have joined the Network. It is a very long story how that came about and I will tell you of it one day. Today, I wish only to tell you I am listening and I do understand.

Affectionately,
Simon

Lillian did not know what to think of it. She and Simon had always been at odds with each other, but she had never fully understood why. She had merely assumed he was sick of dealing with a sister with such a huge problem. Perhaps all this time she had been wrong. She felt warmth blossom in her chest when she read her brother's kind words.

She refolded the letter and looked across the expanse of new garden and the small green shoots cropping up here and there. She had spent enough time resting. Now it was time to get to work.

Lillian began experimenting with her gift, starting with Sarah. She did not merely attempt to call it into action, but she worked with the newest facet—pushing healing emotions toward those she touched. She had realized because she had avoided touching people for so long, she had failed to learn about the best part of her ability. She felt a deep pang of regret.

As soon as she gained more control by practicing on the family's servants, she branched out with local community members. She sat covertly nearby and pulled information from them. She repeatedly started and stopped her ability, learning how to prevent unwanted visions. Those people she was more comfortable with, she took their hands or touched their arms and gave them comfort and light.

Silvano was correct—the best way to harness her power was to experiment, learning what did and did not work. She had also wasted enough years hoping for what did not exist. 'Normal' was a construct of society. Now she was building her own version of normal.

As the hottest days of summer finally arrived, she started to feel hope in a way she never had before.

Lillian had received word from Fran that she had fully recovered from the night of the performance and that she too was working to practice and take command of her gift. However, her friend said it was different since her gift was active all the time. She was trying to learn how to shut it off. Lillian was pleased Fran was at least attempting to take control. From what she had read in letters from school friends, she knew others were also using Christopher's new technique with some success.

When she was not working with her ability, she wrote. To her great delight, she finally finished and sent in her manuscript to the publisher before the end of June. Barely a month later, Sarah entered her sitting room one day carrying a paper wrapped package tied with string. "Something has arrived for you, Lillian. Is this what I think it is?"

Lillian's heart sped up in anticipation. Sarah handed her the package, and she cut the strings with scissors. She slowly opened the brown paper and found a green leather-bound book with gold embossed lettering: "A Global Guide to Herbs," by L. Hargraves. Lillian's dream of compiling the information and seeing it published had come true. She hugged the book to her chest and breathed in the scent of new leather.

Now she could do anything she wanted with her life.

Lillian knew her solitude at home could not last, as it was the family's habit to return to Norfolk by the end of summer. She and Sarah were writing letters in the drawing room one afternoon when she heard the carriage wheels crunching on the graveled drive. Prince Albert had been lazing on her shoulder, nipping occasionally at her ear. Dropping the quill, she jumped up, smoothed the skirts of her gown, and took a deep breath. It had been more than two months since they had all seen each other, and she hoped they would see a positive change in her.

"Come Sarah, it appears the family has arrived. We should probably go greet them."

Sarah gave a laughing smile. "Probably so."

On the front steps, Lillian shaded her eyes from the mid-day sun as she watched the carriages slow to a halt. She blinked. There were four of them. That was an unusually high number, even for her mother who traveled with all her comforts. On her shoulder, Prince Albert bobbed up and down in excitement.

Anne was the first to alight. She saw Lillian immediately and rushed to her, hands outstretched. "Oh Lillian! It is so good to see you again. I have missed you terribly."

Lillian took her cousin's hands and bussed her on the cheek. "And I have missed you. I am sure there will be plenty for you to tell me about the season that you did not include in your letters."

"Could that be possible? I wrote to you nearly every day." Both laughed. "Hello, Prince Albert," Anne said, patting the ferret on his head. Her pet chirped a greeting.

Her mother came next. She hurried up to her daughter and immediately said, "Please do not be angry with me, dearest, but they asked to come, and I could not very well say no. However, they did say if you were displeased they would find a way to take themselves off again." Lady Wentworth finally took a breath allowing Lillian to get a word in.

"They, Mother?"

However, she did not need an answer, for from the second coach the Duke of Wyvern exited and turned to assist the duchess down. Lillian's heart skipped a beat. Gabriel was as handsome as ever. He looked more relaxed than when she had last seen him. Perhaps finishing the business with his cousin had finally given him some of his light back.

Gabriel turned and noticed her. His blue eyes met hers and he smiled, but it was tentative, as if uncertain of his reception. Lillian took the initiative and met them halfway. She was no longer the weak girl who constantly flinched.

She curtsied with a smile. "Your grace, Gabriel. Welcome to Wentworth Manor. You are most welcome. I hope you will make yourself at home here." She could see both duke and duchess release some of the tension they had been holding.

Gabriel took her hand, bent over it, and kissed her knuckles. "You have been sorely missed, Lillian. I am pleased to see you again."

"And I as well," the duchess said. "I could really use a cup of tea about now, however, and since I am a duchess I will not think it rude to ask." She said this most severely, but her eyes twinkled.

Lillian laughed. "Most certainly. Please come inside and we will have a tea tray brought to us at once." She turned again to Gabriel and said with a grin, "I assume that you would like the best tea cakes the manor has to offer?"

"Of course." He smiled.

Prince Albert jumped from her shoulder to his and bounced up and down several times. Her pet had missed the duke too.

Gabriel chuckled and scratched the little rascal under the chin. The Rom had been correct—anyone who gave Prince Albert a good scratch would be his friend for life.

"There is someone else who has come and would like to

greet you, Lillian," Gabriel said, looking back over his shoulder toward the carriage.

Lillian peered around him and saw a man with dark wavy hair and twinkling blue eyes, standing back, watching in clear amusement.

"Michael!" she cried, rushing toward him, hands outstretched. He took them and bowed. "You have come home at last!"

"Lillian! I do hope it is acceptable to call you Lillian. How delightful it is to see you again," he said with a grin. "I never in a million years would have expected we would meet again, and never under such circumstances."

"Circumstances?" she asked.

"First, I always thought I would be the one whose heart was captured long before Gabe's, but here he is, a fallen victim of cupid's arrow, and the mysterious lady I met along the road to London the cause of it." He shook his head, as if in disbelief. "Then, to find out you were the reason I was able to come home to my family after so much time in hiding. I was beginning to think it might never happen. Consider me astonished." He bent and kissed each of her gloved hands, which he still held.

Gabriel took her arm and pulled it through his own, breaking her connection with his twin. "That is enough now, Michael," he said with narrowed eyes. "I was promised tea and I intend to take advantage of such an offer." He led her toward the front door where everyone else had already disappeared, and left his brother to follow.

Lillian kept pace, itching her nose in an attempt to hide her smile.

Somehow, she had ended up sitting between her mother and the duchess during tea. A part of her longed to speak to Gabriel privately and see how he fared, but the other part feared the coming confrontation. The last thing she wished was to hurt him further.

Michael approached her and bowed. "Lillian, would you do me the honor of a turn about the room?"

She stood, smiling, and took his arm. "Of course."

"I had hoped for a few moments alone with you, as I felt an explanation was in order."

"An explanation for what?" she asked, perplexed.

"For how I came to help you along the road to London."

She looked up and saw Gabriel and her father speaking together near the opposite end of the room. "I believe it was Gabriel who was more concerned about that event due to your public visibility."

"After my brother brought me up to date with details from the past months, I gave him a satisfactory accounting, as I will do for you now." His blue eyes met hers. "You see, it was Catriona who sent me there that April morning."

Lillian looked up and gasped. "What—How?" she stammered.

Michael ran a hand through his hair, a gesture that reminded her of Gabriel when he was flustered. "I cannot explain as fully as I would like, as there are still secrets I must keep for the protection of another, but I am connected with someone like you who is close to Catriona. It was through her that I received word."

By the words 'like you' she assumed he meant someone from the Society.

They had reached the end of the room and turned to complete the circle. She saw Gabriel's eyebrows drawn together as he watched them pass by. Perhaps the shock showed too strongly on her face. She smoothed her expression and gave him a brief smile.

"Did Catriona say why she sent you?" Lillian asked.

"Not in so many words," Michael said. "It was more along the lines of you needing assistance and I should be there to give it."

"How entirely strange," she said. "I suppose there is no point in wondering what she meant by it. I will simply have to write her and ask." She looked up at Michael. "Do you not find that people's lives seem to be inexplicably interweaved? Who knew the day I first met you that a few weeks later I would meet your twin and not long after agree to embark on an investigation that would eventually enable you to come home."

Michael gave a bark of laughter. "It is a mind puzzle, I fully agree." He stopped and faced her. "I do want to thank you with more than words can ever express for what you did for Gabriel—for all of us. It is a debt we can never repay."

"It is I who am indebted. If Gabriel had not had such a

strong belief in me, I may never have learned to master my ability to the degree I have."

Michael tilted his head and smiled. "When my brother believes in something, he holds tightly to it." He placed her hand on his elbow and began walking once more. "I know what I am about to say is none of my business, but I am going to say it regardless for my twin's sake. He cares for you deeply, and falling in love is never something he would do lightly. I do hope you will think long and hard before you make any irrevocable decisions."

"When faced with great trials, love is not always enough, Michael," she said softly.

"I think that is only true for weak people, Lillian. You and my brother both have strength in abundance." He stopped and grinned widely. "Listen to me spouting off philosophy as if I know what I am talking about."

She smiled back. "I do thank you for your concern. I will keep what you said in mind." She turned to look at Gabriel. "Speaking of philosophy, do you not find it interesting how I did not spare more than a thought for you after the day we met, but then fell in love with your twin?"

He held a hand over his heart. "Ouch, that hurt!" He laughed. "Gabriel and I may look exactly alike, but we are very different."

"True, but I would argue that you do not look exactly alike."

"Oh? Could you tell the difference between us from across a crowded room?"

"In a heartbeat," she declared.

He clasped his hands behind his back and began walking. "I had a feeling you would say that, and I believe you."

"I am beyond pleased you decided to come visit," she said.

"I only wish I could stay longer, but I will need to leave the day after tomorrow to return to my duties."

"Duties?" she asked, stopping to look up at him.

"Yes, I am in the middle of an important Network investigation. I am certain Gabriel will tell you more about it in time." He took her hand and bowed over it. "I want you to know before I leave that I fully support Gabriel's choice in bride and how happy I will be to call you sister one day. Knowing my twin so well, I have every confidence he will win you over."

"Thank you," she whispered. Her throat felt suddenly tight when she realized if she chose not to marry Gabriel, he would not be the only one she hurt.

In the drawing room that evening after dinner, Gabriel came to stand at Lillian's side. "I know it might be better if I waited to speak, but it has already been several weeks past time for me. Is there somewhere we can go to talk privately?"

"Yes." She took him by the arm and out to the hallway.

"Higgins," she said to their butler, "would you send a footman to light some candles in the blue sitting room please?"

Higgins bowed. "Of course, my lady."

Lillian's heart sped up. She had both wanted and feared this conversation for some time. She had imagined a million times what the two of them might say and how it would end.

Inside the sitting room, she sat on a sofa and invited Gabriel to do the same, with an uncertain smile.

Gabriel took her hand. "I was going to give you more time once I arrived, but when I saw your favorable welcome, I did not want to delay one more minute."

Before he could continue, Lillian interrupted, hoping to stall the inevitable a little longer. "I have not had a chance to tell you how sorry I am about your cousin's death. Not that he died, but the circumstances that led to it. Turpentine informed me of the facts."

Gabriel nodded. "Your friend was instrumental once again in saving my life on that occasion," he said. "I cannot truly regret Howard's death."

"Nor should you," she said.

"Enough about me, please tell me how you are after the events of the house party," he said earnestly. "I have been impatient to know ever since that night."

"I am well, Gabriel. At first, I was overwhelmed both physically and emotionally after all I had experienced that week and that final night. My ability had grown stronger and had pulled farther from my reach."

Gabriel's face fell. "My desire to find my father's killer blinded me to how badly you were being affected. I never meant to hurt you."

"I know. It is not your fault. It is mine. I spent so many years hiding away from my gift that I allowed it to control me. When I needed to use it for good, I had no power over it. It became evident to me that my attitude must change. This is why I came here to be by myself. I needed to explore my gift and see if I could control it."

"And can you?" Gabriel asked.

"Not fully, no, but I have made a good start. I have also discovered an entirely new aspect of my gift." She told him about her experience with Turpentine and how she had been practicing the healing side of her ability ever since.

Gabriel smiled. "That is amazing—you are amazing. I am proud of you for facing your fears to overcome what you have always seen as a such great challenge in your life." He looked down and ran a thumb over her hand, then looked up and met her eyes. "While we were parted, I was miserable, especially not knowing whether you were well or whether you had decided with finality that we could not be together. I not only want to spend my life with you, but I never want to be away from you like that again."

Lillian squeezed her left hand—the one Gabriel was not holding—tightly at her side. "Gabriel." Anguish filled her voice. "Although I have made some progress, touching people is still uncomfortable and unpredictable. How then would it be between us?"

"How do you know it would be a problem?" he asked. "You have never had difficulty when I take your hand such as now."

"I am wearing gloves and always do. I fear what would happen if I were to take them off." Unbidden, tears trickled down her cheeks.

"Let us try, Lillian," Gabriel said quietly. "How else are we to know? You may be running from a possibility that will never become a reality."

Lillian began to shake. She had only recently begun to remove her gloves around the house, and only on occasion. Could she do this? Should she do this? If she found out evil lurked inside of Gabriel, she might never recover. If she refused, she could remain in ignorant bliss, but she would be alone forever.

The worst that could happen was the entire shattering of her world.

She took a deep breath and remembered she had made the decision to stop running.

Gabriel reached for her left hand while looking directly into her eyes. "May I?"

She could not speak, instead she swallowed hard and nodded.

He held her cloth-covered forearm and slowly pulled on one finger of the glove at a time until the entire thing came loose. Laying the glove in his lap, he held up his hand, palm out.

"I am afraid," Lillian whispered.

"Be brave Lillian, and know that whatever happens, I am here to catch you," Gabriel said.

She lifted her trembling hand and gently placed it against his palm. She took a deep breath, then another.

She had expected a jolt at the first touch, but it did not come. Instead, a warm, golden light filled her mind as she pushed love in his direction. It started as only a glow, as small as a candle flame, but it slowly grew until it filled the whole room.

Tears streamed down her cheeks, but not tears of distress. These were tears of relief—of joy.

"Tell me," Gabriel gently said as he ran the fingers of his left hand upwards on each of her cheeks, wiping the tears away.

Lillian opened her eyes and said, "I see nothing but light filling the room. I have never experienced anything like this before." She felt confused. "I do not understand it."

Gabriel intertwined their fingers. "Perhaps we do not need to understand, but instead to believe in the hope it brings?" He leaned forward and gently touched his lips to hers, letting them linger. When he broke away, he said softly, "Will you give us a chance?"

Lillian touched her right hand to her lips in astonishment at the beautiful sensation. She was not certain she could surrender this easily. "What if things change, Gabriel, and I grow worse again?"

"I remember you saying to me once that we should not trade in what ifs. Instead, let us take one day at a time. Know that I love you and would do anything in my power to make you happy. Whatever happens, I will be right here by your side."

"What if we were to have children with the same ability as mine?" Lillian's heart pounded at the thought. "My aunt had it, so it could be possible."

Gabriel touched his forehead to hers and looked directly into her eyes. "I would love them just as I love you." He paused, then said again, "Will you give us a chance?"

Lillian had never thought to be loved so unconditionally. If her intention was to take her power back, control the gift and her life, she needed to act like it. Happier than she had ever imagined she could be, she threw her arms around Gabriel's neck. His arms went around her in response.

"Yes, Gabriel, I will. I love you too. I believe I have from the very beginning, but would never admit it, even to myself."

Gabriel chuckled lightly. He pulled back enough that he could look into her eyes. "Will you marry me then?"

Lillian could not speak for the fresh tears welling in her eyes, so she nodded vigorously, making Gabriel smile. He leaned in and kissed her again until they were both breathless.

EPILOGUE

Three weeks later, Lillian breezed into Gabriel's study at Wyvern House with a light step.

Before she could greet her fiancé, he asked, "How about a quick trip to Scotland? We could elope while there." His blue eyes twinkled in merriment. "This year-long engagement is killing me."

"You know both of our mothers would cheerfully strangle us if we eloped, but why a trip to Scotland?"

Gabriel picked up a letter from the desk. "Michael has sent me a message. He says, and I quote, 'All is well up here. Autumn has not yet arrived, but it is already deuced cold. I am still dealing with that spot of bother that sent me up here in the first place. If you could spare a few men, perhaps you could send them my way? I also have the news you seek on the other matter and would ask you to take a little jaunt to Scotland so we can further discuss it,' and he closes with the usual, 'Yours, et cetera.' " He looked up at Lillian. "What do you think?"

"What is the other matter?"

"French spies," he said.

"Ah. Well, it sounds as if you need to make a trip up north to assist Michael. Whether I can get away with going as well or not is another matter."

Gabriel held out his hand and pulled Lillian onto his lap. "Come sit with me."

"This is highly improper, sir," Lillian teased.

Gabriel gave her a brief kiss on the lips. "Perhaps if someone catches us at it, they will make us marry with all haste."

"Oh, I see what game you are playing now." Lillian laughed. It felt so good to be able to joke and tease openly like this. It had become a regular part of her version of what a normal life looked like. "I almost forgot. I came here for a reason."

"What was that, love?" Gabriel asked.

"I received a letter from Francesca. She told me that all is going well and she is very pleased with the cottage you have lent to her. Also, she wanted me to tell you the redecorating work she is overseeing is progressing nicely." Lillian put her arms around Gabriel's neck. "It was cunning of you to hire her for the task to protect her pride, so she would have an income of her own while she recovers."

Gabriel shrugged nonchalantly. "It benefits us both. The cottage has been sadly neglected for too long."

"Do not pretend you are a coldhearted man with me, Gabriel Ramsay. You cannot fool me!"

Gabriel was swooping down for another kiss when Jersey interrupted, entering the study without knocking.

"Jersey," Gabriel growled.

"Forgive me, Your Graciousness," Jersey said with a bow and—goodness, was that a blush? "But you asked me to remind you when it was time to leave for the Society meeting."

Lillian jumped up. "Yes! Thank you, Jersey. We do not want to be late. We are voting tonight on whether the Society will collaborate in future Network endeavors." Signor Silvano agreed that it was a genius idea—a chance for the Society members to use their gifts in the real world and to find purpose. Lillian turned back to Gabriel. "Everyone in the Society I have spoken to so far has been favorable of the proposal, with some reservations of course, but as long as they have the choice in how much they participate, I think all will be well."

"I am glad to hear it. I believe it will be good for all of us in the end." He stood and hastened to add, "As long as they are the ones to decide of course."

She looked up and gave him a cheeky grin. "That is why I will be the one in charge of the Society side of the Network —so it will be good for all of us."

He grinned back. "Indeed."

"Do you have an update on the new training facility in Rochester?" She moved toward the door.

"With Simon's help, we have been able to get it ready ahead of schedule. As soon as the vote passes, we can begin training," Gabriel said.

She shook her head. "I never in a million years would have imagined my brother training to become part of a spy organization alongside my Society friends."

"I have always believed the world is full of endless possibilities." Gabriel said. He looked at Jersey. "Go away. Now."

The valet scuttled out and slammed the door behind him.

"That was rude, Gabriel," Lillian said with a light laugh.

"I do not care. I want another kiss before we leave to tide me over through the evening."

Lillian swatted his shoulder lightly but gave in. She had found it was difficult to resist giving Gabriel anything he asked for.

She cupped his cheeks with her ungloved hands and gazed into his midnight blue eyes. When his lips skimmed across hers, they were soft and warm. His hands came up to cover hers. She felt the transfer of love in the touch. He deepened the kiss until they were both breathing hard, then slowly pulled away.

Lillian smiled and pushed a lock of dark hair away from Gabriel's forehead. "We need to go."

"Yes," he said softly.

They left the study arm in arm, smiling as if the world could give them everything.

Four months ago, when Lillian had made her bargain with a duke, she had had no idea what changes were in store. She could not regret any of them. She had learned to look beyond her fears and trust in her own strength. The darkness that had once overshadowed her life had been overcome by a light that would only become brighter with each passing day.

If Lillian could see into the future instead of the past, it would look exactly like happily ever after.

The best way you can say thank you
to an author is to write a review for a book.
**Please write a review on the page where
you discovered this book.**

Sign up for Emmaline Rose's Newsletter

to find out about new releases, give aways, free writing

classes for teens, and positive stories

www.emmalinerosebooks.com

ACKNOWLEDGMENTS

Thank you to my editor Josiah Davis

for helping me to grow.

To fellow author Alex Boast

for too many things to name, so I won't even try.

To my super readers Marva and Paula

for your many suggestions.

Thank you to Meghan, Kestral and Tara

for helping to make all this possible.

Thank you to Charlotte who liked this story

back when it was still just a lump of clay.

And thank you to Ryan, Cameron, and Olivia,

my personal cheer section.

**But most especially, thanks to you,
the readers, who I wrote this book for**

ABOUT THE AUTHOR

Emmaline Rose is a Young Adult and Middle Grade author who writes stories where anything is possible. Limitations? Not a word in her vocabulary. She believes in humor, fun, positive twists, and happy endings--even when life isn't playing nice.

Emmaline loves to boast about the following quirky things about herself: One, she's a leap year baby (born on February 29th). Two, she's ambidextrous (able to write with her left or her right hand). Three, she has the coolest writing partners (the current one is a yellow dinosaur named Sunshine). Four, when she's not writing, she works as a genetic genealogist, solving family mysteries using DNA.

Emmaline lives in the Pacific Northwest with her two amazing sons and daughter-in-law who she really really really likes to boast about.

9 781732 407381